# THE FAMIL`

**The second book in the *Hunted* t**
**thriller of crime, lov**

**A controlling mother. Three Men.**
**Love. Hate. Betrayal. Lies.**

As well as her controlling mother, Tori Morgan's life revolves around
three men: the fiancé forced upon her, the man she loves beyond life
itself, but who has deserted her and lastly, her father – whose murder
continues to haunt her.

Unsure of whether Matt or Hunter has fathered the child growing inside
her, Tori's unwanted wedding grows closer, but is there light at the end
of the tunnel? Could she reconnect with the man she loves?

Unfortunately, Tori hasn't counted on another man present in her life.
One who is more instrumental in her misery than she realises and the
crux in the legacy that plagues her.

Sometimes the truth is too late in coming… Other times it makes bad
things happen…
And in the worst of cases it can cause the unthinkable…

**Can a family legacy have the power to take away the most precious
thing of all?**

**What readers are saying about *The Family Legacy*:**

- *"…Makes Romeo and Juliet seem like a children's book…"*
- *"Suspense at its best…"*
- *"Stuffed with heart-wrenching truths…"*
- *"The twists and turns just keep going in this unpredictable wild ride
of a book…"*

## Also by Edie Baylis

### *Hunted Series*
*The Status Debt (Hunted #1)*
*The Target of Lies (Hunted #3)*
*The Hunted Series Box Set*

### *Allegiance Series*
*Takeover (Allegiance #1)*
*Fallout (Allegiance #2)*
*Vendetta (Allegiance #3)*
*Payback (Allegiance #4)*

### *Retribution Series*
*An Old Score (Retribution #1)*
*Finders Keepers (Retribution #2)*
*The Final Take (Retribution #3)*
*The Retribution Box Set*

### *Downfall Series*
*Until the End of Time (Downfall #1)*
*Escaping the Past (Downfall #2)*
*Vengeful Payback (Downfall #3)*
*The Downfall Series Box Set*

### *Scarred Series*
*Mirrors Never Lie (Scarred #1)*

# THE FAMILY LEGACY

## HUNTED SERIES #2

## EDIE BAYLIS

ATHAME press
· LONDON ·

Athame Press
Unit 13230 - PO Box 6945 – London – W1A 6US

**1991**

HUNTER TURNED OVER uncomfortably in his sleeping bag. No matter how many times he'd camped rough over the years, he never failed to consistently find a large rock inconveniently situated underneath wherever he pitched his small tent.

Sitting up groggily, he raked his fingers through his long unkempt dark blond hair and rolled his big shoulders to loosen them from the stiffness he always felt in the early morning when sleeping on damp ground.

He didn't mind. He'd much rather have the peace of the great outdoors, in comparison to being cooped up in a soulless guest house where constant questions from inquisitive busybodies were relentless. Especially when the object of their nosiness was a biker. *Or should he say ex-biker.*

Hunter reached over to his jacket and extracted a packet of cigarettes from his pocket. His eyes focused on the now plain back of the jacket, where for so long he'd proudly worn the Reaper's colours. It was all he'd ever known. Removing the patch had verged on being physically painful and he felt naked each time he'd shrugged the jacket onto his massive shoulders since.

He ran his hand over his untidy beard - well overdue for a trim and expected he looked every inch the hobo he presently lived like. He inwardly shrugged. It made no difference to him. He'd quite happily walk around dressed like Darth Vader or wear a pink sequined tutu, if it meant he could get the answers he needed to get Tori back. *That's if she'd have him.*

A wave of desolation ran through him as the vivid image of Tori Morgan's exquisitely beautiful face manifested in his mind. There had hardly been a minute since he'd left that she hadn't been ingrained in his brain.

Whether he'd ever experience her delights again and make her his own was as up in the air and unreachable now as it was the day he'd left.

It had only been two weeks since he'd stepped down as President of the Gypsy Reapers motorcycle club. Two weeks since he'd lied to Tori about his love for her being false and two weeks since he'd handed the coveted president patch to that two-faced bastard, Noel.

Hunter grated his teeth, imagining how much damage his ex-Vice President would have already wreaked since his departure. He could only hope Grin and the others were handling it. Grin knew he would return as soon as possible, but he hadn't been able to explain *why* he was leaving, or why Noel had been placed in charge.

He knew it was a big ask expecting Grin to have faith with no information to go on, but he'd no choice.

Hunter sighed. If he hadn't been forced to say what he'd said he'd be with Tori by now. She would have left that ponce, Matt, and been with *him* like they'd planned.

Lighting a cigarette, he sighed in frustration at the aftertaste of last night's rancid beer and lay back on a rolled-up jumper he used as a pillow, exhaling smoke towards the low canvas roof of the tent. His eyebrows furrowed together, thinking back to the night which had ruined everything and led him to where he was now.

He'd been all set to expose Noel and Matt's underhand deals over the dodgy regeneration project. If he'd succeeded, the club would have had Noel's guts for garters for attempting to turn them and half of the people in the area that they looked after, over.

Matt, the poncey twat, would have lost everything and the sad conniving schemes he'd cooked up to further his career at the bank would have gone down the sewer. *Along with his impending marriage to Tori Morgan.*

A slight smile formed across Hunter's face with the memory of when it had hit him how he really felt about the girl from a class he'd always despised. After much struggling with self-denial and ever since Georgie had died with his unborn baby inside her, he'd decided life was too short to keep his heart closed and he was willing to take the chance and drop everything for Tori Morgan. Regardless of Matt and Noel's plan to use him and Tori to play each other off, it had backfired. He was in love with her and she'd made him feel in a way that he hadn't thought himself capable.

Hunter reached for the small bottle of water he'd had the foresight to fill up after leaving that pub last night and grimaced as the tepid liquid flowed into his dry mouth.

He sighed. Whatever he'd felt for Tori hadn't been destined to pan out the way he'd wanted. That night, Noel had threatened that if he exposed him and Matt, then *he'd* tell the club what had been concealed years ago.

Hunter was well aware he'd ID'd the wrong target for his initiation hit and it had haunted him ever since. He knew it was wrong of Rafe, the then president, to cover his mistake, but it had been partly for Noel's sake. The hit was for the man who had raped Noel's mother and Rafe had felt it better if Noel believed his mother had been properly avenged.

The trouble was, Noel had heard them talking and all these years he'd known everything. Hunter knew, when he'd become president of the Reapers after Rafe's death, it had only compounded Noel's hidden resentment. The man had never been happy with the club's choice of him taking the reins.

Hunter clenched his jaw and took another swig of the slightly warm water. He'd thought he'd got it sorted. Noel didn't need to expose his past to the club because he'd been set to tell them himself. He'd always been willing to admit the major balls up he'd made and, in all truth, he'd have preferred to have done it years back.

He knew his admission may mean being banished from the Reapers. Hardly ideal – the club was his life, but it was worth it, if it meant Matt and Noel were exposed and he could have Tori. Losing everything was worth it if it meant he could be with the only woman he'd ever wanted. And he wanted Tori. He needed her like he needed air.

Hunter pushed his cigarette butt into the bottle of water and listened to it extinguish. *Like he wished he'd extinguished Noel and Matt.*

He hadn't expected Noel to pull out a second trump card and inform him the man he'd wrongly killed was none other than Tori's father.

Sitting up in his makeshift bed, Hunter rubbed his hand over his face. Even now, after the news had plenty of time to sink in, it still made him feel utterly nauseous.

Unfortunately, Noel hadn't been bluffing like he'd initially suspected. Tori confirmed certain things he'd needed to be sure of the authenticity. The most glaring one being the photograph she'd shown him of her father.

Hunter had forced himself to look into the face of the man he'd savagely butchered and knew then he had no choice but to walk away, rather than break Tori's heart with what he now knew to be true.

Having to abandon her to that bastard, Matt, bothered him every single second of every single day. The way he treated her made him sick. Just as sick as her arranged betrothal, courtesy of her selfish greedy bitch of a mother and Matt's parents after the death of Tori's father. *After the death he'd caused.*

But once he finally discovered who the real target should

be, then he was returning. If he had the full truth to give Tori, there was a small chance that she loved him enough to work through it. At least that was what he kept telling himself, but nothing was looking promising. Nothing at all and he was finding it harder and harder not to lose his drive.

Since he'd been on the road, he'd followed up as many leads as possible to gain more information on Leila Cooper's rapist, but was getting nowhere fast. And if he had no proof to give Tori, how could he stop her wedding to Matt?

Hunter frowned. The marriage was due to take place in July. July the 10th, he recalled her saying, which, if he was right, gave him a few more weeks to get what was needed. After he'd told her, she could then make the decision whether she belonged with him, or not.

Either way he had to try, no matter what.

*But was Tori ok*? Maybe he should phone Sarah? He'd thought about phoning plenty of times. Ten times a day, to be precise. She worked with Tori, so would know what was going on, but he couldn't. Being landlady of the White Hart, it was too risky to call. Sarah would only be there at night after she'd finished at her day job and by that time it was likely the Reapers would be present and in earshot. He couldn't risk them knowing he was in contact.

He needed to wrack his brains. And he needed to wrack them good. *Time was of the essence.*

When he'd been searching for information on his initiation target all those years ago, it had taken him months and months of painstakingly sifting through details and following up the tiniest leads and despite all that, look where it had got him. Precisely nowhere – apart from completely bloody wrong and he hadn't got anywhere near that amount of time.

But there was someone – someone he remembered back in the recesses of his mind that kept jiggling at his memory, but he couldn't put his finger on who it was. And he needed to.

**One Month Later**

TORI GAZED FROM the balcony onto the beautifully manicured park opposite. It was rare to get a house in the centre of a city with a decent view and greenery surrounding it, but when Matt had taken the short-term contract as assistant bank manager, he'd also taken the lease of a house the bank let to certain employees. And regardless of her feelings, it was a nice house.

Moving had happened quickly. After that night in the White Hart when, despite the fallout she'd been set to leave to be with Hunter, she'd barely stopped for breath. Within three days of that awful night, she'd left her job, moved out of her mother's house and relocated eighty miles away to a city where she knew not a soul, so Matt could take the temporary six-month contract position.

Matt's father had rapidly pulled out all the stops and due to the speed at which it had all moved, Tori suspected Richard had decided this was the best route to take to ensure there were no repercussions on Matt for his involvement with the Reapers.

Tori hadn't yet got her head around Hunter abandoning her

and forcing her to swallow that their relationship had only been part of the plan. But to then be forced to leave her job too, which meant leaving Sarah, had been almost more than she could bear.

*Six weeks she'd been here with no Hunter, no job and no Sarah.*

She'd lost count of the number of times she'd picked up the phone to call Sarah, both at work and at the pub, but after dialling the numbers she'd quickly replacing the handset before it connected. She'd seen Sarah's face the night she'd walked out of the White Hart with Matt. She'd seen her disbelief and anger over her decision to go back on her word.

Tori accepted it may have looked that way, but she'd been so floored by Hunter's disappearance she hadn't been thinking clearly. She'd acted like a robot. How she wished she'd found the inner strength to ride it out, rather than dumbly following Matt back to continue their hateful false existence.

With every day that passed it got harder to call. Tori blinked away unshed tears. Sarah must think so badly of her. They were such good friends and the woman had done so much for her, but she hadn't even let Sarah know she was alright.

In hindsight it was probably a good job she hadn't called because after a couple of weeks she'd realised Matt was checking to see what calls she'd made, so he would have known *exactly* who she'd called and when. He'd made it clear after her plans to betray him had come to light that she was to have nothing to do with *anyone*.

Tori admitted she was terrified what Matt might to do if he discovered she was attempting to get into contact with Sarah because she didn't have just herself to worry about anymore.

Her hand moved unconsciously to her belly, now showing a distinct bump. Her clothes were snug on her thickening waist and most no longer fully did up.

Her hand tenderly caressed the small bump. This had to be Hunter's child. No one as evil as Matt could be capable of fathering a baby, surely?

Tori hadn't breathed a word to Matt about her pregnancy

and he'd taken so little notice of her that he hadn't spotted the roundness of her belly when he'd forced himself on her. She'd conceal it from him for as long as she could. She didn't want *anything* from him. Luckily most of the time he was content to leave her sitting in the house whilst he went out 'getting to know' his new colleagues. Most nights, judging by the strong smell of women's perfume on him when he returned home drunk in the early hours, that wasn't *all* he was doing, but that was nothing new. Besides, the less time she spent with him, the better.

She hadn't even gone to the doctor's – she couldn't face it and on top of that, her mother, nor Matt's parents were aware either – although it would probably be sooner rather than later that Matt and *everyone* discovered her secret.

Tori felt a rush of helplessness course through her. When Matt returned home, they were making the trip back to their hometown and she was dreading it for more reasons than she could possibly list.

The thought of staying at Richard and Susan's house was not a good one, albeit marginally more palatable than staying at her mother's. Predictably, a family dinner had been arranged where she'd be forced to listen to everyone congratulate Matt on his career progression and discuss the upcoming wedding, whilst she received jibes, digs and the usual listing of her seemingly never-ending failures.

It was no secret that neither her mother or Susan were happy with her and Matt living together before they wed, but strangely Richard had insisted it was the right thing to do.

Tori knew Matt must have been forced to tell his father of his underhand dealings with the Reapers – not that he'd admitted that, but it had been obvious – at least to *her*. Why else would Richard have pulled so many strings to ensure the move went ahead so rapidly? And why else would he have worked so hard to convince her mother and his own wife that living together for a few weeks before a wedding didn't bring shame on the family?

*'It was 1990 now not 1960',* he'd said, adding that the temporary move would undeniably help Matt's career. This was what had swung her mother's and Susan's grudging acceptance because neither of them wanted to look unreasonable in front of the other.

The only thing Tori didn't understand was *why* Richard had been so insistent. She'd genuinely thought when he'd discovered the underhand games his son had been playing with the Reapers – the sort he despised so much – that he'd have personally ensured Matt lost everything, but weirdly it had achieved the opposite effect. It was niggling at her and she couldn't make any sense out of it, but no longer had the energy for guessing games.

· · · ·

AS THEY SPED along the motorway, Matt scowled. The last thing he wanted was to be stuck in the car with this bleating cow. He'd have much preferred carrying on the pleasant session he'd had with Debs at lunchtime. His dinner hour had been most enjoyably spent sinking a few drinks and then sinking into *her*.

Admittedly he'd probably had a few more drinks than he should have, but that was *ages* ago so it hardly mattered.

He gritted his teeth. Debs and the rest of his colleagues were hitting a club tonight and he'd been well up for that – especially being as it meant he'd get another round in with her or perhaps even a bit more than that if there were any decent lookers in the club up for some fun.

Debs wouldn't have any problems with additional company – she was a goer that one and could only thank his lucky stars she worked at this new branch of the bank. Meeting her on the first day had been just what he'd needed. He'd presumed it would have taken at least a week or two to source a woman happy for no-strings-attached sex, with the added bonus of being fantastic between the sheets.

Matt glanced at Tori. *Unlike her.* Still, at least she was on hand to empty his balls into on the rare nights he couldn't see

Debs – like tonight. He smiled. He'd only been here a few weeks, yet had a good thing going – personally *and* professionally.

When his father insisted he take this six month assignment whilst all the Reapers stuff blew over, eradicating the chances of reprisals, he hadn't been happy. He hadn't wanted to 'run away'. Those toss pot bikers didn't scare him. Noel had got what he wanted with that massive pay-out and Hunter was no longer on the scene, so he couldn't see what possible 'reprisals' there were to worry about.

He'd also been equally miffed to lose what had become frequent sessions with Ginny. Ginny was another one who knew her stuff between the sheets. If Jeremy had been bothered about regularly sharing his girlfriend, he hadn't said, but then the man didn't have too much to gripe about, considering.

But by God, his father had been right that taking the assignment was the best thing to do. The difference in responsibility he'd been given was astronomical. Christ, it gave him a hard on just *thinking* about it. People did as he said and he had full control – apart from still being accountable to the branch manager himself, but Bob Greaves and his father went way back, so it was all good.

Yes, he'd be ready for the final move into the position of manager at his father's bank when the time came – which hopefully wouldn't be too far off and he couldn't wait.

He smiled to himself. Tori wasn't much trouble either since her plans to run off with that baboon had been squashed. She knew it was all over and she'd had no choice but to play things his way. The only downside was that he was stuck in the same house with her, but at least Debs had a nice place they used most of the time. Not that Tori would have any say in it if he decided to bring people back. She *owed* him after the stunts she'd pulled.

Matt glanced at Tori and scowled at her morose face. 'What's the matter?' he barked. 'Aren't you looking forward to seeing your mother?'

Tori continued staring blankly out of the window. *No, she wasn't looking forward it. Not looking forward to it at all.*

'You could have made more of an effort,' Matt said, snatching a look at Tori's peach-coloured dress and loose jacket. 'You look like you're wearing something from a charity shop, rather than the fiancée of someone like *me*!'

Tori remained silent. There was little point in saying anything. Nothing she did would ever be good enough. Besides, she was limited in what she could wear that disguised her growing bump. She'd have to buy some new clothes soon, but she didn't have any money of her own now Matt had stopped her working and he'd demand to know why she needed more clothes when she already had a full wardrobe.

Matt prodded Tori's stomach. 'You want to watch that. Now you're doing nothing all day you're getting lardy. At this rate that wedding dress of yours won't fit, so cut back on the biscuits, you lazy cow!'

Tori swallowed her frustration and pulled her jacket across her.

Matt's irritation levels rose. *He didn't want a fat, dowdy wife.* 'It will be *you* who'll be embarrassed at your dress fitting tonight. You've got a week to get rid of those extra pounds before our wedding.'

Colour drained from Tori's face. 'D-Dress fitting?'

Matt grinned. 'Oh, did I forget to mention that? Yes, Lillian's arranged a final fitting of your dress whilst we're visiting. The seamstress is due before dinner.'

Feeling slightly faint, Tori opened the window a crack. That horrendous dress forced on her, courtesy of her mother and Susan, was very closely fitted. Why had she not foreseen this problem?

'Stop hyperventilating, it's pathetic! It's *you* who's let yourself go over the past few weeks, not me,' Matt barked. 'You'll have to hit the treadmill and *fast*. I can't believe you'd allow th…'

'I-I'm pregnant…' Tori whispered.

Matt almost lost control of the car. '*What?*' Had he heard correctly? Did Tori just say she was pregnant? Had those dummy pills his father gave him to swap out with her contraceptives months ago finally worked?

'I-I said, I'm pregnant,' Tori repeated, hating the smug expression plastered across Matt's face.

'Well, that's *great* news!' Matt cried. *He had to pretend to be happy about this. Well, he was… sort of…*

Tori looked up in surprise. 'You're *happy* about it?'

'Of course!' Matt smiled. 'You know I want children as soon as possible.' *Because it will keep you out of my way.*

Forcing himself not to recoil, he placed his hand on Tori's stomach. 'Wow! I can feel it now you've said. I thought you were just getting fat! I can't believe I didn't put two and two together. How far along are you?'

'About four months,' Tori answered quietly, inwardly cringing at the feel of Matt's hand on her.

'And you didn't think to tell me?' Matt said, his tone sharp. *He'd been beginning to suspect he was firing blanks.* 'Why would you hide this from me?'

'I-I wasn't hiding it,' Tori lied. *She had to pretend that was the case.* 'I-I thought you'd be cross. Our parents will be angry too. Angry I'm pregnant before the wedding. You know how they feel about th…'

'They'll be *fine*.' Matt felt his cock stir within his trousers. Not from the news of Tori's pregnancy – far from it. Christ, the thought of that turned his stomach, but *everything* to do with this now meant he had all the time in the world to spend with whoever he wanted, *when* he wanted. His father would smooth things over with Lillian and his mother. 'We're getting married next week, Tori. It's not like the baby will be born out of wedlock.'

Despite herself, tears rolled down Tori's cheeks.

'Don't worry, we'll tell them tonight,' Matt said, proud about how well he was handling this situation. It gave him more leverage on her which was always useful.

Tori dabbed at her face as the hopelessness of the situation engulfed her. She didn't want to get married. Not to Matt. She wanted to marry Hunter and wanted this to be *his* child growing inside her, but even that wasn't guaranteed. This child could well be Matt's.

She wanted to run away, but was stuck fast and after next week she would be glued into place with this hateful man for ever more.

'We'll be there in half an hour so let's just concentrate on getting there rather than you being upset, shall we?' Matt said, hoping the evening would pass quickly. Keeping up the pretence to be nice to this two-faced lying cow was terribly difficult.

## TWO

LILLIAN WANTED TO choke on her own tongue after her daughter had stripped down to her underwear in the privacy of the large bedroom allotted for the dress fitting. Shame and humiliation engulfed her as she scrutinised Tori's body. 'Move your hands away, girl,' Lillian snapped, irritably watching her daughter's attempt of covering herself.

She took a sharp intake of breath as her eyes ran over the unmistakeable shape of pregnancy jutting from her daughter's belly. 'Oh my God!' she gasped.

The seamstress moved closer. 'I don't think it's as bad as it looks.'

'What do you mean it's not as bad as it looks? Are you blind? Look at the shape of her!' Lillian screeched.

The seamstress bustled around. 'What I mean is that the pregnancy won't be too visible, thanks to the full skirt of the dress. We're lucky it isn't a straight cut design.'

Tori miserably eyed the meringue monstrosity hanging heavily on a girder-like hanger opposite.

'The dress is fitted at the waist though, so...' The seamstress wrapped a tape measure first around Tori's middle, then around her hips. Pursing her lips, she jotted down the measurements in her notepad and then moved to measure Tori's bust. 'Hmm…'

'Hmm, what?' Susan snapped, also in shock from what they'd been told the second her son and Victoria had walked into the house. Only Richard had taken this well and for once she completely shared Lillian Morgan's opinion.

Tori stared at the wall feeling numb. She'd wanted to pass out when, as they'd stepped into the large entrance hall of Richard and Susan's lavish home, Matt had greeted the welcome committee of his parents and her mother. Running his hand down over her dress to make sure the bump was suitably outlined for all to see, he'd announced the unexpected news.

Susan had turned green and sickly, her candyfloss hair quivering worryingly, whereas her mother had wasted no time in slapping her around the face before dissolving into loud, wailing tears.

Richard had quickly pulled both women into a side room whilst Matt left to make an 'important telephone call', leaving Tori standing alone in the large entrance hall. Her face burnt from both the sting of her mother's slap and humiliation as she listened to her mother alternate from screaming in rage to sobbing and then hushed conversation.

Half an hour later, they all emerged from the room. Tori had no idea what Richard had said to either of them, but everyone acted like the previous episode had not occurred.

Tori fixed her concentration back to the seamstress who was comparing her latest measurements with the originals.

'It's not quite as simple as I thought. There's an additional seven inches from hip to hip compared with the initial measurements, but that's not the issue as, like I said, the majority will be hidden by the skirts. The problem is the waist. It's already thickened by three inches and that will make fitting into this dress impossible.'

'Oh my God!' Lillian wailed. 'What are we going to do?'

'Plus, the bust has increased by two cup sizes,' the seamstress continued.

Tori felt like climbing into a hole. Even though she was wearing underwear she felt naked standing here being measured, analysed and discussed like a piece of meat. Her bottom lip wobbled and tears fell from her eyes.

Susan turned to the seamstress. 'What do we need to do to get this rectified? Cost is not an issue.'

'Let's get the dress on her and I'll see if there's an option of inserting panels to widen the bodice. The only other way is to get a dress a couple of sizes bigger,' the seamstress said, struggling to lift the heavy dress from its hanger.

'But you've done all the alterations and added the unique embellishments on this one!' Lillian cried. She glared at her daughter. 'How could you be so thoroughly irresponsible, Victoria?'

'I-I don't know how it happened,' Tori whispered.

'I think it's *obvious* how it happened, you wanton little bitch!' Lillian barked. 'For God's sake, you only had a few months to wait before getting yourself with child!'

'I-I was on the Pill. I don't know wh…'

'How far along are you, Victoria?' Susan asked. Despite her disappointment, she felt herself softening towards the girl.

'Four months, I think,' Tori answered, staring at the floor in humiliation.

'My, that's going to be a big baby in there!' Susan smiled. 'My Matthew was the same though. I was like a tank by six months.'

Tori reddened with the thought that she hoped with every ounce of her being that this baby wasn't anything to do with Matt.

Susan moved towards Tori. 'Don't be upset. What's done is done.' She placed her hand on Tori's bump. 'Let's not forget Lillian, this is our grandchild in here.'

Lillian's mouth fixed into a thin line. She wouldn't be as easily swayed as Susan. She was horrified. She'd known she was right when she'd asked Victoria *months* ago if she was pregnant and it wouldn't surprise her if Richard and Susan

20

Stevens knew about this the whole time.

· · · ·

THIS WAS WORSE than Tori had imagined. She pushed food around her plate, keeping her eyes fixed downwards so not to draw any more attention than she already had. Her mother's eyes steadily burnt a hole of hate into the side of her head despite her putting on a show of being outwardly grudgingly accepting of the shock news.

At least one hurdle was over and done with. The seamstress had left with the dress, the new measurements and the instructions to 'make it fit'. With the prospect of a lot of money up for grabs she'd assured them they'd have a dress to fit by next week, joking that in the worst case scenario there was always 'strategically held bouquets'.

Even though Susan and Lillian had tittered pointlessly at this supposedly humorous comment, Tori knew neither of them were finding any of it remotely funny. Only Richard was being cordial, but the more whisky he drank over dinner, the more grating his comments became.

'Are you not going to eat that, Victoria?' Lillian snapped. 'If not, then please stop playing with your food.'

Tori scowled inwardly at her mother's insistence of talking to her like a naughty child in the constant pursuit of keeping some form of control.

'Yes, Victoria,' Richard boomed, a big grin on his face. 'You need to start eating properly now you're eating for two.' He nudged Matthew and winked, missing the expression on everyone else's faces.

'She already looks like she's eaten for two. I don't want her getting any fatter than she already is!' Matt laughed, having partaken in as many whiskies as his father.

'Oh, you don't have any choice about that, son!' Richard laughed, slapping Matt on the back. 'I'm afraid that's what happens when you procreate. Your wife ends up waddling around like a barrage balloon! You should have seen the size of your mother!'

'*Richard*!' Susan snapped. 'I think that's enough, don't you?'

'And she's not even your *wife* yet!' Lillian hissed. 'Let's not forget that small detail, shall we?'

Richard rolled his eyes, too drunk to care if his comments riled the women. His plan had worked and it was simply perfect. Victoria hadn't said a *word* all dinner and was as meek as a mouse, just like he knew she'd be the minute she had a baby inside her. Women were all the same.

Yes, giving Matthew those dummy pills to swap for Victoria's was just what the doctor ordered. 'Don't take any notice of them, son. Pregnant wives exude your virility. That's *always* something to be proud of. The bigger her belly, the more of a man!'

Matt smiled. Maybe his father was right. Tori being pregnant *did* show he was a man, didn't it?

'Let's just hope we can keep this under wraps until after the wedding,' Lillian muttered, glaring at both Matt and Richard. 'It won't look too great in the magazine and papers otherwise.'

Richard waved his hand dismissively. 'It will be fine, Lillian. The seamstress will do what's needed and we'll officially announce it a month after the wedding.'

Standing up, he made a big show of tapping his fork against the side of his crystal tumbler. 'And now if I can have your attention please…'

Tori forced herself to look up. *What now?*

'Firstly, I'd like to congratulate Matthew and Victoria on the news of their first child. *Our* first grandchild.'

Tori swallowed down bile. This *had* to be Hunter's child. She *needed* it to be Hunter's child. *Please don't let it be Matt's.*

'And secondly,' Richard continued. 'I'd also like to congratulate Matthew for doing me proud at the bank.'

Tori stared back down at the table. *Here we go… More 'isn't Matt wonderful' speeches.*

Richard proudly puffed out his chest. 'We all know

Matthew has made the intelligent, yet difficult decision to undertake the temporary assistant manager position, which unfortunately involved the upheaval of relocating…'

Tori clutched at the hem of her dress in frustration. How much more of this would she have to endure before she could make excuses to go to bed? It wasn't just Matt who had been uprooted. It was *her* who was stuck in a city where she knew no one and had nothing to do apart from stare at the four walls of a house that wasn't even hers. It was her who had to wait for Matt to return after bedding someone else, only to moan at her or worse, insist on sleeping with her.

After what had happened with Hunter, Matt had made it clear she would not be allowed *anywhere* without him ever again. She hadn't been allowed to return to work after that night at the White Hart, neither had she been able to say goodbye to Sarah before they'd moved. She had no life whatsoever and she could only foresee it getting worse.

Tears burnt at the back of Tori's eyes and she fought to contain them. The last thing she needed was to burst out crying. How she missed Hunter. She would do anything to feel his strong arms around her again. Why had left her? She couldn't believe he hadn't loved her. *She most definitely still loved him.*

Tori ran her hand over her belly, consoling herself that if this baby was his, at least she'd always have a part of him with her.

'Victoria?' Richard boomed. 'Are you listening?'

'Concentrate!' Matt hissed under his breath, gripping Tori's thigh below the table.

'Hormones getting to you?' Richard laughed loudly.

Flustered, Tori bit down on her bottom lip to control the scream of rage lurking in her throat. The scream that she badly needed to let escape to underline the unfairness of this whole situation.

Richard cleared his throat. 'As I was saying… Matthew has done us proud; he's taken to this temporary assignment like a duck to water. Bob Greaves speaks *extremely* highly of his aptitude and ability, as well as his capability in the role.'

Susan smiled gratifyingly. 'That's fantastic,' she simpered. She'd thought both her children's lives were going to plan, but after receiving that call from Carmen earlier, she didn't know what to think. She wasn't sure how she would break the news to Richard that their daughter was no longer coming to Matthew's wedding.

It was extremely disappointing. She didn't see Carmen much since she'd moved abroad. Her lifestyle meant regular visits back to England were impossible, but at least they spoke often on the phone and she loved regaling her friends with stories of Carmen and Luca's lavish and exciting lifestyle.

Susan watched Richard beaming widely at Matthew. She wouldn't say anything just yet. She didn't want to spoil the evening and besides, Carmen hadn't said *why* she was unable to make it. She'd just said she'd call another time, so maybe the issue would rectify itself.

In fact, there may not even be a problem, Susan thought hopefully. What if her daughter was expecting too and didn't want to travel? It was more than feasible. She'd been married over four years, so it was about time she had children. That would be *wonderful* news. Two grandchildren at the same time.

Feeling slightly less concerned, Susan concentrated back on the conversation.

Richard grinned. 'Now, I haven't even told Susan this yet, so this really is an important announcement. Matthew, I'm pleased to inform you that you will take over my position of Bank Manager following the end of your temporary assignment.'

He paused, relishing the gasps of surprise from around the table. 'Yes, that's right. I'm retiring and this afternoon headquarters officially signed off and accepted my recommendation that Matthew takes the position.'

Matt stood up, whooping with delight. 'Did you hear that everyone? I'm the new bank manager!'

Susan rose from her seat and gave her son the obligatory air kisses. 'Congratulations, darling. That's superb news!' She glanced at Richard. *If he was retiring it meant he'd receive his more than comfortable financial package...* She refrained from rubbing her hands together imagining the extended holiday she'd be booking on Monday. *This was just what she needed to take her mind off Carmen and finally justify her own dull existence.*

Susan turned to Lillian. 'Isn't that great news?'

Lillian's smile said it all. This promotion slightly softened the blow of her daughter's shameful behaviour. 'Fantastic news! Well done Matthew and congratulations. And congratulations on your well-deserved retirement too, Richard. Wonderful news, isn't it, Victoria?'

Tori nodded, forcing a smile as she reached for a wine glass.

'You can't drink that, you silly girl! You're pregnant remember? Not that any of us are likely to forget that!' Lillian snatched the glass from Tori's hand.

'So, Matthew... once the wedding's out of the way next week and the honeymoon is over and done with, you must look for a house back here,' Richard said.

Tori felt sick. She wanted to down that wine and a couple more bottles besides. *Returning here?* Although she was excruciatingly lonely, it was easier being away from all of the memories where she'd been so close to being happy. And what honeymoon? No mention had been made of that.

Sensing Tori's confusion, Matt smiled condescendingly. 'Sorry darling. Did I forget to tell you that my parents are kindly sending us on a cruise as one of our wedding presents.'

Susan smiled widely, her fuchsia lips resembling a surgical gash. 'Matthew chose the cruise as he thought you would enjoy it, didn't you darling?'

Matt nodded. 'I certainly did.' He'd made sure it was a liner hosting a smart casino and evening entertainment which would surely have a selection of saucy chicks to choose from. *It would be a very welcome distraction.*

'And make sure you get some house viewings lined up

when you return because you'll be starting the position literally a week after your contract finishes,' Richard added. 'And of course, I don't need to tell you that you won't have a problem securing a mortgage of any size, do I?'

Tori quickly did some mental calculations. The end of Matt's assignment was just over four months away which meant she would be almost full term by that point.

Richard watched Tori. 'I know what you're thinking, Victoria, but no one expected you to get yourself pregnant, did they? If you'd only waited until *after* you married. Still, you must have wanted to make sure Matthew couldn't back out!' He laughed heartily and slapped the table with his own amusement.

Tori rose from her seat. She couldn't stand any more of this. 'Please excuse me. I'm feeling a little unwell. I need to lie down for a while.'

She stumbled from the large dining room leaving Matt and the others staring after her in contempt.

# Three

AT THE BAR, Hunter downed his fifth pint and crushed his cigarette butt in the ashtray. For the last hour he'd been ignoring several women giving him the eye, as well as hostile looks from various men.

He shrugged inwardly with indifference. These men were obviously uncomfortable with any newcomers – especially those who caught the attention of the local women. They didn't need to worry – he wasn't interested. He wasn't interested in women right now, nor was he interested if these no-necks in this shithole had an issue with him. He just wanted to drink. In fact, about thirty pints would be a decent number, would go down nicely and with any luck, do the trick.

He glanced around the ramshackle collection of people in the bar who had a problem if anyone who hadn't lived in this street for the last thirty years dared to walk through the door.

Hunter clenched his jaw. Let them start if they wanted to. He'd happily offload his frustration into someone's face, but he'd still rather get drunk. He'd only come in here because it was the closest boozer to where he'd pitched his tent and being as his plans were to numb his brain with alcohol, he'd walked. It was only a short way, so it hadn't been too much of a burden, plus he'd hoped the fresh air would grant him an epiphany over what to do next. Unfortunately, that hadn't happened, so the beer solution it was. Not that it looked like he would get any peace in here.

He scowled. Over the last few weeks he'd spent more time than he'd have preferred taking refuge in the fuzziness of alcohol. He'd drawn a complete blank getting any further leads with finding information he desperately needed and was no further along than he had been to start with. He necked the remains of his pint and motioned to the barmaid for a refill.

Moving towards the large handsome stranger, the barmaid leant on the sticky surface of the bar, her large cleavage purposefully positioned. She smiled coquettishly. 'You've been in here a couple of times now, haven't you?' she purred, picking up the empty pint glass and turning it around in her hand. 'Setting down roots?'

'I doubt that. I have no roots.' Hunter didn't want to be rude, but he had absolutely no interest in attention from this woman – or *any* of them. Even that distraction would do nothing to get his mind off the woman he loved.

The barmaid pouted. 'You haven't seen anything worth hanging around for?' She trailed her chipped fingernails along the sleeve of his leather jacket. 'Are you a biker?' She ran her tongue suggestively along her bottom lip. 'I love bikers. They make me horny.'

Hunter sighed. 'I have a bike, yes, but I'm not a *biker* anymore.' How it pained him to say that out loud. But it was true. As far as he was concerned, he was no longer a 'true' biker because he wasn't associated with a club – or more importantly, *his* club, any longer.

'Well, you look like one to me,' the barmaid whispered, touching a strand of hair which had worked loose from Hunter's ponytail. 'You've got the hair and everything…'

Hunter felt his irritation bristling, despite his intention to stay calm and disassociated. He shook the woman's hand away and gripped her wrist. 'Just get me a drink please,' he growled.

'Here! Don't you be using that tone of voice with our Billie, you city bastard. We respect women around these parts.'

Hunter shot to his feet, his stool toppling over. His steely grey glare fixed on the man further along the bar who had called him out. He hadn't wanted trouble, but wouldn't take being told he was being disrespectful by this piece of shit.

'Want to have a go, do you?' The man's missing front teeth were obvious as he sneered with contempt and folded his arms, pleased he'd got everyone's attention. 'Did you hear that?' he shouted to the room. 'This muppet thinks he can come into our pub and treat our women like crap!'

'Mark, leave it, will you?' the barmaid cried, aware the angry gleam visible in the big man's eyes showed he would not be a pushover.

Hunter's eyes locked on the man unsteadily moving closer. 'I treat women very well, actually,' he growled. 'I just want a drink, that's all.'

The man threw his hands up in the air theatrically. 'Oh, he just wants a drink!' He squared up to Hunter. 'Why don't you just fucking have one somewhere else then and keep your filthy mitts off our women!'

Hunter had heard enough. He grabbed the man around the neck and tightened his grip. Pulling him close, he winced at the stench of the man's rotten teeth. 'Get out of my fucking face, you inbred wanker!'

The man's eyes bulged at the unexpected vice-like chokehold and before he could utter another word, Hunter's fist crashed into his jaw, sending him sprawling to the floor.

Witnessing the commotion, another man rushed forward swinging for Hunter, only to receive a crushing head-butt to the bridge of the nose.

Hunter smiled as the man reeled, blood pouring down his shirt. Grabbing him, he pulled him along, stopping to yank the other man off the floor by the lapels and manhandled them both to the rickety main door of the pub. 'Now fuck off and let me drink in peace!' he screamed, throwing both men through the doorway to land face-down on the pavement outside.

Irritably wiping his hands down his jeans, Hunter exhaled loudly before barging back into the pub. Standing in the doorway, his eyes travelled from left to right across the now completely silent room. 'Anyone else want to have a fucking go?' he roared. 'Or can I have a drink in *peace*, which is what I came in for?'

Hunter watched everyone silently look down at their tables or to the floor uncomfortably. Casually striding back towards the bar, he righted the stool he'd previously knocked over, then sat down and smiled at the barmaid. 'I'll have that refill now please.'

· · · ·

THE REST OF the evening passed without event. No one looked in Hunter's direction again, having correctly worked out it was best to leave the big stranger well alone.

Hunter sparked up a cigarette and quietly continued drinking his now fifteenth pint. The alcohol had taken effect and he was feeling a lot more relaxed and well on the way to being drunk.

Despite promising himself that he would have a well-needed break from the turmoil going on in his mind and the seemingly fruitless search for answers, he found his brain returning to the missing piece of the jigsaw. *The invisible person who had been niggling at the back of his mind.*

Tuning into a song playing on the pub jukebox, Hunter found himself singing along. He hadn't heard this tune for yonks.

Yes, he remembered it well:

> '*...I'm just sitting watching flowers in the rain
> Feel the power of the rain making the garden grow...*'

Jolting forwards, a memory shot into his head as clear as day. He could see it vividly. It was September. *September 1967 and he was five years old.*

He was in that caravan – the one he used to go to regularly and a woman was singing along to that same song playing on the radio. She was dancing around the tiny kitchen area busying herself frying eggs. The delicious smell had made his stomach rumble and he'd hungrily eyed the awaiting buttered bread on a small plate in front of him.

That woman – the nice kind one. She was very pretty. Both her and her equally pretty friend.

That was it!

Jeanie! *Auntie Jeanie.*

Hunter shouted up another drink and leant heavily on the bar in a combination of shock and drunkenness. He couldn't believe something so glaringly simple had bypassed his memory for so long. If he'd remembered this in the first place, then it was unlikely he'd have got the ID wrong to start with. His initiation target would have been correct if his hunch about this was right.

He sighed in frustration. He would be the first to admit that a lot of his childhood memories were purposely filed away so that they were difficult to access. If he were to be plagued with constant memories of what had happened all those years ago, he strongly believed he'd be a lot less in control of himself than he was. The innate ability to *not* remember certain parts of his life had kept him sane, but unlocking these painful memories might also be the key required to shed light on what he needed to get Tori back.

Hunter forced a smile as the barmaid deposited a fresh pint on the soggy beer towel in front of him.

That day his family was killed by the rich businessman too drunk to be behind the wheel of a car, he was being looked after by Auntie Jeanie and Leila – the woman who would become Noel's mother.

He smiled fondly as the image of the woman who had been like a second mother flashed into his mind again. Jeanie wasn't an auntie at all, but she'd acted like one. As the sister of one of the Reapers she was frequently called upon to look after the member's children when the need arose.

Jeanie and Leila had taken care of him on many occasions – especially around the run up to his brother's birth. His mother had been suffering with pregnancy-related problems so needed frequent hospital check-ups. His father had faithfully taken her in one of the pool cars the club reserved for members should they require four wheels, rather than two, and because hospitals, not being a place for boisterous young boys, he'd been left with either one of the member's wives or usually, Auntie Jeanie. As his father had been the Reapers' President there was never any shortage of offers to look after him, but Hunter had always had a special connection with Jeanie.

When his heavily pregnant mother had doubled over, calling to his father that *'it was time'*, Hunter was excited. It meant his long awaited brother was on the way…

With his mother's contractions coming thick and fast, he'd gone to Aunt Jeanie's where she'd kept him entertained, fed him and tirelessly answered his constant questions of *'how long before I get to meet my brother?'*

Aunt Jeanie had been the one who had said the baby his mother was expecting was a boy. From a long line of gypsies, predicting the sex of an unborn baby with the aid of a wedding ring suspended on a piece of thread was something she was bang on with every time. Each time one of the member's wives got to a certain stage in their pregnancies, Jeanie would see which way the wedding ring swung and as far as Hunter knew she'd never been wrong with any of her predictions.

However, the one thing *no one* had predicted was that his parents wouldn't return and he'd never get to meet his new-born brother.

Hunter shuddered, anger seeping up from his feet as the memory of Jeanie sitting him down and telling him about the car crash filtered into his mind.

He knew she'd begged to look after him full time. She'd tried everything by all accounts, but as a single woman – especially a gypsy living in a caravan, the authorities hadn't entertained the thought. Within a matter of hours of his family being exterminated he'd been ripped away from his extended Reaper family too, along with everything he'd ever known and dumped in a kids' home where no one gave a flying fuck. This became his life for several years until Rafe – the Vice President, now President, since his father's death, and his wife finally extracted him from the care system, legally adopting him.

At the age of twelve Hunter had returned to the Gypsy Reapers club.

One of the first people he'd been desperate to see on his return was Aunt Jeanie, but she'd been *different*. Her light had gone out. *Extinguished*. She'd been strange, although as a young lad he couldn't work out why. All he'd known was she wasn't the same as he'd remembered, so his visits had quickly tailed off.

Shortly after, Jeanie disassociated herself from the club and moved away.

Life moved on and Hunter admitted he hadn't thought much about it after a while – until now.

His eyebrows knitted together. Of course, it was now easy to see that Jeanie's change had occurred because of Leila. Whilst Hunter was in care, Leila - Jeanie's best friend, had a baby and then taken her own life, but he hadn't been aware of this when he'd returned. He hadn't even questioned who Noel was or even where he'd come from. Why would he? There were lots of kids associated with the club and they were around the Chapter House or between everyone's houses or vans, so it certainly wasn't unusual. After all, he'd been away seven years and a lot had changed during that time. At twelve years old, things like new kids weren't top of the list to bother thinking about.

It was when Hunter reached eighteen, with his initiation looming, he'd been informed of the circumstances surrounding Noel's conception and why his mother had killed herself shortly after his birth. It had then made a lot more sense why Jeanie had become insular and a shadow of her former self.

Hunter ran his hand through his hair in irritation. He could barely believe Jeanie's possible importance in all of this, both at initiation time and now. How had this memory evaded him for quite so bloody long? How could he have skirted around that glaringly obvious connection?

Jeanie Fletcher could very well have the answers he needed. She was Leila's best friend and they were like sisters. Leila must have told her about the rape and Jeanie would have definitely been the one to support her through the resulting pregnancy, so she must also know who was responsible for her friend's situation.

Hunter tipped his final pint down his throat and swallowed down a belch. He pushed himself to his feet and considering how drunk he was, he crossed the bar and left the pub surprisingly steadily.

Now it was *his* turn to find who should have been the target and this time there was no one to tell him not to. It would go a short way in righting his wrong in mistakenly murdering Tori's father and he'd be making sure he brought the right culprit to justice this time.

But first he needed to locate Jeanie Fletcher and more importantly, get her to talk.

# FOUR

HUNTER SLAMMED THE receiver back on the cradle. He leant against a cracked pane of glass in the telephone box and sighed loudly.

He felt deflated. This was a needle in a bloody haystack and he'd got a banging headache from being enclosed in this box all day surrounded by the stench of tramps' piss.

His excitement from his drunken revelation the other night of his lost memory of Jeanie Fletcher being the missing part of the jigsaw had failed to include exactly how he'd locate the woman. She hadn't been seen or heard of for eighteen years and he could hardly return to the Reapers to ask any of the remaining ancient members if they knew of her whereabouts, could he? Apart from it being imperative that no one, especially Noel, got wind that he was digging around over a subject that, according to popular belief, had been dealt with and was closed, neither could he wander through the city looking for Jeanie.

He'd barely known where to begin, but had started with the obvious step of riding back as close to the city as he'd dared to get access to the local phone directories to see if she was listed.

'J Fletcher' was listed alright – about five hundred times...

He'd stood in countless phone boxes over the last two days

thumbing through the damp pages of the resident directories, then proceeded to use endless amounts of change ringing all of the people on the list and today had been no different.

He hadn't of course asked outright if any of the people answering were Jeanie Fletcher. For a start, some of them were male, so they were easily ruled out, plus he'd have recognised her voice the minute he'd heard it, but not one of the people on the list had owned the voice he was listening for.

Hunter pressed his forehead against the cool glass. *This was ridiculous.* For all he knew in the eighteen years since she'd left, she could have married and if she had, then she'd have a different surname.

The only other option was to ride to St Catherine's House in London and scour through every single marriage record containing her original name. But there was also another option and judging by the way Jeanie had probably felt about men after what had happened to Leila, it was more plausible than her getting married... She could have moved.

Although Hunter knew she'd moved from where she used to live and disassociated herself from the Reapers, she may have moved away *entirely* – far away from the city where she'd been raised, grown up and lived. Again, this was more than feasible, but where the hell did he start? If this option was correct, that meant the whole country would need investigating. *It was impossible.*

Pulling his crash helmet off the ledge next to the telephone, Hunter left the phone box in defeat. He'd had enough for today and his head was thoroughly mashed. Jumping on his bike, he fired the engine into life and headed back to where he'd pitched up.

Reaching his tent, he dismounted and as the sky darkened, Hunter lay back on the grass staring up at the stars and let his mind drift.

Against his will, his mind returned to Jeanie Fletcher. A scene from before his parents were killed replayed in his brain and he tried to force it to stop. Then it hit him. Instead, he concentrated on the playback and a smile passed across his face.

*That was it*! Aunt Jeanie always said if she were ever to move anywhere else in the world, she'd go to Polperro! As a child many moons ago, she'd visited the tiny Cornish fishing village and fallen in love with it. He remembered loving listening to her descriptions of the quaint houses and tiny harbour.

Hunter smiled. It would be a hell of a long ride and perhaps a bit of an insane stab in the dark based purely on a hunch, but he wasn't getting anywhere with what he'd been doing, so had nothing to lose and his instinct told him he was on the right track.

Lighting a cigarette, he made the decision to get on the road tomorrow at first light.

**· · · ·**

SARAH PULLED THE hand pump and struggled to keep up with the onslaught of demanding punters baying for attention at the bar. She glanced to her left where Colin was also working like a trojan.

Inwardly grimacing as she heard yet another glass smash somewhere in the main part of the bar, she craned her neck, but couldn't pinpoint where it had come from amongst the crowd.

She sighed dejectedly, spotting two men openly conducting the buying and selling of drugs to the right of the bar. In the seven weeks since Hunter's departure and since Noel had been given the Reapers' coveted reins, her and Colin's beloved pub had lost all manner of control. Everything they had worked so hard for in making the White Hart a jewel in their area had gone down the toilet quicker than she thought possible.

Thanks to Noel's new open-house policy, all the undesirables, junkies and tosspots had quickly filtered back through the old wooden doors and as he'd quite bluntly pointed out to her, there was nothing she could do about it.

Jeremy, Matt's equally disgusting friend, had been in here several times too, which had been a bit of a surprise. He'd been sitting with Noel, making it easy to work out that he was still including the upper class in his drug dealing.

Sarah's immediate instinct was to go over to the slimy pin-striped shirt and ask after Tori, but she couldn't catch a second when the skinny twat wasn't with Noel. The man never even came to the bar for drinks, for God's sake – it was always Noel. Any time she neared the table, Noel's expression clearly translated that if she interrupted *anything* then she would be dealt with and she didn't doubt that without Hunter's influence and control, Noel would lose no sleep over damaging her beyond repair.

He'd already made his point about what he expected within the pub and she was unwilling to do anything further to make Colin's life harder. Things were difficult enough between them as it was.

Damn Ash Hunter and his games. She'd believed in him and yet he'd taken off without a second thought. She'd truly thought him to be in love with Tori. Had he been there that night Tori had walked through those doors – all set to tell that ponce, Matt, where to go, she *knew* he'd admit he'd been lying about their love being a game. She knew Hunter of old, so why on earth had he left? And furthermore, why had he let Matt and Noel get away with what they'd done, leaving Noel to ruin everything he'd worked so hard to change?

Sarah cursed under her breath as the lager pump she'd moved on to ran out. 'Colin, could you change the barrel?' she shouted over the noise.

Colin didn't even glance up. 'You'll have to do it yourself.'

Biting back her hurt, Sarah stomped from the bar down into the cellar and set about dragging a new barrel into place.

Her relationship with Colin had gone down the pan too. It was no secret that he blamed her for what had happened. He'd told her *countless* times not to get involved, yet she had. She hadn't been able to help it. Both Tori and Hunter were her friends, yet here she was in the middle of the shit they had left behind and there was no sign of either of them.

Grunting with exertion, Sarah upended the barrel and secured the line onto it, wiping the back of her hand across her sweaty forehead.

She knew Colin was punishing her for what he believed she'd helped to cause, but none of this was her doing. In all fairness, she'd honestly believed Hunter would have returned in a matter of days. He always had before, but not this time. No one, not even Grin had heard a word from him. Sarah thought he might have called, but each day that passed she'd become a little less hopeful and now after almost two months, it looked pretty certain he'd gone for good.

What did he have to return for anyway? His beloved club was a chaotic violent pile of shite – just like back in the days before he had the reins and Tori had disappeared off the face of the planet.

Sarah trudged back up the cellar steps, not in any rush to face the melee awaiting in her once comfortable bar, but she had to – for Colin's sake more than anything else.

The night Hunter left and Tori walked out with that horrible bastard, Matt, was the last time she'd seen her friend because she'd never returned to her job at the office. Sarah scowled. That was definitely Matt's doing. He'd never liked her working somewhere so far 'below her station', but as to where Tori was now, she had no idea.

After a week of constant worrying, Sarah had made the decision to go to Tori's house. She'd known, parking outside, that it was a stupid idea.

When Tori had finally levelled with Sarah about how her mother treated her and how she'd had no compunction in literally selling her to that despicable wanker, Matt Stevens, to gain access back into the coveted upper class circles that she so craved, she knew Lillian wasn't the sort of woman to be reasonable about *anything*.

Sarah pursed her lips. The woman hadn't even had the decency to tell Tori the truth – or at the very least, everything she knew about her father's death. Oh no, she'd chosen to give her daughter vague snippets and narky comments on her father's alleged double life and drug dealing.

Sarah knew full well Tori didn't think what her mother had said was true, or added up, but what else did she have to go on? The poor girl was in the dark. And then to be controlled, belittled and berated by the vicious old hag, under the pretence that she owed her was the final insult and it sickened her to the core.

Sarah shook her head in irritation. She'd visited Tori's house only once before, but hadn't forgotten where it was. She was hardly likely to forget the palatial style property in its tree-lined avenue, was she? Just as she also hadn't forgotten the blatant contempt that awful woman had shown when she'd begrudgingly ushered her into a posh sitting room that night Tori had gone in search of Hunter. *The night she'd been convinced everything would work out.*

Pushing open the door into the bar area, Sarah was hit in the face with a blast of noise from the heaving room. She glanced at Colin who didn't even look up, just continued serving drinks as if she didn't exist.

Sarah took her place behind the bar and busied herself mechanically pouring another pint for the next waiting customer.

No, she really shouldn't have bothered going around to Tori's again and might have guessed the reception she'd receive would have been less than welcoming, but even now, seven weeks on, it still stung as freshly as it had at the time.

Sarah had pressed the ornate doorbell three times before there was any hint of movement from within the big house. Lillian finally answered the door and Sarah had smiled widely, but the expression she received had been stony. The woman stared through her like she barely existed, her coiffured hair perfectly lacquered and her overly made-up face only accentuating her advancing age.

Lillian's brightly painted mouth had puckered in irritation. 'Yes?' she'd snapped.

Sarah had been determined to be polite, even though the initial urge was to remind the sour-faced woman that she could use some manners. 'Hello, Mrs Morgan,' she'd said pleasantly. 'I don't know if you remember me, but I work with Tori and she hasn't been into work all week, so I thou…'

Lillian had held her hand up, stopping Sarah mid-flow. 'I'll stop you there.' She'd run her eyes over Sarah disapprovingly before continuing. 'I *do* remember you. It's hardly likely I'd forget someone such as *yourself* visiting my house.'

Sarah had bitten back the scathing retort itching to escape from between her lips and was about to continue speaking, until Lillian got in first.

'There's little point coming here looking for Victoria,' Lillian had continued coldly.

'Listen Mrs Morgan, I just want to see her that, that's all. I just want to make sure she's alright and I…'

'Oh, she's alright,' Lillian snapped. 'And she's even *better* now she's away from the likes of *you*!'

'Wh…'

'I don't know what you think you'll achieve or what you're trying to do, young lady,' Lillian had barked. 'But you're not welcome here. Ever since I was stupid enough to allow Victoria to lower herself to work somewhere she should never have been, she'd got very silly ideas. Thankfully, she's now seen sense and won't be returning, so I suggest you take yourself back to wherever you've crawled from.'

Ignoring the rapidly spreading anger, Sarah had smiled once again. 'Can I just see her or if you c…'

'Do you not understand? She's not here,' Lillian interrupted, a smug smile on her withered lips. 'She's moved away with her fiancé to embark on a *proper* life.'

'She's *gone*?' Sarah had been genuinely shocked. 'But where? Can I have her address? I'd really like to keep in touch. Tori was a very good fr…'

Lillian had laughed airily. 'Dear God, girl. Do you *really* think I'd give *you* any information as to where my daughter is?'

She folded her arms across her chest defensively. 'Now get yourself back to your council estate or wherever it is that you reside.'

Lillian had stepped back into the hallway, glaring at Sarah for good measure. 'Are you deaf? Get off my property *right now* and if you *ever* come here again, I'll call the police!'

For once Sarah had been speechless as the heavy door slammed in her face.

Sarah placed the pint she'd poured onto the beer towel for the impatient customer and forced herself to smile and take the money for the drink. Even thinking about Lillian Morgan wound her up.

After that incident she hadn't known what to do. She had no one else to ask of Tori's whereabouts, therefore no means of contacting her. She'd hoped Tori would call. In fact, she'd presumed she would - they'd been friends after all, at least as far as *she* was concerned, but there had been nothing. Not a word. No call, no letter. *Nothing*.

She wouldn't pretend it didn't hurt. It did. But there was always the possibility Matt had done something to her because she wouldn't put anything past him.

She'd done a bit of digging on him too. She'd gone to the bank where he worked, pretending to be interested in some ridiculous financial thing and spoke to a woman, but all she'd managed to get was that Matt Stevens had taken a work transfer and no longer worked at the branch.

When she'd asked which branch he was now at, she'd been snottily informed that *'...the bank was not at liberty to give out such details...'*

Sarah had been at a loss at what to do ever since.

Then she'd seen the notice in the paper. The banns had been posted. *Tori was getting married.*

Sarah glanced sadly at the calendar on the wall behind the bar. *10th June*. It was today.

Tori was marrying that snake later on this very day. Not that she'd been invited, of course. She hadn't expected to be, but it *did* mean that Tori and Matt would be back in the city for the wedding.

She'd been hoping Hunter would return to stop this farce, but there was no sign of him. She'd been sure he was aware of the date for Tori's impending marriage and hadn't thought he'd miss the chance to stop it, so why wasn't he here?

Maybe she'd been wrong all along? With a sinking feeling, Sarah realised she may have to face the possibility that Hunter really wasn't who she'd thought he was.

# FIVE

TORI RESENTED GINNY standing in her bedroom helping to dress her like a maid of honour should. She didn't want the woman as her maid of honour – she never had. She hated the supercilious bitch and she hated this wedding.

Ginny had never liked Tori and didn't shy away from making it obvious. As Matt's best friend's girlfriend, she'd been on the scene for years and like the rest of them, had endlessly enjoyed putting her down and making her feel small.

Tori scowled. If she had to have a maid of honour it should have been Sarah and if she was getting married it should be to Ash Hunter.

Ginny held up a suspender belt and jiggled it in front of Tori's face. 'And this is to add a bit of spice. Let's see if we can get it to fit, shall we?' She ran her eyes scornfully over Tori's body. 'Jeez, Tori, you're massive!'

Standing in her underwear, Tori self-consciously ran her hand over her bump, resenting being scrutinised.

Ginny's bright pink fingernails reached out. 'Can I feel it?' She laid her hand on Tori's belly. 'Oooh! It's all hard!' she giggled, her shrill laugh echoing around the large bedroom.

'Oh God, I couldn't *stand* looking like that! I'd feel *so* paranoid.' She proudly ran her hand over her own flat washboard stomach. 'It'll only get worse, you know. You've got over four and a half months to go yet.' A sly sneer appeared on Ginny's face. 'How's Matt finding your new figure?'

'Matt hasn't said too much,' Tori muttered. 'Apart from that he's pleased.' *They had barely discussed it, but personally she didn't care what he thought.*

Ginny smiled, knowing full well that Matt hated the look of Tori's new shape because he'd told her. She'd been with him only last night and he hadn't been able to get enough of her lithe figure – not that she could blame him, looking at his wife-to-be.

'Is the dress even going to fit?' Ginny eyed the mass of white ruffles laid on the bed, her nose wrinkling with contempt. 'I must say I'm not sure I would have picked this style.'

Tori took the suspender belt from Ginny's hand and attempted to secure it around her waist. She wouldn't have picked the dress either, but when did she ever have a choice over anything? 'The seamstress has altered it. It's supposed to fit now,' she said dully.

Ginny watched Tori fumble with the suspender belt. 'I hope it fits. I did get a size sixteen instead of your usual size ten.' She raised her hand to my mouth. 'I couldn't imagine being a size sixteen. Aaargh! It must feel *awful*.'

Tori rubbed her hand over her bump. It didn't feel awful at all. It felt beautiful. The chance of the baby inside her being Hunter's was an even more beautiful thought, but regardless of whose baby it was, it was *hers*. 'It's strange, but nice at the same time. I feel very womanly.'

Ginny pursed her inflated lips. *There was nothing womanly about looking like a moose as far as she was concerned and would happily stick to her size eight, thank you.* 'I still can't quite believe you got yourself pregnant before the wedding. Lillian must have had a fit!'

Tori smiled despite herself. She hadn't got *herself* pregnant. That would have been a biological mystery. 'She wasn't happy about it, no.'

Ginny sneered. 'Let's just hope no one else finds out when the press are around.'

Tori inwardly sighed, knowing Ginny was probably already working out how she could let the situation 'slip' to the papers and the *Country Life* magazine just to ensure maximum problems.

'Oh, Victoria!' Lillian exclaimed, bustling into the room. 'You're not even half-dressed!' Even though she had told herself a thousand times not to let the sight of her pregnant daughter upset her today, it wasn't working.

Just the sight of the visible result of Victoria's lack of self-control shone like a beacon and it was all she could fix her eyes on.

Tori could see that her mother was struggling to stop herself from coming out with a derogatory remark, but it was only a matter of time before something seeped out of her wrinkled mouth. How she wished she could disappear somewhere that no one would find her. *Like the moon, perhaps?*

It had been bad enough travelling down here last night. Matt had barely spoken a word during the journey, apart from boasting about how well he was doing at the bank and she hadn't seen him since. She'd been deposited at her mother's house whilst Matt had disappeared out with Jeremy and Ginny. She didn't join them because apparently it was unlucky to see the bride the night before the wedding. Not that she felt it would make any difference. It was clear she didn't possess any luck, otherwise she wouldn't be in this position.

Her mother, thankfully, had gone off for her usual drinks with her like-minded gossiping crones, meaning that at least she'd had the evening to herself and feeling an unfamiliar surge of confidence, the minute her mother's taxi had departed, she'd rushed to the phone. It was unlikely Matt would check to see who she'd called whilst she was here.

Her heart had thumped in her chest as the line connected and after what seemed like an immense amount of time, it was answered.

'Yes?' Colin's gruff voice had barked.

Tori's voice had frozen in her throat. She could hear the background noise of the White Hart and it sounded chaotic.

'Who's there?' Colin had yelled at the silent response.

Tori had willed her voice box to work, but it hadn't. She hadn't expected Colin to answer and hadn't weighed up what to do should that happen.

'Listen, I haven't got time for fuckwits who don't speak. Fuck off, whoever you are and stop pissing around!'

Tori had remained standing with the phone in her hand long after Colin had slammed his end down.

Dejectedly, she'd gone to her old bedroom and sat on the bed, grateful that her mother hadn't felt the need to remove her belongings the minute she'd left like she'd done with her father's possessions almost immediately after his death.

Everything was still just as she'd left it. She hadn't taken much with her because that was what Matt had insisted on. He'd used the term 'fresh start', when in reality it was just another form of control.

Taking the shoebox holding her father's personal keepsakes from the bottom of her bureau, she'd spent the remainder of the evening perusing the contents, enjoying the solace it brought. She'd still no idea where the rest of the photographs that had been in here had gone, but was glad for the two remaining. She'd stared at the pictures, transfixed by the expression of pure love on her father's handsome face for the unknown woman with him.

If he was here, there would be no way he'd allow this wedding to happen. He'd have done everything and more to ensure his daughter was with the man she wanted to be with, not because of an 'agreement'.

Tori glanced up when her mother muttered something as she busied herself arranging the dreadful wedding dress, then stared over to the large window which opened out onto a huge expanse of landscaped gardens, feeling the hint of an ironic smile creep onto her face.

Last night she'd been praying to hear the roar of Hunter's huge motorbike pull up outside to save her at the last moment, like Rapunzel. She'd have gladly, despite her fears, jumped onto the back and let him take her far, far away where they could raise this baby in peace. Her life would be joyful and perfect.

Of course, the motorbike hadn't come and wasn't going to. She'd known that in reality but had clung to any slight strands of hope. *Even they were now gone.*

'Victoria! Stop daydreaming!' Lillian's voice was more screechy than usual. 'Get into your dress immediately. The car will be here any minute!'

Taking a deep breath, Tori stepped towards the bed and prepared to get smothered by flounces and frills.

*It was time and there was nothing she could do about it.*

· · · ·

JEREMY GRINNED. 'Let's just have one more quick line before Tori arrives. She's bound to be late.'

Matt glanced down the nave of the church. All the pews were full and the congregation chatted excitedly amongst themselves.

Pulling up the starched white cuff of his shirt he looked at his watch. There was more than enough time to go and have a cheeky snort and he definitely wouldn't say no to another blast of powder.

Matt nodded to the vicar standing to one side waiting patiently for the arrival of the bride. 'We're just popping to the toilet before this starts.'

Seeing the vicar smile benevolently, Matt walked through the side door of the church with Jeremy close on his heels.

In the safety of the small toilets, Jeremy exhaled loudly. 'Christ, I don't know why I'm so nervous. It's you who's getting married, not me!'

Matt grinned and short of nothing else to use, cut a line of cocaine on the flat surface of his monogrammed leather wallet.

Sniffing it up, he breathed deeply, savouring the rush to his brain. Soon all of this pretence and bullshit of formalities would be over and he'd be free to continue making his way up the ladder with a sizeable pay-out to boot. Now he'd secured the bank manager position he was all set and it couldn't be better. He would be every inch the success he knew he was. In an hour or so he'd be married and could get on with his bloody life. Then within a few months, not only would he have his feet well under the desk as the manager, he'd own a nice big house and have a kid, which would tick all of the boxes required. *Job done.*

Jeremy took the rolled up twenty pound note from Matt's hand and snorted the fresh line cut for him. 'What happened to Carmen? Do you know why she couldn't make it?'

Matt shrugged. 'I only found out myself last night.' He admitted there was a part of him that was disappointed that his sister had pulled out of coming to his wedding at the last minute. His mother had seemed reluctant to go into detail and had been purposefully vague. He wasn't bothered Carmen was missing the actual wedding; it was hardly a 'real' one. His sister knew it had been an arrangement for as long as he had, but he had been looking forward to boasting about his career progress. They'd always been competitive – even as kids and that hadn't changed. He'd been green with envy when she'd landed on her feet by marrying Luca, but now he was on the up. His achievements weren't through marriage and he wanted to rub her face in that.

Matt glanced at Jeremy and smiled widely. 'Her and Luca are no doubt somewhere like the Cannes Film Festival or sailing around St Tropez on their yacht.'

Jeremy laughed. Matt's sister did indeed have a very luxurious lifestyle. 'Changing the subject - you're a sly old dog aren't you! Why didn't you tell me Tori was pregnant? I take it that it was an accident?'

Matt smiled. 'Not exactly, no. I planned it.'

Jeremy frowned at Matt's answer, still unable to believe he would be a father within a matter of months, but then nothing should surprise him. And as for Matt not telling him about this, he expected nothing less in reality.

He'd also been shocked when it was announced Richard Stevens was retiring and Matt would take over the post of bank manager. Jeremy had always known it would happen eventually, just not so soon.

Jeremy leaned forward. He needed to remind himself that Matt only liked it when all conversation was centred around him. 'What's it like with Tori being pregnant?'

Matt frowned. 'It's alright as long as I don't look at her. Take her from behind so it's not off-putting – that's my theory anyhow. But you know me. I'm not intending on spending too much time with her. Better places to be!' *Actually, it was off-putting. A woman's body should be thin and beautiful, not bulging in strange places.*

He was just grateful Ginny had been around last night for a decent session. How on earth he'd stand a whole week stuck on a cruise liner without her or Debs on hand was anyone's guess, but there would be other women on the bloody boat who hadn't eaten all the pies, surely?

'Sir, the bride's car has arrived,' a voice said loudly from the other side of the door.

Matt jerked his head at Jeremy. 'Right, let's do this.' He strode confidently out to the main body of the church, seeing his father nod approvingly from the front row, whilst his mother daintily dabbed her eyes with a lace-edged handkerchief.

# Six

TORI WAS DETERMINED to make an effort. After dinner they had drinks booked with the captain and to her surprise, she found herself looking forward to it. Despite Matt's behaviour during the first exceptionally long and lonely days of their honeymoon cruise she had found the inner resolve from somewhere to make the best of things.

Whilst Matt spent the entire afternoon in one of the many bars, she'd plucked up the courage to book an appointment at the most expensive hair salon on board. She'd also treated herself to a manicure, pedicure and massage and was now feeling both relaxed and pampered.

Staring at her reflection in dressing room the mirror of their sumptuous suite, she felt strangely pleased with what she saw. Her newly cut and styled hair looked fantastic. It was pinned up, leaving a handful of loose soft curls tumbling down around her face and shoulders. Her make-up was light but dewy, giving her glowing complexion an added layer of beauty and the touch of mascara she'd applied to her thick lashes framed her bright blue eyes perfectly.

The sun she'd soaked up for want of nothing else to do whilst Matt had been 'elsewhere' the last couple of days had already given her previously pale skin a healthy light tan and she looked radiant. Even the hairdresser had remarked how healthy she looked.

Standing up from the velvet cushioned stool, Tori turned to admire herself in the floor length mirror on the wall. The crystal-studded halter neck straps of her dress emphasised her bust and pink chiffon draped from an empire-line cut to hang in soft folds, tastefully skimming her growing figure.

Tori's heart jumped with excitement feeling a flurry of faint movement and her hand immediately went to her bump. She'd started feeling what she could only describe as 'butterflies' a couple of weeks ago, but this intermittent sensation was getting stronger and she had no doubt it was from her baby.

Glowing inwardly with happiness, Tori applied a layer of clear lip gloss, put in diamond stud earrings and slipped on heeled sandals. She walked across to the large patio door opening out onto their private balcony and stared out at the dipping sun over the sea. Scanning from left to right, she could see no land and became mesmerised by the steady movement of the sea as the large liner continued its slow passage through the ocean.

Tori found her mind wandering back to Hunter, like it invariably did and mused as to what he was doing right now. Did he ever think of her? Did he wonder what would have happened if he hadn't left? Was he aware she'd come to the White Hart to be with him?

Did he know that she didn't believe what he'd said and she loved him above all? Would it have changed his mind? Would he have stayed? And how would he feel if he knew this baby could be his? Would he want her regardless if it wasn't?

· · · ·

SCOWLING, MATT STUMBLED along the corridor back towards his suite. He couldn't believe he'd been so close to bedding that tasty woman when they'd been interrupted. *Damn it.* If they'd only left the bar to go to her cabin half an hour earlier, he'd be done and dusted by now.

The woman had been halfway through giving him long awaited head when there was a knock on her cabin door. She'd tried ignoring it, but it was insistent. Pulling a satin robe over her splendid naked body, the hard nipples of her large breasts clearly visible through the thin silky material, she'd sashayed to the door.

Matt had been forced to conceal himself in the bathroom to wait impatiently. When she finally opened the bathroom door, he'd almost pinned her to the wall with his need for release until she'd said she'd forgotten her hair appointment.

He'd questioned whether it was *that* important, but clearly it had been because he'd had no choice but to cram his engorged cock back into his trousers and vacate her cabin. She'd promised to 'pick this up later', but he couldn't be bothered. Fuck it. If her hair was more important than spending an afternoon in bed with him, then she wasn't worth his time. Nah, he'd find someone else.

Matt drunkenly palmed his hand over his still semi-hard crotch. He was as horny as fuck and hadn't had hardly any action since his damn marriage. It was near on killing him and now he'd got an evening with the bloody captain.

He had no idea why he'd arranged that either. It wasn't like he needed to impress anyone. He was about to become a *bank manager*, for God's sake, so everyone should be impressing *him*, not the other way around. Still, he might meet a few potential clients, so it may not be a total waste of time.

Matt continued striding down the corridor, backtracking slightly when he drunkenly wandered past his own cabin door. Unlocking it, he stumbled into the room seeing Tori on the balcony. The floaty material of her dress blew with the breeze. *She'd do, providing she didn't turn around.*

'Oh, you're back,' Tori exclaimed, as Matt approached from behind.

Matt winced seeing the outline of Tori's body through the flimsy material as she turned to face him. Grabbing her shoulders, he spun her around, pressing her against the balcony. 'Face this way, the view's stunning,' he said, yanking at her dress. *He'd have to try to be nice. He needed sex.*

'W-What are you do…'

'We've got plenty of time before dinner.' Matt growled, freeing himself from his trousers and pushing Tori roughly against the balcony rail.

Tori gasped in pain as the metal rail smacked into her belly. 'Matt, you're hurting me!'

Matt's rage increased. 'For fuck's sake, you whining cow. Nothing's ever good enough for you, is it? It's lovely out here and you don't want to enjoy it.' Grabbing Tori's wrist, he dragged her back into the room.

'Matt, you're drunk! Stop it and…'

'I said shut up, didn't I?' Matt barked, spittle flying from his mouth. He let his trousers fall to the floor and pumped his fist down his shaft. He refused to lose his erection because of her bleating. 'Take your stuff off.'

'B-But I'm ready to go out. We…'

'Fine! I'll take it off then, you insolent bitch,' Matt yelled, his hand yanking at the halter neck of Tori's dress. He smiled widely at the loud ripping noise as the flimsy fabric ripped to the waist and Tori's swollen breasts were exposed. 'Well that's one thing, I guess. You're not wearing one of those fucking girder-like bras for once. I prefer your tits bigger.'

Tori yelped in pain when Matt sank his teeth into her sensitive flesh.

'Lighten up!' Matt snarled. 'I'm your husband, so do your duty!'

As the remains of Tori's ruined dress fell to the floor, Matt scowled in contempt. 'Urgh, don't put me off by shoving your belly in my face. Get on the fucking bed.'

'Matt, please. Can't we j…'

'I said, get on the bed,' he roared, pushing Tori to her knees on the mattress. Grabbing the back of her neck, he pushed her face down into the pillow, the clips of her perfectly styled hair flying out. 'Now *stay* there.'

Roughly shoving himself into her, Matt groaned loudly. 'That's better. Oh yeah, that's it.' Digging his fingers into Tori's hips, he thrust harder.

Tears spilt from Tori's eyes as her head repeatedly smacked into the headboard.

Matt stared down at Tori's slender back and dug his fingers into her buttocks. She looked fine from this angle, but he needed it harder. A lot harder. All the coke he took made him horny, but it took ages to get off and he had to soon because his balls were fit to burst.

Matt slammed into Tori at breakneck speed, shunting her even further into the headboard. His nails raked down her back as he grunted in exertion.

'Matt, you're hurting me,' Tori sobbed, her voice muffled by the pillow. 'The baby?'

'Sod the baby,' Matt muttered. *He needed to come. Almost there, almost there.* Upping his pace, he roared as his long awaited orgasm rushed over him before heavily collapsing.

Forcing herself out from under Matt's weight as he lay snoring, clearly spent from his exertions, Tori jumped off the bed and stumbled into the bathroom.

Leaning against the washstand, she gulped in large mouthfuls of air to tone down the rising nausea and panic. She stared in the mirror at her reflection. Streaks of black mascara covered her cheeks and her hair hung in a tangled mess around her face. She gingerly touched the angry bite marks on her left breast, turning to see deep scratches on her hips, back and buttocks.

With mounting dread, she laid her fingers on the bruises already forming across her belly and winced.

Standing motionless in a combination of shock and fear, she held her breath in the hope that she would feel fluttery movements from inside her, but there was nothing.

## SEVEN

'A TOP UP, MATTHEW?' Lillian gushed, pouring more wine into Matt's glass.

'I don't mind if I do,' Matt smiled ingratiatingly. 'Obviously none for you, Victoria.'

Tori clenched her jaw as her mother's false tittering laughter echoed around the large dining room.

'How's married life treating you?' Lillian asked. 'I didn't expect to see you quite so soon after your honeymoon – not that I mind, of course.'

'We got back two weeks ago,' Tori mumbled, managing to keep the irritation from her voice.

'We've got house viewings tomorrow,' Matt said. 'So we thought it would be good to come and see you at the same time.'

Tori scowled. *WE hadn't thought that, Matt had*, she thought. *This was the last place she wanted to be.*

Lillian's magenta lips formed into a tight line eyeing her daughter's shapeless dress. 'I hope you've brought along more suitable clothes than *those* to wear, Victoria? You look like a factory worker!'

'I-I didn't get chance to change. I didn't know we were coming until Matt returned from work and we left straight away.' Tori reddened, despising her need to justify herself.

'I can assure you she won't be wearing *that* tomorrow.' Matt laughed loudly. 'Can you imagine it? I won't be taken seriously about purchasing the type of houses we're looking at if my wife turns up looking like a dustman!'

The truth was Tori wouldn't be accompanying him *anywhere* if she wore those cheap things again. It was a complete travesty. How dare she embarrass him like this.

'I must say, Victoria, those clothes are in no way, shape or form *remotely* flattering. Just looking at you makes me feel quite ill,' Lillian scoffed.

Tori reddened further, self-consciously smoothing the material over her bump. She liked this dress – it was comfortable. Besides, she was more than grateful her baby was safe after what had happened on the cruise and personally, she didn't care if her mother or Matt thought she looked ridiculous.

Matt glared at his wife. 'Your mother's right, Tori. You must stop wearing those revolting things. You make no effort at all!'

Lillian chuckled loudly at Matt's comment. It was more than nice having a such a good man as her son-in-law.

'I'll go and change,' Tori said quietly. *As usual she'd have to play it their way.*

Lillian nodded, pleased she'd made her point. 'How was the honeymoon? I bet it was wonderful.' She was envious. She'd have loved to have gone on a cruise for *her* honeymoon, angrily remembering the only thing Jack had been able to afford was two nights in a Blackpool guesthouse.

'It was great!' Matt helped himself to another glass of wine. At least some of it was - the parts when he wasn't stuck with his frigid wife, or being interrupted whilst getting it on with eligible women, that was. The second half of the week was good after he'd hooked up with that hot little croupier from the casino.

'Of course, Tori insisted on being melodramatic,' he added.

Tori's eyes remained locked on the deep pile carpet. She

knew what Matt was going to say. She'd heard him recount this story to several people now.

'What did she do this time? Split her wine over the captain's wife or something equally embarrassing?' Lillian laughed.

'Almost, but not quite. In fact, it was *worse*,' Matt said, enjoying Tori's expression. 'We were supposed to be having after dinner drinks with the captain, except Tori being Tori, forgot she'd placed a pair of shoes on the balcony. And what did she do?'

Lillian sat entranced listening to Matt, more than proud she was now officially part of his family. 'Don't keep me in suspense! What, dare I ask? Did she drop them in the sea?'

'Nope!' Matt raised his hands theatrically. 'She only went and tripped over them and fell against the balcony rails!'

'Oh Victoria!' Lillian said. 'How dreadfully stupid of you. Where you late for dinner because of this clumsiness?'

'Well that's just it. We didn't go. Tori was upset – almost hysterical, in fact,' Matt continued. 'She hit herself here.' He motioned to his stomach. 'I insisted she go and see the ship's doctor to make sure the baby was alright. You can't afford to be too careful with things like that. She didn't want to go, but I insisted.'

'Victoria, you're so lucky to have such a caring husband and you can't even do him the decency of making an effort?' Lillian snapped, cutting her daughter a withering look. 'How could you be so careless?'

Tori forced a smile. After what Matt had done, she'd looked a complete mess and besides, he'd passed out on the bed. It had then taken her until the next morning when Matt had finally woken up to get him to take her to see the doctor. He hadn't wanted to, but made sure he gave the doctor the same story.

'Me and the doctor had a laugh about it,' Matt grinned. 'He said being clumsy and forgetful was common in pregnancy. His wife had been the same with each of their children. He said it used to drive him mad!'

Lillian laughed loudly. 'Victoria's clumsier than most at the best of times. She's always been uncoordinated and ungainly.'

Tori sat in silence. Like at the doctors, she hadn't dared explain what had *really* happened to cause the line of bruises across her belly.

'Because of her stupidity, the doctor said she must spend the next few days on bed rest just to be on the safe side, so we never did get our drinks with the captain,' Matt added.

'Oh, what a shame!' Lillian exclaimed. 'That sort of chance doesn't happen every day.' She glared at Tori. 'You silly girl! Only *you* could ruin your own honeymoon.'

'The fact that the baby's ok is all that matters.' Matt forced himself to lay his hand on Tori's bump, ignoring her flinch at his touch. 'I offered to stay with her in the cabin the whole time of course, but she didn't want that.'

'Always been ungrateful, that one,' Lillian spat.

Tori remained staring at the carpet. Matt had certainly not offered to stay with her, which she'd been glad about. She hadn't wanted him anywhere *near* her and had been relieved to barely see him for the rest of the cruise.

'Oh, I've just remembered,' Matt said, changing the subject. 'I'm popping over to see Jeremy tonight as I'm not sure I'll get time after all these house viewings tomorrow.'

'Are you going, Victoria?' Lillian asked.

'No, she's not,' Matt added, quickly turning to Tori. 'Don't bother yourself with that, darling. Have a nice bath, relax and put your feet up. I won't be long.' He didn't want *her* coming. His plan, as well as seeing Jeremy, was to have a bit of a session with Ginny and pick up where they left off before he'd moved.

'What a gentleman! Thinking of you like that. A lot of men would insist on dragging you along regardless. I hope you realise what you've got here, Victoria?' Lillian cried.

'I do,' Tori muttered. *Yeah, she was more than aware what she'd got.*

• • • •

THINGS COULDN'T HAVE worked out better even if Matt

had set it up himself. Jeremy hadn't been at the flat when he'd arrived, but Ginny was and they hadn't wasted any time tumbling into bed.

Now replete, Matt rolled onto his back and sighed with satisfaction. 'Where's Jeremy tonight?' he asked. He'd been glad the man wasn't here so he could get a decent shag, but on the same vein he was curious as to where he was.

Ginny ran a trail of light kisses over Matt's chest. 'I don't know,' she said indifferently. 'I don't bother asking much these days.'

Matt raised an eyebrow. 'Things not good?'

'No worse than usual.' Her hand trailed slowly down Matt's chest.

Matt smiled. It was no surprise that Ginny should prefer him over Jeremy. He was better looking for a start – not to mention a hell of a lot more successful.

Ginny sighed petulantly. 'He reckons he'll hit the big time soon. I can't see it myself. I mean, he's not like *you* when it comes to deals, is he?'

Matt puffed his chest out in gratification at her words. 'No, he hasn't quite got the same drive.' Actually, Jeremy had very little drive and didn't have a clue what he was doing. Poor bloke – he'd never amount to anything – not without someone like *him* leading the way.

Ginny's fingernails traced the line of hair running down from Matt's belly button teasingly. She was doing well. Men loved having their ego inflated as well as their cock and she was happy to take care of both of those things if it bought her a decent bank balance. 'Yeah and it's hardly like he'll rake in too much hanging around that White Hart dump.'

Matt's smile fell. 'What's he doing there?'

'No idea. I won't step foot in that dive unless I have to.'

Matt frowned. He'd wouldn't have thought Jeremy would continue dealing with the Reapers, but what did it matter? It wasn't like he'd ever attain *his* level of success.

Ginny's hand ran along Matt's inner thigh. 'Don't waste

time thinking about that. It's not important. It's great to see you, Matt. I've missed you.'

Feeling his cock swell with Ginny tantalisingly close to it, Matt grinned. 'I've missed you too. You've no idea how much.' Well, not *all* that much whilst Debs was available, but if she hadn't been, then that wasn't something he could bear thinking about. The prospect of being stuck with Tori and *just* Tori was not something he wanted to entertain.

'How long is it now until you move back here for good?' Ginny asked.

'Two months, near on. That's why I'm hoping one of these houses we're seeing tomorrow will be what I'm looking for.'

Ginny's mouth set in a hard line. Why should Tori reap the benefits of Matt's success? It wasn't fair. He didn't even want the miserable cow. 'How is Tori?' she asked bitterly.

'Fucking fat!' Matt snarled. 'You should have seen the state of her tonight.'

Ginny smiled. 'You've always got my body to look forward to, babe.'

# EIGHT

HUNTER SAT IMPATIENTLY in the small room at the front of the garage and glanced at the plastic clock hanging crookedly on the oil-stained wall.

This was the downside of not having any of his tools with him. If something went wrong with his bike, then he had no choice but to pay someone else to fix it. He rolled his eyes. God only knows how much this would cost. It was only the brakes, which he could have easily replaced himself if he'd had his kit, but he didn't.

He glanced at the clock again in the hope that somehow more time had elapsed in the minute since he'd last looked at it. It was so frustrating. He'd wanted to leave at dawn – planning to be in Polperro by midday at the latest, but there was no way that could happen now. He was all for living dangerously, but that didn't include something as inane as slamming into the back of a truck because he had flaky brakes.

Out of all the days for his bike to play up it would have to be today, wouldn't it?

Snatching a magazine from the collection dumped on the small table in front of him, he stared blankly at the cover. *Bloody Country Life? How many people waiting in a car repair* garage would be avid readers of this high-brow rubbish? Didn't they have any newspapers?

He glanced around the room in the hope that someone had left todays' copy of *The Sun* behind, but there was nothing, so with want of nothing better to look at, Hunter flicked through the glossy pages of the magazine in his hand.

### Best Country Homes For Sale This Week.
*A unique Grade II listed penthouse apartment in the heart of Belgravia converted across three buildings with an abundance of exquisite outside space.*

*For sale with Savills, London – Price on Application*

Hunter rolled his eyes. 'Price on application?' Yeah of course - it would be. His eyes scanned the list of other properties: a grand farmhouse in Gloucestershire, a ten-bedroom country residence with equestrian facilities in Somerset and a gentleman's residence with five acres of land in Yorkshire…

Swallowing down his irritation, he thumbed past the rest of the overpriced luxurious dwellings on to the next page.

### Review of the new model Bentley

*A slick rugged powerhouse for those with class…*

Hunter snarled, quickly turning over. *'For those with class'?* Like the wanker driving that Bentley who had killed his family? Trying not to lose his temper completely, he flicked through several more pages.

### Rabbit and Venison Pie with Orange Jus

*The most delicious cut of a fresh rabbit is the…*

What? Jesus Christ! Oh, he couldn't read this drivel. Closing the magazine, he was about to launch it back on the table in disgust when a photograph caught his eye.

He hastily located the page where he'd seen what he'd thought for a minute to be…

Hunter's heart stopped in its tracks as the colour photograph of Tori and Matt burnt onto his retinas. His throat became dry and he blinked rapidly.

Tori was breathtakingly beautiful - her dark hair piled high on her head, loose curls framing her perfect face and her bright blue eyes staring hauntingly at him from the image. The eyes he could drown in – the eyes that conveyed deep despair.

They'd got married? The wedding wasn't until July was it? *What was going on?*

He frantically read the article:

### Sumptuous Wedding for Bright Young Couple

*Victoria Elizabeth Morgan – the only daughter of Mrs Lillian Ann Morgan, proudly married Mr Matthew Richard Stevens – son of Richard Cuthbert and Susan Madelaine Stevens on 10th June at 2.30pm.*

*The bride looked dazzling as she embarked on life with her successful new husband, who will be shortly commencing his position as bank manager, following in the footsteps of his well-respected and highly successful father.*

*The wedding party was completed by Miss Virginia Howlett – Victoria's Maid of Honour and Mr Jeremy Seaton-Masters – Matthew's best man, along with bridesmaids: Ruth Charcote, Lucinda Greaves, Matilda Southwall, Bettina Landrew and three flower girls: Ruby and Harriet Andrews and Sally Thirlow. The Pageboy was Master Teddy Greaves.*

Hunter felt sick. Sick to the core. How had he got this so wrong? *Fuck, fuck, FUCK!*

Throwing the magazine against the wall of the waiting room, he collapsed back in the plastic chair. Putting his head in his hands, he raked angrily at his hair. *He'd thought the wedding was July, not June! What was he going to do now? He was too late!*

Hunter's entire body shook from rage and pent up aggression. He knew he should have phoned Sarah. She'd have known his dates were wrong and then he could have gone back to beg Tori not to marry that prick. He'd hadn't meant what he'd said. He hadn't fucking meant it and she *had* to believe him.

The door between the waiting room and the workshop opened. 'Mr Hunter?'

Hunter looked up, his grey eyes cold. 'What?' he snapped.

'Erm, your bike is ready,' the man muttered, hastily retreating back into the workshop.

Hunter stood up. Tori may be married, but there was nothing to stop him getting her back. His jaw set determinedly. He wouldn't let Matthew-Fucking-Stevens win. Over his dead body.

He would go and find the truth from Jeanie and then when he'd put everything together, he'd go and see Tori. She'd have the truth – *all* of it and then the ball would be in her court.

Hunter strode into the workshop to collect his bike.

# Nine

JEANIE WAS AT home when she had that *thing*. That creeping sensation she got each time something was about to happen. She'd always had the ability to sense things – even as a little girl. It was in her blood, her mother had said and was what came with being a gypsy.

She stiffened and stood motionless, listening intently – not to anything in particular, but to see if she could pick up any further information.

This gift had been useful in a lot of respects, but sometimes she wished she hadn't ever had the ability because there was always the risk she might ignore warnings when she shouldn't and then bad things would happen. *And bad things did happen.*

The one day she'd ignored a warning was the last time she'd allowed herself to tune in. Since then, she'd purposefully bypassed the feeling whenever it occurred and refused to listen. Not that it happened much anymore these days.

Still, regardless of her resolution to pay no attention, this one was strong. *Really* strong. She frowned, unable to distinguish whether whatever was inbound was good or bad.

For the last eighteen years she'd lived in peace with no hassle, no grief and less guilt. She'd even abandoned her roots and bought a house, which had been weird to start with.

She smiled as she looked around the tiny cottage she owned near the Polperro harbour. She could sit all day watching the little fishing boats come and go whilst everyone quietly went about their business. The only time, if any, that she least preferred it was in the height of summer when, as years passed, more and more holiday makers discovered the quaint little fishing village unchanged by progress and flocked to see its unspoilt beauty. But that was a small price to pay for the place that held fond memories from her childhood and was the perfect escape from the event which had sent her adult hopes and dreams into meltdown.

As a child she'd stayed here for a few months. Her family had been travelling gypsies – never in one place for too long and this was one of the many places they had stopped. And it was the place she'd always dreamt of returning to one day.

Even though her family and the rest of the gypsies they'd moved around with had eventually made the decision to stay in one place and her brother had joined that club, they had never given up their culture by living in a house and she'd been very happy about that. She'd been proud of who she was, as they all had and it was just a shame other people didn't see them in the same light.

It had been difficult to make the decision to buy a house, but she knew how people were and regardless of anything else, she'd needed somewhere with no questions. She'd needed to settle in like anyone else with nothing around her neck impeding that. And she'd settled here nicely.

Jeanie knew virtually all the locals and spent many a pleasant evening in the pubs around the small harbour watching the sun set.

Walking to the window of her cottage, she peered out, grateful to see everything was as it should be and absentmindedly rearranged her china ornaments on the wide sill. She'd wander down the village shortly to buy some freshly baked bread to go with her soup.

• • • •

HUNTER WAS EXHAUSTED. His backside felt as stiff as a board. Although his low-ride chop had a lovely deeply-cushioned seat, *no* seat was particularly comfortable after six and a half hours.

Still, he was here now, albeit a lot later than planned. With reluctance, he realised he had little choice but to get a room for the night being as there was no chance of getting back to his tent tonight after his late start.

Riding into the centre of the village, Hunter kept his eyes peeled for a public phone box, although after the last three days of virtually living in the bloody things, it was the *last* place he wanted to be, but needs must.

Despite his exhaustion, he loved the look and feel of the small village. It really was a pretty little place, but was Auntie Jeanie actually here?

Seeing a red phone box come into view, Hunter pulled to a halt, put his side stand down and hobbled off his bike. Hanging his helmet over the handlebars, he shook his tousled hair, convinced his head must have assumed the shape of the helmet he'd had it on that long. Pulling his cigarettes from his pocket, he lit one and inhaled pleasurably whilst graciously ignoring the withering glares from an old couple on the opposite side of the road.

He yanked the telephone box door open, dismayed to see no telephone directory inside. He stood for a few moments, completely unsure of what to do. He hadn't thought about *that* being a possibility. *Every phone box had a telephone directory in it - that was the bloody point, wasn't it?*

Hunter looked closer at the shelf where the directories were usually kept, seeing the chain attaching them had been snapped. *Some low life had nicked the bloody telephone directory! Seriously?*

Raking his hands through his hair, Hunter left the phone box and slowly walked back to his bike, not looking forward to getting back on that seat. *So, where was the next phone box? Down the road perhaps?*

He glanced around, noticing the old couple who had given him disapproving glances were now standing in the tiny front garden of their little house. They must be the sort to feel uncomfortable at the sight of a biker, having probably never left this village all their lives, but he had no choice but to approach them because there wasn't anyone else around. He really couldn't face riding around aimlessly; the villages and towns around this neck of the woods were few and far between – he'd seen that much on his ride in.

Crossing the road, Hunter strode purposefully towards the couple, dismayed to see the old man grab a large garden fork and raise it in his direction. He held his hands up in submission. 'I'm not going to attack you,' he smiled. 'Can you tell me where the next phone box is?'

The man lowered the fork a little, but refrained from putting it down entirely. 'Phone box?' he repeated, his Cornish accent strong.

Hunter nodded. 'Yeah, the directory's missing in that one.'

'We don't have much need for directories around here,' the old man muttered. 'And that's the only phone box. Next one's probably back in Looe.' He pursed his lips and eyed Hunter suspiciously. 'Who you looking for?'

Hunter knew well enough not to give any information away. 'No one in particular. Somewhere to stay perhaps?'

The man shrugged. 'There's a pub down the harbour that does rooms. Don't know whether they'll have vacancies.' He glared at the motorbike.

Nodding his thanks, Hunter returned to his bike. He'd take his chance. Maybe the people in the pub wouldn't be so uptight and would have a directory he could use.

Firing the engine, he roared off in the direction of the harbour.

· · · ·

JEANIE SAT IN her usual window seat at the Mackerel and Hook enjoying a glass of red wine. She smiled at Joe as he recounted his day at sea.

'I've had a good catch.' Joe's weathered face beamed with his good fortune.

Jeanie smiled. 'Glad to hear it, Joe. That's great news.' She had a lot of time for this man. It was no secret he'd held a torch for her for years, but she'd stuck to her guns not to get involved with a man, however nice he seemed.

In a way it made her a little sad. Sometimes she got lonely and she'd be lying if she hadn't wondered what it would be like to be with a man – a *good* man, who loved her and treated her right, but she'd never been able to let her guard down enough. *Not after what she'd witnessed what could happen.*

Now in her mid-fifties, she'd long since accepted she'd never know the joy of having children and then grandchildren around her. But that was life and it was just how it was. She'd promised herself that what she had would be enough and it was. *Most of the time.*

Joe had eventually accepted they could be nothing more than friends and had proved to be a particularly good one at that, but sometimes Jeanie felt she'd missed out.

'Can I get you another?' Joe asked, nodding towards Jeanie's glass. 'Then tell me what you've been up to today, yes?'

Jeanie smiled, but then her face froze as the roar of a big motorbike assaulted her ears, drowning out all background noise.

Joe's face creased with concern. 'What? What is it, Jeanie? What's the matter?' He placed his hand over hers.

'I-I don't... The motorbike...?' she whispered. Every time she heard a motorbike like *that* it transported her back to a time she wanted to forget. The time where everything she believed to be decent and true had been blown out of the water. The feeling she'd experienced earlier washed over her again and she shivered with apprehension.

The roar stopped as the bike pulled up outside and the pub fell silent when the door opened and the huge man walked in.

The barmaid's eyes lit up as the large handsome stranger strode up to the bar. 'And what can I get for you?' she asked, eyeing the man's square jaw and tousled hair in appreciation.

'Pint of lager please, love,' Hunter smiled, fishing money out of his pocket.

Jeanie stared as the large man leaning against the bar with his back to her and a strong buzzing radiated through her body. *That man – who was he?* Something was jangling inside her. She had the overwhelming sense that she knew this person, but didn't know why. Her fingers visibly shook as she picked up her wine glass.

'Jeanie, are you ok?' Joe asked, concerned by the look on her face.

'Y-Yes, it's just… I don't know… I…' She stared at the man's back. He wore a leather jacket, but there was no patch. She peered closer. There *had* been a patch though. Her nerves jangled louder as the pull towards the stranger became stronger.

'Do you have a phone directory?' Hunter asked the barmaid as she placed a pint of lager in front of him.

'Yes, there's one over there, next to the pay phone.' She pointed towards the corner and smiled. 'Looking for someone?'

'Maybe,' Hunter winked. He'd look through it in a minute, but first he'd have this long-awaited pint. 'Got any rooms? It's been a long day!'

The barmaid grinned. 'I think there's one free. I'll check for you.' She pulled a small book from under the till and flicked through the pages. 'Yes, here we are, but it's only a single.'

'There's only me, so that will be fine.' Picking up his drink, Hunter smiled, already liking the atmosphere.

Jeanie felt the strange sensation get stronger than ever as the man at the bar turned. *His eyes… Those grey eyes… Was it…? No, it couldn't be…*

Shakily she got to her feet and left Joe staring after her with a worried look. Approaching the large man, she tapped him gently on the shoulder. She didn't think it was possible that she could be imagining things, but either way she had to know. 'Ashley?'

Hunter swung around, his face a mask of confusion. He hadn't been called by his first name for years. He looked down at the tiny woman and gasped. Her hair was no longer jet black, but her eyes were still sparkling green. 'Auntie Jeanie?' he cried in amazement. *She was here!*

He scooped her up into a big hug. 'Oh, Auntie Jeanie! I can't believe it's you! Fancy you being here of all places!' He hadn't actually thought if he located her how he'd explain his presence, let alone broach the subject he needed to talk to her about.

'My son!' Jeanie cried, tears of happiness rolling down her face.

The barmaid's mouth hung open in shock. 'Jeanie? This is your *son*? You've never said.'

Extracting herself from Hunter's embrace, Jeanie shook her head. 'He was like a son to me.' *Well, he was.* She'd loved Ashley Hunter. He was such a sweet little boy and she'd tried so hard to keep him after that dreadful thing with his parents' death. It had always haunted her. She should have fought harder to keep him, but she'd lost all sense after what had happened… What had happened to… *Don't think about that!*

Seeing this boy – now a man, brought the memories crashing into her brains like an avalanche and Jeanie fought to keep herself in check.

Smiling, she looked up into his rugged face and placed her hand on his thickly bearded cheek. 'My, you've grown up!' She took in his massive frame. 'You look just like your father, but with your mother's eyes.' *His parents – they'd been such a loving couple.*

Hunter smiled. 'You look great, Auntie Jeanie. You haven't changed a bit!'

Jeanie laughed. 'That's hardly true, but I'll forgive you for lying in this instance.'

'Let me get you a drink.' Hunter nodded to the barmaid to get Jeanie whatever she was drinking.

'Come and sit down.' Jeanie excitedly took her new glass of wine.

Joe stood up as Hunter approached, finding the man completely dwarfed him. He shook his hand and laughed good-naturedly. 'Jeez, you're a big bloke! I'm Joe.'

'Pleased to meet you, Joe.' Hunter glanced inquisitively at Jeanie and then back at Joe.

'I can see what you're thinking and no, I'm not Jeanie's husband. I would be if she'd let me, but alas, she won't!' Joe smiled.

Hunter smiled, liking the man immediately. He'd been right about Jeanie's reticence to marry and it looked like she'd stuck to it.

'I'll leave you two to catch up,' Joe said jovially. 'I'll see you later.'

Nodding gratefully, Hunter pulled the chair out so Jeanie could sit down. He sat down opposite and smiled widely. 'So, how are you?'

Jeanie could tell Ashley Hunter's presence was no coincidence, regardless of his making out this was a chance meeting. Even after all of this time she knew him too well and her senses had been right. *But what was this about?* She had the distinct feeling it would be something she didn't want to hear, but she'd worry about that later. Right now she didn't want anything spoiling the happiness of seeing the little boy she'd loved so much. Besides, judging by the new wave of instinct which had just flashed into her mind there were also happier things to discuss.

'On Ashley,' she cried, grasping his hand. 'You're all grown up and a fine specimen of a man too! Your parents would be so proud. And you have a son yourself too, yes?'

Hunter frowned. 'I haven't any children.'

Jeanie smiled. 'Oh, but you have. There's definitely one on the way.'

Hunter's face grew sad, suspecting he knew what Jeanie was picking up on. 'I used to know a girl. She was pregnant, but died.'

Jeanie shook her head. 'I'm sorry to hear that, sweetheart, but that's not what I'm getting here. This one is your wife.'

'I haven't got a wife either,' Hunter laughed. *Maybe Jeanie had gone a bit funny?*

Jeanie studied his face. 'Ashley. You forget I can sense things. I'm not losing my mind.'

Hunter reddened. He should have known she hadn't lost her touch in that respect.

Jeanie smiled. 'This woman... The one with the big blue eyes. If she's not your wife, then she should be. She's pregnant with your son.'

Hunter paled. *Blue eyes? Tori?* 'Are you sure?'

Jeanie frowned. 'Of course I'm sure, when have you known me to be wrong.' Her eyebrows knitted together in deep concentration. 'I can see her. She's with someone else, but she wants you.' *There was something dark here. A cloud. A dark cloud. She couldn't quite see what it represented.*

Jeanie took Hunter's hand. 'The child is definitely yours.'

Hunter was gobsmacked. *Could Jeanie be right? Was Tori pregnant with his child?*

Jeanie squeezed his hand and looked him square in the eyes. 'Now, why are you *really* here, Ashley? It's no accident you're in Polperro, is it?'

# TEN

HUNTER SMILED AS Jeanie placed a can of beer in front of him on her little table. He looked around the tiny sitting room of the cottage. He'd never thought she'd give up her caravan and live in a house, but he was wrong. He eyed the line of ornaments along the windowsill and grinned. They were the same ones she'd had in the caravan, he remembered them well.

He watched Jeanie bustle around the small kitchen leading off from the sitting room. He was still floored by what she'd disclosed about Tori. Could it possibly be true she was carrying his child?

Despite his reasons for being here, it was nice seeing Jeanie again. As a boy she'd always had a calming effect on him and that serene peacefulness still radiated from her. However, he'd have to broach the subject as to why he was here very soon.

In the pub, when Jeanie had asked why he was *really* here and received an awkward glance, she'd suggested they go to her cottage just around the corner to talk and Hunter was more than happy to do that. He didn't want an audience.

'Here we are.' Jeanie placed a bowl of steaming hot soup in front of Hunter and sat opposite with a bowl for herself. 'Eat up.'

Hunter eagerly tucked in. 'This is delicious!' he grinned, spooning it greedily into his mouth. He was famished. He'd been so eager to get here, he hadn't stopped for food and his stomach was eternally grateful to finally receive something.

Jeanie watched the man she'd known as a boy closely. She knew he was delaying what he needed to talk about, but she wanted to know. Placing her spoon on the table, she knitted her fingers together. 'Now tell me why you're here.'

Hunter cleared his throat. He wasn't relishing discussing a subject which he knew would upset Jeanie, but it had to be done. His hand reached over the table and rested on hers. 'I need to talk to you about Leila.'

Jeanie paled, her eyes wide with shock. *She wasn't expecting that.* 'L-Leila?' She looked away, panicked. 'I-I…'

'I know it's a difficult subject and won't be easy, but I have to find out what went on.'

Jeanie shook her head resolutely. She hadn't ever spoken about this and didn't want to start now. *It hurt too much.* 'I really don't want to discuss that, Ashley. It's taken me a long time to move on. I'm sure you know Leila's death hit me very hard.'

Hunter nodded sadly. 'I do. When I got out of care you seemed different and I'm ashamed to admit that I couldn't handle how you'd changed. I should have made more effort. At the time I didn't understand what had happened, but I…'

'That's the other thing,' Jeanie cried. 'I've always felt guilty that I couldn't stop you getting taken away.' She felt her hands trembling as memories flooded into her mind.

Hunter raised his hand. 'That wasn't your fault, Auntie Jeanie! How could it have been?'

'I should have tried harder,' she snapped, still angry with herself.

Hunter opened his can of beer. 'I don't think you could have, but it doesn't matter now. What matters is that I put right some wrongs and try to make everything better. At least as much as I can.'

• • • •

IT WAS A LONG and painful discussion for Hunter to explain his gross mistake in who he had wrongly taken out in revenge for Leila and how Noel had, unbeknownst to him, known the truth all along and then used it against him, but it was a discussion he had to have if he wanted Jeanie to tell him what she knew.

Jeanie sat quietly the entire time and Hunter was unable to decide whether she hated him for his lack of judgment, whether she was angry or disappointed about what he'd done since or whether she was horrified that he loved the daughter of the man he'd wrongly murdered.

Even though he'd finished speaking, Jeanie remained silent. She hadn't made one comment, nor had she asked any questions, just stared blankly at the wall behind his head. 'Are you not going to say anything? Even if it's to shout at me?'

Jeanie shook her head slightly. She'd never wanted this sweet boy to have to take over the Reapers reins. She hadn't wanted him to have to be vicious and she *certainly* hadn't wanted him to be given the task of avenging Leila as his initiation. *Damn that bloody club.*

However, she could tell from what Ashley had told her about everything else, he'd tried his best to run the Reapers in a decent way which showed that, despite what he'd done or had to do, his baseline was still good, of which she was very glad about.

It didn't change that she was angry that the boy she'd loved with all her heart had been forced into being a killer. A killer with a conscience, meaning he had to live with his actions and error of judgement. And now his error was haunting him and ruining his life in additional ways.

Ashley loved the woman she could see in her mind and could read it distinctly in his eyes. And Noel – what a disappointment he'd turned out to be. She pursed her lips. It was a blessing in disguise that Leila was not around to witness it.

However, her son's attitude was only to be expected if the genes from the man who'd fathered him dripped through him like poison.

Jeanie looked up sadly. 'What do you want me to say? Apart from you need to get that woman back. You say she's got married? Something bad will happen there, Ashley, I can feel it. You need to get her away from him.'

Hunter looked desperate. 'That's partly why I need your help. I need to tell Tori the truth, but I need to know how I screwed this up so badly with her father. I have to know why, at the time, everything pointed to Jack Jacobs as the culprit if it wasn't him?'

Jeanie rose from the table and fetched another can of beer and a bottle of wine which she slowly poured into a glass for herself. 'It wasn't Jack Jacobs,' she stated clearly. 'That much I *do* know. That man wouldn't have hurt a hair on Leila's head.'

She could remember it as clear as day, even now. Jack and Leila were perfect for each other from the day they'd met and they were so in love. Jeanie sighed wistfully. The gypsies had a lot to answer for in all of this. Jack wasn't a gypsy, so there was no way they would have approved. Leila hid their relationship, but had been determined to be with Jack, despite how difficult her family would make it when the truth came out. She was set on marrying him - it was all planned, but then everything got ruined.

'Aunt Jeanie, *please*? Anything you can think of, anything at all. I have to make sense of this,' Hunter grasped Jeanie's hand once again. 'I want to put things right.'

'How can you put things right?' Jeanie cried, shaking Hunter's hand away and reached for her wine. 'It won't bring Leila or Jack back, will it? It won't remove the stain on Leila's reputation and neither will it change the fact that you murdered the father of the woman you want to marry!' She put her head in her hands. 'Dear God, Ashley. Why Jack Jacobs? He was a lovely man.'

Hunter frowned. 'All the leads I got at the time pointed to

him. I searched for months. People had heard Jack had an interest in Leila and that it would never have been allowed, so that was a motive.'

'Leila hid their relationship well. She knew their association would not be approved of, but she knew her own mind.'

Hunter raised his eyebrows. 'You knew Jack?'

Jeanie smiled wistfully. 'Of course! Leila was my best friend and I covered for her several times.' She sighed sadly. 'Jack respected Leila and loved her beyond anything. Everyone would have come round eventually, but they never got the chance.' She shook her head. 'Leila couldn't have had a more decent man – unlike the rest of them.'

Hunter's ears pricked up. 'The *rest* of them, you say?'

Jeanie's eyes flashed with hate. 'Bastards. That's who they were. Utter *bastards* wo masquerading behind money and status. Made me sick, it did.'

'Who were they?' Hunter pressed.

'People Jack knew. Not that they were friends. They treated him like dirt. Why he put up with them, I'll never know.' She shook her head in frustration. 'Probably because he was too bloody nice.'

The question Hunter needed to ask stuck in his throat. 'W-Was it one of them who… who…'

'Who *raped* her, you mean?' Jeanie spat. 'Yes. That sort took what they wanted and they did that time too!'

'Who was it?' Hunter held his breath. He was so close. *So close to discovering the scum he should have removed.*

Hot tears spilt from Jeanie's eyes. 'I don't know his name. I never did. The only name I ever heard relating to them was 'Bob', but I can tell you now that it wasn't him. I know which of them it was though. He was the worst. I met them briefly twice and both times he was the most obnoxious damn awful creature.'

'Didn't Leila tell you his name?' Hunter asked.

Jeanie shook her head. 'She wouldn't utter a word. She

vowed *never* to speak of him. I knew something had happened before she'd even said. The minute I saw her, I knew. I should have been there. I…'

Hunter grasped Jeanie's shaking hands. 'You weren't to know.'

'I should have, or rather, I *did*. I sensed something bad would happen that day and I ignored it. I've never forgiven myself.'

'What day? The day Leila was attacked?'

Jeanie nodded. 'Yes. It came through strong first thing that morning. I thought it was about me and I ignored everything it was trying to tell me. Stupid, *stupid* woman that I am.'

Hunter could see Jeanie's mounting distress. He topped up her wine and remained silent, watching her brain work overtime.

'They were going for a picnic - just her and Jack,' Jeanie continued. 'Leila said I was welcome to join them, but that warning in my head put me off. I was too concerned about myself to think for one moment it might have been meant for *her*.' She cleared her throat and flapped her hand in front of her flushed face. 'Oh God!'

'Take it steady, Auntie Jeanie. I know it's hard.' Hunter soothed her as best as he could.

'When Leila returned… I knew. I *knew* something awful had happened, but she wouldn't speak of it. Eventually she told me a man had raped her in the woods that day whilst the others watched.'

'Jack Jacobs watched?' Hunter asked incredulously. 'I thought you said he was decent?'

Jeanie shook her head furiously. No, no! Not him. Jack didn't know what happened and never found out as far as I know. Leila walked to a stream to wash up the cups and plates and the others followed, leaving Jack to pack the car. Jack thought they were playing silly devils and had run off to hide.'

'But why were those others there in the first place?' Hunter asked.

'Leila said they invited themselves along when her and Jack stopped in town to pick up drinks. Jack was too much of a gentleman to say no.'

'And Leila didn't tell Jack?'

'Oh God, no. How could she? She believed she'd brought it on herself. Leila was a good gypsy girl and was saving herself for marriage. Jack respected that and was waiting for her. He *loved* her.'

'Why didn't she tell him? From what you've said about the man he'd have understood.'

'That's what I said, but she was adamant. As far as she was concerned now this had happened she was tainted. *Ruined.* And nothing would change her mind.'

'Did Jack sense something was wrong?'

'I think he must have, but she never saw him again. God, he was broken-hearted. He came looking for her several times and eventually got warned off by her brothers. He wasn't a gypsy, remember? They didn't want him sniffing around. She did write, telling him it was all over and she wouldn't be marrying him. He was devastated apparently.'

'And what happened with…'

'When Leila discovered she was pregnant, there was no going back. Her family went mad with the thought she'd been putting herself around when they found out. Her reputation and life were in tatters. Her family believed she was a tart, but she still wouldn't tell them the truth. They locked her away. Even I only got to see her occasionally in secret. No one wanted my virtue sullied by association...'

Hunter felt quite nauseous. *How sad. How incredibly sad.*

'The last time I saw her, she was almost nine months pregnant. That bastard ruined her life and walked off like nothing had happened. Leila wanted the baby - she said it was *hers* and that she'd deal with how it came into existence somehow. I wasn't so sure, but she was insistent. She'd planned to move away after the birth and go incognito – to start again.'

'I promised her I'd come again as soon as I could. Despite

her brave words I knew the whole thing was destroying her. Family and virtue were the most important things to Leila – they were to all of us, but she'd lost both. I can still see her now – her belly huge and her eyes dead. She was broken.' A lone tear escaped from Jeanie's eye.

'She gave birth alone that very same night and by morning she'd ended her life, leaving a note, asking for her baby, Noel, to be taken care of. I wish she'd told me she was on the edge. Again, I should have known.'

'Did the note name the man?'

Jeanie shook her head. 'No, just the facts. Of course, her family were devastated. One that she was dead and two that they'd doubted her morals. At least someone found her that day, otherwise Noel would have been a further casualty, I don't doubt.'

'Everything about what had happened was kept under wraps, but the club and gypsies went mad wanting to avenge her death. They scoured *everywhere*, but couldn't find anything to go on. I heard on the grapevine that nothing happened for years – until Jack...'

Hunter scowled, knowing he'd been the one responsible for ruining an innocent man's life. 'Did they ask you if you knew anything?'

Jeanie smiled weakly. 'Yes, but I lied. I said I knew nothing. I was beside myself with grief, rage, despair and guilt and I've never breathed a word about any of it. Until now.'

# ELEVEN

'DON'T SAY A WORD. Speak as if I'm a double glazing salesman or someone.' Not the usual way to start a conversation with someone who had been left in the lurch, but Hunter knew this was the only way he stood a chance of speaking with Sarah without anyone else getting wind.

Regardless of it being a huge risk calling, he had no choice. He'd ridden back from Polperro, armed with a lot more knowledge than he'd arrived with, but still not anywhere near enough to give him any idea where to go next.

Hunter knew it had been difficult for Jeanie to talk about the subject, but he didn't think she'd withheld any information. It had gone round and round in his mind how he could find out who these other men were and then it had hit him. He'd been about an hour away from his tent when he remembered that photograph Tori had shown him.

The night he'd told her he no longer loved her and walked out of her life was the night she'd shown him the picture of her father. He wasn't likely to forget that as the picture confirmed the man he'd wrongly murdered was the one and the same. His main focus was coming face to face with the man he'd killed and then the shock of seeing Leila Cooper, so he hadn't paid too much attention to anyone else on the photograph, but as he focused his mind, he recalled the picture showed a group and it *had* included other men.

Leila was sitting on a tree trunk, so it stood to reason the picture had been taken in a wood. Jeanie had said Leila had been attacked in a wood after a picnic. Had it been the day the photo had been taken? If so, one of those men in the photograph must be the rapist, unless it was the one taking the picture. Either way, there was only one way to find out and that was to get his hands on the picture, but how could he get into Tori's house without her or her mother seeing him? Furthermore, where would she have put it?

It was at this point he knew he had to risk it and call Sarah.

'Sarah? Can you hear me?' Hunter could tell from the stunned silence on the other end of the line that Sarah was struggling to think of something to say, other than the questions he knew she would be desperate to ask.

'I'm sorry I haven't been in contact. It was unavoidable. Listen, I know you can't say much, so I'll do the talking. I'll tell you as much as I can, but if I ask the questions, can you give me the answers as best as you can?'

'Ok,' Sarah muttered.

Hunter's heart lurched when Colin asked Sarah who was on the phone and listened with bated breath as she made an excuse about a brewery survey.

'I know Colin won't think much of me right now and I also know you don't understand why I left or put Noel in charge. Have things been difficult?'

'Yes, that's definitely correct,' Sarah snapped. 'You could also make a note that doing that *ruins* the beer!'

Hunter got the gist and his heart sank, knowing his decision had caused problems for Colin and Sarah.

'Shit, Sarah. I'm sorry, I really am. I had to leave to find information. Noel has something on me – something *big* and let's just say, part of what he's got was news to me. However, I checked it out and he was bloody right. It's bad – *really* fucking bad and that's why I pulled out of exposing him and Matt. I couldn't let Tori find out that way - it affects her too.'

'I don't understand,' Sarah muttered.

'I've tracked someone down. Someone from my past. I can't say who, but they told me things I can work on.' Hunter spoke quickly. He had so much he needed to say. 'I can't say much over the phone, but you need to trust me when I say I need to put everything together before I can tell you, Tori, or *anyone* anything further.' Hunter sighed. 'Sarah, can you trust what I'm saying?'

'I'm not sure,' Sarah said bluntly.

'I don't blame you, but everything I said and did was for a very good reason and you'll understand that soon. I need to get something from Tori but without her being aware of it.'

Aside from needing that photograph, he also needed to make sure Tori was ok. If Jeanie was right and Tori was pregnant, then surely Sarah would know? He wanted Tori like no other and if she had his child in her, then it was even more imperative that he put this right. 'Sarah, how's Tori?' Hunter held his breath.

'I can't answer that, I'm afraid,' Sarah replied.

Hunter paused. 'Because you won't or because you can't?'

'The second option. What you require isn't in the area any longer.'

Hunter felt sick. 'Tori's gone? Left town? Where?' *Oh Christ, this complicated things even more.*

'I don't know the answer to that either.'

Hunter's mind swam. 'I know she got married. I got the bloody dates wrong. I need to know where she is. I need to get…'

'Like I said, I can't help with that. I don't know.'

'Fuck, Sarah! Can you find out? *Please*? I need to know if she's ok. Plus, she has something - something I need. She showed me a photograph. Listen, I love her and I need…'

'I previously attempted that but it didn't work. I can confirm it's definitely not stocked around here any longer.'

'Did she say anything before she left? Anything *personal*, you know – about me, or erm…'

'I'm not sure quite what you mean, but I don't think so.'

Hunter heard Colin tell Sarah to put the phone down and stop wasting time on 'damn surveys'.

Hunter felt a fresh wave of guilt wash over him. What he'd left them with had clearly had a detrimental effect on their previously good relationship. 'So, you tried to find her, but couldn't and she's definitely left? Is her mother still there?'

'Correct on all those points. Thank you for calling.'

'I'll be in touch as s…'

Hunter blankly stared at the receiver when Sarah hung up, cutting him off mid-sentence. Placing it back on the cradle, he leant against the wall of the phone box and exhaled slowly.

*Where had Tori gone and would she come back? How would he find her?*

He gritted his teeth in determination. What was he talking about? If he'd found Jeanie after almost twenty years, surely he could track Tori down? *He had to, but first he'd got to get his hands on that photograph.*

Realising an old lady was peering into the phone box, bluntly hinting that she wanted to use it, Hunter grabbed his crash helmet and pulled the door, holding it open for the old woman as he left.

Getting back on to his bike, Hunter fired the engine. Sarah had said Tori's mother hadn't left, so maybe he should try her? Rapidly realising that was a ridiculous notion, based on what Tori had previously said about the woman, he snarled in frustration and pulling back on the throttle, roared down the road.

Wait! Tori may have left, but could she have left some of her belongings? Would she have left that box of her father's things behind being as they were so important to her?

It was the only option he'd got, so he'd have to gamble on the long shot that she'd left the box at her mother's house.

. . . .

'I REALLY LOVE this one.' Susan gushed, flicking through the wedding photographs. 'Look how handsome Matthew is. He reminds me so much of you when you were younger.'

Richard puffed out his chest. 'Well, of course, but I trust that I haven't lost *all* my looks yet?'

Susan laughed. 'No, of course not.' She turned to another photograph and looked at it, a trace of sadness on her face.

Richard knew what Susan was thinking, but it didn't change the facts. 'You're thinking about Carmen, aren't you?'

Susan looked up. 'I am and I'm worried.'

Richard waved his hand dismissively. 'It's a storm in a teacup. I told you this before. It'll blow over, if it hasn't already.'

When Susan had told him that Carmen wasn't coming to Matthew's wedding he'd been both surprised, but mainly irritated. Carmen didn't get over all that often and Richard hadn't thought she'd miss her own brother's wedding, but to cite the reason as having problems with Luca? It was ridiculous.

He'd been more than annoyed. Why was his daughter being so melodramatic if her husband had strayed once or twice? He presumed it was something along those lines? What else could it be?

Nothing, that's what. He'd previously assured Luca his daughter would be no bother. She was like her mother – too invested in glitz and glamour to care much about anything else. The man kept her in a lifestyle that most women, even in *their* circles, could only dream of, so it was damn wrong full stop if she'd dreamt up a pathetic reason to cause problems. She should quit pushing her luck. He'd brought her up better than that and she knew it. And now Susan was bloody mithering and driving him mad. He sighed deeply.

'It must be more complicated than we think, Richard,' Susan said, wringing her hands. It was true. She'd spoken to her daughter again last week and the girl was deflated. All of

Carmen's usual boisterous chat about dinner parties and fashion shows was missing from the conversation, but she still wouldn't elaborate about the problem and Susan couldn't understand why. However, unlike her husband, she knew what Carmen *was* planning.

Richard huffed loudly. 'You know what she's like. She'll be fine.' To Carmen, the world was ending if one of her twice-weekly salon appointments was changed. She didn't know the *meaning* of upset.

Susan pursed her lips, unsure whether to say anything. Richard wouldn't like it, but he would have to know sooner rather than later. 'She's talking about coming home…'

Richard spluttered into his glass of whisky. 'Coming home? Is she kidding? She missed the wedding and now, a matter of weeks later, she's coming for a bloody visit? Oh, that girl, she…'

'No.' Susan shook her head. *She might as well tell him.* 'She means for good. She wants a divorce.'

Richard's mouth hung open in shock. *Was he hearing correctly?* This couldn't be right. That's why he'd set up his daughter's marriage to Luca LeVere in the bloody first place! He'd been confident the man would experience no issues or problems with the girl - this he'd felt able to guarantee because Luca had more than enough money to keep her happy, but if she'd had a personality transplant and was making waves, it would cause all manner of unpalatable problems.

Richard wiped his hand across his chin in agitation. Luca would quite rightly question the terms of the agreement. After all, he'd assured the man that the association would be life-long. And if he started questioning things, the big problem was neither Carmen nor Susan were aware of the arrangement.

He hadn't seen why he needed to tell his wife or daughter, Susan wouldn't have approved of the man's history – he didn't even know that much himself, but it had been too good an offer to turn down. Plus, it had looked good at the bank.

Susan must be mistaken. Carmen was far from stupid –

she'd never throw away that money and status. Richard fixed his gaze back on his wife. 'Did you say *divorcing* Luca?'

Seeing Susan nod, Richard slammed his glass down on the coffee table. He'd have to play this to reflect on Carmen, rather than what it would mean to him if Luca decided to discuss the finer points of their contract. 'Oh, for God's sake! What the hell is she talking about? Why would she want to divorce Luca over what's probably a few simple indiscretions? She can't do that, she'll be ostracised! We'll *all* be ostr…'

'Like I said, I think it may be more complicated,' Susan interrupted.

'How? What could the man have possibly done to warrant a bloody divorce? It's ludicrous! The girl's an idiot and I won't have it!'

Had Carmen found out about the arrangement all these years later? Luca wouldn't have told her, he was sure of that, so how was it possible that she could have discovered it? It wasn't. She knew Matt's nuptials were agreed, but she'd only asked once if hers had been and of course he'd had the sense to flatly deny it.

'I don't know what the problem is. She won't say,' Susan said quietly.

Richard banged his fist on the table. 'She can't pull a stunt like that. She'll make our family a bloody laughing stock, don't you realise?' *And that was an understatement.*

Susan realised alright. The thought of everybody finding out their rich and successfully married daughter was getting divorced was her worst nightmare. What would she say to the ladies? This sort of thing didn't happen in their circles. It was *unheard* of. If it wasn't so taboo, she'd have done it herself years ago!

Richard scowled. Bloody women. They were more trouble than they were worth. Carmen was his daughter, but he'd be damned if she would waltz back into their lives, dragging shame down on the family's good name. And just when Matthew's career was taking off too.

He folded his arms defensively across his chest. 'I won't allow it,' he boomed. 'I'll not let her embarrass us. I suggest you find out what's going on and tell her to stop being so bloody childish.'

He slugged down the remains of his whisky. 'She's *not* getting divorced and that's the end of it!'

# TWELVE

LILLIAN SWUNG HER legs daintily into the footwell of the back of the taxi and balanced her Gucci handbag on her lap whilst she secured her seat belt.

'The Polo Club, please,' she said to the driver, eyeing his slicked back dark hair. She really must reiterate to the taxi firm not to send foreigners. She screwed her nose up in contempt. She'd already mentioned *twice* before that she felt uncomfortable with it and now they'd done it again. They *knew* she liked the same driver each time and they'd always made sure that was the case until recently. Now she was getting every Tom, Dick and Harry.

What must it look like, arriving somewhere with a bloody foreigner behind the wheel? She involuntarily shuddered. Damn right embarrassing, it was. When she saw who they'd sent tonight, she was tempted to refuse to get in the car and demand they send another driver. The only reason she hadn't, was because she'd have been late and she didn't want to miss anything.

Punctuality was important. Being tardy for her drinks evenings was out of the question. She would not give any of those women a chance to say *anything* that she wasn't there to hear. Especially if it was about *her*.

But this shoddy service by the taxi firm had to stop. She spent enough money paying them and was such a regular and distinguished customer they had better pull their socks up before she took her damn business elsewhere.

In fact, it may be worth looking into getting a chauffeur. She'd never learnt to drive – it wasn't fitting for a woman of her calibre to be behind the wheel of a car, but once Matthew and Victoria had moved back, perhaps it would be sensible, what with Matthews position, if she had a more upmarket mode of transport. A chauffeur would be more acceptable than a taxi – especially if they kept insisting sending ones like this.

Lillian stared out of the window, thankful the third time she ignored the driver's attempt at conversation, he'd got the hint. She didn't want to engage in small talk – especially with *him*.

As the car wound its way along the roads she pursed her lips in annoyance. Staring out of the window, her mind wandered and she found herself thinking about her daughter. As usual, the thought of Victoria brought Lillian instant irritation. That the girl had made things so difficult for everybody by being so ridiculously stupid with her lack of control still bothered her virtually every second of every day.

Victoria was just lucky that her loose morals hadn't been discovered prior to, or during the wedding, but it was only a matter of time before *everyone* found out she was expecting.

Lillian didn't know how she would deal with that, or the countless questions she would receive over the subject, but she needed to think about the awkward situation sooner rather than later.

Her over-coiffed hair quivered and she sniffed in derision imagining the host of barbed comments made by all the ladies when they discovered Victoria was pregnant *before* she married. She'd never hear the end of it. It almost neutralised the stature she'd gained by having Matthew Stevens, the soon-to-be bank manager, as her son-in-law.

Lillian's nose wrinkled in disdain. Yes, the ladies in her

circles would enjoy having something unsavoury to throw at her and it was hardly something that could be continued to be hidden. The more Victoria and Matthew returned to look at houses, the more chance *someone* would spot them. Or more to the point, spot that belly of hers. The ultimate poster for lack of virtue. It went against *everything* she'd worked to achieve all of these years where their reputation was concerned. The silly, *silly* girl.

Lillian glanced back out of the window, spotting one of those large motorbikes parked up on the side of the road. It looked like the same one she'd seen near her house a few months ago. She'd spoken to the Neighbourhood Watch people, as well as the City Council about getting a *'No Motorbikes'* sign erected in their area and they had *assured* her they would look into it.

She craned her neck as the taxi drove past and stared at the large man sitting astride the bike. It looked like he was waiting for something or someone.

Oh, she didn't like this one bit. Ok, so it wasn't on *her* road, but it was close enough. She didn't want *that* sort with their dirty long hair and foul way of dressing lurking around. She'd been promised this would be nipped in the bud, but if the council thought she'd sit here allowing the tone of the neighbourhood to be lowered by undesirables loitering, no doubt looking for houses to burgle, or women to rape, then they were very much mistaken.

• • • •

HUNTER GROUND HIS cigarette on the tarmac and glanced at his watch. He'd give it a bit longer so twilight would be a little more advanced and then he'd make tracks. He was pushing his luck as it was, but he had little choice.

In the two weeks since talking to Sarah, he'd been back and forth to the city, but thankfully hadn't been spotted by anyone. Not least anyone that mattered anyway.

It had taken all his power not to swing by the Factory and

see what, if anything, had happened to it. It had been so tempting to do a rapid ride-by just to look, but he knew the mere sound of his bike would be picked up from streets away. It had a very distinctive sound and he was certain that they, especially Noel, would have an ear open for a surprise return.

However, as much as he'd wanted to, he'd had to refrain and instead fully concentrate on the careful watch he had on Lillian Morgan. He'd been watching her on a nightly basis for two weeks and now had enough information on her movements to enable him to finally make a move.

Tonight was Wednesday and Wednesday, as well as Thursday and Monday were the nights Lillian went out at 8pm on the dot. From there she'd be out for at least three and a half hours and would be picked up and dropped back by the same taxi firm each time.

Hunter glanced at his watch once again: 8.15.

Wiping a film of sweat from his forehead, he pulled his crash helmet on and fired his bike's engine, silently praying that this wasn't the one night out of all of them that Lillian had decided to give her night out a miss.

• • • •

SARAH FORCED A smile and served up yet another pint. Her arms were aching and she had a splitting headache. It had been awful at the office since Tori had left. Aside from missing having her to chat to, the firm hadn't replaced her. Being as she was the only other typist, she was now lumbered with doing two people's jobs.

That miserable bastard of a boss enjoyed that she was run off her feet – always giving her additional crap to deal with and if her and Colin didn't need the money, she'd tell the moaning old toad where to stick his bloody job.

She'd barely got back tonight before she'd had to jump behind the bar. It was hectic and regardless of whether she could do with lying down to shift this headache, or something to eat, she had no choice but to get stuck in.

Sarah scowled hearing Noel's raucous voice over the relentless noise in the tap room. *How she hated that man.* She followed his trademark laugh over to the dart board area where he and the rest of the Reapers sat and wondered what he was scheming this time. Grin was sitting opposite Noel, staring blankly at his pint. He hadn't looked the same at all since Hunter had left.

Sarah felt bad. Grin must find it extremely hard being on his own when it came to having someone to bounce off. Although Noel had been Hunter's vice president, it was Grin who Hunter trusted, so she couldn't begin to work out why he'd chosen the worst possible contender to take his place when he'd stepped down.

Sarah sighed. It would have been so much easier if she'd spoken to Hunter properly when he'd called, but that was out of the question whilst Colin had been around. If he'd have caught wind it was Hunter on the phone, he'd have gone berserk and she couldn't say she'd have blamed him.

Her first reaction on hearing Hunter's voice had been to tell him to sling his hook. She was still angry and hurt by his actions, but also relieved to know he was alright. But what he'd said had puzzled her and she was desperate to get further details.

She needed to see him and find out what was *really* going on. He owed her that after leaving her in the shit, but all she could do was hope he got back in contact shortly, or even better, returned to rectify everything that had manifested in his absence.

At least Hunter had admitted that his feelings for Tori were true and Sarah was glad about that. But what was this stuff that Tori needed to know? What could Noel possibly have on Hunter that could be so bad?

Sarah's eyebrows knitted together. Noel was hardly the brightest button at the best of times, so for him to have something to stop Hunter exposing his and Matt's shitty behaviour and make him walk away from the woman he loved, was a complete surprise.

And whatever Noel had, Hunter hadn't been aware of half of it? And it involved Tori too? None of it made sense.

Sarah glanced around, irritably clocking the drug deals going on everywhere she looked. They'd get closed down at this rate, but she couldn't do a thing to stop it because with Noel calling the shots, it was *encouraged*. She knew damn well he took a commission off the dealers and was raking it in.

Her and Colin were no match for taking on the hordes of undesirables that now frequented the White Hart and without the Reapers' backing, she stood no chance.

'Are you serving anyone, or are you just standing there catching flies?' Colin snapped, pulling Sarah from her thoughts.

Quickly taking a pint glass from the nearest outstretched hand, Sarah held it under the lager tap. Things weren't getting any better with Colin either - they were getting worse if anything. She bit her lip. It was heart-breaking, but she didn't know what to do to mend it.

$$\bullet \ \bullet \ \bullet \ \bullet$$

DESPITE HIS MASSIVE FRAME, Hunter pulled himself effortlessly onto a ledge at the side of Lillian's house. Glad the building was secluded from prying neighbour's eyes by a line of trees separating the properties, he held his torch between his teeth and slipped a wire into the window lock. With a bit of fiddling, he slipped the catch and released the latch.

Slowly squeezing his body through the tight opening of the utility room window, he eased himself onto the countertop, taking extra care not to knock anything over, courtesy of his large steel toe-capped boots.

Feet firmly on the floor, Hunter took a few seconds to catch his breath and get his bearings. He tuned his hearing into any sign of movement from within the main body of the house. He couldn't afford to be too careful. The last thing he wanted was alerting someone to his presence either from inside or outside. Finding an uninvited biker in a posh house would not go down well should the police arrive. Furthermore, being arrested would guarantee an abrupt halt to further progress with his mission.

Satisfied the house was empty, he made his way as quietly as possible into the hallway, trying to recall exactly which way it was and which room was Tori's. He'd only been here twice before and both times at night. Both of those times he'd left in a rush without paying too much attention to his surroundings.

His mind returned to the first time he'd been here. The night he'd first made love to Tori. The first time he'd experienced the exquisite delights of her body and the raging desire and love she'd awakened in him. His heart beat faster with the memory until the thought of the second time he'd been here drifted into his brain. The time when he'd broken her heart, lied and left the woman he was so in love with sobbing on the bed.

Flicking off his torch to remove any illumination being spotted from outside, Hunter continued along the hall, grateful for the small table lamp Lillian had left on for her return which cast a dim glow from the other end of the long hallway.

Making his way up the stairs, Hunter tried the doors of two rooms, seeing immediately they were not the one he'd been in before and berated himself for being unable to locate Tori's bedroom straight away. Feeling panic flutter, he hastily pushed open another door, relieved to see the correct room. He moved towards the window, pulling the curtains shut. Satisfied the curtains were fully closed, Hunter flicked the torch on and breathed in the faint scent of the room. Despite her absence, Tori's perfume lingered and made his senses tingle.

Remembering he had a job to do rather than reminisce, Hunter scanned around, unsure where to start. He checked under the bed and in the drawer of the bedside cabinet for anything resembling the box he remembered her looking in that contained the photographs, but there was nothing of that sort here.

He felt uncomfortable rifling through Tori's belongings, even though he had a very pressing reason for doing so. He also needed to make sure he didn't make it obvious someone had been in here.

Hearing a noise, Hunter froze. Surely the mother couldn't have returned already? Waiting patiently with bated breath until satisfied the noise wasn't connected, he moved to a chest of drawers. Glancing inside, he pulled out a white top and pressed it against his face.

Whatever Tori had taken when she'd moved was minimal and finding what he was looking for became a real possibility.

*Now, where was this box?* He racked his brains, wishing he'd paid more attention to where she'd got it from, rather than the unsavoury task of what he'd been there to do that night. Moving to the bureau, he eyed the neatly stacked writing paper and envelopes. *Clearly no box there.*

Pulling open the drawers at the base of the bureau, he hastily yanked a shoebox out. *This was it!*

Hardly able to contain his haste, he lifted the lid and breathed a sigh of relief to spot the photo he needed amongst the various items.

Not wanting to again meet the eyes of the man he'd murdered, Hunter quickly stuffed the photograph into the inside pocket of his leather jacket and replaced the box. Now he had to get out of here sharpish.

## THIRTEEN

'CARMEN?' TORI BLINKED several times in quick succession staring at the stunning blonde standing in her doorway.

'Victoria!' Carmen cried, leaning in for the obligatory air kiss, then walking uninvited straight into the hallway of Tori's house.

Tori hovered nervously by the door. She hadn't seen Matt's sister for years. In fact, she'd barely ever met her, short of the occasional and brief meetings they'd had at garden parties. Being five years older than Matt, Carmen hadn't been around that much and by the time Tori and Matt had officially got together, Carmen was married and living in France.

She rarely visited – it was always Matt's parents visiting her. This was preferable as it gave Susan and Richard the excuse to live it up in Carmen's chateau and accompany her to the many elite functions she spent so much time attending. Tori knew this because she'd listened to Susan and Richard boasting incessantly about their daughter's lavish lifestyle for *weeks* after they'd returned from one of their visits.

Tori watched Carmen inspecting the décor of the hallway. *What should she do?* Matt hadn't said his sister was visiting, although that wasn't altogether surprising. He didn't tell her anything anyway, but she'd heard that Carmen was having problems with her husband. She was certain she wasn't supposed to know this, but had overheard Susan talking to Richard about it when they'd thought she'd gone to bed.

But why would Carmen come here rather than her parents' house? From what she understood, Matt and his sister hadn't ever had a close relationship.

Tori studied Carmen's immaculately styled light blonde hair draping around her shoulders. Tall and slim, her catwalk-worthy figure showed off the extortionately expensive designer clothes down to a tee. She smoothed her dress down, feeling immediately inferior and dowdy next to the woman who could have quite easily walked straight off the cover of *Vogue*.

'Oh, I'm being rude, aren't I?' Carmen exclaimed. 'I'm so sorry I didn't make it to your wedding. I got sent some pictures though and you looked *divine*.'

Tori managed to smile, knowing that was in no way true. Even Carmen couldn't have made that wedding dress look anything other than horrible.

'And look at you!' Carmen gushed, moving towards Tori, placing her manicured hand on her bump. 'Another little Matt growing in there.'

Tori winced. There was absolutely nothing good about the possibility of the baby being 'another little Matt'. The thought alone caused bile to rise. 'Erm, Matt's not here at the moment. He's at wo…'

'I didn't expect him to be,' Carmen interrupted. 'I'll surprise him when he gets back tonight.'

Tori smiled. *That's if he came back tonight.* So far, he'd been out every night this week and tonight probably wouldn't be any different and the thought of keeping Carmen company for the entire evening was not something she was looking forward to. It wasn't like they had anything in common.

'Are you planning on visiting your parents?' Tori asked, ushering Carmen into the sitting room and gesturing towards the sofa.

'Oh, how delightful,' Carmen exclaimed, seeing the balcony overlooking the park.

'I don't expect it's much of a view compared to what you see at the chateau,' Tori said, realising Carmen had side-tracked her question and then asking herself why she was justifying where she lived.

Carmen faced Tori. 'I won't see much of that anymore.'

Seeing Tori frown, Carmen smiled. 'I'm surprised you haven't already heard. I'm getting divorced.'

'Divorced? I'm sorry to he…'

'I'm not sorry,' Carmen said. 'But my parents will be, which is why I'm here. I haven't told them I'm back in England yet.'

It didn't take Tori long to work out that Carmen would be staying with them for the foreseeable future. Susan and Richard would not like this and it looked like they were taking sides. She felt the urge to ask what had happened to make Carmen leave her husband that, by all reports, she was blissfully happy with, but refrained. Even though she had the distinct impression that Carmen was inwardly nowhere near as together as she outwardly projected, Tori didn't know her well enough to pry.

'Let me make you some tea.'

'I'd prefer wine if you have any?' Carmen stretched her long legs out in front of her as she sat down on the sofa and kicked off her Christian Louboutin heels. 'We don't drink much tea in France, although I'd best get used to it now I'm back.'

'I'm sure Matt has some wine,' Tori said.

'This is a very nice place,' Carmen said. 'I take it you'll be buying your own place now Matt has finally got his dream job, courtesy of Daddy.'

Tori glanced up, not missing Carmen's hint of sarcasm. 'Yes, we'll be looking over the next few weeks. We need to find somewhere soon because Matt's new position starts the week before the baby's due.'

'Impeccable timing by my dearest brother, I see,' Carmen

griped. 'I'm sure Daddy will help him find somewhere *suitable*.'

Tori raised an eyebrow. There was definitely an unspoken issue between Carmen and Matt and, from what she could gather, her father too. Maybe the woman wasn't so bad after all, but the glimmer of the possibility of having an ally flashing into her mind, was quickly dismissed. It was unrealistic to expect Carmen to be on her side.

'Let me get you that wine,' she smiled.

· · · ·

'I DIDN'T EXPECT to see you again so soon, Ashley,' Jeanie said, ushering Hunter into the cottage. It taken her *days* to gather herself together after the last time he was here opening all those old wounds.

Hunter's face fell. He could immediately tell that Jeanie was uncomfortable. 'I'm sorry to have to co…'

She raised her hand. 'Don't get me wrong. It's lovely to see you, I didn't mean it like that. I can just tell that, again, this visit isn't a social one.'

Hunter plonked himself down dwarfing the small two-seater floral sofa. 'I'm afraid you're right. I would have called, but you don't have a phone.'

'Never needed one,' Jeanie smiled.

Hunter adjusted himself slightly. He hadn't been relishing the long ride back down to Polperro – or rather his backside hadn't and it had fared just as painfully this time as the last.

Jeanie sat opposite Hunter on the matching wingback armchair. 'First of all, tell me – did you make things right with that lady of yours?'

Hunter shook his head sadly. 'Not yet. I still have to get all the info before I can do that.'

Jeanie frowned. She could still see the woman for Ashley in her minds' eye. 'You should forget about getting the information first. I feel that being there for her takes a higher priority.'

She could see the woman's face. She was desperately unhappy and there was impending danger lurking. She couldn't see what sort – just that it was there and wasn't good. *That man…*

'What?' Hunter asked. He'd always been able to tell when Jeanie concentrated on what she sensed. 'What can you see?'

'Was I right about the baby?' Jeanie asked, knowing without any shadow of a doubt she was. She could see it as clear as day.

Hunter shrugged. 'I don't know. I haven't seen Tori, but I did find out that she's moved away. I don't know where at the moment, but I'm working on that too.'

Jeanie clutched Hunter's hand. 'You must find her.'

'But I need to tell her the truth so she can make the choice to be with me, or not…' Hunter argued.

Jeanie frowned. Personally, she was getting it loud and clear that Ashley needed to be with this woman and speak the truth later. It was more important to remove her from whatever the bad situation was. In an ideal world, yes – tell her the truth, but there was something infringing on this. Something that wouldn't wait.

She needed quiet to work out what it was and then she'd have something solid to say. She knew Ashley too well. He was stubborn and almost too righteous to do so otherwise. In the meantime, she'd have to let him do it his way.

Jeanie smiled. 'Come on then. What do you need to ask?'

'Do you mind if I…' Hunter pulled out his cigarette packet.

'Not at all, but I take it that isn't the question?' Jeanie reached for a small glass ashtray and placed it on the little table in front of Hunter.

Hunter lit a cigarette and retrieved an envelope from his inside pocket. 'I managed to get this. I remembered something based on what you said last time. I think this may have been taken the day Leila was attacked.' He watched Jeanie's face turn ashen. 'I want to know if any of these men was the one who did it.'

Jeanie's fingers visibly shook as she reluctantly took the photograph. She forced herself to stare at the image, bile rising immediately as she focused on the faces. There was Leila – her beautiful Leila and dear Jack. And there was that bastard. She'd recognise him anywhere. She could still hear his nasally voice after all these years.

'Is the man on the picture?' Hunter pushed, knowing already by Jeanie's expression that he was. 'Which one is it?'

Jeanie viciously prodded at the man on the end. 'That's the bastard. *Him.*'

Hunter stared at who Jeanie was pointing to. Now he knew what the man looked like. Or at least what he *used* to look like

'And no, I don't know his name before you ask me again. I've already told you that,' Jeanie said, feeling uncomfortably light-headed.

'And you're sure it's him?'

'Of *course* I'm sure, I'll never forget him. God knows I've tried!' Jeanie said, tears brimming in her green eyes.

Hunter squeezed her hand. 'I'm sorry for all this, Jeanie, I really am.' He felt bad for upsetting her yet again. He could see how much this hurt her.

'You're a good boy, Ashley. You must do what you need to do.'

Hunter frowned. 'You mentioned before you heard one of their names. Bob, wasn't it? Can you remember which one Bob is?'

Jeanie forced herself to look back down at the photograph and pointed to a short stocky man standing next to Jack Jacobs. 'This one. His was the only one whose name I heard. No idea of a surname – just Bob.'

Hunter nodded. 'And you said they had or were studying together?'

Jeanie pursed her lips. 'That's what I'm sure Leila said. Business and economics or something like that.' She traced her finger lightly over Leila's face as it stared out of the photograph. 'Leila always said that lot had high aspirations of getting into finance.'

'What? Jack Jacobs?'

Jeanie shook her head. 'No, not him. The rest of them.' She snorted derisively. 'Always thought they were something special. Destined for great things, top jobs – bank managers - you know the sort.'

Hunter removed the photo from the table and stared at the man on the end. *So that was who should have been his target?*

His jaw clenched. He'd never set eyes on the man before and had no clue where to start, but at least he knew that one of them was called Bob. *Bob who may or may not be a bank manager or something similar.*

Putting the photo back in the envelope, he secured it safely back in his inside pocket. 'Thank you, Jeanie,' he smiled. 'Now how about I treat you to a glass of wine down the Mackerel and Hook? Your friend Joe might be there and I'd like to see him again. He seems like a nice chap.'

Jeanie smiled, glad for the diversion. 'Alright, if you insist…'

## FOURTEEN

WHEN MATT ANSWERED the phone he hadn't expected his bloody mother. 'What's happened? Are you alright?'

Although slightly hungover, the coke he'd taken this morning had brightened him up somewhat, but the prospect of something having befallen his mother was sobering. She wouldn't have called him at work if it wasn't an emergency. Maybe his father had had a heart attack? Oh no, if that had happened wouldn't it balls up or slow down his taking up the position?

'I'm fine,' Susan snapped. 'I've been trying to reach you for two days!'

Matt became irritated. *Two days? That was hardly an emergency.* 'You've called me at work? For what? It's emergencies only! You know that beca…'

'Perhaps if you were ever at home with your pregnant wife then I wouldn't be forced to call you at work!' Susan cried. Oh yes, she'd called several times over the last two days and each time Victoria had said Matthew wasn't there.

She didn't believe Victoria was making it up. She could tell the poor girl was making excuses for her husband's whereabouts, even though it was obvious she had no clue where he was.

Matt sighed. *He didn't need this.* 'Listen, I'll call you tonight. I have an important meeting shortly and I ne…'

'Matthew,' Susan barked. 'You may be able to lie to your wife about where you are, but not to me!' She could hazard a guess that her son was out – busy putting it about with all sort of floozies. His father had been just the same. She was not impressed that Matthew would do this to Victoria in her fragile condition and that was only the *start* of it. 'You should be at home!'

Matt reddened. Even though he had his own office with no chance of anyone overhearing the conversation, he wouldn't have his mother phoning him at work, having a go at him like a naughty child. 'With all due respect, I don't have to explain that to you. I ca…'

'If you were ever there, then maybe you'd realise your *sister* has moved into your house!' Susan interrupted.

Matt stared at the receiver in shock. 'She's *what*?' *Carmen was in his house? Since when?*

'Like I just said, your sister's taken it upon herself to move in. She hasn't told *me* this – I only know because I eventually forced your wife to admit that Carmen's been there for the past two days.'

Matt spluttered in disbelief. 'She's been… Tori said… I…'

'Luca called three days ago demanding to speak to Carmen,' Susan said. 'Well, of course, I hadn't seen her and told him so, but she told him she was visiting all of us. Being as she isn't with us, who else does that leave, apart from *you*?'

'But, I…'

'But nothing! I've wasted two days trying to get hold of you,' Susan continued. 'I suggest you pull yourself away from whoever you've been spending your time with and get yourself home. Myself and your father will be coming to sort this mess out that your sister has caused. Do you understand?'

Before Matt could answer, his mother hung up. He silently fumed. *Well, that put paid to another session with Debs tonight.*

He grated his teeth. Tori would be loving this. The bitch wouldn't have been able to wait to tell his mother of his absence and now he'd got his bloody sister there too.

• • • •

'ARE YOU OK, SARAH?'

Sarah glanced up to see Grin, more than aware she'd been in a world of her own. She smiled weakly. 'Not really, no…'

Grin leant on the bar, oblivious that he'd just rested his elbows in a large pool of beer. 'I'm sure things will get better.'

'I hope so,' Sarah muttered, glancing around the tap room.

Grin leant closer. 'Have you heard anything?'

Sarah looked up sharply. 'Heard anything?' She knew what Grin was asking, but she needed to deflect this. It was not a question she wanted to answer.

'From Hunter?' Grin hissed. 'You need to tell me if you have, even if he told you not to. I need to know the score.'

Sarah bit her lip. What should she do? She knew what Hunter said, but Grin needed to know what was going on too. Having someone to talk to about everything would also be a weight off her mind because she sure as hell couldn't tell Colin – he'd made it clear that pretty much *anything* she said and did was wrong these days.

'Sarah?'

Sarah saw the worry behind Grin's eyes. 'Well, I…'

'Grin!' Noel slapped Grin hard on the back whilst eyeing Sarah curiously. 'Too busy having a conversation to get the drinks in?'

Sarah watched Grin straighten himself up, a nerve in his neck twitching with suppressed rage.

'Are you two going to include *me* in this little chat?' Noel's eyes gleamed nastily. 'You know I don't like being left out and the rules are that we all keep each other informed.' He sneered at Sarah. 'That way things don't go wrong…'

Sarah quelled the urge to smash a glass in Noel's teeth. 'I'm afraid not everything is interesting, Noel,' she smiled. 'Just chatting, that's all. We've run out of whisky.' She gestured towards the empty optic on the wall behind her. 'Colin's gone to fetch some more.'

'Fucked up the spirit order, did you?' Noel said, raising his eyebrows. He scathingly chucked a five pound note onto the bar. 'Keep the change,' he sneered. 'Not that you need it.' He looked around the packed room pointedly. 'No need to thank me for the increase in customers, by the way.'

Sarah scowled at Noel's retreating back as he made his way with Grin over to the dart board area and was thankful to see Colin return through the rickety door. She hated being around Noel. His very presence made her skin crawl.

'You managed to get a bottle?' she said chirpily.

Colin didn't bother answering, instead he concentrated on fixing the new bottle of whisky to the optic.

The shrill and sudden ring of the telephone made Sarah jump out of her skin. *It might be Hunter.* She rushed towards the handset, but Colin beat her to it.

'Yes?' he barked.

Sarah held her breath, pretending to busy herself with wiping up more spillage.

'Who is this?' Colin shouted.

Sarah froze. *It must be Hunter. Shit!*

Colin angrily slammed the receiver down. 'For fuck's sake!'

'Who was it?'

'Well that's just it. No one! I'm sick of this happening!'

Sarah frowned. How many times had this happened? Had Hunter been trying to reach her? Or Tori?

'That's the *third* bloody silent call. I know someone's on the other end, but they never speak,' Colin ranted. 'Can you shed any light on that?'

'M-Me? What do you mean?' Sarah said quietly, aware that the general noise level had dropped with Colin's raised voice.

'Has Hunter called you?' Colin raged. 'Or that two-faced little bitch? Is this what it's all about?' His eyes narrowed. 'I'm warning you, Sarah. If you're speaking to *either* of them or anyone to do with them after everything we've been through and everything I've said about it, then we're *over*!'

Feeling the stress rise like a volcano, Sarah rushed out from behind the bar and pushed blindly through the crowd. She didn't care if everyone could see the tears streaming down her face.

Needing some air, she rushed into the back corridor and yanked open the door to the small enclosed courtyard, glad to see there was no one else out there. She leant back against the wall and tilted her head up towards the sky, breathing deeply and frantically wiped away her tears with the back of her hand.

Were things really that bad that Colin would consider leaving her? Over *this*?

Before she could think any further, Sarah yelped as she was grabbed around the throat. Her eyes shot open in panic, only to see Noel's manic glare inches from hers. 'What the...'

'Listen here, you meddling witch. What the fuck's going on?'

Sarah pulled at Noel's hand around her throat, but couldn't budge it.

'I heard what Colin said. Are you in contact with Hunter?' Noel spat.

Sarah shook her head defiantly. She was damned if she would tell Noel a thing. She'd rather he strangled her.

Noel pushed his body up against Sarah's, crushing her further into the wall. His proximity made her feel sick, but when he yanked at her skirt, pulling it up, panic formed in the pit of her stomach. His calloused fingers ran down the outside of her thighs. *Surely he wasn't going to...*

'Get off!' Sarah cried, twisting her body away.

'I could teach you a lesson you sorely need if I wished,' Noel sneered, releasing her skirt. 'But you're not worth the effort.'

Despite her fear and revulsion, it was vital to give Noel the impression she wasn't scared, even though she was utterly terrified. 'How dare you make such disgusting threats. I thought you were better than that!'

'Just shows how wrong you can be then, doesn't it?' Noel sneered, his face still inches from Sarah's. 'You've got Hunter wrong. Don't for one minute fall for his shit. He's not who you think he is. There are lots of things you don't know.'

Sarah's false confidence evaporated fast. 'I need to get back in there. Colin will wonder wh…'

'By the sounds of it, Colin wants the truth too.' Noel barred Sarah's way, folding his arms across his large chest. 'I'll ask you once more… Has Hunter made contact?'

Sarah forced herself to look Noel straight in the eyes. 'No!' she hissed. 'No, he hasn't.'

Noel's face broke into a sneering smile. 'I hope for *your* sake you're telling me the truth because you'll be very sorry if you're not.' Stepping aside, he bowed theatrically. 'Thank you for your time and remember to let me know *when* he gets in contact. Because both you and I know he will eventually.'

Nodding briefly, Sarah pushed her way back into the bar. She smiled as expected at all the waiting customers and made her body override the trembling which was gaining momentum through her.

She even ignored Colin's sideways glances. She felt sick to the very root of her being.

· · · ·

'I'M NOT HAVING IT, RICHARD,' Susan whined, inspecting her bright pink lipstick in the passenger seat vanity mirror.

'Put that bloody thing away,' Richard barked, pushing the sun visor back into position. 'I can't see with that in the way!'

Why did the stupid woman insist on looking at herself when he was driving? She did this every time they were in the car and each time he told her not to. It got on his nerves, but not quite as much as having to drive to Matthew's. He'd planned a nice quiet evening in watching a video, but he'd stepped through the door to find Susan waiting in her coat, informing him that they were going straight back out.

He'd wished he'd had a hint something was afoot because he'd have made an excuse to work late under the proviso of doing something 'really important'. But no - now he was driving almost one hundred miles to sort out his bloody daughter.

'If Luca phoned three days ago, why have you not told me about this before?' Richard snapped, eyeing Susan frostily.

He swallowed nervously. By God, if Carmen divorced Luca, then he'd be well and truly in the proverbial shit. He had a good enough idea what Luca really was and if his daughter's games continued, there would not be a good end result. Neither would it be good if Susan, or Carmen, come to think of it, discovered anything. On top of that, if Carmen pushed for divorce everyone would presume he'd raised an awful disobedient daughter and it would ruin their social standing.

'I didn't want to worry you,' Susan muttered.

Richard angrily wiped the sweat off his brow. '*Worry* me? What makes you think I'd be even marginally concerned that our daughter wants to throw away a perfectly good marriage and hasn't been seen since? She could have been lying dead in a skip for all you knew!' And Carmen may well still be doing that if the girl didn't get her act together and return to her husband immediately.

'There's no point being facetious. I knew you'd be irrational.' Susan watched a vein in Richard's temple twitching ominously. 'I was trying to get hold of Matthew, but it seems that he's following in your footsteps in more ways than one.'

'And what's that supposed to mean?' Richard barked, feeling the urge to push Susan out of his car onto the hard shoulder just so he wouldn't have to listen to her voice going on and on and bloody *on*.

Susan pursed her lips. She knew she was riling Richard, but she'd had enough. 'He's never home. He's off out with God knows who. He should be with Victoria. What will people think?'

'What do you mean, what will people think?' Richard said.

'Not everyone's as suspicious as you. Having a job like that requires a lot of extra work – networking and all sorts.'

He knew full well Susan was alluding to his own frequent disappearances in the past, but he'd never admitted to any indiscretions and was damned if he would start now. 'And why are you suddenly so bothered about Victoria? She's doing alright.'

'How would *you* know?' Susan yelled. 'I know how she must feel. It's horrible being pregnant and your husband disappearing. You were exactly the same and it made me feel awful.'

*That's because you looked like a tank and did nothing but eat and moan*, Richard thought, his stomach turning from the memory. 'I was working to provide the house and lifestyle you wanted, Susan.'

'If that's how you see it…' Susan sniffed. 'I'm not stupid. I know you were with other women, but the difference is I was brought up to accept that as part and parcel of marriage. It didn't make it any easier though and Victoria… well, she's more fragile I suppose. This pregnancy is taking it out of her and Lillian isn't exactly much help.'

Richard felt this was a good time to change the subject. 'Lillian's *never* been anything other than Lillian. Look, are we going to Matthew's to sort out our daughter or to worry about Victoria?'

Yes, he'd spent time with other women and why the hell not? He'd be disappointed in Matthew if he wasn't doing the same thing, not that he'd admit that to Susan.

These women – sitting around all day doing nothing but happily taking money to keep them looking nice and living somewhere plush. They wanted everything their way, but they never saw it like that, did they? No logic – *any* of them.

Richard gripped the steering wheel harder. This was not the way he'd wanted to spend his night and could only envisage it getting a lot worse. If he knew Carmen at all, everything that came out of her mouth would be overdressed and exaggerated bullshit, just like her mother.

Susan stared out of the window. Admittedly, she was brought up to expect this, but sometimes, just *sometimes* it got her down. There really wasn't any point reasoning with Richard. It was his way or the highway. She'd never had anyone she could talk to. All the people she spoke of as friends, weren't - they were all equally trapped, pretending to be happy with their successful husbands, nice clothes and big houses, when in reality they were miserable. Either that, or too stupid or indoctrinated to notice or care their marriages were as fake as a plastic Christmas tree.

Richard glanced at Susan and decided to make an effort. They'd be at Matthew's soon and it wouldn't look good if they lectured their daughter about her marriage when it was clear they had been arguing throughout the whole journey.

'If you're worried about Victoria, you should tell Lillian to make more of an effort. She's her mother, after all.'

Susan snorted. 'I doubt she cares if Victoria's unhappy or not.'

Richard laughed. 'Yes, she's a bit of a tough one!' *Actually, Lillian was more mercenary than anyone he knew and that was saying something.*

'Besides, she's got more pressing things worrying her,' Susan added thoughtfully. The last time she'd seen Lillian she really had wondered whether the woman was losing her mind.

Richard sighed. 'What this time?'

'While she was out the other week, she was convinced someone had been in her house.' Susan had listened for a good two hours whilst Lillian recounted every minute detail.

'They'd be brave if they had! The last thing I'd want would be stuck unexpectedly in a house with Lillian Morgan!' Richard quipped. 'What made her think that?'

'She was sure a door she'd closed was ajar when she returned.'

'What?' Richard chortled. 'And that's the reason she thought someone was in her house?'

'There were other things too,' Susan added. All rather irrelevant, but she hadn't said that to Lillian.

'What had been taken?'

'Nothing,' Susan laughed, now slightly more relaxed. 'Nothing at all.'

'Dear God,' Richard laughed. 'She's got more antiques and expensive stuff than a shop on the King's Road and nothing was taken? It was either a very dense burglar, or Lillian had quaffed too much champagne.'

'That's what I thought!' Susan agreed. 'I think she spooked herself because she'd said she'd seen one of those bikers on her way out. You know one of them from that dreadful club.'

The hackles rose on Richard's neck. 'And was it?'

Susan shrugged. 'I don't know. Lillian thinks she's seen them hanging around before. Just the one, mind. She believes they're casing houses to burgle. She's spoken to the Neighbourhood Watch team and the local council who said they'll look into it, but if it's true, then it's worrying.'

'Hmm,' Richard mumbled. *It was more than worrying.* If Lillian was right, why were the Reapers hanging around neighbourhoods such as theirs? He hadn't dug Matthew out of the hole he'd created for himself with that despicable motorbike group for it all to start up again.

He also hadn't fixed Matthew's post with Bob Greaves out of the goodness of his heart. He'd had to make sure his son was out of town until any fallout with the Reapers had died down. And he certainly hadn't got together the money for Matthew to pay off that psycho that he'd been stupid enough to enter into deals with for any other reason other than it stopped anything going any further. *Or stopped the past from rearing its ugly head.*

The bank still hadn't discovered he'd moved the money to pay the Reapers off with from various holding accounts, but he'd only got a few more weeks until his retirement and then he'd be in the clear on that score.

*So why were the Reapers sniffing about?* This was supposed

to be over. There was nothing left to link him to them or theirs, especially since he'd destroyed those photos Tori had found.

'What's the matter?' Susan asked, eyeing Richard's pale complexion. 'Do you think our house will be broken into?'

Richard quickly castigated himself. He was being ridiculous. He didn't even know if the Reapers were on his tail or even it if had been a Reaper Lillian had seen. Even if it was, it was most likely nothing to do with him. Why would it be? *No reason. He was being daft.*

Richard squeezed Susan's hand. 'No, of course not. I doubt whether it was anything. Lillian's always on the lookout for a drama. Take what she says with a pinch of salt.' He smiled widely. 'Now, we'll be arriving at Matthew's in the next ten minutes, so we need to agree on how the hell to deal with Carmen.'

## FIFTEEN

HUNTER HAD MOVED on yet again and was getting thoroughly sick of living in a tent. It had been *months*. He had a perfectly good place back in the city – even if it was a dilapidated and half-converted Victorian factory, but it was *his* – providing Noel hadn't razed it to the ground in his absence of course. Either way he should be there, rather than in a field full of cow pats.

His brows furrowed together. He hadn't dreamt it would be so painstakingly slow getting to the bottom of everything, although he should have guessed it wouldn't be easy. *Nothing ever was.*

Every time he thought he was on to something, he hit another brick wall. His forehead creased in concentration. It wasn't like he'd got too much to go on, was it? Locating a bloke called 'Bob', who may or may not be a bank manager – *somewhere…*

Would he have ever left if he had known it would take this long? It didn't have to be like this – he could have said nothing and been with Tori as planned. She may have never found out about his secret and sometimes his insistence of trying to do things in the 'right' way irritated him. Who was he trying to kid? After the things he'd done, he wondered why he bothered trying to be honourable at all.

Hunter exhaled slowly. It may not make sense to anyone else. It barely made sense to him half the time. Even Jeanie suggested he put the truth to one side for now, but it mattered to *him*. His heart ached thinking of Tori, imagining her exquisite face looking up at him with that deep intense love. Feeling his cock stir, Hunter reprimanded himself. Had he forgotten the last time he'd seen her, she'd been broken and destroyed? *Thanks to him.*

Pulling out his notebook, he despondently flicked through the pages. Getting names of bank managers was a feat upon itself. For a start, there were thousands of banks across the country and most places wouldn't give out names over the phone to a random man asking. Why would they? From the handful who had, none of the managers were called Bob or Robert.

However, he'd had a brainwave. After a few days of fruitless phone calls and being dismissed as a random nutter, he'd morphed into Edward Taylor – a rep from *Business Weekly*.

He should have been a *Mastermind* contestant, he thought ruefully. Putting on his most eloquent voice, Hunter had confidently announced to whoever had answered the phone that their manager was nominated as a finalist for *Business Weekly's* esteemed 'Bank Manager of The Year' award.

When hearing the added bonus that the manager would be attending the finalist ceremony at London's Savoy Hotel, strangely excited at this prospect, every single person he'd spoken to had hardly been able to wait to give their manager's name so that the relevant invitations could be sent.

It was a long and laborious process, but he was finally getting somewhere and it had been so easy he wondered why he hadn't thought of it before.

In his hometown there was not *one* manager of that name and also no one in the next couple of cities either. He'd had a few possibilities from the next city, which meant he'd had to take a trip. Staking the bank in question out, he'd waited patiently for the 'Reserved – Bank Manager' space in the car park to be filled, only to see that one of the contenders was at least twenty years too old and the other, too young, so that had been a dead loss.

Pulling off the top of a bottle of beer with his teeth, Hunter took a gulp, trying his best to bypass that the beer was decidedly warm and instead scanned the list he'd made from today's countless hours in the phone box. He was developing a phobia of bloody phone boxes and after this was all over, if he *ever* stepped foot inside one again, it would be too soon.

He squinted over his own scrawl. Three potential contenders to check out tomorrow which would take more than one day if the relevant person wasn't there.

Hunter sighed, wishing he could have got hold of Sarah when he'd called. That Tori might be pregnant was weighing heavily on his mind and Sarah may well have heard something by now, or even know where Tori had moved to, but when Colin answered, he'd had no choice but to hang up.

He raked his hands through his unkempt hair, picking a twig out of it. *Christ, this was no good. He was turning into a scarecrow.*

Too many things were going on that he needed to get on top of, but it wasn't for lack of trying. He just had to make things quicker.

• • • •

'I TAKE IT Matt isn't coming back tonight?' Carmen said, mindlessly twirling the stem of her wine glass around in her fingers.

Tori moved her gaze from the window. Carmen must presume she was staring in the hope of spotting Matt's car, but she couldn't have been more wrong. She was actually wondering what it would be like if she could walk out of the door and not return. 'He's going to a work function tonight.'

Carmen raised an eyebrow. 'And you're not accompanying him? I bet he didn't like that. It's always good to show off the wives.'

Tori smiled weakly. She hadn't wanted to go in the first place – she hated those pretentious events where everyone sat around a table, giggling nonsensically at some in-joke from a stranger.

'It was Matt who insisted I didn't go. I don't think he wanted me to embarrass him.' Tori glanced down at her belly.

'Embarrass him?' Carmen cried, sitting up sharply, sloshing wine over herself. She'd almost finished the second bottle of the evening and it showed. 'He's got a cheek! Men love showing off their virility at corporate functions. I'm surprised he didn't drag you there.'

Actually, she wasn't. Carmen saw how her brother spoke to Tori during the time she'd been here and it was irritating her. In fact, everything about him was irritating. The more time she spent with Tori, the more she found herself liking the woman, even though she hadn't expected to. And the angrier she became with men. Especially men like Matt. And her father. *And Luca.*

Carmen forced herself not to grind her teeth, still unable to believe she'd been lied to all of this time.

Tori watched Carmen dab at the wine on her cream top. 'Let me get you a cloth. It will stain your lovely top otherwise.' She hefted herself to the edge of the armchair.

'You stay there,' Carmen said. 'And it's not a lovely top. Luca chose it and I fucking hate it!'

Tori sat back in shock. Carmen always seemed so poised and ladylike, but these last few days she'd seen a different side of her. There was a lot more to this woman.

'Are you missing your husband?' Tori asked. *Maybe Carmen was having second thoughts over the divorce?*

Carmen stared at Tori incredulously. 'You *are* joking? By God, not after wh...' Stopping suddenly, she reined herself back in. 'Never mind, but no I'm not.'

She clumsily refilled her glass from the bottle on the coffee table. 'I expect he's mercilessly hounding my parents over my whereabouts as we speak! They certainly won't be encouraging him and will pretend they know nothing about it. Even mentioning my name is a no-no at the moment because we all know how 'embarrassing' a divorced daughter would be...' They could shout, scream, threaten and do what they liked, but it wouldn't change her mind. *Nothing would. And it was their own fault.*

Tori smiled. 'They weren't very happy, were they?' *That was probably the understatement of the year.*

After their wasted journey last week to get their daughter to accompany them back to their house and then put things right with Luca, Richard and Susan had left empty-handed. Tori had been embarrassed witnessing Richard giving his grown daughter a dressing down about her 'unacceptable' behaviour. Carmen had stood her ground though and Tori admired her greatly for that, but would still love to know the real reason behind her departure.

'They certainly weren't happy, but it's one thing I won't be agreeing to in order to make their social standing more acceptable.'

Carmen brushed her hair away from her face in agitation. She could still barely believe any of it and hadn't, for one minute, assumed her father would do this to her. She knew Matt's wedding to Tori was arranged and had always disagreed with that. *No one* should marry purely to make someone else's life better, but she hadn't expected in a *million* years that her parents had done the same to her.

Well, her father had. As far as she was aware, her mother was unaware of Luca and her father's agreement.

Oh yes, *her* marriage had also been arranged, completely for her father's benefit, despite him vehemently denying it when she'd asked.

Carmen scowled. For nearly five years, she'd believed Luca had *wanted* to marry her. Ok, so he hadn't set her on fire, but he'd offered a wonderful lifestyle and wasn't quite as boring as the other men in the circles she'd frequented. She'd thought it was a good move. Things like that had once seemed important. *Not anymore.*

'I'm sorry for burdening you. I expect you could do without me adding to your problems, what with…' She nodded towards Tori's belly.

'Not at all,' Tori smiled. 'I'm enjoying your company.' She didn't want to get her hopes up, but was starting to feel she was silently making an unexpected ally in Carmen.

Frowning, Carmen studied Tori. 'How are things with you and Matt? I mean, *really*? I know he's my brother, but you don't seem very – how can I put it? Happy?' She wanted to know if Tori's marriage was as miserable as it looked.

Tori's face fell. She could hardly admit what had really been going on, even though she wanted to. She may be getting on with Carmen to a larger extent than expected, but it didn't mean the woman was trustworthy. She could report everything back to Matt, Richard and Susan for all she knew.

Tori tried to say something plausible. 'Oh, there's been a lot going on the past few months. The wedding, the move and now preparing to move again!' She rubbed her growing bump. 'And of course, this one. Anyway, I hardly see Matt he's so busy…'

Carmen sat forward. 'The way he talks to you…'

Tori smiled weakly. *So she'd noticed.* 'He gets stressed…'

Carmen pursed her lips. 'Hmm. That's what all men say to give their disgusting behaviour an excuse!'

Tori saw the anger on Carmen's face. 'What happened with Luca?'

'Oh, let's not bother talking about that!' Carmen said, quickly standing up. 'I'm going to grab another bottle of wine.'

## Sixteen

'OH, LOOK AT YOU!' Susan cried, holding Tori at arms' length and staring at her appraisingly. 'Look Richard, doesn't Victoria look positively glowing?'

Richard stared at Victoria impassively. *What was 'glowing' supposed to mean?* Was that a female description of being pregnant because she didn't look much other than that. At least Matthew was fortunate that she hadn't piled weight on anywhere else apart from out front. Susan on the other hand, had put it on *everywhere* when she'd had Matthew and Carmen and it had taken her *years* to lose it.

Still, he'd been right in as much as believing that Susan would love a grandchild being on the way, even if it hadn't been in the order she preferred. If she wanted him to gush compliments all over his daughter-in-law, then he'd do it if it kept her happy.

He knew Susan was worrying about Carmen and he was less than impressed that his daughter was still playing silly devils at Matthew's house. He'd been so humiliated she'd refused point blank to return home, but Susan insisted they give their daughter space. How long did that damn well take? It had been three weeks now and she *still* refused to take their calls.

However, Richard had managed to touch base with Luca. Unbeknown to Susan, he'd called him last week and tested the water. Obviously, he hadn't mentioned divorce, and it was a good job, because Luca was under the impression his wife was visiting Matthew and Victoria to spend time with them before the baby was born. Richard had even made a joke about the possibility of Carmen becoming broody. He'd often wondered why Luca hadn't insisted on Carmen popping out a few kids by now as they'd been married for nearly five years.

Of course, he really wanted to broach the subject of whether Carmen had somehow discovered their 'arrangement', but hadn't. Luca wasn't the sort of man who took kindly to questioning and it was imperative he kept him on side. The good news was Luca hadn't mentioned anything, so providing his daughter returned to her rightful place before too long, he didn't foresee any major problems.

Richard's lips set in a thin line. The man wasn't stupid. He wouldn't swallow Carmen being absent for too long before taking it upon himself to come over in person to collect her. And what would *that* look like to everyone?

*Bloody embarrassing, that's what.*

The last thing he wanted was to offend his son-in-law. He needed their relationship to stay on track and that would not happen if Carmen broke the arrangement.

Susan had also been stupid enough to mention something to at least one of the other women because whilst he'd been playing golf yesterday, someone remarked about 'social fall out when children divorce…'

Richard laughed it off as nonsensical gossip, but how could Susan have been so careless? She knew none of those women could keep their mouths in gear and shut. That's what made the stunt Carmen was pulling even more frustrating. Their family had enough on at the moment as it was without her rocking the boat.

He hadn't been able to have too much of a go at Susan for opening her mouth though because he'd need her on side later to help explain Lillian's actions. Even though she'd initially been horrified when learning what Lillian had planned, she'd soon realised it was the only thing to do to remove the chance of any embarrassment. Besides, it was too late now to change anything Lillian had said now as it had already been done and there was no turning back.

Stepping towards his daughter-in-law, Richard air-kissed Victoria's cheek and smiled warmly. 'You look absolutely beautiful - a picture of health and happiness. Marriage and babies obviously suits you.'

Tori smiled, sure her face would shatter into a thousand pieces. She might look ok, but she certainly didn't feel it. Things had deteriorated further with Matt over the last month. They barely spoke and no matter what she said or did to make the atmosphere at home more palatable, he was dreadful to her. Most nights he didn't return home and on the nights he did, that Deborah woman was in tow and she'd have no choice but to listen to them having very loud sex from the guest room. At least she had Carmen for a bit of company, although she must think her a complete laughing stock.

'What a lovely dress, dear,' Susan said, admiring Tori's clothes.

'Thank you,' Tori muttered shyly and smiled. Susan's attitude towards her had changed since her pregnancy and she and Carmen were the only people to show any pleasantry or kindness. Admittedly, she'd made a special point of spending hours on her hair and makeup tonight. She'd also worn one of the expensive designer dresses Matt insisted on buying to ensure she didn't humiliate him with her choice of clothes.

The light blue dress set off the blue of her eyes. A sweetheart neckline emphasised her full breasts and the stretchy under-fabric clung to her body, outlining her shape, whilst the looser outer fabric of light chiffon covered in a butterfly print, softly skimmed her curves. It highlighted her new body spectacularly, but tastefully.

Of course, Tori knew Matt liked to accentuate and show off

her advancing pregnancy at times when it offered him a suitable advantage – like tonight, whereas the rest of the time she knew he could barely stand looking at her. For once she felt beautiful tonight, which was a rarity after Matt's consistent put downs and unsavoury remarks.

'I can't believe how much you've changed since we last saw you.' Susan placed her hand on Tori's belly. 'It can only have been a month and well…'

Tori smiled, this time genuinely. It was true that she'd grown over the last four weeks, her perfectly formed symmetrical bump sat high on her small frame.

'Do you know?' Susan said, eyeing Tori closely. 'By the shape of you, I'd say it's a girl. I was that shape with Carmen, but Matthew I carried a lot lower. That happens with boys, I'm told.'

Susan lowered her voice, almost to a whisper. 'By the way, how's Carmen? Has she spoken to you about anything? Has she said what she's planning? She can't stay at yours for ever, after all.'

Tori hesitated. Carmen had still said nothing about what had occurred with her husband, but it was clear something was bothering her deeply. Whatever happened, she wasn't about to tell Susan that.

'Oh, erm… she's ok. She hasn't said a lot, but oh…!' Tori felt a sharp flurry of kicks and drew in her breath sharply.

Susan smiled. 'Come and sit down, Victoria. I shouldn't put more pressure on you by asking questions about my selfish daughter. You've had a long day looking around those houses so you must be tired. I'll get you a glass of water and you can rest before your mother arrives.'

. . . .

'I'M PLEASED TO say that today we found the perfect house,' Matt announced.

Tori almost choked on her dessert. *Matt had made a decision without telling her?* She glanced at him sharply.

Matt smiled graciously. 'I haven't said anything to Tori as I didn't want her getting her hopes up. I know how much she loved this particular property and I didn't want anything to stress her.'

Tori stared uncomprehendingly at Matt. She hadn't liked *any* of the houses they'd viewed. In fact, she'd *hated* them. They were soulless - too big and palatial for anything she'd ever be comfortable living in. 'Which one?' she asked weakly, not sure she wanted to hear the answer.

Matt smiled. 'Your *favourite*, silly!' He patted her hand patronisingly. 'Don't tell me you've forgotten already? This little one really has turned your brain to mush hasn't it, darling.'

'That's wonderful news!' Susan gushed. 'I was beginning to think you'd never find a house you both loved that is fitting to your position. I mean, how many have you looked out over the last few weeks? It must be several?'

'Twenty, to be precise,' Matt answered smugly. 'And the best news is that I put in an offer this afternoon which had been accepted!'

Lillian raised her hands to her mouth. 'Fabulous! I'm so pleased. Well, don't keep us in suspense. Tell us more!'

'Yes, Matt,' Tori said. 'Tell everyone which house it is.' *She, for one, would love to know.*

Matt dramatically glanced around the expectant faces, eking out the suspense for as long as he could. 'It's in Walnut Park…' he said proudly.

'*Walnut Park*? Oh bravo, son! Fantastic choice.' Richard boomed.

'Walnut Park?' Lillian echoed. 'Oh my word! Tell us all about it.' Walnut Park was one of the most expensive and exclusive areas in the city and *her* daughter would be living there. She, of course, would be a regular visitor and couldn't *wait* to tell her acquaintances so.

'I can do better than that,' Matt grinned, fishing out the estate agent's particulars from the inside pocket of his blazer. 'Have a look yourself.' He passed the paperwork across the table.

'Nine bedrooms, two self-contained annexes for servants if required, three acres of grounds, four double garages, a tennis court and a swimming pool,' Matt said proudly.

Lillian almost fainted with glee. 'Oh, that's amazing! You must be so happy, Victoria?'

Tori forced another smile, contradicting that her heart was sinking faster than a brick. She didn't need to see the paperwork Susan and her mother were poring over; she knew *exactly* which property Matt had bought. It was the most pretentious over-priced monstrosity of the lot and she detested it.

'Annexes are always a good idea. You'll need one of those for the live-in nanny,' Richard added pompously.

Matt raised his wine glass in agreement. 'Exactly!'

Tori stared at Matt. *Live-in Nanny? She'd be looking after her own child, thank you.* Matt made it clear that under no circumstances would she return to work *ever* and there was no way she'd let a stranger raise her child.

'We haven't discussed anything like that yet,' Tori added quickly.

'Oh, Victoria. You haven't got the deluded assumption that you want to look after a baby, have you?' Lillian said scathingly. 'Someone of your standing doesn't deal with *children.*'

Jack had been so useless he never earnt enough to offer the basic necessity of a Nanny and she'd resented every minute of looking after Victoria. To lower herself to the same level as the masses had been utterly humiliating.

'Don't leave it to the last minute, Victoria. Good recommended nannies are unsurprisingly thin on the ground at short notice.'

'I'll get it sorted,' Matt said smugly, ignoring Tori's expression. 'Also, I'm planning to complete and move to the house the weekend my contract finishes.'

'What's that now, six weeks?' Richard asked. 'That will mean your new position commences a week after. Superb timing!'

Tori felt even more nauseous. In six weeks' time there would only be a week before the baby was due.

Susan patted Tori's hand reassuringly. 'Matthew will take care of everything, Victoria. You won't need to lift a finger.'

'Of course she won't,' Matt smiled. 'I'll not have my pregnant wife worrying about anything.' He kissed Tori on the cheek. 'You leave everything to me.'

Lillian sighed with pleasure at her daughter's good fortune. Now was a good a time as any to let her know what had been said.

• • • •

TORI COULD BARELY believe her ears and stared at her mother in amazement. 'You said *what*?'

Lillian smiled patronisingly. 'Like I said, I gave the paper a story. They approached *me* and after discussing it between ourselves, we felt this was the most sensible route to take.'

Tori glanced between Richard and Susan. 'You all decided this without thinking to speak to me?' She felt she might hyperventilate. She'd never heard anything so offensive. She turned to Matt for support, but he only shrugged.

'You knew about this too?'

'I just said to say whatever was best for the family and the business, then let us know what had been decided,' Matt replied.

Tori was speechless. She looked around the table at each of them in turn. She hadn't thought this evening could possibly get any worse. First the news that she'd be moving to that monstrous house and now *this*.

Richard sighed theatrically. He'd suspected Victoria might be surprised, but he wasn't overly impressed that she was acting so defensively. 'Victoria, what did you expect? The press got a photograph of you and Matthew whilst you were last house-hunting a couple of weeks ago. Your pregnancy is glaringly obvious and we were approached for a story. We needed to put a stop to any speculation.'

Lillian looked her daughter up and down pointedly. 'You hardly gave us a great deal of choice. You married and then within three months you're clearly pregnant from *way* before the honeymoon!'

Tori mutely took the paper that Susan handed to her from the sideboard. It was open at a page containing a large colour photograph of her and Matt. She stared at the picture taken as they left the viewing of a house with a massive orangery and the longest gravelled drive ever.

Matt was wearing his standard 'wear-to-impress' tailored suit from Saville Row and she had on a loose lilac dress with a pretty matching bolero jacket. The camera had cleverly caught the images just as the breeze blew the light material of her dress against the obvious large bump under her clothes.

Her eyes lowered to the article:

### The Patter of Tiny Feet Comes Four-fold to the Recently Married Mr and Mrs Stevens

*What a wonderful way to embark on married life for the recently wed Matthew and Victoria Stevens.*

*The happy couple were snapped leaving a house viewing in preparation for returning to the city to start Matthew's role as Bank Manager. The photograph leaves no doubt that the couple are expecting a lot more than a house move and Mr and Mrs Stevens are reported to be ecstatic to conceive during their romantic honeymoon cruise.*

*Mrs Lillian Morgan, mother of Victoria, happily confirmed these speculations: 'It is my great pleasure to announce that my daughter is indeed pregnant. As you may expect we are all over the moon, but even happier to discover she is expecting quads.'*

*'The babies aren't due for a further six months,' Mrs*

*Morgan continued. 'As you can appreciate this is a very taxing and strenuous time for my daughter, so we will all be making sure she receives the best possible care.'*

*The Daily Echo would like to offer Mr and Mrs Stevens our congratulations over their exciting news.*

Tori slammed the paper down. She couldn't read anymore. She glared at her mother. 'Quads? That's insane!'

Susan wanted to keep things calm. Lillian wasn't the most tactful in dealing with her daughter. She didn't agree with what had been said either, but Richard made it clear it was the only thing to be done, given the circumstances and it wasn't like she had any sway in what was decided. 'Victoria, sweetheart, you're seven months pregnant. The only way to possibly explain the size of you without sullying your reputation is if it's multiple babies. Surely you can understand that?'

Tori stared at the ceiling in exasperation. 'And whose idea was this? Yours, I presume?' She glared at Lillian. 'Have you ever stopped to think about what will happen after I've had the baby? You know, the *single* baby? According to what you've said, I'll give birth over four months early!'

Lillian smiled. 'Oh, that's the easy bit. I've already worked that out. We'll say it was a premature birth – that's common with multiples, but everyone knows a birth that early on is extremely dangerous, so it won't be a shock that only one baby survives.'

Tori stood up in rage. 'How dare you! That's disgusting!'

'Don't be overdramatic, Victoria,' Richard snapped. 'It's not real, is it? That's just what the papers will be told after you've had the baby. Lillian's story merely prepares for that. They had to be told *something*, otherwise it makes you out to have no morals. We have a reputation to uphold, after all.'

Tori stormed towards the door. She needed to escape from them. Her anger and disbelief were threatening to spiral out of control and that would only cause more problems. Her life was bad enough as it was.

'Oh dear God, Victoria. Do you have no control over your gait? You're waddling. You look like a duck!' Lillian tittered loudly as Tori crossed the room. 'Please don't do that, you look ridiculous.'

Tori had no idea how else she could walk, apart from forwards and swallowed the urge to scream.

'And you really need to get some supportive bras. You'll end up with droopy breasts at this rate and you don't want that.' Lillian sighed dramatically. 'Seriously, Victoria, straighten your back and sort yourself out. You've still got two months to go and you need to learn how to hold yourself.'

Tori continued towards the downstairs cloakroom, still unable to quite believe they were expecting her to lie and say three out of four babies had died. Apparently, *she* was the unreasonable one for thinking this unacceptable? What sort of people were they?

Tori sighed in resignation. She knew *exactly* what sort of people they were.

Locking the toilet door behind her, she closed her eyes and took deep breaths. Feeling a sharp kick in the base of her belly, she smiled through her despair.

Her baby deserved better than this and so did she. She had to find a way to get away from these poisonous people and should have done it long before now, despite Hunter disappearing. All of this would have to stop.

## SEVENTEEN

MATT GRINNED SMUGLY when Bob Greaves slapped him on the back and handed him a whisky. 'Well, I must say Matthew, I could hardly believe my ears when your father told me that you and your wife are expecting quads!'

'Ah, you know what us Stevens' are like. Exceptional in *every* aspect!' Matt laughed. He'd felt almost like a celebrity since the news had spread.

He'd previously warned Jeremy about the coming article in the paper. He understood, of course he did – he knew how it all worked and had assured him that he wouldn't let on and neither would Ginny. But as far as everyone else was concerned, he was the proud father-to-be of four babies.

'I hope your wife will come to the dinner at the end of next week? I know we're all looking forward to seeing her,' Bob smiled.

Matt swallowed uncomfortably. He didn't want Tori there. He'd booked a nice suite at a plush hotel and intended on getting some good use of it with Debs. 'I hope so too,' he lied. 'But she's very tired at the moment, as expected with this sort of pregnancy and I don't want her overdoing anything as I'm sure you can appreciate.'

Bob nodded. 'Yes, of course. See how she is closer to the time and if she feels up to it, that would be fabulous.'

Walking around to his side of the desk Bob glanced out of the large window overlooking the precinct. 'I must say we'll miss you once you leave, Matthew. You've been an asset to the bank and of course to your father.'

Matt puffed with pride. 'Thank you, Bob.' *Yeah, he'd done well.* He'd enjoyed it here in more ways than one, but was more than ready to settle into his rightful permanent position.

'I guess it's true what they say though. Our loss is another's gain. I'm sure you'll do your father proud when taking over his role and wh…'

Matt looked up as Bob stopped mid-sentence and watched him staring intensely from the window to the scene below. 'Are you alright?'

Turning, Bob nervously straightened his tie. 'Yes. Yes, of course. I just thought I saw something.'

Matt frowned. 'Like what?'

'Oh, it's nothing. I must be getting paranoid. It's just that's three times now I'm sure I've seen the same person hanging around.'

Matt got up and looked down upon the expanse of precinct below. 'Who?'

Bob turned back to the window and smiled. 'That's the point. He's gone now, so I'm probably imagining it. As a bank manager, it's natural being on alert when you see a suspicious type. I'm sure your father will second that. It's something you'll no doubt get to learn. It never hurts to be too aware.'

Inwardly Bob felt uncomfortable, but he didn't want Matthew Stevens to know just how much. He'd be straight on the phone to his father, which would then give Richard something to use for amusement the next time he saw him.

However much he didn't want it to be he would swear that man was the one he'd seen yesterday in the car park and indeed the same one the day before that. He was a huge beast of a man – the type not to be easily confused for someone else.

Matt scanned the area. 'I can't see anyone overly suspicious. Although I do know what you mean. Back home we have a high percentage of undesirables. One half of the city is full of them. We're lumbered with a disgusting motorbike group too.'

'This man looked that sort, but thankfully we don't have any of those dirty clubs here.'

Matt's hackles rose, before controlling his irrational thoughts. *It would hardly be the Reapers here.* 'There's a steady stream of riff-raff everywhere.'

'I couldn't agree more.' Bob gestured for Matt to sit back down. 'On another subject. My wife heard your sister's back, but I told her that couldn't be right. Your sister lives in France, doesn't she?'

Flushing, Matt brushed off his uncomfortableness over this unexpected situation. 'She's only back for a fleeting visit, that's all.' He wiped his sweaty hands down his trousers hoping Bob wouldn't notice. 'She popped over as a surprise whilst she had a couple of days spare.'

Bob nodded. 'That explains it. Janet's got all sorts of weird notions in her head. These women don't half know how to make mountains out of molehills, don't they?'

Matt forced a smile. Carmen was causing problems. Furthermore, why was she still here? He'd told her in no uncertain terms that her stay could only be short, but what was it now? Bloody weeks!

He'd hardly even spoken to her since she'd arrived. She had a chip on her shoulder and he didn't want to listen to her bleating. Besides, he hadn't been there much anyway. It was bad enough returning home to his whale of a wife, but to have his sister in his face too was not high on his priority list.

He was damned if Carmen was accompanying them when they moved. *No way.* She'd have to swallow whatever had got her knickers in a twist with Luca and go home with her tail between her legs. Either that or find somewhere of her own. He didn't really care. She was a stuck up bitch who got everything for nothing at the best of times, but whatever was going on in her life wouldn't be infringing on *him*. His life was going very well at the moment and it was all set only to get better and he wanted that to remain so.

. . . .

SARAH WAS STILL ON EDGE. She'd faced Noel multiple times since he'd threatened her and it didn't get any easier. He watched her like a hawk – as did Colin.

She hadn't told Colin about it and maybe she should have, but after what he'd said himself that night, she'd been too scared to add further fuel to the fire, or load more pressure for him to have to deal with.

Well, she'd like to think he'd deal with it, or at least do *something* about Noel. Colin wouldn't normally think twice, but now she genuinely wasn't so sure. Surely Colin wouldn't *seriously* leave her? They had too much together to throw away, didn't they?

Sarah swallowed uneasily. Maybe they didn't? Maybe in Colin's mind she'd betrayed him too much by her decisions which had made such a mess of everything?

She glanced at the clock. 10 am on a Saturday, meaning only another bloody hour before opening. She was dreading it because undoubtedly it would be busy.

Reaching for the local paper, thinking she might as well have a quick flick through whilst she had the chance, Sarah steadied herself against the bar seeing a photo of Tori staring back at her. The blood drained from her face as she scanned the article.

Dear God, the woman was now completely finished. That bastard hadn't just managed to marry her, but he'd also got her pregnant the minute they'd wed? He hadn't wasted any time. And with *four*? She hadn't thought the weasely scrote had it in him.

'Hey, have you seen this?' Sarah glanced at Colin and pointed to the article.

Making his way behind the bar, Colin glanced at the paper and shrugged dismissively.

'Aren't you going to say anything?' Sarah cried in exasperation. 'That horrible bastard has got Tori just where he wants her.'

Colin's jaw set tightly. 'Don't you think you should spend less time worrying about that stupid cow?'

'W-What?' Sarah spluttered.

Colin rubbed his hand over his chin in irritation. 'For Christ's sake, Sarah! Your blinkered attitude is driving me mad! How many times do I have to explain it to you? That lot have ruined enough things for us as it is, so no – I really don't give a toss if Tori and her new husband are expecting one or *ten* kids, to be frank and neither should you!'

He poured himself a pint and greedily slurped at it. 'For some reason it hasn't yet sunk in that your *perfect* Tori must have been part of all that business from the off! Jesus, you've always been astute, so I can't believe you've been so fucking blind!'

Sarah stood motionless, her mouth flapping open and closed as she struggled to reply. *Was that what Colin really thought? That Tori had purposefully helped set up those dodgy deals and that everything she'd said had been a lie?*

Finding her voice, Sarah stared at her husband. 'Tori wasn't part of *that*. You heard what she said herself. She told us th…'

'Yeah, *she* told us,' Colin snarled. 'Your friend, was she? Funny how you haven't seen her for dust since… If she was *really* your friend and *so* bothered about you and if what she had with Hunter was as true as she made you believe – made us *all* believe, then she wouldn't have disappeared without a trace. She'd have found a way to get in contact – unless she already has, of course…'

Colin had to admit that half the reason he was angry with Sarah was because she'd put him in the position of being involved in all that business with Tori, Hunter, Matt and Noel and it had ruined everything. It wasn't just the state of his bloody pub; he'd fallen for the lies too. *He felt stupid.*

He'd believed Tori and in hindsight felt ridiculous he'd allowed himself to be sucked in, only to be made an utter fool of. Now to make matters worse, he was convinced Sarah was in contact with her or Hunter, or both. She must have been in contact with *one* of them.

Sarah pursed her lips. 'You don't know Matt! He's capable of a lot of things.'

'And nor do *you*!' Colin snapped. He poked his finger at the photograph in the paper. 'Look at them! They look alright to me. Look at the size of that house they're viewing. Oh yeah, they're having a real tough time, aren't they! Come on, Sarah – that pair have it sussed. Hasn't it crossed your mind they got exactly what they wanted at everyone else's expense?'

He angrily refilled his pint. 'Do you not think the 'woe-is-me' act Tori pulled off so well was exactly that. An *act*?'

'I worked with her a long time, Colin,' Sarah fumed. 'I would have known.' She couldn't quite believe he would think Tori to be so devious and her to be so stupid not to see through it if that were the case.

'And what about Golden Boy?' Colin raged. 'Where's he? Oh look, he's miraculously disappeared too. I think it's fairly obvious the whole lot of them took us for a ride. Hunter was in on it with Noel, Matt and Tori. Why can't you see that?'

'What?' Sarah couldn't believe what she was hearing. 'Hunter wouldn't do that. I've known him for ye…'

'Yeah, you've known him for years. So you keep saying,' Colin interrupted. 'Both he and Tori have cunted you off, Sarah. Just fucking accept it, but don't expect me to be happy that you dragged me into this stupid game. Have you not noticed the pile of shite they've left us with?

Colin waved his arms around the expanse of the empty tap room. It was all in order at this precise moment, but he knew as well as she did, that within an hour of opening the doors the place would be chaos and full of every toe-rag this side of the city, thanks to the portal opened by trusting her so-called friends.

Sarah felt like she'd been slapped. *This was a mess.* She was angry too, but when Hunter called, she'd believed what he'd said. But what if Colin was right?

No. Hunter *would* return when he knew what to do and Tori, well, she didn't know what she was doing, but was fairly confident whatever it was, she had little choice in it.

Sarah had to speak to Hunter again and tell him about Tori's pregnancy before he heard it from somewhere else. It would kill him, but might make a difference to what he had planned.

'What are you thinking now? Planning on running to Golden Boy and telling him how obnoxious I am?'

'Don't be so bloody ridiculous!' Sarah snapped.

'What about Noel? Why don't you get on side with him? He might have a new plan to rip us off even more. Maybe this time you'll be quick enough to get a commission!'

Sarah gasped. 'What's happened to you? Why would you say such things?'

Colin sighed, his anger diminishing. 'I believe you lied, Sarah. I still think you are. I feel betrayed and I don't like it. You're putting everyone else before me – before *us*.'

Sarah swallowed the lump in her throat and shook her head sadly. 'That's not the case, you should know that. I love you and I'm trying to make things right for everyone. Don't you love me anymore?'

Colin stared at the floor and remained silent for far too long. Sarah hardly dared to breath; his silence worrying. 'C-Colin?'

Colin looked her straight in the eyes. 'I do you love you. I always have, but I don't know whether I can do this anymore.'

Sarah was unable to hold back the tears from cascading down her cheeks as Colin walked from the bar and headed upstairs.

# Eighteen

THE ADRENALIN POUNDED through Hunter's veins as he waited. His patience was paying off. This could be a hit or another miss – it was impossible to tell.

He'd thought he'd nailed it last week when he'd located a bank manager with the correct age and name. After staking him out for a couple of days, he'd made his move. He'd been sure he'd been on to a winner, but within minutes of speaking to the man and loading a shed load of fear onto him it was evident he was not the right person.

Hunter knew immediately he was hearing the truth. The man knew nothing, so he'd had no choice but to continue his search. This time though, he wouldn't get his hopes up too high.

Again, this man had the correct name and appeared to be the right age, but whether it was the man on the photo from thirty-odd years ago, it was difficult to tell. All he could possibly work on was the body language when he questioned him.

Spotting the man walking to his car, Hunter cracked his knuckles and waited until the suspect got in before making his move.

Lurching from the shadows, Hunter yanked the passenger

door open and threw himself into the car.

'What the…' Bob Greaves scrabbled for the door handle, only for the intruder to lean over, lock the door and remove his keys from the ignition. 'H-Have the car. Take it! I…'

Hunter studied the panicking man. He *could* be the man on the photograph. From what he could see there were certain similarities and his heart raced with hope. 'I don't want your car and I don't want to hurt you,' he growled. 'Providing you give me the right answers, that is.'

Bob stared at the man's piercing grey eyes drilling into his and took in the sheer size of him. His biceps were bigger than both of his own arms put together. *It was that man – the one he'd seen hanging around.* 'W-Who are you?'

Hunter smiled but his eyes remained ice cold. 'It doesn't matter who I am, I'm only interested in who *you* are.'

Bob blinked rapidly. 'M-My wife will worry if I'm late. I'm very punctual and she'll call the police, th…'

'Let's hope not, although I doubt she'll notice, being as she's gone out herself.'

Bob's eyes widened. 'H-How do y…' He swallowed hard against the tight constriction in his throat. *This man knew where he lived?* 'I don't understand what I've done. I…'

Hunter smiled lazily and pulled his cigarettes from his pocket, lighting one. Winding the window down slightly, he offered the packet. 'Smoke?'

Bob shook his head. *This guy was offering him cigarettes whilst car-jacking him? Was he insane?*

'I don't think *you* have done anything. I need information, but first I want your name. Just a pointer, but I suggest you give me your *real* name, rather than a bullshit one.'

'R-Robert. Robert Greaves.'

Hunter studied the man intently. 'How old are you, Robert?'

'I-I'm 55.'

Hunter smiled. *That added up.* 'Do you know a woman called Leila? Leila Cooper?'

Bob blinked rapidly. 'I don't... I don't think so.'

Hunter exhaled smoke towards the roof of the Range Rover, where it hung in a thick cloud. 'Think back...'

'T-Think back?' Bob repeated. *Was this guy one of those crazies?* 'I don't know what you me...'

'Think back to your college days.'

'College? Erm... I don't...'

'Alright, let's try this one. Did you have a friend called Jacobs? Jack Jacobs?'

Hunter smiled menacingly watching the man's face instantly pale. *Bingo! This was his man.* 'I asked you a question, Robert.'

Bob breathed heavily. He remembered Jack Jacobs. Of course he did. He was the one Richard took the mick out of. The one who lived in a council house. He hadn't known the guy personally, but did know Richard had resented him. He was dead now, by all accounts.

Hunter watched the man's brain ticking. 'I haven't got all day, but I'll sit here for as long as it takes, so I'll ask again... Did you know Jack Jacobs?'

Bob forced himself to face the scary-looking man. *This couldn't be Jack's son, could it? Had he even had children? Christ, he didn't know.* 'I-I didn't really know Jack. I knew *of* him, but only met him a couple of times. I...'

'And would one of those times have been during a picnic?' Hunter asked, his voice quiet but menacing. 'A picnic in the woods?'

'P-Picnic?' Bob spluttered. *Oh no. He couldn't mean...*

'With a woman called Leila?' Hunter added. *This was definitely the right guy. It was all over his fucking face.*

Bob become cold with fear as the penny dropped. *Leila.* Yes, he remembered, although he'd tried for many years to forget. He'd virtually managed it, but not completely. He couldn't totally forget something like *that.*

'Who *are* you?' Bob asked again. He didn't know what else to say. He didn't want to talk about that day, now or *ever.*

'Like I said the last time you asked, it doesn't matter who I am. It's of no importance. Tell me about Leila,' Hunter growled. He could see the man knew where he was going with this.

'I don't know a…'

Lurching forwards, Hunter gripped the man around the throat. 'I'm running out of patience, you bastard. I know you know what I'm talking about, so *talk*!' He glared into the man's frightened eyes and pulled him closer. 'I know Leila Cooper was raped that day.'

'I-It wasn't me, I swear!' Bob spluttered, his eyes bulging.

'Relax, I know it wasn't you,' Hunter hissed. 'If it was, do you think I wouldn't have killed you by now? I want you to tell me *who* it was.'

Bob's mouth flapped open and shut as he gasped for air. He couldn't tell this lunatic that. He hadn't wanted it to happen in the first place. He'd known it was wrong and that he should have done something, but he'd been too weak. Too scared of not being liked…. *He still was…* 'I-I don't know…'

Hunter slammed the man's head into the driver's window. 'Don't be a fool, Robert. I said I wouldn't hurt you, but my patience is wearing thin. You fucking *watched* the woman get attacked, you pervert. People would be *very* interested to hear that, I'm sure. But to avoid that, all you need to do is tell me who did it.'

He watched the man spluttering and choking. 'I think you've kept it to yourself for far too long, Robert, don't you? Now, tell me what I need to know and then you can go home to your wife. But if you don't… well…'

Bob wished he could be anywhere else but here. If he told this psycho what he knew then this life would be ruined, but if he didn't tell him, it would also be ruined. *Jesus Christ.*

'Leila Cooper killed herself because of what your *friend* did. It ruined her. Did you know that?' Hunter roared, his temper spiking. 'And on top of that a man died for another man's crime, so speak, you spineless bastard!'

Salty tears spilled from Bob's eyes. How he wished he'd never tagged along that day. Richard always said he'd make sure everyone knew he'd been part of it if he ever opened his mouth, but he *hadn't* been part of it. He'd been told to watch and he'd always done what he was told. And what did this thug mean by 'another man died?'

Hunter released his grip. 'Looks like I'll be paying your wife a visit…'

Bob stiffened, his eyes panicked. 'Don't hurt my wife! She's got nothing to do with this!' *Furthermore, she didn't know anything about it and he wanted it to stay that way.*

Hunter had no intention of hurting the man's wife, but he'd let him think what he wanted. He pulled the photograph from the inside pocket of his leather jacket and held it up. 'Tell me who these people are. *All* of them.'

Bob stared at the picture, nausea rising. There was Jack Jacobs and Leila. He could clearly remember Richard's anger that Jack – the cheap council house boy, as he was commonly known, should get such a looker, even if she was a gypsy. *'Why should Jack be the only one',* Richard had said. And there was Ed, himself and of course Richard.

'I didn't know any of them that well…' Bob lied.

Hunter sneered. 'I doubt that… That's Leila, right?'

Bob nodded, his neck feeling like it had been surrounded by concrete. 'I-I didn't agree with it. It shouldn't have happened. I…'

'Well it did and you didn't stop it, you sick fucking wa…'

'Don't you think I know that?' Bob cried defensively.

'Did Jacob's know what was going to happen? Did he watch?' Hunter had to know. He knew what Jeanie had said, but he wanted to hear it from someone who'd been there. He had to know if the man he'd killed had any trace of guilt which could *slightly* warrant what had been done to him.

Bob shook his head. 'No, he didn't have a clue. He was back at the car.'

Hunter's intense hatred for the pathetic man in front of him increased. 'Was it planned?'

'I-I don't know. All I know is that I was told to follow. I didn't realise what was going to happen. I wouldn't have gone…'

Hunter was fed up of listening to this prick feel sorry for himself. He pointed to the photograph. 'Which one did it?' *This had to match what Jeanie said.*

Bob stared blindly at the picture. *Oh God, this was hopeless. He was finished.* With trembling fingers, he slowly pointed to the man on the end.

Hunter's face contorted into a snarl. *That matched what Jeanie had said.* He glared at the condescending expression on the man's face as it stared out of the photograph at him. 'Name?'

Bob took a deep breath. 'E-Ed…' He knew he was doing the wrong thing. He shouldn't be giving this thug the wrong name, but what else could he do? Whatever Richard had done, he couldn't serve him up to this loony. He could hardly say the man he was searching for had a son working in his bank right at this very moment and that he also knew exactly where he lived either. *God no.*

Whereas Ed… Ed had never liked him and he hadn't seen him for years. The man could be dead for all he knew! No, he'd made the best and most sensible choice under the circumstances.

Hunter moved closer. 'Surname?'

'I-I can't remember…'

'Fucking *surname*!' Hunter roared. 'You've got two seconds…'

'Barratt. Edward Barratt,' Bob blurted.

Hunter exhaled. *Edward Barratt.* He finally had a name. 'And where's this Edward-fucking-Barratt?'

Bob stared at the dashboard, desperate to get away. He'd already said too much. *Far* too much. 'I don't know. I haven't seen him for years. Not since we left college. After that, we all lost touch.' *At least that bit was true.*

Hunter eyed the man suspiciously. He knew more than he was letting on. 'I think you're being stupid for not telling me everything. It will make things easier in the long run.'

He placed the photograph back in his pocket and reached for the door handle. What he'd got was enough to go on for now. He'd let this gimp worry for a while and then pay him another visit if he needed to.

Hunter got out of the car and turned back to the man frozen in his seat. 'Thanks for the chat. I trust our conversation won't be relayed to anyone?' He smiled coldly. 'I'll return if I discover you've lied or if I need more information.'

Bob blinked. What did he mean? What was he going to do and when would he be coming back? Oh Christ, he should just tell him it was Richard. What would happen if he found out he'd lied? He didn't want this man hurting Janet or saying anything.

He wound down the window. 'Wait!' Bob shouted, but the big man had already disappeared.

· · · ·

SEEING BOB GREAVES with the telephone receiver in his hand, Matt knocked on the office door before entering. 'Sorry to interrupt, but I...'

Bob swivelled around in his leather chair and slammed the receiver down. 'For God's sake, what is it?' he barked. 'I was about to make an important phone call.'

Matt stared at Bob in surprise. He hadn't heard him raise his voice at anyone before and he certainly hadn't raised it to him. The man was one of the easiest-going people about. 'Er, I'm sorry... I just th...'

'Whatever it is will have to wait. I need to speak to someone,' Bob yelled, scowling as Matt hovered in the doorway. 'In *private!*'

Having made his point loud and clear, Bob waited until Matt left and then got up, pulling the shutters down over the window in his door and across the window facing the open-plan office behind. Making sure the door was locked, he returned to his desk.

Sitting back down, Bob sighed dejectedly. Matthew Stevens being in his face wasn't helping his state of mind. It was because of his bloody father he was in this mess.

When he'd returned after speaking to that lunatic the other night, Janet had immediately noticed something was very wrong. Of course she'd asked, but it wasn't like he could tell her. She'd go berserk if she knew he'd been involved in anything like that. Not that he'd actually *done* anything, but he'd witnessed it and hadn't spoken up.

Bob wiped his hand across his brow. Janet would take him to the cleaners. She'd divorce him, then tell all of her cronies exactly *why* and everyone would see him as being as bad as Richard. *Which he wasn't. He wasn't anything like Richard Stevens.*

But that was the dilemma. What on earth did he do? He should have told that man the truth, but he hadn't and instead he'd made everything worse. He was on tenterhooks waiting for that angry giant to reappear when he discovered he'd been given the wrong name. He'd be tortured, or worse, the lunatic might tell Janet or hurt her. He couldn't bear that.

Two days now he'd procrastinated over what to do. His fingers visibly trembled as he picked up the telephone again. Whether he liked it or not he'd have to tell Richard what had happened.

Taking a deep breath, Bob dialled Richard's direct work number. It wasn't like he could call from home in case Janet overheard and likewise, he suspected Richard wouldn't want Susan hearing any part of the conversation either.

A voice barked down the line with its usual hint of arrogance. 'Richard Stevens – bank manager.'

'Richard, it's Bob. Sorry to call you at work but…'

'Bob? This had better be important. I was about to leave early to catch a round of golf.'

Bob was tempted to say he'd call later and then not bother, but decided against it. 'Something's happened and you'll want to hear about it.'

Richard sighed. 'Has Matthew done something he shouldn't? I'm sure we can sort it out, Bob. We go back a long way, remember?'

Bob scowled, not missing the veiled reference *yet again* that Richard had something on him that he didn't want anyone to know. 'It's nothing to do with Matthew. They know what happened with you... With you and Leila...'

There was a long pause down the other end of the line and Bob wondered whether he'd got cut off. 'Richard? Are you still there?' He heard a beep.

'Madelaine, hold all my calls,' Richard said. 'I don't want any interruptions.'

'Richard?' Bob repeated.

'Yes, yes, I'm still here,' Richard hissed. 'Now, tell me what the hell you're talking about.'

Bob hastily relayed what had happened with the man in the car, making sure he didn't mention giving Ed's name up instead.

Richard listened to everything Bob said incredulously. 'Who was this man?'

'No idea,' Bob said. 'Although I'd seen him hanging around for a few days and the next thing I knew, he jumped in my car.'

'What did he look like?' Richard barked. He didn't want the Gettysburg Address - just the facts.

'Scary - a massive bloke. Long hair and a leather jacket. Not a lot else to say about him.'

Richard went cold. *Surely it couldn't be, could it?* 'A biker?'

'Maybe. He was that sort, but I didn't see a bike.'

'Any patch?' *It was the bloody Reapers again, wasn't it?*

'Patch?'

'On the jacket,' Richard snapped. 'It shows what club they belong to, like the fucking sheep they are.'

Bob frowned. *How did Richard know so much about*

*bikers?* 'I didn't see one, no…'

'What colour hair?'

'Lightish, from what I remember.'

Richard scowled. It wasn't that revolting man Matthew had been cutting deals with and if it wasn't him, then who was it? And how did they know about Leila?

'He's bluffing, trying to extort money,' Richard said, attempting to play it down even though it was pointless.

'I can't see how. How could anyone know those details if they were bluffing and why would they approach *me*?' Bob argued.

Richard ignored the trickle of sweat making its way between his shoulder blades and adjusted himself in his chair. 'Yes, why *did* he come to you?' *If Bob had breathed a word to anyone, he'd…*

'He had a photograph. A photograph of all of us. Me, you, Ed, Jack and Leila. It was taken that day… that day you…'

'Are you *serious*?' Richard screeched. *Jesus Christ*! How could this be? He'd got rid of those photographs. Matthew had sworn he'd taken everything Victoria had found. She had no clue what they were or how important it was that no one ever saw them and neither did Matthew, so how could there be more? And why did this man have them?

'I thought for a moment it was Jack's son because he mentioned him too,' Bob said.

'Jack didn't have a son. What did he ask?'

Bob swallowed nervously. 'He knew it was you. He pointed you out on the photo. He wanted to know your name and where you are. I-I made a name up…'

Freezing dread spread up Richard's legs. 'So, you didn't tell him anything else? You're sure you didn't give my name.'

'Of course I'm sure!' Bob cried. *That was partly true… He'd given Ed's instead…* 'I don't think he believed me. He said he'd come back and tell Janet. If that happens, I'll be ruined and…'

'I don't give a fuck about that!' Richard roared. 'What

about me? I'm the one in the shit here.'

Bob was speechless. Richard was thinking about himself like he always had. He should have just told that man everything.

'For God's sake, this was done and dusted years ago – or so I thought,' Richard ranted. 'Jacobs took the blame for it, don't you realise? He was the only one linked to that gypsy slut.'

Bob remained silent as the extent of Richard's words sunk in. Jack Jacobs had died *years* after and he'd heard it was because of drug dealing. 'Are you saying Jack was killed because of…'

'Jack was always useful for something!' Richard laughed, despite the gravity of the situation.

'But what will you do?' Bob blathered.

Richard frowned. He didn't honestly know, but he *did* know one thing and that was he couldn't let Bob know that any of this unsettled him. 'It's rubbish. They don't know where I am and as far as the law's concerned, who'd believe something like that about *me* – especially coming from that sort of person?'

'But that man knows where *I* am, where I live and everything!'

'Like I said, don't worry about it. He'll get bored. If he comes back, keep denying everything. Not a word, remember?'

Bob didn't know what to say. All he could do was listen to Richard's nasally voice.

'Right, got to go, Bob. Thanks for letting me know about this and I'm pleased you're honouring what you've always promised. I'm off to have that game of golf before it gets too late. Let me know if you hear anything else.'

Richard hastily hung up the receiver. He stared at it for a few moments before putting his head in his hands. *Shit, shit, SHIT!* What the hell was he going to do now?

This was too much of a coincidence for it not to be the Reapers. It *had* to be them. Thanks to Leila's links to that bloody group they'd been looking for the culprit at the time and even though it had taken them years with him looking over his shoulder at every opportunity, they'd managed to pick the wrong man.

But they didn't know that. It *was* finished as far as they were concerned, so why had it been resurrected?

Richard poured himself a large whisky and raised it to his mouth with a shaking hand.

# NINETEEN

BENDING HIS HEAD, Hunter trailed kisses along Tori's neck, his hand gently caressing her breasts, her nipples hardening at his touch to form hard, aching points.

'Hunter... I...' she whispered, as he pressed his lips on hers, his tongue slowly exploring her mouth whilst his hand gently ran from her breasts over her swollen belly and down between her legs.

Burning with rapidly building desire, she wound her fingers in Hunter's long hair, his beard scraping deliciously against her soft skin and relished the taste of his mouth on hers.

'I've missed you, Tori,' he whispered. 'You're having *my* baby and we're going to be together. I'll look after you.'

Tori smiled with renewed happiness. She was lucky. She'd got a second chance with this man. This wonderful man who loved her unconditionally. He would be a great father. An absolutely *wonderful* father and she loved him. Loved him so much.

Tori gasped for breath, pure pleasure making her delirious as his fingers brought her closer to a slow, but heady climax. 'Yes, yes. That's what I want. I love you,' she panted, her back arching. 'Oh God, oh, oh...'

Tori moaned loudly as the orgasm burst through her body and sent her straight into freefall.

'Tori!' Matt's loud voice boomed in the silence of the room, jolting Tori awake. He pulled her blanket aside, scowling to see her loose dress pulled up and her hand inside her knickers. 'You dirty bitch! I get home from work to find you frigging yourself off on the sofa in your sleep! What's the matter with you?'

Tori looked around, confused. She squinted as her eyes adjusted to the daylight and Matt's face came into focus. Her heart crashed to her feet and she felt like crying. *It was a dream, yet it had been so real.*

'I-I'm really tired, I must have fallen asleep.'

'You weren't asleep in your dream, were you!' Matt spat. 'It sounded like you were having an orgasm when I walked in. Who were you having sex with, you dirty whore?'

Tori reddened. She didn't think she'd ever had a dream like that before. She didn't ever touch herself and couldn't understand what had happened. She felt embarrassed and uncomfortable.

'Come on!' Matt snapped. 'Tell me who you were dreaming of? That overgrown baboon, was it?'

Tori panicked. 'What? No! I don't know what you're talking about. I wasn't dreaming about anyone or anything like that.'

*Oh, but she had. She'd most definitely been dreaming of Hunter and sex and how the baby was his and that everything was good...*

'Don't fucking lie!' Matt laughed. 'Your hand was in your knickers! I saw you!'

Utterly humiliated, Tori struggled to her feet and made to walk off.

'Where are you going? For God's sake, Tori. You say you're not up to sex and too tired or some other bloody excuse, but you seemed pretty into that! Good job I've no desire to fuck a whale, otherwise I'd be even more pissed off.'

Tori sighed. *Damn right she didn't want him to touch her.*

*She wanted him nowhere near her.*

'I've heard pregnancy raises a lot of women's sex drives – apart from yours. That is of course, unless it's with your own hand!' Matt sniped.

'I didn't get *myself* pregnant, Matt,' Tori muttered.

'You think it was an accident? You don't know how it happened?' Matt was irritated. *The horrible bitch had got on his wick for far too long.* 'Of course it wasn't an accident, you stupid cow!'

Tori stared at Matt in confusion. He knew she'd been on the Pill when she'd fallen pregnant. 'Are you saying that I did it on purpose? Why would I do that? Don't you think I knew it would cause problems for everyone?'

Matt grinned smugly. 'Yes, it was a gamble, but my father was right. It paid off and put you in your place. It's made you a lot more pliable.'

Tori couldn't process what Matt was saying. 'I-I don't understand. What was a gamble?'

Matt prodded Tori's protruding belly. 'You think *this* would have happened if I hadn't made sure of it? You're pregnant, Tori because I made it that way.'

Tori bit back the itching need to point out that she hoped he wasn't the father of the child inside her and instead protectively rubbed the spot that he'd poked.

Matt realised Tori still didn't grasp what he was saying in a roundabout fashion. *He'd have to spell it out to the thick cow.* 'You haven't got it yet, have you? I know I *made* you pregnant – I mean, I stuck my dick in you, for my sins, but I arranged it so that you had no choice. It was a necessity.'

A sly grin spread across his face. 'I swapped your pills for fake ones. A suggestion by my father as a means of quietening you down.' He ran his eyes contemptuously over Tori. 'And it worked. Let's face it, you've got no choice but to toe the line. You won't get very far otherwise, will you?'

Matt's face screwed up in contempt. 'Though I have to say I'll be glad when you look less offensive again. It's like being married to a rhino! At least when it's out I'll be able to face screwing you again. Until you get as big with the second kid, of course.'

Tears rolled down Tori's face as Matt's words sank in. *How could he do this? And his own father had suggested it? This was sick.*

A spark of defiance crept into her mind. Matt believed that she'd used protection with Hunter, but she hadn't. Oh no, he hadn't thought of that that, had he? He'd trifled with her contraception whilst also instructing her to sleep with another man. *The man she loved.*

Matt chucked loudly at Tori's expression. 'Your face is a picture. You didn't expect that, did you? When you've had this one, you'll be expecting another within a few months. It'll keep you nicely tame. You're my obedient baby machine and next time you'll do it voluntarily, so it won't come as a shock.'

In a rare display of uncontrolled anger, Tori raised her hand and slapped Matt hard around the face. 'You're disgusting and evil. Both you and your father.'

Matt's face twisted first in shock, then rage. The imprint of Tori's hand burned. *How dare she have the impertinence to strike him.*

Grabbing Tori around the face, Matt pushed her against the wall, crushing her with his weight. Lowering his face, his voice was low and menacing. 'You silly little cow. You think you can do that to *me*?' Yanking at her dress, he shoved his hand into her knickers.

Terrified, Tori pressed as far back as possible against the wall to take as much pressure off her belly that Matt was crushing with his weight.

Matt savagely forced three fingers into Tori, jabbing them roughly into her soft flesh with each word he spat. 'You're. The. Fucking. Disgusting. One.'

Removing his hand, Matt snarled with contempt. 'Nah, I won't even bother reminding you whose wife you are. You make me sick, you ugly fat slut. Now get away from me. I'm out of here.'

Backhanding Tori around the face, Matt stormed from the room as she sank to her knees on the floor, her body wracked with heavy sobs.

As Matt stomped down the hallway Carmen quickly closed the bedroom door and retreated back into her bedroom.

. . . .

'NO, SUSAN, I'M completely fine,' Richard said, controlling the urge to shove his wife's face into the souffle. He plastered on a smile and pretended to admire the dessert she'd placed in front of him.

'You don't look it to me. You're pale. Has something happened at work?' Susan asked, eyeing Richard suspiciously. For a start, he'd been late and she'd reached the point where she'd been both worried and annoyed.

She'd been about to throw Richard's dinner in the bin when he'd walked through the door looking, well, all she could describe it as was 'stressed', but that didn't adequately sum up his combined appearance and demeanour.

Knowing Richard, something had happened which could infringe or affect his retirement package. There had better have been no hiccups as she'd already booked and paid for a cruise. She hadn't mentioned it to him yet because if this business with Carmen wasn't sorted soon, then it was unlikely they'd even be able to go.

Aware Richard still hadn't said anything, Susan lightly touched his arm. 'Is this something to do with Carmen? Have you heard something?'

Richard looked up. *Carmen*? He wished it *was* to do with Carmen. However unpalatable the game she was playing was, it was a thousand times better than what was really going on.

'No, it's nothing to do with her. If you must know, I lost at golf, that's all. And some stuff at work. All in all, not a great day.'

*Understatement of the year.* He hadn't been to golf. Ok, so he'd planned to, but after Bob's phone call how was he supposed to do that? He'd remained holed up in his office, needing space in which to think.

'Oh, how utterly annoying!' Susan remarked.

'What? Oh yes.' Richard had forgotten what he'd said for a moment. Even though he'd been trying to think in the quiet of his office, it was impossible to concentrate. He was unsure of what to do or where to start and hadn't wanted to react too hastily, but after an hour he still hadn't arrived at any brilliant ideas how to get further with this latest pile of shite.

He'd thought about calling Ed to let him know what had happened with Bob, but then thought better of it. Between Ed and Bob, Ed was the one back then who'd had the biggest bee in his bonnet over what had happened.

Richard sneered. That supercilious bastard, like Bob, had been happy to bloody watch. The last thing he'd heard, Ed, like the rest of them, had done alright for himself, but that was about it because he hadn't seen him for years.

He'd even invited the man to Carmen's wedding a few years ago, but he'd declined. Because of that, he hadn't bothered inviting him to Matthew's. Oh yes, Ed Barratt had made it clear he no longer wanted anything to do with the Stevens' and that worked both ways... Richard wouldn't warn Ed that he was on a photo some psycho had hold of.

The trouble was, *he* was also on that photo, but at least Bob had sent the nutter in a different direction. Anyway, these days he didn't look much like he used to. There were some upsides of getting old, he mused.

'So,' Susan said suddenly, not at all convinced by Richard's previous explanation. 'What's *really* happened? I'm quite sure you wouldn't be so on edge purely from a lost game of golf!'

Feeling the urge to slam his spoon between Susan's teeth in protest at her constant haranguing, Richard refrained. He had to think of something else now. *Something feasible.*

He'd sneak in a phone call to Matthew at some point soon, having already decided to ask him if he could discover anything on the grapevine. As much as he didn't want his son involved with the Reapers again, whether he liked it or not, Matthew had contacts there and being as he'd paid them an awful amount of money, it was the least they could do. He'd call tonight if Susan ever stopped interrogating him. *Actually, that gave him an idea!*

Richard gently placed his spoon down and looked suitably forlorn. 'I had a phone call from Bob Greaves... about Matthew.'

Susan's eyebrows knitted together. 'What about him? Has Matthew done something wrong?'

Richard shook his head. 'I don't think so. Bob just wanted to warn me that there's been a spate of fraudulent deals happening at his branch and...'

'What? And he thinks it's Matthew?'

'Let me finish, will you?' Richard barked. He'd never get used to Susan jumping to conclusions. It drove him crazy. 'As I was saying, these instances of fraud have been occurring for a few weeks. They're fairly sure they know who's behind it, but because Matthew's the acting manager, it will be him that's initially answerable to head office.'

'Oh my God!' Susan screeched. 'This will ruin his position and then you won't be able to retire! Our names will be dragged through the mud and...'

'*Susan*!' Richard yelled. 'It's standard procedure. It will be wrapped up shortly and won't have any bearing on Matthew's promotion. Bob was merely keeping me in the loop, but I do need to speak to Matthew and give him some pointers.'

Susan wrung her hands together in worry. 'Are you *sure*?'

Richard patted his wife's hand reassuringly. 'It will be alright, you'll see.'

Now that was something *else* he'd have to remember to tell Matthew just in case Susan ever mentioned it.

## TWENTY

MATT WASN'T LOOKING forward to making the call to his parents, but it had to be done. He listened to the ringing and willed it to be his father who answered, rather than his mother. *Come on, come on – pick up.*

At least once he'd made this call, he was free to get on with what he *really* wanted to do. He ran his finger between Deb's large breasts as she lay naked in front of him, her hand tantalisingly stroking between her thighs.

'Hello?' Richard answered, his voice gruff.

'Dad, it's Matt.' *Thank God. His mother would ask far too many questions.*

'Matthew! I tried calling last night, but no one answered.'

'Erm… yes, I was working late and I think Carmen and Tori went out.'

'Tori? My God, I doubt whether she'd fit through a door now, based on the size of her the last time we saw her!' Richard guffawed.

Matt scowled. *That much was true.* Personally, he was glad he didn't have to face the revolting cow resembling a beach ball with tits leaking milk all over the place for a while. It was hardly attractive, however he'd have to word this carefully so as not to raise suspicion.

'She's not coping too well at the moment. The baby's taking it out of her and I'm so busy I'm not around as much as she needs. Plus, I need to prepare the house ready for moving – it's not long now.'

Richard paused. 'Ok and?'

'Well, we decided it would be best if Tori went to Lillian's for a while – just for a bit of a break,' Matt said, hoping it sounded plausible.

He hadn't actually decided that at all. *Carmen* had and Tori had done what she'd said. It was none of his sister's fucking business what happened between him and his wife the other night. She shouldn't even have been there, but like the nosy interfering shit she'd always been, she'd witnessed everything. Not that he'd known that at the time.

It was only when he'd returned the next evening after spending a thoroughly enjoyable night with Debs did he realise his wife was missing. Carmen, however, wasn't...

'I've told Tori to go to her mother's,' Carmen had spat. 'What you did was *disgusting*, Matt! I know you're a dick, but that was totally wrong. She's your wife and heavily pregnant too. You *hit* her!'

Matt had been furious. What the hell did Carmen know about the situation and what gave her the right to dictate what he could and couldn't do?

'I'm sick to the back teeth of men and how you all behave!' Carmen had screamed.

Matt had quite rightly pointed out that it was none of her concern. More to the point, she shouldn't take her marital issues out on *him*. He'd been about to give her a slap too and say that if she didn't like the way he worked, she could pack her bags and sling her hook, leaving him to retrieve Tori from Lillian's. That was until she'd said that if he forced Tori to come back with him then she'd tell their mother *everything* she'd witnessed.

Matt's first reaction had been to laugh. He could easily talk his way out of that one. It was well-known that he and his sister had always been competitive, but then she'd pointed out she'd also heard what had been done to Tori's contraception...

'You think it's *normal* for a man and his father to trick a woman into pregnancy on the basis of keeping her quiet? That's not normal – that's fucking *twisted*!' Carmen had screeched.

She'd heard *exactly* how they'd done it too and it had been that which forced his hand and let his sister get her way. *For now.* But if she thought her dirty game-playing wouldn't be equalised then she was more arrogant than she looked. Besides, it was fine by him. Tori could stay away for as long as she liked. *Forever* as far as he was concerned, providing that, from the outside, it didn't look like anything was amiss.

Matt had almost forgotten his father was on the other end of the phone. His attention was fully on Debs wrapping her lips around his cock and he struggled not to groan out loud.

'Are you telling me Tori has moved out?' Richard barked. 'What do you think that will look like?'

'No, she hasn't moved out. Of course she hasn't. She's just getting a bit of rest and relaxation at her mother's. Don't forget it's the only chance they'll get to spend time together – just the two of them, for a very long time once the baby comes.'

'What? And Tori want to spend time with Lillian?' Richard laughed. 'Her hormones must be completely haywire!'

Matt chortled. 'Something like that, but she really needs a break and some company.'

'She's got your sister, hasn't she?' Richard queried.

'Ah... well, Carmen's moving to Jeremy's,' Matt added quickly. It had been the only place he could think of when she'd refused to spend another night under the same roof as him.

Again, she'd used her ill-gotten knowledge to blackmail him into finding somewhere for her to stay. He knew Jeremy wouldn't mind – he'd had a bit of thing for Carmen ever since they'd been teenagers and, as expected, he was more than happy for Carmen to take his spare room.

'She's gone to *Jeremy's*?' Richard said. 'Why?'

'To be honest Dad, she's been causing problems,' Matt lied. 'I didn't want to say anything, but whatever's going on with Luca is affecting her and she's not herself. She'll be better off at Jeremy's with him and Ginny. Besides, how can I get this place packed up with her here?' *Like he would be doing it himself. As if!*

'Hmm, I see your point. Well, as long as everything's ok?' Richard said.

Matt fidgeted as Deb's experienced mouth continued to work him and he desperately tried to concentrate on what his father was saying. 'Yes, everything's absolutely fine. I'm just busy.'

'Well, you'll need to free up some time because I want you to do something for me,' Richard added. 'I think the Reapers may be trying to set me up.'

Matt lost his erection at speed. 'What? Why?' he spluttered. 'What could they have on you?'

'Nothing, obviously. The whole thing's absurd. I think they're trying to extort money. After the last huge pay out they're probably trying their luck,' Richard lied. He could hardly tell Matthew why they were *really* digging around.

'I wouldn't worry.' Matt eyed Debs enticingly tracing her fingernails over her breasts and wished his father would go away.

'That's not the point. I want to know what they're saying,' Richard snapped. 'I know I told you not to get involved with them again, but if you could just find out if and what they're doing, I...'

'How can I do that from here?' Matt asked.

'You'll think of something. It's important.'

Matt blinked, wondering why a bit of possible hearsay had unnerved his father so much. 'Ok. I'll ask Jeremy. I have an inkling he's still on speaking terms with them.'

'Good, good,' Richard muttered. 'Soon as you can then son, yes?'

'Yes, ok. I'll call you when I've got something to report.'

'Appreciated,' Richard said stiffly before promptly hanging up.

Matt wasted no time in putting the phone down himself. He'd call Jeremy later. He was damned if he was doing it now.

Grabbing Debs around her small waist, he pulled her across the bed. 'Sorry about that. Now, where were we?'

· · · ·

'ARE YOU ON YOUR OWN?'

Sarah gasped. 'Hunter? Is that you? Yes, I'm on my own, I...'

'I haven't got long, so I'll be quick. I just wanted to let you know that I'm getting somewhere with what I need to do. Have you h...'

'When are you coming back?' Sarah blurted.

'As soon as I can. Have you heard from Tori?'

'No, but...'

'Sarah, I know you were good friends, but it's important you tell me. Even the smallest detail about where she might be.' *He'd have to tell Sarah. He couldn't leave it any longer.* 'I think Tori's pregnant...'

Sarah bit her lip. 'Hunter, I...'

'I went to see someone...an old friend, to help with... to... it doesn't matter... She told me Tori's pregnant with my child. I've known for a few weeks, but I really have to find her.'

Sarah took a deep breath. *This would hit him hard.* 'Tori is pregnant, yes.'

'You knew?' Hunter yelped. 'Why didn't you tell me? Never mind... Is she ok? Is the baby alright? How m...'

'Hunter,' Sarah interrupted. 'Whoever your friend is, they were wrong on one count. A rather important one... The babies aren't yours.'

'W-What? What do you mean?'

'Everyone knows about it. Tori's expecting quads. With *Matt*.'

'*Quads*?' Hunter repeated incredulously.

Sarah could hear his disbelief. 'It was in the paper. Tori's only three or four months pregnant. The babies can't be yours. I-I'm sorry.'

There was a long pause. 'Hunter? Are you still there?'

'Yes, I'm here. Are you sure? Jeanie's adamant the baby's mine.'

'That's what the article said. I haven't seen her myself.' Sarah wasn't sure what else to say. 'I really am sorry. Will this affect your plans?'

'Affect my plans?'

'You must see now it's pointless trying to get Tori back? Not only is she married, but she'll have *four* children with another man. Matt will never let his children go so y...'

'Don't mention that bastard's name,' Hunter growled. 'I don't care what you think, I'm still going to try. What else can I do? I love her, Sarah and she needs to know the truth. About *everything*. You don't understand.'

Sarah was completely exasperated. Hunter was plain deluded. Either that or obsessed. He had to think about the bigger picture too – like returning to sort all of this mess out.

Should she tell him about what Noel had done, about her and Colin and about the state of the White Hart? No, she couldn't. Not now. She could sense his pain even though she couldn't see him. 'You should come back. We coul...'

'I need the information first,' he said, his voice steady.

By his change of voice alone, Sarah pictured the mask of neutrality falling firmly back over Hunter's face like it always did when emotions threatened to engulf him.

'Is everything ok your end?' Hunter continued.

'Oh, erm... yes. Well, it's...' Hearing the main door, Sarah's heart lurched into her mouth. *Colin's back.* 'I've got to go. Call me next week. *Please.* Whatever happens, call me, ok?'

Not giving Hunter the chance to respond, Sarah replaced the receiver and grabbed a cloth to wipe down the bar just as Colin walked in.

## TWENTY ONE

'I STILL DON'T understand why you felt the need to come back here?' Lillian sniffed. 'It's a bit strange. You should be with your husband.'

Tori placed down the magazine she was reading and looked at her mother. She'd had nothing but the Spanish inquisition since arriving – not that she'd expected anything else. She did however feel slightly more empowered. Thanks to Carmen, she'd found both the energy and the courage to do this. She knew she'd have to return to Matt when the house sale finalised, but for now, at least, she had a couple of weeks of peace. Well, peace in comparison to what Matt had done.

Tori realised she must stick to the story Carmen outlined. It would be the same one Matt would use. 'It's not strange at all,' she said brightly. 'Matt's up to his neck with work getting everything ready for the handover and I'm exhausted.' *More likely up to his neck in that woman's knickers that he kept bringing round.*

'Yes, but…'

'Then there's the house. That will be impossible to pack with me in the way. It's not like I'm up to doing much or coping with people bustling around. On top of that, I need to register at the doctors here, ready for the birth.' Straightening her back, Tori winced as a flurry of hard kicks beat against her rib cage. 'Ooh, that was a hard one.'

Lillian cringed watching her daughter caressing her belly. 'You act like you're enjoying this.'

Tori smiled. 'I am, that's why.'

'I absolutely *loathed* being pregnant. Why do you think I only had the one? I couldn't wait to get you out,' Lillian scoffed.

Tori sighed. *That remark came as no surprise.* Even though Matt had engineered this and it was unplanned, it still stood more than a good chance this baby was from the man she loved, rather than from the man she hated. And it was that thought which kept her going. If the worst came to the worst and Matt was the father, it didn't matter. This was *her* baby.

'Matt must be so worried with you being so far away now you've not long to go,' Lillian said. 'He rings twice a day.'

Tori forced a smile. Matt was checking up on her, that's all. She knew her mother had strict instructions not to let her out of her sight. Matt would have pretended it was because she was so 'frail' and 'unhinged', but in reality, she hadn't felt this strong for a long time.

She didn't know how she would do it yet, but as soon as the baby was born, she'd leave Matt and the rest of them. What he did the other night was the last straw and there was no *way* she'd bring up a child around that man. He'd crossed the line and there was no turning back. Her eyes were well and truly open.

It hadn't escaped her notice either that her mother had, yet again, turned a blind eye to the myriad of bruises over her arms which she must have seen, but it didn't matter.

Carmen was her surprise fairy godmother. She was leaving too and said she'd be in touch as soon as she'd found somewhere. Tori smiled. *She hoped so.*

• • • •

EVEN THOUGH JEANIE hated discussing Leila, she'd been hoping Ashley would return with further questions. Not because she wanted to answer them, but because she needed to talk to him. Her sense of him needing to act now rather than later had reached an all-time high. She still couldn't put her finger on exactly what would happen, but she knew for certain that the woman – Tori – was in grave danger. *Both her and her baby.*

It was vital Ashley stepped in and removed her and his unborn child away from the man, whoever he was, that she could see in her mind and get somewhere safe.

Jeanie closed her eyes in concentration, hoping the exact danger would be revealed so she could be more specific, but it wasn't. It was just *DANGER* loud and clear.

Ashley must put aside this silly notion of getting all of the information to tell Tori the truth. Protecting her was *far* more important. He had to act and act now because she didn't know what window of time was available and it worried her deeply.

Jeanie stared out of the window in frustration. It had been bothering her for weeks, but she'd now reached the point where the incessant voices wouldn't let her sleep. She had to reach Ashley, but how? She had no car, but even if she had, where would she go? It was hopeless. It was all very well returning to where she came from, but Ashley had said he was on the road most of the time and living in a tent, so she wouldn't know where to start. He could be in Scotland for all she knew.

It was dangerous to ask after him in his hometown, so what could she do? She must think of something and very soon because she didn't want to be too late. Or rather, she didn't want *him* to be too late.

Jeanie padded across the quarry tiled floor of her small lounge to the kitchen and picked up the kettle. Filling it up, she ran through every conversation she and Ashley had had during both of his visits. There must be a hint of *something* to lead to a point of contact, surely?

Standing waiting for the kettle to boil, Jeanie worked through all of the names he'd mentioned. She prided herself on her good memory, although sometimes remembering every single detail was more of a curse than a benefit.

There was a pub he'd talked about - somewhere that the Reapers gathered and one of the places involved in those contract deals that kicked all of this off in the first place.

Ashley respected the couple who ran that pub. What were their names? That was it. *Colin and Sarah.* It shouldn't be too difficult to find the number for that place. It was the White Hart, wasn't it? Heart or Hart?

Jeanie shook her head in frustration. It hardly mattered. There wouldn't be too many pubs in one city called that with either spelling, but who should she ask for? Colin or Sarah? And was either of them in contact with Ashley?

Maybe Colin was the most obvious choice? Jeanie frowned, recalling Ashley mentioning Sarah more. Didn't the woman work with Tori? Or at least, had done?

One of them must have heard from him by now and know where he was to be able to pass on a message?

Jeanie flicked the kettle off. That was decided. She'd go to the Mackerel and Hook and use their phone. Directory Enquiries could get the number for that pub and there was no time like the present.

· · · ·

WHEN THE MAN answered the phone Jeanie immediately sensed sadness. She sensed a feeling of betrayal and doubt as well as stomach-wrenching worry, but it was unfounded – at least in the way he believed.

This was the problem when she allowed her gift in. Even if the door was only slightly open she was swamped with a deluge of information from everywhere, which was part of the reason she'd switched off from it all those years ago. But whether she liked it or not, it had come back to her with a vengeance.

'Is that Colin?'

'Who wants to know?' Colin said gruffly.

'I'm looking to speak to Colin or Sarah,' Jeanie pushed. 'It's important.'

'They all say that,' Colin muttered. 'If it's about double

glazing or driveways then we don't want either.'

Jeanie paused. 'I need to talk to Colin or Sarah. It's about Ashley.'

'I don't know any Ashley. Look, is this a joke?' Colin barked. 'I'm fed up with stupid phone calls.'

Sarah glanced up. *Who was that on the phone?*

'I'm telling you, I don't know anyone called Ashley,' Colin snapped as Jeanie repeated the question.

Jeanie felt the sudden urge to tell this man he needn't worry. 'Can I just say that whatever is troubling you isn't as you think. Your wife is on your side.'

'What the hell are you talking about?' Colin gasped.

'Your wife loves you and only wants what's best for everyone. She's a good person.'

Colin stared at the receiver in shock. *What on earth? Had they emptied the loony bin again?* 'Listen, love. I don't know who you are, but you're clearly cracked in the head so go and have a look for this Ashley, or whoever he is, somewhere else. If it's that important I'm sure you'll find him – probably on the moon.'

'Wait!' Sarah rushed towards Colin. 'Let me speak to them.' *Hunter's name was Ashley. Not that many people knew that, so could this be to do with him?*

'What do you want to speak to them for?' Colin stared at Sarah as she snatched the phone.

'Hello? This is Sarah. Can I help?'

Jeanie breathed a sigh of relief. 'Sarah, my dear. I need to speak to Ashley. It's very *very* important.'

Sarah glanced at Colin watching her strangely. She needed to ask questions, but couldn't with him there. 'I-I don't think I...'

'Don't worry about your husband. He'll come around.'

'W-Who are y…'

'I'm Jeanie, dear. Did Ashley mention me? He visited me in Polperro. I need you to get a message to him urgently.'

Sarah swallowed nervously. *She was right. This was about*

*Hunter.* 'Is everything alright? I don't have a number for him.'
She could feel Colin's stare bristling in the back of her head.
She'd blown her cover and she knew it.

'No, I'm afraid things are far from alright. Ashley will be
in contact soon, I know he will. Tell him Jeanie said to forget
the truth. He needs to go to his woman. I'm seeing danger.'

Sarah frowned. 'Danger?'

Colin stepped forward. 'Sarah? Who is th…'

Sarah held her hand up to silence Colin. *She had to hear
this.*

'The woman is in danger, or she will be. She's carrying
Ashley's child,' Jeanie continued. 'He needs to forget the truth
for now, this is more important. He needs to get her away from
that man.'

'The babies, they're not his, they're…'

'I'm telling you there's only one baby, my darling and it's
definitely Ashley's. A son. A beautiful bonny boy.'

Colin knew the instant Sarah mentioned 'babies' that
whoever was on the phone was calling about Tori and Hunter.
*He knew it. He just bloody knew it.*

## Twenty Two

IRRITABLY GULPING DOWN A large mouthful of wine for want of nothing better to do, Ginny glared at the back of Jeremy's head. Her eyes narrowed jealously watching him hanging off Carmen's every word.

He'd been thoroughly engrossed in whatever amusing and fascinating account spouted from between Carmen's perfect lips. Jeremy was *her* boyfriend, yet she was the one sitting here like a spare part! What was he thinking of, letting that woman stay? Did how *she* feel about it not count for anything?

*Well, she'd had enough.*

Putting her glass down heavily on the table to gain some attention, Ginny cleared her throat noisily. 'I thought you had to go out tonight, Jeremy?' she said haughtily, making a show of glancing at her Rolex. 'Shouldn't you be thinking about making a move? I'm sure Carmen has better things to do than sit here with you all night!'

Jeremy glanced at Ginny. He could tell from her badly concealed expression that she was not happy, but he was enjoying Carmen's company. More than enjoying it as it was hardly a chore. The only thing that was a chore right now, was Ginny trying her best to make the situation awkward and embarrass him. That and Matt loading the pressure on by asking him to do some digging on the Reapers. Why couldn't he do it himself if it was so important?

He didn't want anything to upset the good thing he'd got going with Noel and hadn't quite understood why Matt wanted him to find out if they were nosing around in his or his father's business anyway. Why the hell would the Reapers be digging around on Richard?

He sighed. He said he'd try and find out if anything was afoot, but only because it was another good excuse to get a little more in Noel's pocket – which would only mean more deals and money for him.

Jeremy smiled at Ginny. 'Yes, you're right. I'd better go shortly.'

Smiling widely, Ginny got up. 'I'll just go and get my jacket.'

'You won't want to come. I'm going to the White Hart.'

'That's ok. I fancy a change.'

Jeremy stared at her incredulously. 'But you *hate* it there! You said you'd never step foot in that dump again even if th…'

'I've changed my mind,' Ginny snapped. She wanted to get away from Carmen and if that meant spending the evening surrounded by the scourge of society, then so be it.

'Sometimes a change is as good as a rest,' Carmen piped up, glancing at her empty wine glass.

'Why don't *you* join us?' Jeremy asked. 'It's a dreadful place – full of people that you could base a film on, but it would be a laugh!'

Ginny's mouth set in a hard line. *He couldn't be serious?*

'Why not!' Carmen said. 'I could use a laugh. Can we just have a couple more before we go?'

'Sure, no problem,' Jeremy said, smiling widely.

Ginny rolled her eyes noticing Carmen's manicured hand resting lightly on Jeremy's arm. When she'd angrily asked him about this inconvenience the other night, he'd looked at her as if she'd dropped down from outer space.

'Carmen's Matt's sister,' he'd barked. 'I've known her for as long as I've known Matt, which is *forever*!'

Ginny pursed her lips. He'd clearly forgotten that she'd heard Matt's good-natured digs more than several times about the 'thing' Jeremy had always had about Carmen. Was she supposed to be ok with a woman that her boyfriend had dreamt about for *years* living in his apartment? *She thought not.*

Well, it was time to do something about it.

Standing up, Ginny walked over and picked up Carmen's empty glass. 'I'll get you a top up, shall I?'

'Oh, thank you. That's *so* sweet of you,' Carmen smiled, flashing her white teeth.

Ginny studied Carmen. Most of her was probably surgically enhanced and it wasn't like *she* was successful. The woman's lifestyle and money were entirely down to her luck in bagging that French man.

She could almost feel new wrinkles permanently ingraining themselves on her face as she scowled. *She* should be living in luxury – not Carmen. And the woman had the cheek to have some kind of hissy-fit and talk about leaving her husband? Was she mad?

In the kitchen, Ginny filled Carmen's glass with white wine from the fridge. A small smile passed over her face as she slipped a small white pill from her bag into the glass. Stepping back, she folded her arms and waited as it dissolved. Time to show Jeremy that Carmen shouldn't be on the pedestal he'd put her on. It would be fun to see how the mixture of Ecstasy and several more glasses of wine had on her.

Pleased, Ginny topped up her own drink and took both glasses back into the lounge.

• • • •

CARMEN MADE QUITE a show of complementing Jeremy on everything, from his shirt to his driving ability. She knew it was needling Ginny, which was why she was enjoying it so much. If she'd met Ginny before moving into Jeremy's, then the woman hadn't made enough of an impression to warrant filing into her memory, but Carmen thought she'd at least have the good grace to have some manners.

Carmen found it difficult not to laugh out loud. She could still picture the expression on the miserable cow's face when she'd been forced to walk behind when she'd linked her arm through Jeremy's as they'd walked into the White Hart.

She felt a little mean. She knew Jeremy had always had a soft spot for her, but she'd never be able to see him as anything other than a little brother, like Matt. Not that she saw Matt as *anything* right now, short of a manipulative bastard.

It was probably a good job she'd had hold of Jeremy's arm. She felt quite drunk already and she'd only had a couple. Still, it was taking the edge off her anger over her brother's behaviour, which was good. She didn't want to even think about Matt or her father. Neither did she want to think about Luca.

She'd been doing more than enough thinking lately to last a lifetime. She'd done nothing *but* think on the run-up to leaving France. Since getting to Matt's it had continued, but for slightly different reasons. Witnessing the way Matt treated Tori and then how he behaved only backed up her own thoughts about where her life was heading and she was done with it.

She'd had enough of playing the dutiful wife and acting up to appearances. Especially when it had all been a lie from the start.

Carmen glanced around the tap room of the White Hart with ill-concealed delight. Jeremy was correct. This place was a complete and utter abysmal dump and *exactly* the sort of place she felt like being in at the moment.

She smiled thinly. The state of the place almost mirrored the wreck her life had become. Six months ago she wouldn't have dreamt in a million years of stepping foot in somewhere like this, let alone sitting *down*, but that was six months ago.

*A lot changed in six months.*

Carmen slugged down her wine and waved the empty glass in Jeremy's direction. 'Fill it up then, honey,' she smiled, enjoying the venom dripping from Ginny's face.

At least Jeremy was half-decent, so Ginny was lucky in that respect, but then who knew if he was decent behind the scenes. He could be like every other man she knew – including her own bloody father. Men were off her agenda now – unless it was on *her* terms. She was done with lies, betrayal and bullshit.

· · · ·

JEREMY MADE HIS way back from the bar yet again with a refill for Carmen. He eyed her through the crowd. Although she hadn't had that much to drink, she was acting wasted and seemed a lot drunker than she should be. She was even chatting to all the locals like she knew them.

He scowled as someone nudged into him as he fought his way back to the table, avoiding looking at Ginny. She was fuming. He wasn't daft. He knew she only wanted to come tonight to get him away from Carmen and then he'd invited her too, much to her annoyance. Although he'd been quite clever, making sure he hadn't given her any opportunity of cornering him to moan, but he also knew it was only a matter of time before that happened. There was only so long he could avoid getting it in the neck and worse, Noel hadn't even been in yet to use as an excuse to disappear.

When Jeremy was elbowed in the back for the second time, he was about to glare at the perpetrator when he heard the unmistakeable voice.

'What brings you in here tonight, Jezza?'

Turning quickly, Jeremy could almost kiss Noel with gratitude. Now he was here, he could stall Ginny's diatribe for even *longer*. 'Looking for you, as it happens,' he smiled. 'I need to speak to you about something.'

Noel hooked his leather-jacketed arm roughly around Jeremy's neck, causing the wine glass he was holding to slop down his blue shirt. 'And what do you need to talk about?' he drawled.

'Well, I'm not sure exactly, but I need to as…'

'Hold your horses!' Noel interrupted, his eyes fixed across the room. 'Looks like we've got a fresh bit of totty in here. Haven't seen that one before. Very nice… *Very* nice…'

Jeremy followed Noel's gaze and to his horror, found his sights set on Carmen. *This was all he needed.* 'Oh, she's with me,' he said, flinching as Noel swung around to face him.

'With *you*? What's happened to your usual bird? You know, the plastic one?'

Jeremy flushed red. 'I'm still with Ginny. I…'

Noel quickly made his way towards Carmen who was leaning unsteadily against the cigarette machine.

Feeling a horrible sinking sensation, despite wanting to go in the opposite direction, Jeremy forced himself to follow and pulled at Noel's arm. 'Wait, don't g…'

Noel spun around, his eyes flashing menacingly. 'Are you telling me I can't talk to that woman? What the fuck is it to you? She's not yours, so what's the problem?'

Jeremy swallowed. He had to get this back on the correct footing. He didn't want to rub Noel up the wrong way. 'Sorry, I should have explained. That's Carmen. She's staying with me at the moment as a favour.'

Noel arched an eyebrow. 'A *favour*?'

'I've known her for years. She's having marriage problems, so I said she could stay with me for a while.'

Noel grinned widely. 'She's fair game then. Good. Don't worry, Jezza - I'll take her mind off her crap marriage.'

Jeremy pulled Noel's arm once more as he made to walk away. 'Please don't. I'm keeping an eye on her for Matt. Remember Matt?'

'Matt?' Noel's teeth ground together. 'I'm hardly going to forget that prick, am I?'

'Carmen's Matt's sister,' Jeremy explained. *Noel would definitely give her a wide berth now.*

'That makes it even *better*,' Noel winked, nodding towards the half-empty wine glass in Jeremy's hand. 'Was that supposed to be for her?'

Jeremy looked desperately at the glass. 'Erm, yes, but I still haven't told you what I want to speak to you ab…'

Snatching the wine glass, Noel tipped the remains down Jeremy's already wet shirt. 'Oh, whoops. Look! You've spilt the wine you've bought for the lady. I'll go and get her a fresh one.'

'But when can I talk to you ab…'

'Later,' Noel said, pushing his way back to the bar.

• • • •

GINNY'S MOOD HAD lifted considerably. As she'd watched the mixture of drugs and alcohol kick in, causing Carmen's behaviour to become consistently erratic and loud, she'd found herself enjoying the scene – even if it was in this dump.

It was even more hilarious when that disgusting greaser, Noel, had arrived with a drink for Carmen. She'd gladly swapped seats so he could sit next to the woman and struggled to hold her laughter in. This would give Carmen her just desserts for inviting herself out with them and commanding her boyfriend's attention. Now she had to put up with the resident psycho leering all over her.

Ginny was unable to contain her glee, until she slowly realised Carmen was enjoying Noel's company. She watched Noel push yet another glass of wine in Carmen's direction and screwed her nose up in disgust as she swayed accepting a light for the cigarette he'd also handed her.

Ginny nudged Jeremy under the table. 'How long are you going to let this go on for?' she hissed.

Jeremy ignored Ginny. He was well aware what she'd said, but had no idea how to answer her. He'd tried to stop it. He'd even collared Carmen as she'd left the Ladies toilets. He'd suggested he took her home, explaining she was drunk and if she carried on, then she'd be in a right state because it was still quite early. He'd also warned her that Noel probably wasn't someone she should get too friendly with.

After draping herself around Jeremy's neck and tracing a

long fingernail down his cheek, Carmen had informed him, in no uncertain terms, to mind his own business. She was enjoying herself, she'd said.

Jeremy had watched Carmen stagger back out into the bar and admitted defeat. There was no point trying to appeal to Noel's better nature. Namely because he didn't have one and the worst thing was he still hadn't spoken to the man about what he'd come in here for in the first place.

Jeremy took a swig from his bottle of lager. *Sod it.* He'd spent years running around for Matt. Everyone was adults here and as for him finding out if the Reapers were doing any digging on the Stevens, what a load of paranoid bollocks. He'd tell Matt he'd done all the digging required and there was absolutely nothing going on. It was a bloody embarrassing waste of time asking him to do it in the first place anyway, so he wouldn't.

As long as Carmen was happy, then what she did was her own concern, not his. He was sick of worrying about everything and everyone.

Feeling a lot better now he'd come to this conclusion, Jeremy walked back into the bar and over to the table, pleased to see that even Ginny now had a smile on her face, which was good because he had no intention of putting up with her moaning tonight either. 'Another drink?' he smiled.

• • • •

SARAH DRAGGED THE newly washed glasses, still piping hot, out of the glass washer, and ignored her burning fingers as she placed them on their shelves under the bar. She was flat out and hadn't had time to catch her breath all night. At least it wasn't long before she could ring the bell for last orders.

She glanced around the tap room, her eyes narrowing at Noel and several of the Reapers clapping and jeering at a woman dancing on a tabletop. She wasn't happy about Colin agreeing to Noel's suggestion of installing a jukebox, but he'd reminded her that it was thanks to *her* they had to agree with everything the new Reapers President wanted. Sarah hadn't bothered arguing. They'd done enough of that after she'd taken the call from Jeanie.

Colin had easily put two and two together. Again, she'd denied it, but he hadn't believed a word of her excuses and Sarah couldn't say she blamed him. She'd been outed as lying, backing up his theory and there was absolutely *nothing* she could do about it. Since then, he hadn't shouted at her, but he hadn't spoken to her either. She only hoped what that woman said was right and that Colin would eventually understand. Preferably before it was too late.

Hearing even louder jeering, Sarah glanced back to where Noel stood, dismayed to see the woman on the table had now progressed to removing her clothes. As Black Sabbath boomed from the speakers, the woman swayed drunkenly on the table, her hand fumbling for her bra clip.

She looked at Colin. *Surely he would stop this?* That woman was drunk and clearly out of control. She didn't know her, but someone needed to step in. 'Colin!' Sarah hissed. 'Don't you think you should stop that. The woman's wasted and the Reapers are taking advantage.'

'She's one of your perfect *friend's* mates, by the looks of it,' he spat, nodding towards the group. 'She came in with that pair.'

Frowning, Sarah craned her neck over the crowd and spotted that dreadful plastic woman whose name she could never remember, and Jeremy. Her jaw clenched watching, amid much cheering, Noel clambering on the table behind the gyrating half-naked woman and placing a big meaty hand on her toned stomach. Pulling her backward, he thrust his hips, mimicking taking the woman from behind, whilst his other hand expertly unclipped her bra. A huge cheer went up as the woman's large breasts fell from her lacy bra that Noel then threw into the jeering crowd.

'Colin?' Sarah cried, unable to believe he wasn't intervening.

Shrugging, Colin continued serving. 'She looks quite happy

to me! Besides, you know as well as I do that we have no say with what goes on here anymore.' He'd given up trying to keep order. His pub was ruined, as was his marriage. Sarah was lying and now he'd no choice but to accept he wasn't as important to her as he'd thought. With that in mind, not much else mattered. *Actually, nothing did.*

Looking back, Sarah saw the woman kissing Noel, her fingers winding in his slicked-back hair. Noel's hands greedily massaged the woman's breasts, much to the delight of the audience and when she saw one of his hands trailing down towards the woman's black lace knickers, she slammed the half-poured pint down and angrily pushed her way through the crowd.

*She wasn't having this. This was a boozer, not a bloody knocking shop!*

'Oih! Pack that in!' Sarah yelled as she came within shouting distance.

The woman briefly glanced over at her, unable to focus her glazed eyes, yet smiled and continued unzipping Noel's jeans. 'Oh God,' Sarah muttered. 'NOEL!' she screamed.

His face feral, Noel jumped from the table, scooping the drunk woman into his arms and placed her on the floor. Turning to Sarah, he grabbed his erection through his jeans. 'You miserable bitch! What makes you think I'd let *you* get a free look at what you can't have anyway?'

He turned back to the woman now draped under his arm and ran his tongue down her flushed cheek. 'Come on, baby, we'll finish this somewhere else.'

When Noel booted open the front door and staggered out with the half-dressed stranger, Sarah could only glare at everyone and walk back towards the bar.

## TWENTY THREE

JEREMY WASN'T IN THE MOOD. He'd had virtually no sleep, thanks to Ginny's relentless whining and now, within ten minutes of getting to work, he'd got Matt bothering him. The man knew full well he worked in an open plan office and couldn't have a telephone conversation without people overhearing, but he was somehow expected to transcend this limitation and explain everything in minute detail.

Jeremy stared at his screen that was still booting up. Another upgrade by the dweebs in the IT department, no doubt.

'Are you going to tell me what happened, or what? I'm busy. Probably a whole lot busier than *you*,' Matt snapped. 'What did you find out? It's not a difficult question!'

Jeremy wanted to slam the receiver down, but refrained. He'd tell Matt what he wanted to hear. At least, that way he'd be off his back. It was a ridiculous thing to request in the first place and Matt would never know he hadn't bothered. 'There's nothing to tell you.'

'What's that supposed to mean?'

Jeremy glanced up, well aware the inhabitants of the desks around him were earwigging. 'I asked and there's nothing going on for you to be concerned about.'

'Ssshh!' Matt hissed. 'Don't say too much! I know where you sit in that office, remember?'

Jeremy rolled his eyes. 'How am I supposed to answer your questions if you're insisting I tell you, but don't speak?'

'Don't get snarky. Are you one hundred percent sure they're not digging on me or my father? What about Noel?'

'That's who I spoke to,' Jeremy lied, making the contents of the conversation slightly less obvious to those around him. 'As I said, neither of you figure.' *It was enjoyable saying that.* What he'd really wanted to say was not everyone's lives revolved around Matt or Richard, but decided against it. Partly because he hadn't asked Noel anything and partly because he still wanted a job and if Richard discovered he was discussing him across the office, it was likely he wouldn't have one for much longer.

'Neither of us *figure*?' Matt spat. 'Are you taking the piss?'

'Couldn't think of another way to say it,' Jeremy lied. 'It's not quiet in here, if you get my drift? And I'm very tired, which isn't helping.'

Matt laughed, swallowing the half-hearted apology. 'Stay up all night, did you?'

'No, but the other half wasn't very happy.'

'Ah, arguing with Ginny again?' Matt sneered. 'Tut, tut. You'll never marry anyone at this rate. What's her problem this time? Has her nail varnish run out?'

Jeremy's mouth set in a thin line. 'Actually, it was about the *lodger*.'

'Carmen? What's she done now?' Matt laughed. 'I was about to ask how she was settling in.'

Jeremy scowled. *It was all a big joke to Matt, wasn't it? Well, let's see how he liked this.* 'She accompanied us out last night and let's just say, she didn't come home...'

There was a long pause from the other end of the line and Jeremy could imagine Matt blinking rapidly, his mind processing what he'd heard, whilst thinking of a witty, sarcastic or insulting retort. 'Matt, I'd better go. I've got a meeting shortly.'

'No!' Matt yelled. 'I need more information than that! I don't understand. Has Carmen moved out?'

Jeremy swallowed a smile. *Would he really have to spell it out in front of the office?* 'I'm guessing she stayed at a *friend's*.'

'What are you talking about?' Matt yelled.

'She left with *Noel*,' Jeremy hissed.

'WHAT? Are you su…'

'Got to go. Talk later.' Jeremy replaced the handset and smiled. Picking it up again, he dialled reception. 'Hold all of my calls for the next hour, please.'

He put the phone down happily. Matt would have given up trying to call back by then.

• • • •

CARMEN BRUSHED HER knotted hair away from her face and with effort, turned over onto her front. Bypassing her pounding head as much as possible, she tried to swallow, but her mouth was as dry as a bone. Her hand moved to her neck and gingerly ran her fingers over various sore patches. Pressing her finger down onto one of them, she winced.

'You've finally surfaced?' A deep gravelly voice came from somewhere. 'I was beginning to think you were dead!'

Carmen willed her eyes to open. She hadn't even managed that yet. *Who was that? It wasn't Jeremy.*

Finally getting her eyelids to crank open, Carmen blearily peered around the darkened room. Confusion flooded through her as she took in the darkly-painted walls. A stained mirror hung at an angle above a wooden chest of drawers that had seen better days and piles of magazines, books and bits and pieces were heaped on top of it. *Where on earth was she?*

Propping herself up on one elbow, she pulled the itchy blanket further up over her naked body, panic setting in, until the memories of the night before seeped into her hungover brain.

She'd been dancing. Dancing on the tables to something.

Some heavy metal tune. She'd been taking her clothes off...
Kissing someone...

With a jolt, the memory of kissing the dark-haired biker
returned in technicolour. *How had she got so drunk? So
wasted?*

Noel opened the thin, grey curtains across his window a
crack, giving the room some light which illuminated him from
the shadows. 'Get that down your neck. It'll take the edge off a
tad.'

Carmen stared at the warm can of lager and then up at the
man who had handed it to her. *She'd slept with him?*

She studied the man's thick dark hair, slicked back into a
ponytail and his brawny arms sticking out of the short sleeved
T-shirt. He was attractive in a savage way.

Noel watched Carmen weighing him up and laughed
heartily. He could hardly wait to see her expression when she
clocked the mass of love bites he'd left all over her neck.
'Coming back to you is it, baby?' He cracked a can open for
himself and poured some into his mouth. 'You were good,
honey. *Real* good!

Carmen felt embarrassed. She'd made it obvious to this
poor man that she was struggling to remember what had
occurred. *How rude was she being?* 'I-I'm sorry... I... erm...'

Noel sat heavily on the end of the bed. 'Noel. My name's
Noel,' he laughed.

Despite her embarrassment, Carmen found herself breaking
into a smile. 'Think I had too much to drink last night. I meant
no offence. It's gradually coming back... I...'

'No worries, sweetheart. No offence taken.' How could he
possibly take offence after spending the night with his dick in
this delectably upper-crust bird that was Matt's sister –
whatever her name was. *Oh, how he'd love to see Matt's face if
he knew he'd boned his big sister.*

'You going to drink that, or what?' Noel nodded towards
the can Carmen was clutching.

Carmen pulled her eyes away from Noel and looked at the

can of lager. There was something about this man, but she couldn't put her finger on it. Hesitantly, she tugged the ring pull and sipped at the tepid liquid, grimacing at the sour taste. It made her stomach want to heave, but at least it was wet and she was desperate for a drink.

Noel studied Carmen intently. She may be a posh bird, but she was damn fine looking and that no one could argue with. He smiled widely, his hand resting on her thigh covered by the blanket. 'That's right girl, get it down your neck. It'll make you feel better once you've had a few.'

He hadn't got to be anywhere for an hour or two, so may as well see if his luck still prevailed. 'Have you got somewhere you need to be?' Noel asked, his eyes resting on the diamond-encrusted wedding band on Carmen's left hand. 'A husband, perhaps?'

Carmen followed Noel's eyes. She had no idea why she was still wearing that. She didn't want to be associated with Luca LeVere in any shape, way or form. *Not after his lies.* Two could play at that game. Not that she'd be telling him. She never wanted to see him again in her life.

She smiled inwardly as she gulped more of the lager, her mojo returning. For a moment there she'd lost sight and almost slipped back into the way she *used* to think. *That woman no longer existed.*

Pulling her wedding ring off, Carmen slung it across the room into the far corner. 'I have nowhere I need to be right now.' Her eyes met Noel's and she gave him a suggestive look.

Noel made a mental note of where the ring had landed. He didn't expect any of the sparklies on that baby were cubic zirconia. Oh no, they'd be kosher diamonds and he'd be sure to get a nice few quid for them.

Taking the look he could see in Carmen's eyes as a green light, Noel smiled. *Well, why not?*

He moved his hand from her thigh, slowly pulling the blanket away, exposing her nakedness and lowered his mouth between her legs.

. . . .

'I TOLD YOU that you had no need to worry,' Matt said confidently. He'd been looking forward to giving his father the good news. No doubt another feather in his cap for getting the required information so quickly.

'And you're absolutely *sure*?' Richard asked.

Matt could hear the relief in his father's voice. It still intrigued him why he would think anything was amiss in the first place. Any debts with the Reapers were settled the minute Noel was paid off. The bank was none the wiser, so it was all good. *His father worried too much.*

'I'm absolutely sure. Jeremy spoke directly to Noel. You know who Noel is, so I su…'

'I'd hardly forget *that* man, would I? The freak was in my own kitchen with *you*, remember?' Richard snapped. He knew Matthew didn't understand his need to know whether anything was being investigated by that despicable bunch. As far as his son was concerned, it was over. Well, Matthew's part of it was.

'And nothing was said about me? You did ask Jeremy to ask about me too, didn't you? I made it quite clear th…'

'Yes, he asked about everything.' Matt sighed inwardly. 'Apparently, Noel didn't have a clue why Jeremy would even ask! He didn't even know who you were!'

'And now he does?' Richard tried not to let the panic show in his voice.

'Please, Dad. You've got nothing to worry about.'

Richard swallowed a mouthful of whisky and kept the phone close to his ear. He knew he shouldn't be drinking this time of the morning, but his nerves had got the better of him. He'd hardly been able to wait to get to work to call Matthew to see if there were any updates.

'Jeremy did well by acting so quickly on your instructions,' he added.

Matt bristled. Why Jeremy should get any credit? The man had all but hung up on him earlier.

Richard decided he should change the subject. 'How's Victoria?'

'I called last night and spoke to Lillian. Tori had gone to bed, tired. Getting bigger by the day, apparently,' Matt said, trying not to picture his wife's misshapen body.

'Susan said she'd try to pop around and see her this afternoon,' Richard added, knowing she was hoping to get more information from Victoria about Carmen.

'Tori's got an appointment for a check-up today, so she might not be there.'

Matt was proud he'd remembered something that made him appear to find that sort of thing important. The truth was, the only reason he remembered was because he'd reiterated to Lillian to accompany Tori wherever she went – *including* the doctors. He couldn't risk giving her an opportunity to run or speak to anyone. Not that she'd be doing much running, the state she was in.

'Oh, well, your mother will have to catch her another day,' Richard muttered.

'Right,' Matt said brightly, wanting to wrap the conversation up. 'I'd best be go…'

'And how's Carmen?'

Matt paused. His initial reaction was to blurt out that from what he'd gathered, she'd landed herself in Noel's bed, but thought better of it. If his father found that out, he'd storm round there and ruin his other plan.

Matt smiled to himself. Oh yes, Carmen thought she was being clever taking Tori's side and causing ructions, but it would backfire in her face. He'd had it up to the back teeth with his sister's interference and for once, she'd experience the boot on the other bloody foot. He'd get in touch with Luca and fill him in with what his wife had been up to. Carmen would then find out what it was like to be the talking point of the town and be left with nothing. He'd slap that smarmy smile off her scheming face this time. All these years he'd been forced to live in her shadow. Well, no more. Her involvement with what was right, wrong or indifferent in his marriage and calling the shots about it, was the final straw.

Carmen would be the black sheep of the family after he'd finished. He'd take the place of the esteemed one in everyone else's eyes. He just needed this kid out of Tori and get her back where she was supposed to be and everything would be hunky dory.

'Matthew? Did you hear me? I asked about your sister,' Richard repeated.

'Sorry,' Matt said quickly. 'The line went funny. Yes, Jeremy said Carmen's fine.'

'Good, good,' Richard said. At least he'd got an update to keep Susan's constant mithering at bay for a while. 'Your mother's very worried. She was going to go round an…'

'I wouldn't interfere. It might make things worse,' Matt interrupted. He didn't want anyone sticking their oar in. He'd never had an opportunity to balls his sister's life up like this and didn't intend on having it diluted, or losing it.

'I wouldn't class that as 'interference', Matthew,' Richard snapped, frostily. *He wanted Susan to find out what had really gone on, being as he had more riding on it than anyone realised.*

'I didn't mean it like that,' Matt backtracked. 'Tell mum it's all looking good but to give Carmen space. You know what she's like.'

Richard chuckled. 'Seems you've learnt a bit from me about understanding women, Matthew. They really are in a league of their own!'

Matt laughed. It was false, but he'd learnt enough from his father to ensure it sounded genuine. 'Indeed. Now, I really must go. A meeting…'

'Yes, of course. Let me know if there are any further developments on any front.'

Putting the phone down, Matt leant back in his chair and exhaled deeply. The question was, what to do about Carmen? He'd only spoken to Luca about five times in his life, but this was the one thing that, if he knew anything at all, the man would not want to be kept in the dark about.

It also gave him the perfect opportunity to get his own back.

## Twenty Four

HUNTER WAS THE first to admit he hadn't taken what Sarah had said the other day very well. Actually, he'd taken it *really* badly. He may have outwardly made out it wasn't a big deal and that he still intended to get Tori back, but in real life, it wasn't that simple. In fact, it was bloody pointless.

Since finding out Tori was expecting Matt's quads, all manner of things had lurched through his mind. He'd really believed Jeanie was right that Tori was expecting *his* child, but she'd clearly lost her ability over the years and whether he wanted to admit it or not, Sarah was right.

He'd really thought he'd been getting somewhere on *all* levels, but how could he expect Tori to run off with him to a life where he could offer nothing, with four kids in tow. *Four kids that weren't his.*

Hunter fumbled drunkenly for his cigarettes. It was futile. All completely futile.

Just before he'd found out about Tori's quads, he reckoned he'd hit the jackpot regarding Leila Cooper. He hadn't even had to pay that Bob Greaves bloke a second visit and had been overjoyed when preliminary digging uncovered only one man with the name of Ed Barratt. An Edward Barratt of the right age, with the right type of job. Yes, he'd been extremely pleased until further digging revealed that the tosser had only gone and died of a bloody heart attack six months ago.

He was too bloody late. *Everything* was too bloody late. This now meant he couldn't put it right and things were ruined with Tori on both counts. Why had that bastard got her pregnant? Out of anyone, it should have been *him*. Matt didn't love Tori, but *he* did. He loved her more than *anything*. If only… if only it could have been him…

'Same again, please,' Hunter slurred, glancing up at the barmaid who was eyeing him questioningly.

He knew he was a mess and being so drunk mid-afternoon was not a good look. He also knew he should pull himself together, but Sarah's news had knocked the wind out of his sails and he'd lost sight of everything. Getting to the bottom of who had attacked Leila Cooper was now irrelevant. The real culprit was dead and so he couldn't take out the correct person.

But even if he'd been able to, it wouldn't make any difference to Tori. Not now. The only outcome would have been to make *him* feel better and now even that wasn't an option. Saying that, he didn't *want* to ease his own conscience, however slightly. He *deserved* to suffer and feel bad. He *deserved* to lose everything.

Wondering why his glass was still empty, Hunter raised his bloodshot eyes. 'Where's my drink?'

The barmaid gently laid her hand on Hunter's arm. She had no idea what was eating the man, but this was the third day in a row he'd openly drowned his sorrows. He hadn't said a word to anyone, short of asking for refills – and he'd asked for *lots* of those.

'I think you've had enough,' she said gently.

Hunter's eyes narrowed. *He was paying, wasn't he, so what business was it of anyone else?* 'I don't expect to justify whether I've had enough or not, but for the record, I haven't.'

Grabbing the woman's hand, he picked up his empty glass and wrapped her fingers around it. 'Now, please fill this up.'

Shaking her head sadly, the barmaid poured another pint. 'I can see you're not alright. Is there anything I can do to help?'

Hunter's drunken annoyance faded into desolation. He ran his thick fingers through his unkempt hair. 'There's nothing *anyone* can do.'

The barmaid placed Hunter's fresh pint in front of him and let her fingers rest on his. 'Maybe not, but I might be able to think of something that could at least get your mind off things for a while...' She winked suggestively. 'I finish at 5...'

Hunter glanced up. 'Thanks, but no thanks.' *If he couldn't have Tori, he didn't want anyone.*

. . . .

SARAH WAITED IMPATIENTLY at the small pharmacy located inside the doctor's surgery whilst they put together her prescription. She didn't go to the doctors at the best of times and would usually find an excuse to avoid the place, even if she was bleeding from the eyes, but after pulling her neck last night, she had little choice.

She knew she'd done something bad when she'd dragged that barrel into place because she'd distinctly felt something go. The doctor said she'd trapped a nerve and had thankfully prescribed her heavy duty painkillers.

Sarah sighed. It was her own fault. She should have asked Colin to help, but they were barely speaking. They'd always had a wonderful relationship, but now it was steadily falling apart. She loved him to pieces and couldn't imagine her life without him, but until she found a solution to put everything right, she had no clue how to start rectifying it.

Colin was her rock; he always had been and it was awful feeling that he despised her. It was like she didn't know him anymore; like he'd lost a part of himself - the part that made him *Colin*. It seemed he'd given up on everything he stood for and what mattered – including *her*.

*And it was her own fault.*

Sarah glanced around impatiently. *How long did it take to*

*put a packet of pills in a paper bag?*

Suddenly hearing her name, Sarah stood up, wincing as she moved towards the pharmacy counter. Gratefully taking the bag, she was stuffing it into her handbag just as the door to the nurse's room opened. Her mouth hung open in shock as Tori waddled out.

'Tori?'

Tori glanced up nervously, her tired-looking face breaking into a smile. 'Sarah!' she cried.

Sarah's immediate reaction was to run over and hug her friend, until she was sharply reminded of Colin's words. *'She would have been in touch if she was really your friend...'*

Whether she wanted to believe it or not, there was a possibility that what Colin had said was true and if it was, then she'd already made enough of a fool of herself as it was.

Sarah felt torn. Despite everything, she couldn't turn off how she felt and what her instinct was telling her. It was screaming that something was very wrong and Tori needed her now more than ever.

Sarah could see the dark circles around Tori's eyes, her gaunt face completely at odds with the huge mound of her belly. 'What brings you here?' she asked, a hint of coldness in her voice. 'I didn't think you'd moved back yet?'

Tori's elation at seeing Sarah faded at her coolness. She couldn't blame her. After all she hadn't been in touch – not that it was for want of trying. 'I'm staying at my mother's for a few days,' she mumbled.

She hadn't stepped foot outside the house for days. The one exception was for this appointment and that was in a taxi which picked her up and was patiently waiting outside to take her straight back. *She was a prisoner and she knew it.*

Tori could tell Sarah was attempting to read her and she hesitantly glanced down at her protruding belly. 'I had an appointment with the nurse to check on the baby.'

Sarah raised an eyebrow. 'Don't you mean, *babies*?'

'Oh, erm, yes... that's what I meant,' Tori blustered. She'd forgotten she was supposed to be carrying quads.

'I must say, you're noticeably big for, what – four months?' Sarah wasn't fooled. Tori had always been a bad liar. *If this woman was only four months' pregnant, then she was Florence bloody Nightingale!*

'Erm, yes… I suppose so.' Tori glanced at the door, self-consciously smoothing her dress over her bump. The urge to tell Sarah the truth was overwhelming. *She should leave.* 'I'd better get going.'

'Matt not with you?'

Tori shook her head. 'No, he's busy at work, but I've got a taxi waiting.'

Sarah watched Tori pull her loose jacket around her, the shoulder slipping to reveal several clear finger-shaped bruise marks along the top of her arm. *This was bullshit. Total and utter bullshit.*

The act of remaining distant flew out of the window. 'Keeping you under lock and key, is he?' Sarah snapped. 'And the bruises? Are you going to tell me what the fuck is going on?'

Tori felt her resolve crumble. 'Everything's fine. I'm just tired and…'

'What's he doing this time?'

'I-I don't know wh…'

'Cut the shite!' Sarah snapped. 'You look like crap and you've got bruises. You're pregnant, Tori. *Heavily*, by the looks of it...'

Grabbing Tori's arm, Sarah steered her to a secluded corner and helped her into a chair. 'The least you can do is have the decency to be honest after you fucked off leaving me to deal with all of your shit.'

'I-I tried to call you. I really did. Several times, but I…'

'Are there *really* four babies in there, Tori?' Sarah hissed. 'The truth?'

When Tori shook her head, Sarah frowned. 'It said in the pa…'

'My mother gave the press that story because she didn't want it known I was pregnant before I married.' Tori answered bitterly.

'So, how far along are you really?'

'Eight months,' Tori whispered, glancing around nervously. 'Matt swapped my contraception with dummy pills, that's how I fell pregnant,' Tori whispered, her voice dripping with humiliation. 'He said I would be easier to control.'

'Holy fuck!' Sarah could barely believe what she was hearing, unable to think even Matt would stoop so low. She could almost taste the pain radiating from her friend. 'That man! He's…'

The words Jeanie had spoken during the phone call rushed into her mind. *She'd said Tori was in danger. She'd said Hunter needed to get her away from that man…* 'Tori, you can't st…'

'I'm leaving him, Sarah. The minute this baby's born and I can function properly.' She glanced down at her belly. 'He's despicable. The things he does… I…'

'I've heard all this before,' Sarah said coolly, remembering all too well the night Tori had stood in the White Hart, all set to tell Matt where to go and leave with Hunter.

'I should have done it before, I know, *regardless* of Hunter disappearing, but this time I am. I'm *not* bringing my child up with that man around,' Tori spat. She'd thought of nothing else the last few days.

'Why not do it now?'

'I can't until I've had the baby because it's hard to do anything, but I don't trust him. I-I don't trust him not to do something to hurt us.' She wrapped her arms protectively across her bump.

Sarah was surprised to see the determination behind Tori's tired eyes.

'H-Have you seen him?' Tori asked, her voice barely more than a whisper. *She had to ask. She needed to know.* 'Hunter, I mean. Have you seen him?'

Sarah shook her head. She hadn't 'seen' Hunter, only

spoken to him. She wanted to tell Tori that Hunter had done what he'd done for a reason and to be patient, but she couldn't. She didn't want to get involved. Not this time. Although this latest development put a slightly different slant on things.

A large tear rolled from Tori's eye. 'He's gone for good then?'

Sarah glanced at Tori's distended belly, a creeping thought snaking into her mind. She hadn't forgotten Jeanie being adamant Tori was carrying Hunter's child and she'd been right about there being only one baby... 'Is this child Hunter's?' she asked, watching Tori closely.

Tori looked at the floor. 'I-I don't know... Matt presumed I used added protection with Hunter, but I didn't... It could be either of them... You mustn't say anything, Sarah, promise me?' She felt so ashamed. She'd never thought she'd be in a position where she wasn't sure of her baby's father. *What would she tell her child?*

'Oh my,' Sarah gasped. *So, Jeanie was right.* 'You think it's Hunter's, though, don't you?'

Tori nodded. 'Yes.'

'How sure are you?'

'I can't be 100%. I wish I could, but instinct tells me this baby isn't Matt's.' A small smiled passed over Tori's face. 'It's the only thing keeping me sane at the moment.'

Sarah eyed Tori quizzically. *She wasn't playing.* 'Well, you'll know for sure the moment it's born. I can't imagine Hunter's metal grey eyes not being passed down the bloodline.'

Tori managed a small smile. 'Whatever you think of me Sarah, I don't blame you, but I *will* leave Matt, regardless of whether I'm on my own or not.'

Sarah squeezed her hand. 'I believe you, but y...'

'Mrs Stevens?' The receptionist poked her head around the corner. 'The taxi driver is asking for you.'

Tori grabbed her handbag. 'I must go. My mother will tell Matt I disappeared otherwise. She reports to him every night.' She pulled Sarah into a hug. 'It's lovely to see you. I've missed you so much and I'm truly sorry you feel I disappeared on you. I swear it wasn't like that. If I could have come to you, I would have. I've thought of little else.'

'Apart from Hunter…'

Tori blushed. 'Yes, apart from him. I wish I could say I'll see you soon, but I don't know whether I will.' She struggled to her feet. 'Give my love to Colin.'

'Phone me when you can,' Sarah said sadly as Tori walked towards the door.

So, there was a good chance Tori was carrying Hunter's baby and Matt was still definitely being an abusive bastard. Whatever Colin believed, he was wrong. Tori was not making this up. She believed every single word and she would make sure Hunter was informed. What she'd told him was incorrect and she had to let him know.

## TWENTY FIVE

MATT SCOWLED IRRITABLY at the hand-painted porcelain in the glass-fronted cabinet. It was things like that which required individually wrapping and packing.

He'd hardly been back to the house since Tori had run off to Lillian's. The last time he'd been here, he'd been too busy arguing with his bloody sister to notice the box he'd left for Tori to make a start packing the fragile items in was still on the floor. It was even in the *exact* spot he'd left it. His face twisted into a sneer. *The selfish lazy cow.*

Striding over to the cabinet, he pulled open one of the carved wooden doors. The whole dinner service was in there and Tori knew as well as he did that it cost a bloody fortune.

For God's sake. He'd paid a lot of money for a removal firm to come and pack the house up at the end of this week, but he wouldn't chance having those gorilla-like imbeciles pack the special dinner service his parents had bought them as part of their wedding present. It was a limited edition and it wasn't like he could replace the odd plate, cup or saucer if any got broken.

No, he'd asked Tori to do *one* thing and she hadn't bothered. Now she'd fucked off and left him to cope with it. Well, if she thought she wouldn't be unpacking the other end, she was sadly mistaken. Besides, the exercise would do her good.

Christ, he hoped her extra weight came off as soon as the kid came out. They'd got that important function to go to a couple of weeks after he started his new position and he didn't want his wife looking like a goddamn pig on his arm.

Matt glanced at his watch and then back at the cabinet. There wasn't time to make a start on this now, he'd got things to do. Tonight was the first lot of farewell drinks with the work crowd and he'd also planned seeing Debs. Maybe he could get *her* to pack this stuff up. *Now that was an idea.*

Shame he had to give her up now they were returning back to the city, but there were always silver linings. Once he was back, he'd be bank manager and secondly, Ginny would be an acceptable replacement.

The house he'd bought was top notch too. Thanks to his connections he'd had no problem singly-handedly securing a massive mortgage for the huge property. He snorted derisively to himself. Even though he'd made sure Tori wasn't working in a ridiculous job any longer, it was hardly like her wages would have counted towards anything anyhow. Besides, women didn't go onto mortgages; everyone knew that was a man's job. She wouldn't be on the deeds either. That idiot solicitor had even had the cheek to point out if the paperwork remained as it stood, then his wife would have absolutely no rights to the house. *No shit, Sherlock!*

Of course she didn't. And she wouldn't get any rights either. To *anything*. Tori Morgan – or should he say – Tori *Stevens* as her name now was, would have *nothing* of his - apart from his name, his children and some spending money. She gave up her right to everything else when she'd made the decision to try and humiliate him by choosing that silverbacked low-life biker over him.

No, she'd well and truly shot herself in the foot. As his wife, she could have had it all, but now she was his wife in name *only* and under *his* rules. She'd move into this new house with him, deliver their child and accompany him to work functions when her presence would prove useful.

He'd also put his plan for Carmen into motion. He'd got hold of Luca. Well, he hadn't actually got hold of him, but he'd left a message with his secretary asking him to call back. He hadn't yet, but he'd be sure to soon. And if he didn't, then he'd just call again.

. . . .

'JUST MEET ME SOMEWHERE,' Sarah hissed. 'I can't talk here.' She glanced over the bar, knowing Colin was only in the cellar and would be back up any minute.

She'd been hoping Hunter would have called before now, but at least he had finally done so. But things weren't right. She could tell he'd been drinking and drinking a lot. He could normally sink plenty before any trace of alcohol was audible in his voice and being as heard a definite slur, he must have put away a shed load. She also didn't like the slight dismissive tone when he spoke.

'There's no point meeting up, Sarah,' Hunter said coolly. 'I've shelved my plans. You were right. There's no point. I was too late on *both* counts.'

Sarah blanched. She knew it. He'd given up on things after what she'd said. *Oh God. More stuff that was her fault.* Maybe Colin was right from the start and her interference *had* caused all the problems. Maybe everyone would be just fine if it wasn't for her. 'NO! You don't understand. I've discovered what I said isn't true.'

There was a pause from the other end of the line and then a woman's voice in the background. 'Who's that?' Sarah asked.

'No one,' Hunter said gruffly. He wasn't in the mood. Bella was a bit offhand with him since he'd turned her down. Still, it wasn't like he could ignore her. Not if he wanted a drink and use the pub's phone, that was.

'Did you hear what I said?' Sarah pressed. She had to get through to him. 'Where are you? Tell me where you are. I need to see you.'

'Why,' Hunter said dully. He didn't want to see Sarah. He didn't want to see *anyone*. He'd only phoned because he'd promised to.

'It's Jeanie,' Sarah said quickly. Ok, so it was a lie, well, partly, but it was all she could think of to get his attention. He'd switched off and she had to explain it was *vital* that he didn't. *And she needed to do that as soon as possible.*

Mentioning Jeanie did the trick. Frantically scribbling down the name of the pub and the town where Hunter was right at this very minute, Sarah hung up. Grabbing her car keys, she raced out of the White Hart. There was little point explaining to Colin that she needed to go out and why. He'd probably divorce her on the spot if he knew where she was heading.

Running out to her car, Sarah had little idea of where she was going, apart from that it was about fifty miles away, but whatever happened, she needed to get a move on.

# TWENTY SIX

TORI WAS SURPRISED, yet pleased, to be informed that Carmen was downstairs asking to see her. Unexpectedly meeting Sarah at the doctors yesterday had affected her greatly and brought the constant thoughts of Hunter even more to the forefront, so a distraction was welcome. She followed her mother down the stairs as quickly as her cumbersome body would allow.

Yesterday also served to strengthen her resolve over leaving Matt. She knew Sarah didn't believe she would do it, but she would. She really would this time.

'Carmen's in the drawing room,' Lillian said over her shoulder. 'I must say, I didn't recognise her at first, although I haven't seen her for some time.' She frowned disparagingly. 'I didn't realise you two were such good *friends*.'

Tori refused to rise to her mother's 'friend' barb and also didn't wish to give her any information about Carmen's estrangement from her husband. 'Carmen's staying around here for a while. She said she'd come and see me as soon as she could.'

'Well, that's good. She can help to keep an eye on you until Matt is back,' Lillian simpered.

Lillian smiled to herself. It was a godsend, to be honest. She was getting increasingly frustrated remaining in the house every evening babysitting her grown-up daughter under the express wishes of Matthew. She'd already cancelled several drink nights with the ladies, as well as a bridge evening and dreaded to think exactly how much she'd missed out on with her absence.

However, she'd drawn the line at accompanying Victoria to the doctors yesterday. It would have meant missing her appointment at the hair salon and that was *not* happening. Besides, the taxi she'd booked waited for Victoria, with strict instructions not to accept any requests to go anywhere other than back to this address.

Now Carmen had been cleverly placed by Matthew, no doubt to ensure there were two pairs of eyes on his wife, she could take some nights off. Thankfully, it was only a couple of weeks before Matthew and Victoria's house purchase completed and then she'd get back to normal.

Lillian pushed open the drawing room door and breezed in. 'Here she is. So sorry to keep you waiting, Carmen. Victoria takes an excruciating amount of time to waddle down the stairs these days.' She tittered loudly at her own remark.

Carmen ignored Lillian's comment and smiled at Tori. 'Hello, darling,' she said, rising from her chair, ensuring the silk scarf hanging around her neck did not slip. 'How are you?'

Tori smiled. 'I'm ok, considering!' She looked at her huge bump and rubbed it.

Lillian grimaced in distaste at her daughter's need to gleefully draw attention to her condition. 'What would you like to drink, Carmen?'

'Nothing, thank you,' Carmen smiled. 'I'm not stopping. I've come to take Tori out for the afternoon.'

Tori's heart lurched with the prospect of escaping somewhere, still shocked to have found an ally in Matt's sister.

Lillian frowned. 'Oh, I don't know whether that's wise, dear. Victoria's very fragile. She's only got three weeks to go and Matthew said th…'

Carmen waved her hand dismissively. 'Nonsense. I lived with my brother long enough to know that he doesn't always know best.' *Like, never, from what she'd seen with her own eyes.* 'It doesn't do any good being cooped up inside all the time. Come on, Tori, put your jacket on. We're going for some pampering at the spa.'

'That's out of the question!' Lillian barked. 'We're keeping Victoria out of the public eye as much as possible.'

Carmen pulled Tori's hand. She wouldn't let Lillian dictate to her as well as everyone else. She hadn't seen the woman for a long time, but from what she remembered, she'd always been a vicious sour woman and it seemed absolutely nothing had changed. She was still a miserable old boot. 'I'll make sure Tori's left alone.'

As well as out of principle of wanting to give Tori a break from her controlling mother's clutches, Carmen needed some female company with someone she didn't have to put on airs and graces with, or pretend that she was on holiday.

Lillian's mouth set in a hard line. 'Well… if you're *sure*?'

'I'm sure.' Carmen steered Tori from the drawing room and out of the house towards her hire car.

•  •  •  •

TORI WAS INITIALLY horrified when Carmen produced a bikini, informing her they were going in the jacuzzi. That would go against *everything* her mother was worried about. *People would see her.* Besides, she'd look ridiculously blimp-like next to Carmen's immaculate size-eight catwalk figure.

After being promised the booked jacuzzi was *private*, Tori finally acquiesced and was glad she had. Sitting back in the gently bubbling water with a glass of freshly squeezed orange juice, the tenseness and stress lifted from her body like magic.

There was one thing though… Despite Carmen going to great lengths to cover the marks on her neck, she hadn't done a great job because they were visible. *Very* visible. However, she held back the urge to ask where they had come from. Or rather, *who* had done them.

'Thanks for this,' Tori smiled. 'I needed a break from the house.' She winced as a flurry of hard kicks rocked through her and smiled as Carmen stared in fascination at the rolling, waving movements from within her large bump, half-sticking out of the water.

'It wasn't just for your benefit! I had to escape from that awful Ginny woman,' Carmen quipped. 'Christ knows how Jeremy puts up with her.'

Tori bit back a smile. She still couldn't quite believe Matt had arranged for Carmen to stay at Jeremy's.

'The woman *hates* me,' Carmen continued.

Tori laughed. 'Ginny hates everyone,'

'It doesn't help that just to irritate her I purposefully compliment her boyfriend on just about *everything* he does,. I'm sure she thinks I'll run off with him! He's like my brother, so that's *not* going to happen!'

It was no good. Tori had to ask. 'I thought for a minute you were going to tell me that they were off him.' She nodded towards the marks on Carmen's neck.

Self-consciously raising her hand to her throat, Carmen topped up her wine. 'I got a bit carried away the other night! Not with Jeremy, I might add!'

Able to read Tori's thought process, Carmen frowned. 'And for the record, I'm not returning to Luca. Our marriage is over.' She waved her bare wedding ring finger around. 'Everyone will have to accept it. He's not who I thought he was, believe me!'

Tori sipped at her orange juice, waiting.

'I'm so sorry what my brother and father have done to you, Tori. It's unacceptable.'

Tori reddened, embarrassed.

'My brother's always been a prize dick with an inferiority complex, but what I saw him do to you th…'

'Thanks to you, I'm away from him for a while.' Tori interrupted, not wishing to go over the humiliating things

Carmen had witnessed Matt do that night. She certainly didn't want to discuss the ones she hadn't seen either.

'You don't have to go back to him, you know?'

Tori stared at Carmen in shock. *She was advocating that she should leave her own brother?* 'But what ab...'

'What about *what*? Look at what I'm walking away from. Believe me, I know how much fall out it will cause, but I'm done with it. I'm done with doing things for face value when people don't realise what's really going on. Don't get me wrong, I used to love the glitz and the status, but there's a limit to lies.'

Tori frowned. 'Did... did Luca... did he...'

Carmen shook her head. 'Luca's done nothing like what's been done to you, but he lied. He lied and...'

'And?'

Carmen's beautiful face morphed into a snarl. 'Unbeknown to *me* he made an arrangement with my father!' she spat. 'My marriage is as fake as yours. My father's a greedy, manipulative, lying bastard. As is my husband...'

Tori's mouth hung open with shock. 'Are you serious?'

Carmen nodded. 'Deadly. I overheard a conversation and I left. I won't do it! I even used to love that he was a jealous piece of shit, but there was nothing between us. No passion. I was a trophy wife. Nothing more.'

'And they never told you?'

Carmen shook her head. 'Nope. I don't think my mother knows, but I can't be sure. Either way, I wouldn't believe anything they say now. My fucking family is *cursed*!'

Tori shivered with apprehension. *That she would most definitely agree with.*

'They don't know that I know... Yet...' Carmen added.

Tori didn't know what to say. She was shocked. She'd really believed Carmen's marriage was happy and genuine. One of those fairy-tale types, when, like hers, it was just lies. Lies manipulated and dictated by the Stevens'.

'And you haven't heard the worst bit... *Luca*...' Carmen

spat her husband's name. 'Isn't Luca…'

'What on earth do you mean?' Tori asked confused.

'Like I just said, I mean, he isn't *Luca*. He isn't even French!'

'T-Then who is he?'

'That, I have *no* idea… and right now, care even less!' Carmen snapped. She hadn't fully accepted it herself. She was struggling to take on board that she'd been so stupid and it had taken her so long to work out her husband had *never* been what she'd believed him to be.

'Oh my God! That's unbelievable!' Tori exclaimed.

Carmen fumbled over her bottle of wine. 'I bet you wish you could have a glass, don't you?' She felt guilty. How could she bleat on about Luca and her problems when Tori had been tricked into pregnancy and had her arsehole of a brother to deal with? She'd happily help her get away from him.

'I meant what I said. You need to leave Matt and I'll help you in every way I can,' Carmen smiled, squeezing Tori's hand.

Tori returned a grateful smile. 'Thank you. I'm not sure how I'll do it yet, but I will.' She really wanted to tell Carmen about Hunter, but didn't dare risk it. *Yet.*

She watched Carmen clumsily refill her glass. 'So, now are you going to tell me about your neck?'

'You don't give up, do you?' Carmen laughed. 'Just a man. No big deal.' In all truth, she didn't know how to explain it. That Noel was a strange one. She didn't know anything about him, but his utter lack of finesse and roughness had been weirdly refreshing. She'd enjoyed not playing the token wife.

Noel had behaved like she'd *existed*. He'd made her feel passion - like she was *real*. Furthermore, he'd treated her like a rag doll in the bedroom and boy, had she enjoyed it. She'd come several times and surprised herself and if he played his cards right, she'd see him again.

• • • •

AFTER TAKING SEVERAL wrong turns, Sarah pulled up

outside the Ragged Staff and yanked the handbrake on with relief. *Was this the place?*

She looked at the grubby façade of the pub and glanced at the small dashboard clock. Thanks to a traffic jam, a very slow five miles behind a tractor and getting lost several times, it had taken her three hours to get here and she just hoped Hunter had stuck around.

Hurriedly getting out of the car, Sarah pushed open the large pub door and stepped inside. Her eyes scanned the room and ignored the distinct silence which descended with her arrival. Oh, she knew how it worked. *A newcomer! Shock, horror!*

Straightaway, Sarah spotted Hunter sitting at the bar with his back to her. It was impossible to miss his hulking figure, but nevertheless, a wave of relief flooded over her. She made her way over quickly, knowing everyone was looking at her, including the barmaid, who was studying her suspiciously.

'Can I help you?' Bella asked tartly, watching a woman she'd never seen before making a beeline for Hunter. Even though he'd turned her down, she still cared. He was a decent man and was clearly going through a hard time. This woman might be his girlfriend or even his wife? Maybe she'd come to sort things out?

'Pint, please,' Sarah said.

Hearing a familiar voice, Hunter turned around. 'Hello, Sarah.'

Sarah automatically moved to hug him, but stopped, sensing the invisible barrier Hunter had placed between them. Her eyes took in his dishevelled and exhausted appearance and her heart sank. Guilt surfaced and she wished she'd been sure of the facts before she'd said anything. At least now, she was.

Sarah smiled warmly as the barmaid ungraciously deposited a pint on the soggy beer towel. 'Thanks.' Handing over the money, she turned back to Hunter. 'Is there somewhere we can go?'

Nodding, Hunter stood up and motioned to a quiet corner

over the other side of the large room.

## Twenty Seven

'I'M NOT SURE why Carmen would show her face in there again. Not after the spectacle she made of herself the other night?' Ginny said, scrutinising Jeremy for any hidden motive in his suggestion.

Personally, she'd been overcome with happiness watching Carmen humiliate herself with her disgusting whore-like behaviour. If the other night hadn't put Jeremy off his dream-woman, then she didn't know what would! And with Noel? That revolting psycho?

Ginny bit back a smile. She couldn't have engineered it any better herself, but what had actually happened had been far better than what she'd been originally hoping for.

She'd seen the look in Noel's eyes and could see without any shadow of a doubt that he'd got his eye on Carmen. She'd presumed Carmen would have been aghast at someone like Noel's advances and thought it would have caused her to run a mile! A woman with a lifestyle such as hers and married to that amazingly successful rich Frenchman surely should have curled up in horror at a greasy biker's attention, putting her off socialising with her and Jeremy. That way she'd get her manicured claws out of him, but it hadn't worked out like that at all. Much to Ginny's surprise, Carmen had *relished* that riff-raff's come-on and the show she'd made of herself had been gut-clenchingly mortifying.

Ginny shuddered involuntarily. Carmen deserved to lose everything! Look at what her husband provided for her and she still went and did the dirty on him in front of all of those people? But worse than that... with someone like Noel? That was far too insulting.

Ginny looked at Jeremy again, sure he wasn't listening. 'Did you hear what I said? I said, I'm not sure why Carmen would want to show her fa...'

'I heard what you said,' Jeremy snapped. *How could he not?* If he could invent a bullet-proof formula to be selectively deaf to Ginny's voice, then he'd patent it. 'It's not that much of a big deal, is it?'

'Not that much of a big deal?' Ginny squeaked. 'The wife of a tycoon publicly strips off in a flea-pit and then sleeps with one of the local greasers and you're telling me the press won't have a field day?' She arched her eyebrows. 'And I doubt whether Matt will be too impressed by trusting you to look after his sister in her time of *need*...'

'It's not my problem,' Jeremy muttered.

'It probably bothers *you* more than anyone else,' Ginny said, unable to control her jealousy.

Jeremy sighed. *Not this again.* 'That's not true. Anyway, I've got to speak to Noel.'

'What for this time?'

'Just business.' Jeremy had popped into the White Hart yesterday afternoon to have a word with Noel. He'd been planning to talk about Carmen and get the man to see sense – not that he'd tell Ginny that, but he hadn't wanted to deal with the wrath and interrogation from that Sarah woman.

From the window, he saw her behind the bar on the phone, so he'd gone around the back, hovering in the beer garden to see if he could catch sight of Noel. It said 'beer garden', but it was about as much of a garden as a concrete bloody slab. The only greenery in that 'garden' was a collection of weeds sticking through one of the cracked paving slabs in the courtyard and the mould growing on an abandoned shopping trolley in the corner.

He'd tried to surreptitiously peer through one of the windows without Sarah spotting him, but she'd been far too engrossed in whoever she was talking to. He'd lurked near the open sash, seeing the tap room was empty. It must have been the day where all the scum picked up their Giros or something because there was absolutely no one in there, despite being mid-afternoon.

He'd only popped across on the off chance between appointments and couldn't hang around. Noel wasn't there, so he'd been just about to retrace his steps and leave when his ears had pricked up, catching part of Sarah's conversation. He was sure she'd said 'Hunter'. Noel would want to know about that, as would Matt.

Jeremy pulled his jacket on and glanced back at Ginny. 'I'm going and Carmen's coming too, so if you don't want to join us, then we'll see you later.'

Scowling, Ginny slipped her feet into her stilettos. Regardless of whether Carmen was interested in Noel or not, she wasn't giving her any additional free time with Jeremy.

Slinging her handbag over her shoulder, she crossed her arms defensively. Let's go then, shall we? That's if Carmen's ready of course. We couldn't possibly leave without *her*.'

· · · ·

HUNTER PULLED BACK on the throttle and with the engine roaring, raced up the road. He hadn't cared for Sarah's warning to leave this until the morning.

Well, *he* was the judge of that and although he'd had a few drinks, he was more than coherent enough to ride his damn bike. He was all but *born* on a motorbike and could ride one in his bloody sleep. Besides, this was *way* too important to leave until tomorrow. He'd already wasted days with his pointless self-pity trip, but now… Now, things were different.

He hadn't been sure what to think when Sarah blurted out that the paper had been fed false information, courtesy of Lillian Morgan. Far too many people were feeding him information and he was sick to death of being jerked around, left, right and centre. As he'd opened his mouth to tell her to go back to the White Hart and concentrate on her own life, she'd spoken over him. She'd made him listen and he was glad she had.

Sarah had seen Tori. She'd actually *physically* seen her. She'd heard from Tori's own mouth that she was *not* expecting quads and was *eight* months' pregnant, not five. Furthermore, Tori believed her baby was his. Sarah also said Jeanie had phoned, impressing the urgency of Tori being in danger and that he needed to get her away from 'that man'.

*That man had to be Matt Stevens.*

Hunter overtook a car, swinging his bike back into lane and opened the throttle further. There was still a chance. Although he was too late avenging the real target, he had at least uncovered the truth. He had to see Tori and had to see her *now*. Ok, so it wasn't the way he'd wanted it and he'd tell her everything he knew when the time was right, but this was more important. Her *safety* was more important.

Hunter spat out a fly from between his teeth which had taken the opportunity to divebomb his mouth as he steamed up the road and set his jaw determinedly. Although he believed Sarah, he needed to see Tori with his own eyes and read her reaction.

Sarah insisted Tori was still desperately in love with him, but he needed to see it for himself. He'd left her in the lurch, making her believe he'd played her, so she had every right to hate him. What would he say? How would he justify what he'd done the last time he saw her? Should he tell her the real reason as to why he'd left now?

He couldn't. Not whilst she was heavily pregnant. It wasn't right, so she'd have to trust him and that was a big ask, considering.

Hunter's teeth clenched. Sarah had also told him what Matt had done to get Tori pregnant, along with his father, but it looked like it had horribly misfired on the pair of disgusting jumped-up bastards and worked in *his* favour. He had no idea what Matt's father was like, but given his bloody son, he presumed he was of the same ilk. *On their head be it.*

As Hunter had scrambled to get out of the pub, Sarah had begged him to think about what he was doing. How would he get past Lillian Morgan, for instance?

He didn't have time to think about what he was doing and sod Lillian Morgan! He'd get past her and didn't give a rat's arse how he did it. If she called the bloody cops. *Let her.*

*He was going to see Tori and it would happen tonight, regardless.*

## TWENTY EIGHT

NOEL'S EYES LIT UP as the woman he'd bedded the other night strutted into the bar. To her credit, she showed no signs of embarrassment after her display.

Noel nudged Grin and then winked at Carmen as she flashed him a seductive smile. 'My night has just looked up, I see.' *Yeah, he'd happily have another round with her. She had a body to die for and he very much wanted it underneath him again.*

Pushing himself to his feet, he rearranged himself to disguise his arousal and sauntered over to the bar. He placed his hand on the small of Carmen's back, his fingers cheekily brushing lower. 'Whatever the lady's having please, Colin.'

Ignoring the silent glare Colin afforded him, Noel elbowed Jeremy out of the way and leant on the bar.

'Noel, can I...'

Noel glanced at Jeremy. 'Fuck off, Jezza? I'm not buying you a drink.' All he wanted was to concentrate on Carmen.

He smiled inwardly. It wasn't like he had a thing for her, before any of the other Reapers started ribbing him. He wasn't the type to go stupid over a bird. No, this was pure physical lust, coupled with the mental gratification of fucking a blue-blood that did it for him.

Jeremy frowned. 'I-I wasn't asking for a drink. I wanted to tell you someth…'

Noel clenched his teeth. Did the scrawny fuck not get it? He was about to chat to a bird and didn't need him butting in. 'Can't you see I'm fucking busy?' he hissed.

Taking the hint, Jeremy stepped away and Noel turned back to Carmen, plastering on his widest smile. 'Hold that drinks order, Colin. We'll have two bottles of your finest champagne. That's if you've got any in this dump?'

He pulled a wad of notes from the inside pocket of his leather jacket, peeled off five twenties and threw them onto the bar. 'A ton should more than cover it. Bring them over, would you? I'm taking this lady to a table.'

Noel felt like celebrating. It had been a good day. The wedding ring Carmen launched across his room had fetched a tidy sum. It was worth a lot more than what he'd accepted for it, but it wasn't like he could go mainstream with it. Regardless, forty-five grand wasn't to be sniffed at, so the least he could do was buy the woman a drink and hope she didn't ask for her ring back.

Colin glared after Noel as he led Carmen to a table by the dartboard. 'I presume *you'll* take this over?' He dumped the champagne and glasses in front of Jeremy.

'Oh, erm…' Jeremy wasn't sure what to do. Noel didn't seem to want his company and he didn't even *dare* glance at Ginny. Her rage radiated like an open fire and he knew why. She was spitting chips over Carmen being bought champagne whilst she got wine.

'I'll take it over, yes,' Jeremy smiled, making a big show of pulling his monogrammed wallet from his blazer pocket. 'Although, can you get another bottle of champagne out. I think we'll have the same.'

'Does this look like the fucking Ritz?' Colin snarled. 'How many bottles of that stuff do you think we keep here? Those two Noel's got have been sat here ten years and that's all we had. If you want that sort of clobber, you'll have to get it yourself from the off licence.'

Jeremy fiddled uncomfortably, sure the daggers from Ginny's glare had opened several holes along the side of his skull. 'Oh, right... well, I...'

'I'll just have wine,' Ginny barked. 'I'm used to getting second best.'

. . . .

HEARING A NOISE, Tori stirred. Her mother hadn't returned already, had she? *What time was it?* Blearily opening her eyes, she looked at the clock on her bedside table. *It was only 9pm.* She must be hearing things.

Her first reaction when her mother had announced she was going out tonight was surprise at being left alone. Tori's second thought was to phone or visit Sarah. She hadn't though because Matt had probably tapped the phone, plus her mother had a long-standing arrangement with the taxi firm and they'd inform her a request had been made. On top of that, she was so exhausted she could barely function. She could barely keep her eyes open, so had little choice but to give in to what her body needed and get some rest.

She ran her hand over her belly and smiled. This baby had developed a habit of being extremely active during the night and she'd had no sleep for days now and had to admit she was looking forward to getting her body back to herself.

Rearranging the pillows, Tori closed her eyes again. She must be hearing things. Her mother wasn't back and that was all that mattered. On the verge of dropping off, she frowned hearing that unmistakeable noise again. It was something hitting her bedroom window. *Like gravel.*

She flicked on her bedroom light, her heart beating rapidly. The only time she'd heard that sound was when Hunter had thrown gravel at her window months and months ago. *It couldn't be, could it?*

Struggling to manoeuvre out of bed, she pushed herself to

her feet and pulled her robe around her. Padding over to the window, she peered through a crack in the curtains and her heart leapt into her mouth.

*It was him. It was Hunter.*

Tori clung to the window sill, her legs threatening to fold under her. She remained frozen to the spot. She'd waited *months* for this moment and now it was here she had no idea what to do. The last time this man had seen her she'd been a trim size ten. Now she was a *lot* different. Hunter probably didn't even know she was even pregnant, let alone that the baby might be his.

She peeped back out of the curtains, her stomach lurching and frantically glanced around the driveway. Now she couldn't see him anywhere. *Had she dreamt it?*

Slowly moving back to the bed, she questioned her sanity, then froze hearing footsteps pounding up the stairs. Before she could process anything further, her bedroom door burst open.

Hunter slammed the door behind him and leant up against it, panting from the exertion.

Tori stared at the man she'd loved from the start. She took in his square bearded jaw and long tousled hair. He looked exactly the same. Despite her shock, the immediate throbbing in her core reminded her just what effect he had on her.

Hunter's heart crashed noisily in his chest. When he'd arrived at Tori's house, he'd fully expected to have to deal with Lillian Morgan. Sarah had already told him Tori was being kept a virtual prisoner, so he was ready to do whatever he needed to see her.

He'd hurried up the gravelled driveway, spotting a small chink in the downstairs curtains. Peering through, he couldn't tell for sure if anyone was in. There was a light on, but that didn't mean anything. Then he'd remembered the last time he'd needed to get Tori's attention, which now seemed like a thousand years ago. But it had worked. *Thank God.*

Inhaling deeply, Hunter locked eyes with Tori, unable to fully comprehend she was finally in front of him. He had dreamt of this moment for so long. He wasn't sure what he'd expected, but it wasn't quite this.

Her beauty was shimmering even with her mussed bed-hair. Her bright blue eyes studied him intensely and he found himself staring in fascination at her once flat stomach, now transformed into a huge mound, completely out of proportion with her slight frame. *His baby?*

Hunter slowly stepped forwards. 'Tori,' he said softly.

Realisation suddenly hit him like a sledgehammer. He hadn't contemplated feeling like this. In this instant his decision was easy. Even if the baby wasn't his - it didn't matter. It was *Tori's* baby and for that reason alone he didn't care who the father was.

He never thought it would be possible to feel like that. He hadn't thought he could dismiss something so important, but it really didn't matter. He was so in love with this woman he would take her in whatever way enabled him to be with her.

Tori remained motionless as Hunter approached, his metal grey eyes focused on hers. She wanted to reach out and touch him to make sure he was real. *But he'd left her. He'd left, saying his love was a lie.* Despite this, the pull towards him transcended everything else.

'I've missed you,' she whispered, unable to keep the tears from rolling down her cheeks. 'Why did you leave?'

Hunter stared at Tori. There was still about eight feet separating them. The urge to pull her into his arms was suffocating, but he couldn't do that. *Not yet.*

'There was something I needed to do.' He realised this sounded an altogether pathetic justification for how he'd made her feel and wanted to wipe the tears from her face; the tears *he'd* caused by his actions.

Hunter watched Tori's expression change from shock and pain into anger. 'Please listen. I know I hurt you and I'm sorry,' he continued. 'I had no choice.'

'Y-You left me!' Tori added, her voice quiet but her anger evident. 'I came to tell Matt it was over. I was going to be with you like we'd planned… You would expose Noel and Matt but y…'

Hunter put his hand up. 'Things happened which meant I couldn't. Tori, *please*. I don't expect you to understand, not without knowing why, but I can't tell you that yet and…'

'So, why are you here?' Tori's overjoyed reaction to Hunter's appearance morphed into resentment. 'Have you come to play more games? To laugh at me?'

'Games?' Hunter moved towards her. 'No! It was never a game and I've never laughed at y…'

'Stay away from me!' Tori yelled. He wasn't making any sense.

Hunter froze. This was not going well. He hadn't known what her reaction would be, but he wasn't doing a very good job in making her believe or trust him. 'That night I said what I did was because I needed you to think I didn't care. So you'd hate me until I got what I needed to prove that I was sincere.'

Tori's face fell. 'Well, you did a bloody great job in making me believe you didn't care, but I never hated you. That was the problem,' she whispered.

'I'm so sorry,' Hunter murmured, his voice cracking. Tori looked so vulnerable, so hurt, so *beautiful*. 'I love you. I love you more than anything. I always have…'

'I-I don't understand. Why… why would y…'

'I need you to trust me.' Hunter risked stepping forward.

'Trust you?' Tori yelped incredulously.

Hunter's eyes remained locked on Tori's. It was taking all of his resolve not to press his lips hungrily onto hers. Slowly reaching out, he placed his large hand on her belly, heartened that she didn't push him away. 'Is this my baby?'

Tori's bottom lip quivered, her shame bottomless. She'd been wondering when he would mention the elephant in the room. The one which had transformed her washboard stomach into a large mound. 'I-I think so, but I can't be sure.'

Hunter's hand rubbed the large bump, amazed to feel movement under his fingers. 'A woman I trust who knows things believes this baby is mine.'

'What? Someone just came out with that? You expect me to believe that too? Stop this and just tell me why you're here,' Tori said, her voice small.

'I've been planning how to return and get you back since before I left,' Hunter said, his voice low. 'The baby is a bonus and what I said about that woman knowing things is true.'

Trying to quell the desire flooding her, Tori didn't know what to make of any of this. 'I-I'm married now and what if the baby... What if...'

'What if it's Matt's, you mean?' Hunter managed to utter that bastard's name, even though it stuck in his throat. 'Tori, I will love this baby either way because it's part of *you*.' He gently pulled her towards him, his arms enclosing her protectively.

Tears ran down Tori's cheeks and she pressed her face into Hunter's hard chest, almost suffocating with the need to breath in his scent. The scent she'd yearned to smell again for so long.

'You'll be with me now, like we planned. I promise you,' Hunter said. Jeanie was right. This was more important than the truth that no longer mattered. He'd tell her after all of this was sorted and she'd had the baby. It was too late to do it any other way.

'You're in danger if you stay with Matt,' Hunter spat. 'And I won't have him touch you again. Or the baby.'

Tori swallowed nervously. 'You know more than anyone that I don't want to be with him. I never did. Besides, he's not here.'

'But he will be. From what I understand, he'll be expecting you to play happy families very soon,' Hunter said.

Tori frowned. 'Understand from who? Who would kn...'

'I saw Sarah. She told me. It doesn't matter. What's important is that you can't be with Matt. Even if you don't want to be with me, you need to get away from him.'

*So, Sarah had seen Hunter? She said she hadn't been in touch.* 'I've already planned to leave Matt, but I need to wait until I've had the baby. I can't do much at the mo…'

'No, Tori. You need to get away from him *now*. It's important.'

Panic surged and Tori wrapped her arms protectively across her belly. 'If you know he's planning something then you have to tell me.'

Hunter raked his fingers through his hair, admitting to himself that it sounded ridiculous. 'I don't know. All I know is that I've been given a warning and we must act on it. You can't wait until the baby's born.'

'Is this from the woman who 'knows things', by any chance?' Tori said petulantly. 'Matt won't be anywhere near me for at least a week. Until the house sale completes.'

She sighed. She didn't understand what was going on, but if Hunter said she was in danger, regardless of what had happened between them in the past, then perhaps she should believe what he said on this score.

'So, you'll let me take you away somewhere? I can't offer much, but I can offer you my heart,' Hunter took Tori's hand. 'We've got a few days to arrange it.'

'How do I know you won't disappear again?'

'You don't, but I won't. I thought I was doing the right thing before - for everyone, but mainly you. I got it very wrong.' He grasped Tori's face with both hands, then brushed his lips tentatively onto hers.

Tori gasped, her lips parting. The pent up love and passion flooding from her.

Despite not wanting to, Hunter broke the kiss and held Tori at arms' length, not quite believing she was in front of him once more. 'My God, you are so utterly beautiful.'

Tori self-consciously looked down. 'Even with…'

'Even *more* so…' Hunter pulled the tie of her robe, watching as it fell to the floor and his breath hitched seeing Tori's naked body so ripe.

There was something overwhelmingly powerful and amazingly seductive seeing the woman he loved full to bursting with his child. *It was his child. He could sense it.* 'You're stunning.' He needed to touch her, feel her, *love* her.

He ran his finger down between her breasts and traced a line lightly over her bump. 'I want you Tori… so, *so* much…'

Tori felt ridiculous. How she could possibly appear sexy looking like *this.*

Sensing her thoughts, Hunter smiled. 'That's *my* baby in there. I don't doubt that, even if you do. How could you be anything other than beautiful,' he murmured, his mouth coming down onto hers.

Tori allowed herself to be laid gently on the bed and she wrapped her fingers in Hunter's hair as his mouth trailed kisses down her throat and along her collarbone. She felt delirious with both happiness and worry. *Could she trust him again? Could she believe him?*

She had to. She *had* to believe him. Her heart and body already did.

Hunter's mouth moved to Tori's nipple, his tongue gently tracing a circle around the sensitive flesh. Although he was desperate to reclaim her, he needed to take it slow – for her, but also for him. The intensity of his feelings were so strong, they were almost crippling.

Pulling his T-shirt off, he leant back over Tori, his mouth now running over her belly. Feeling strong movement rolling under his lips, he inhaled deeply in amazement and sadness that he'd missed her pregnancy developing. *He should have been here.*

Propping himself back over her, he tenderly kissed her, groaning into her mouth as her fingers ran down his back to his belt.

Tori reached after Hunter when he suddenly got off the bed. Unbuttoning his jeans, he let them fall to the floor and desire throbbed mercilessly as she watched his cock spring out, hard and ready. All notion of her self-consciousness disappeared. She could tell from the way he touched and kissed her that he found her beautiful. Sitting up, she pushed herself to the edge of the bed and ran her fingers lightly over Hunter's cock, smiling as he moaned with need.

Finding her wetness, Hunter lay back on the bed, sitting Tori on top and guided himself into her. He watched her above him, her eyes closed and her head tilted back. Her dark hair fell in waves over her breasts. She was the most beautiful thing he'd ever seen and her dramatically changed figure only deepened his burning love.

Tori moaned loudly with rapidly building pressure, feeling the sensation she'd missed for so long building steadily from deep inside her.

Hunter clenched his jaw in an attempt to control the fast building climax. It was taking all of his power not to flip her over and pound into her, but that was out of the question. Oh God, he loved her. Loved her so much. All of this was so, *so* intense.

'We'll be together this time, Tori. *All* of us. I don't care what it takes…' he groaned.

'Yes, yes that's what I want,' Tori panted, the wave of her climax cresting. 'Oh God… Hunter… I…'

Hunter held Tori as she screamed with pleasure, her orgasm massaging waves along the length of his shaft. *He was back where he belonged. With this woman.*

## TWENTY NINE

'YOU'RE TAKING IT to follow me to the bogs now, are you Jezza?' Noel zipped up his flies and scowled at Jeremy. 'Do you have a habit of doing this to other men, or is it just me?'

Jeremy hovered near the washbasin opposite the line of urinals. The *last* place he wanted to be was in the toilets with Noel, but he had little choice if he wanted ten seconds to speak to the man being as he'd been consumed with Carmen since they'd arrived and she'd been an extremely willing recipient.

Of course, it had made for an excruciatingly awkward atmosphere. He and Ginny sat at the table with Carmen and Noel in silence, like spare parts. Ginny's face couldn't have looked more slapped if she'd tried and just to make him feel that little bit more uncomfortable, she'd stared pointedly at Carmen's champagne, then at her own wine and finally at Jeremy. This she had repeated for what seemed like *hours*. He couldn't wait to go home. This was dire and now Noel was making unpalatable insinuations as to his sexuality?

'You going to say anything, or have you just come to stare at my huge cock?' Noel barked. He began unzipping his jeans. 'For fuck's sake! I've only just put it away and now you want a closer look?'

'Don't be stupid! Of course I don't want that, I...'

Eyes narrowing, Noel slammed Jeremy up against the cracked tiles of the wall by his throat. 'Don't call me stupid, you prick! I'm far from that.'

'I-I didn't mean it like that,' Jeremy spluttered.

Dropping his grip, Noel glared at Jeremy and then sparked up a cigarette. 'What the fuck do you want then? I haven't got any more gear arriving until next week. You know that.'

Jeremy straightened his shirt and hoped the wet he felt on his neck wasn't what he suspected it was, although it looked unlikely to be anything else, being as Noel certainly hadn't just washed his hands. It was best all round if he didn't dwell too much on the more likely alternative. 'It's not about that, it...'

'If you're going to say I shouldn't poke your mate's sister, then *don't*. I fuck who I like and I wo...'

'Sarah's in contact with Hunter,' Jeremy blurted.

Noel flinched. Only very slightly, but enough to be visible. 'Why the fuck didn't you tell me?' he growled.

'I've been tryi...'

'How do you know this?' Noel cut in, barely able to contain his rage. He knew that slag must have maintained contact with Hunter and he was right. *The bitch had lied.*

'I overheard her on the phone this afternoon,' Jeremy replied. 'And before you ask, I was looking for you. But you were right. I *was* planning on speaking to you about Carmen, but to be honest, now I don't give a shit.'

Noel's eyes narrowed even further and he eyed Jeremy suspiciously. *This guy really thought he was funny, didn't he?* Well, he wasn't laughing. However, he'd let the Carmen thing go for now because finding out what was going on with that two-faced slag behind the bar was more important. 'And you're *sure* she was talking to him? You heard her say his name?'

Jeremy shook his head. 'No, not for definite. I *thought* she did and from what she said, I presumed it was him. She kept asking, *'Where are you? I need to see you'*. Things like that.'

'You fucking imbecile. That doesn't mean jack shit! It

might not have been him at all. That could have been *anyone*.'

*It also could well have been Hunter and he'd be finding out.* He'd made it very clear before now that he expected the truth off Sarah and he hadn't thought she'd be so stupid to defy him, but maybe he'd given her too much credit. Noel threw his half-smoked cigarette into a urinal.

'Where are you going now?' Jeremy squeaked.

'Funnily enough, I'm going to see if Sarah's back and then return to the fucking hot chick who's sitting at my table. This may come as a bit of a disappointment, Jezza, but it's not my first choice to spend the remainder of the evening holed up in the bogs with *you*!'

Jeremy watched Noel leave. *Was that it then? Not even a 'thank you for the information?'*

He sighed. Maybe it wasn't Hunter? He may have jumped to conclusions, so he'd better not mention anything to Matt until he knew for certain. In fact, he might not bother at all. Matt was another ungrateful bastard and he was damned if he'd have two people treat him like an idiot in one night.

· · · ·

TORI LAY BETWEEN HUNTER'S LEGS, her back resting against his chest. The hot soapy water lapped around her body and she closed her eyes in tranquil enjoyment as he gently ran a sponge over her arms, breasts and down over her belly rising like an island from below the waterline.

Could she allow herself to believe that her dream had come true? That dream she'd had about Hunter – the one when Matt arrived home and accused her of…

She didn't want to think about Matt. She didn't want *anything* to taint the time she had with this beautiful man.

But could she trust Hunter? Was she being ridiculous? Wasn't she accepting him far too readily, considering how much he'd hurt and let her down? If only she could speak to Sarah, she'd know what to do. Tori frowned. But then, Sarah hadn't been honest about any of this either. Maybe she knew about the things that Hunter said he couldn't yet tell her?

Was she risking her future on a stupid whim?

No, she wasn't. She *loved* him. She loved Ashley Hunter with every fibre of her body.

She would leave with him. They'd got the rest of the week to put things in place before Matt arrived and she'd be long gone before he showed his face. Hunter said first thing in the morning he'd rent somewhere for them to live. *Somewhere away from here.*

Tori wished Hunter could stay with her tonight and although her mother wouldn't be back for some time yet, it was out of the question. *Still, he was here now.*

Tori sighed contentedly and ran her hands up Hunter's thighs under the water.

Hunter suddenly laughed in joy. 'Look! I can see a foot!'

Tori opened one eye. 'What?'

Hunter put his hand to the left of her belly. 'There! Look! A foot!'

Tori stared down and sure enough there was a distinct outline of a tiny foot pushing through her skin. 'Oh my God!' she cried.

Hunter grinned widely and placed a kiss on Tori's throat. 'Fuck me, this pregnancy lark's amazing, isn't it? I wish I'd been here the whole time.'

Tori smiled sadly. 'I wish you had too.' She drew in her breath as a strong flurry of kicks and sudden movement squirmed from inside her. She frowned. 'It's uncomfortable though.'

Hunter laughed. 'Well, I *love* it! How much longer have you got to go?'

Tori sighed. 'Only two weeks and I think I'll have burst by then.'

'Takes after me you see! He'll be big!' Hunter winked.

Tori's face fell. 'W-What if it isn't yours?'

Hunter frowned. 'You keep asking me this, Tori. I've already said I'll love you and the baby regardless and I meant it, but he's *mine*. It's a boy, Tori, I keep telling you.'

He placed his big hands on her huge belly once again. 'This is *my* son. I've been told that on good authority. My Aunt Jeanie hasn't been wrong on this sort of thing yet.'

Tori hoped so. She hoped more than anything else in the world that this Jeanie woman was right.

. . . .

'WHAT THE FU…' Sarah couldn't fathom what had happened when she found herself slammed face-first into the wall. She'd only been popping to the toilets before jumping behind the bar and also trying to think of what she was going to say to Colin. She'd seen his expression as she'd scuttled through the taproom and knew with certainty he'd be asking where she'd disappeared to for the last few hours. *But now this?*

'You've been to see him, haven't you?' A voice hissed close to her ear.

Sarah knew who that voice belonged to. *Noel. Shit.*

Pure panic engulfed her as Noel swung her around and pressed his body tightly up against hers, crushing her painfully against the wall.

'Cat got your tongue?' Noel growled, his eyes shining savagely.

'I don't know what you're talking about!' Sarah muttered.

'Don't play stupid. I *told* you to let me know if you heard from Hunter and you didn't. You fucking *lied*, you bitch!'

Sarah's eyes darted behind Noel's head. *Surely someone must need the toilet?*

'How long have you been in contact for? How long have you been speaking to Hunter since he left? The whole time?'

'I haven't seen anyone and certainly not Hunter,' Sarah cried. 'Now, get off me!' She didn't feel anywhere near brave enough to say this, but she had to do something. How did he find out where she'd been?

Aware tears were threatening to spill, Sarah had no choice but to chance her luck. She could see the manic hate in Noel's face. 'I mean it, Noel. Get the fuck away from me, otherwise I'll yell and everyone will know you've threatened me!'

'I can easily stop you from doing that,' Noel grinned nastily.

'What the fuck's going on out here?' Colin barked, bursting through the door, clocking Noel move quickly away from Sarah. He looked at his wife's reddened face and then looked at Noel, a smirk wide across his mouth.

Noel smiled confidently. 'I suggest you ask your fucking wife that question, Colin.' Turning on his heels, he stalked through the door into the taproom.

Colin stood in front of Sarah. He felt like his heart may break in two. *This was the final insult.* He was too shocked to be angry and slumped backwards against the wall. 'Sarah, how *could* you?'

'What? What do you mean?' Sarah reached out to touch Colin's arm, flinching as he recoiled from her.

'I know you blame me for everything that's happened and that you think Hunter and Tori set us up, but they didn't. Colin, you've got to believe me.'

'What the fuck have they got to do with this? I'm asking about you and Noel! He was all over you!'

'But that's it! It's everything to do with Tori and Hunter. That's what this is all about. That's what I'm trying to tell you!'

Colin said nothing. All his anger from the last few months was replaced by abject desolation. *Sarah hadn't denied sleeping with Noel…*

'Colin? Are you even listening? Tori's baby may be Hunter's. In fact, she's pretty sure it is. Tori's in danger. A woman has confirmed this,' she babbled, realising how ridiculous it sounded. 'You don't understand. I don't understand either, but a lot's going on. Hunter begged me to understand there's a reason why he left us in the lurch. I don't know what it is yet, but I believe him when he said there was no choice and we'll understand when he's able to tell us.'

Sarah sighed in frustration when Colin still made no

response, just stared mutely at her.

'I had to tell him to go and find Tori. I saw her last week. She told me what's been going on. I've been to see Hunter today and he's going to get her. That's where he's gone now. Noel wants to know what I know.'

Suddenly, the truth dawned on Sarah. *Colin thought she was sleeping with Noel, didn't he? Dear God.* 'COLIN! *Nothing's* going on with Noel! Not what you think, anyway. I'm certainly not having an affair with him!' she yelled. 'He's playing games. He's also been threatening me. He suspects I'm in touch with Hunter and wants to know everything, but I can't and *won't* tell him.'

Suddenly everything fell into place in Colin's mind. He loved Sarah for the way she stood up for those she cared about. It was one of the things he'd *always* loved about her, but he'd been so angry and humiliated with what had happened to the White Hart since Hunter's departure, he'd blamed it all on her. And none of this was her fault. And neither, from what she'd said – what she'd *always* said, was this Hunter's or Tori's fault either. *He'd got it wrong.*

Colin's eyebrows knitted together. 'Did you say Noel's been *threatening* you?' His voice was razor sharp.

Sarah nodded. 'He's done so a few times. To be honest, he scares me … I…'

Colin didn't want to ask the question. If he got the answer he didn't want, he didn't know how he would cope, but nevertheless, he had to ask. 'H-Has he…?'

'He hasn't raped me if that's what you're asking. He's pushed me about a bit and another time pulled up my skirt. I was terrified he would, but he hasn't.'

'Why didn't you tell me any of this before?'

A tear rolled down Sarah's cheek and she brushed it away with trembling fingers. 'How could I? You've treated me like I don't exist for *months*. You said our marriage was over if I had anything to do with Hu…'

Colin pulled Sarah into his arms. 'I'm so sorry, Sarah. I

should have been there for you.'

'But I've ruined everything,' she sobbed, relief at being in Colin's arms once more acting like a tonic on her frayed nerves.

'No. Only one person around here has ruined everything,' Colin snarled, glancing towards the door leading into the bar. 'And I'm going to fucking kill him!'

As Colin gently removed Sarah from his embrace and moved towards the doors, she grabbed his arm. 'No, *please*!' she begged.

'You can't be serious. That bastard has threatened and sexually harassed you and you want me to leave it? You really think I won't kill the cunt?'

'Please leave it. If you don't, it will come out about Hunter and I need him to concentrate on Tori. She's about to give birth really soon. *Please* just leave it for now. Until this is all over.'

Colin sighed resolutely. 'Not sure how I'm going to do that, but if that's what you want, then I guess the least I can do with the way I've been, is what you want.'

Sarah breathed a sigh of relief and hugged Colin tightly.

'Come on,' Colin said. 'Let's go and see how much of a good actor I am.'

Jeremy waited a further few minutes before he left the toilets. The burning question now was, did he tell Noel what he had just heard, or did he tell Matt. Or should he tell *both* of them?

# THIRTY

MATT STOMPED INTO THE HOUSE. He hadn't planned on coming back here this morning. It was only when he woke up at Deb's realising he'd brought the wrong shirt with him, that he'd had to make the trip specially to get the right one before work. It was such a pain in the arse.

He could have spent that extra hour between Debs legs, but instead he'd had to use that time driving. There'd been no choice because he had an important lunch meeting with clients today and Bob wanted him there because they had links back in his hometown which could prove useful.

It was the ideal networking opportunity, but he couldn't wear a blue shirt - not with a pinstripe suit. That wasn't an acceptable combination; it was *so* last year and it was important to be on trend and maintain an up-to-date image. That was part of his vision for his new position. A new face for the new bank manager. No offence to his father, but things required updating and *he* was just the person to achieve that.

Quickly changing into the correct shirt, Matt ignored the delicate items dotted around that *still* hadn't been packed and reached for his car keys, but something made him glance at the answerphone. The red light was flashing. He didn't want to waste time, but if he didn't see who it was, it would niggle him all day.

Pressing the 'play' button, he fidgeted impatiently. The automated voice stated a message was left last night at 10.56pm and then, after the customary beep, Jeremy's voice spoke loud and clear.

'Matt, it's Jeremy. Hope you get this... I didn't know whether to call... Erm... something's happened... It's important. Can you call back? Soon as you can... Doesn't matter what time... Ok? It's important... About Tori... Ok? Bye.'

Matt's blood ran cold. Had Tori had gone into labour? She hadn't got long to go now, so it was feasible. He frowned. If she had, he'd be guilted into driving all the way back, just to pointlessly sit in a hospital listening to Tori wail and moan for what would probably be *hours*. He didn't want to get involved in all that rubbish. He'd miss his lunch meeting and *that* was important.

*Hang on... Wouldn't Lillian call rather than Jeremy if Tori was in labour?*

Sighing, Matt glanced at his watch. He should be able to catch Jeremy before he left for work. *Just.* Picking up the phone, he dialled the number.

'Hello?'

'Jeremy? It's Matt. What's so important?'

'Matt! I thought you might have called last night.'

'I've only just got your message, so hurry up and spit it out!' Matt snapped. *He hadn't got all day.*

'I overheard Colin and Sarah an...'

'Colin and Sarah?' *Was this really that important?*

Jeremy could sense Matt's impatience, but he needed to hear this. 'Yes, from the White Hart. You know th...'

'Yeah, I remember them, but what the fuck have they got to do with anything?'

'They were arguing. I overheard that Sarah's been in contact with Hunter and Colin wasn't happy. Noel suspects, but she didn't tell him anything, she only told Colin. I haven't said anything to Noel because I thought you should be the first to know. I don't know whether it's true or not, bu…'

'Has she been in contact with him or not?' The hairs on the back of Matt's neck bristled. He didn't want to hear that man's name ever again. 'Where is the prat?'

'I've no idea, but…'

'Look, is there any point to this? I really don't care if Sarah's been in contact with that overgrown moron, or if her husband or Noel doesn't like it, but wh…'

'She told Colin that Hunter was on his way to visit Tori. She said Tori was in danger and that Hunter needed to get her away.'

'WHAT?' Matt barked, almost choking. *Was he hearing things?* 'What do you mean, in danger? From who? And are you telling me that wanker went to take my wife?'

Jeremy hesitated, sensing Matt's rage down the telephone line loud and clear. 'I don't know. I'm just repeating what was said.'

Matt forced himself not to hyperventilate. 'And this was last night?' *If that man had been anywhere near her…* Trying to embarrass him again, was he? And Tori? He might have bloody known. And what was Lillian doing? He'd instructed her quite clearly to keep him abreast of *all* situations. Tori was to have *no* visitors and to go *nowhere* unaccompanied.

'There's more…' Jeremy knew Matt wouldn't like this one. 'Sarah said Tori thinks the baby is Hunter's…'

Matt laughed loudly. 'Oh, for God's sake. This is a wind-up, right?'

When Jeremy remained silent, Matt's teeth clenched. Why was he letting this bullshit get to him? It was a ridiculous concept. There was *no way* Tori could be pregnant from Hunter. The kid was *his* and his alone.

'That's madness,' Matt interrupted. 'They must have known you were listening and decided to wind you up, unfortunately at my expense.'

Jeremy sighed. He didn't know why he bothered. Let Matt believe what he wanted. He knew what he'd heard and it had been *no* wind up, but if that was what Matt wanted to think, then sod him. 'Maybe you're right.'

Matt pursed his lips. He wouldn't let Jeremy know this rattled him as much as it did. 'Thanks, but none of it's feasible, so I really do think you've been had. You know none of them like you. It was probably Noel's idea.'

Jeremy sniffed uncomfortably. 'It's Carmen who's more interested in Noel, I'm afraid.'

'Seen him again, has she?' Matt sneered. 'Interesting...' That reminded him. He still hadn't heard anything from Luca, so another call would have to be made shortly, but first, he'd call Lillian. Only to confirm that all of this was total and utter rubbish, of course.

'They seem to quite like each other,' Jeremy said. 'Strange, really.' He decided not to mention that he'd listened to Noel noisily rutting on Carmen through the wall in his apartment most of the night. To be honest, he wasn't pleased Carmen thought it acceptable to bring Noel back in the first place, but he liked her too much to hold it against her, even if she was intent on sleeping with that greaser.

Jeremy frowned. Noel pissed him off. The way he'd treated him in the White Hart was crap and for that reason, on principle, he'd made the decision not to tell him anything and just tell Matt, but now he wished he hadn't done that either being as everything he'd said had just been dismissed.

As far as he was now concerned, he'd wash his hands of the lot of them if this was how it would be. 'You're back next week, aren't you?' Jeremy asked.

Matt smiled. *See, this was all about Jeremy's nose being out of joint over his impending return.* 'Yes, the house should have completed by then.' It better had anyway. That was what he was paying the solicitor for, was it not? But if he was wrong and this *wasn't* a wind up and that fucking bonehead was sniffing around his wife again, then he'd be going back a lot sooner. *Hunter's kid, indeed? Stupid bastard.*

'Must dash,' Matt said airily. 'Got a meeting first thing.' He hadn't, but he wanted to speak to Lillian before he got to work and that was his next call.

· · · ·

'IT'S NOT A PROBLEM, MATTHEW. I can understand your worry, but I can assure you that it's unfounded.' Lillian stretched her neck to relieve the building tension caused by the lies she was speaking.

'I presumed that was the case, but I felt it prudent to double check,' Matt said in his best voice. The voice he'd been practicing.

He found raising the intonation of certain words gave him an added edge of authority which he wanted to master before becoming bank manager. He didn't want people presuming they'd receive special treatment because they'd worked together previously at the same level, or they socialised outside of work. And it looked like he couldn't get his authority stamped fast enough because some people were intent on taking the piss.

'So, there's no way anyone could have visited Tori last night?' Matt pressed.

'I don't see how? I was here all night.' Lillian felt the first prickles of sweat at the base of her neck. Matthew must not discover she'd left Victoria in the house alone – he'd go mad. But who on earth did he think would have come round? 'Who's supposed to have been here, Matthew?'

It was pertinent to act on the defensive. After all, she'd already answered Matthew's question, but he'd repeated it, giving the impression he didn't believe her, so it was only right she should feel offended.

Lillian sniffed loudly. 'I must say, I'm rather disappointed that you mistrust my word. You asked me to accompany my daughter when she went out and that she was to receive no visitors and I've adhered to this. Don't forget, it's also in *my* interests that Victoria doesn't get hounded by the press, but I've now missed several important engagements to honour your request, so pl...'

'I apologise if I've come across as mistrustful. That certainly wasn't my intention.' *Bollocks. Now he was being forced to grovel to the old cow.* His reasons weren't about the press, but he could hardly tell her what they were *really* about. He'd have to work it another way.

'I guess I'm overprotective. I heard there's been a spate of recent problems with that dreadful biker gang. They've had a normal person knocking on doors pretending to do surveys and then they barge in and rob the place.' *Ok, so that was a load of bullshit, but he couldn't think of anything else off the top of his head.*

'Urgh. Those damn bikers again! I told your mother I'd seen one hanging around some time ago an...'

'That's why I thought I'd ask,' Matt jumped in. *Bingo! God, he was good.* 'I just wanted to make sure no one had knocked on the door, that's all. Tori may have answered it if you were busy. I wasn't insinuating you had left her alone.'

'No, Matthew, no one's been around at all.' Lillian breathed a quiet sigh of relief. Matthew knew nothing and no one had been round. It was purely his overprotective nature coming to the forefront. *What a good man he is.*

'I'm very relieved to hear that, Lillian.' *Well, he was.* As suspected, Jeremy was spouting bullshit. Did he really think he wouldn't work it out? 'And I very much appreciate what you're doing. I realise you've given up a lot regarding your social engagements, but I'll be back shortly and then everything will return to normal.'

*He'd ramp it up a bit more now...* 'I can't bear being away from Tori – especially not so close to the birth. I worry constantly, you know? How is she?'

Lillian beamed with pride listening to her son-in-law and only hoped her ungrateful daughter finally realised how lucky she was. 'Victoria isn't up yet, the lazy girl! She was exhausted last night and went to bed straight after dinner.'

That was another reason it had been safe to go out. Victoria could barely move and wouldn't have the energy to answer the door, let alone anything else.

'Please tell Tori I called, but it's probably best not to mention anything about the bikers. I know how much they scare her, what with her father and all of that and I don't want her worrying. Not in her condition…'

Lillian bristled at the mention of Tori's father. *Would she ever be allowed to forget the mistake she'd made?* 'I certainly won't mention that.' *Time to change the subject.* 'I expect you're really excited, aren't you? Your child will be here any day now.'

'You've no idea,' Matt simpered. *Yeah, excited when he could properly get on with his life.* The kid was the final piece required to set him in full standing. 'My mother can't wait either. She wanted to visit the other day, but I remembered you were taking Tori to that doctor appointment, so no one would have been in.'

Heat travelled up Lillian's spine. She hadn't accompanied Victoria then either. 'That's a shame, but at least your sister saw her, which was nice. It was good for her to see a fr…'

'Carmen visited?' Matt interjected. *What was this?* She knew full well that he didn't want her having anything to do with Tori. Not after her interference. 'What did she say?' *She'd better not have let anything slip. He'd kill the bitch.*

'Say? She didn't say much. She was too insistent on taking Victoria out for the afternoon.'

'You let her take Tori out?' Matt gasped. *He couldn't believe this. How dare she! How fucking dare she!*

Lillian frowned. 'That's not a problem, is it? Oh, I do hope not. I didn't think not going out or seeing anyone included family members? I did say that perhaps it wasn't a good idea, but Carmen was very insistent.'

Matt swallowed in an attempt to moisten his dry mouth. He had to play it cool. As far as Lillian was concerned, everything was fine. 'No, of course it's not a problem. She's my sister. I'm just surprised. Carmen's been going through a bit of a difficult time recently, so I didn't think she'd be up to it.'

Lillian smirked. *So, it was true what she'd heard?* The ladies were adamant something was afoot in the Stevens' court.

Lillian sniffed airily. Susan had mentioned nothing, of course. That woman wouldn't divulge anything to make her look anything less than perfect, but if what she'd heard was true, then she'd be next in line for questions. She'd heard Carmen was divorcing her husband and she'd only been married four or five years.

She'd listened for *years* about how successful and perfect Carmen was. How the chateau she lived in with her obscenely wealthy husband was 'divine' and how well she'd done. She mixed in all the elite circles and went to the best social events and dinner parties. And now it looked like it had all gone wrong.

Lillian smiled nastily. If this was the case, then it was hardly a surprise Susan had kept it quiet, but she itched to find out the story. It would be nice to have something on Susan to underline her precious daughter wasn't the saint she made her out to be and instead was a social embarrassment. It would be extremely pleasurable, in fact.

'Lillian? Are you still there?' Matt asked.

'Sorry, yes. I heard Carmen's had a few issues, but she seems fine. And as for her and Victoria going out, despite my reservations it probably did them both good.'

'Where did they go?'

'Carmen had booked a spa afternoon, but don't worry, it was private, so no press interference. You know, I didn't know they were such good friends, but obviously I'm pleased that they are.'

Lillian had to say that, but if the rumours were true, Victoria would have no further connection with the woman. She hadn't gone to all this trouble with the pregnancy story for Carmen to ruin it by association.

'I didn't realise they were such good friends either,' Matt

muttered. And that was would be knocked on the head as soon as possible. Once he was back, he'd personally police who Tori spoke to and there would be *no* repeat of this sort of thing.

He must get hold of Luca sooner rather than later so he could fetch his disobedient wife so that she didn't balls up anything further.

'Right, Lillian. I really must get off. I've got to get to work. I've so much to tie up over the next couple of days,' Matt said brightly.

'Alright, dear. I'll see you soon,' Lillian said and gratefully replaced the receiver, breathing a long sigh of relief.

# THIRTY ONE

'AND WHAT ON EARTH is the matter with you?' Lillian asked suspiciously as Tori entered the living room. It was almost lunchtime and she'd only just surfaced, sitting there staring into space wearing a weird expression.

Lillian's face screwed up in revulsion watching her daughter absentmindedly stroking the proof of her wantonness. 'Cover yourself up, girl!' she snapped. 'Have you any idea what you look like?'

Tori smiled dreamily. *She looked beautiful. That's what Hunter had said and that was all that mattered.* Her whole being still thrummed from his touch and the deep warm glow that she was, after everything, going to be with him, radiated pleasurably through her. Even her mother's scathing remarks could do nothing to dampen her happiness.

'Victoria! Are you even on this planet? Why are you sitting smiling at nothing like an imbecile?' Lillian couldn't bear it. She couldn't stand the sight of the girl. This whole thing made her stomach turn. 'And stop running your hands over yourself! You're not an animal!'

Tori glanced up. Soon she wouldn't have to listen to any of this *ever* again. 'I'm just happy. What's wrong with that?'

Lillian pointed at Tori's belly. 'We'll see how happy you are when your contractions start, shall we? Believe me, there's nothing remotely joyful about that, I can tell you!'

The prospect of childbirth didn't faze Tori. The thought of giving birth to Hunter's child only caused more happiness. She rubbed her belly once again, delighting in the hefty kick she received in response. 'It will be worth it though. Isn't that what everyone says?'

Lillian harrumphed. 'I suppose it depends on what they end up with…'

Tori shrugged. 'I'm just feeling really good about myself today.'

'Oh, so you've *finally* realised which side your bread's buttered?' Lillian sneered. 'I should think so too. You're fortunate Matthew has so much love for you. You sure as hell don't deserve it.'

Tori felt like laughing. *Yeah, Matt was just great, wasn't he? Her mother was welcome to him after she'd left.*

'At least he'll be back soon to take you off my hands and so you can act like a proper wife to him.'

Tori smiled sweetly. She could keep up this pretence for a few more days.

'He called this morning, by the way. He's worried about you.'

Tori's smile froze, her senses on red alert. 'Worried about me?'

Lillian flapped her hand. 'He's being overprotective. He doesn't want to miss his child being born and I think he's eager to get settled in your new house.' *She wouldn't mention anything else that Matthew had said.*

With difficulty, Tori hefted herself to her feet and waddling over to the window, staring out longingly. She was eager to get settled into her new home too, but not the one her mother was referring to. She was moving *nowhere* with Matt.

Hunter may have found somewhere for them to live already even though it wasn't yet midday. Her heart quivered in anticipation. The thought of waking up in his arms every morning made her shiver with delight.

Tori could barely conceal her excitement. Hunter said he'd be back as soon as possible, but would definitely return by the end of the week in time to leave the day before Matt arrived.

• • • •

SITTING ON HIS BIKE at the side of the road, Hunter patted his leather jacket pocket, just to make sure the keys were safely stowed.

He smiled. It had taken him the best part of the day and a full tank of fuel to-ing and fro-ing back and forth, but it wasn't bad going considering some people took *months* to find somewhere they wanted to live.

He glanced up at the tiny terraced house in front of him. It was a lot different to what Tori was accustomed to and he wished he was in a position to provide something a little bigger and better for her, but it would have to do for now. It was on the outskirts of the city - a bit close to the old stomping grounds, but on the same vein, he had no intention of letting anything fall by the wayside. His priority was getting Tori settled, then he'd tell her the truth.

His face fell slightly. Would telling her blow his happiness out of the water? Maybe, but judging how she'd reacted to him last night he didn't think *anything* could break their love. *Even the death of her father.*

Secondly, he'd be rectifying the mess Noel and Matt had caused and he didn't want to be too far away for that. No, this was perfect. The area had a line of shops, a little supermarket, a hairdressers and a couple of other places and would do very well. Besides, they didn't have to stay here for ever – just until they'd got everything sorted.

He'd been lucky. The property had only come up to let this very morning. It had been having a lot of work done to it, following the state it had been left in by the previous tenants and the landlord had been unable to rent it until the repairs had been carried out, so was keen to get new tenants in as soon as possible. Hence why Hunter hadn't had to do any arm-bending to get a lease written up and the keys in his hand immediately. It was strange what a six-month upfront payment could achieve.

His heart swelled. This time next week he'd be coming home to the sight of his pregnant wife setting the table for...

A big grin formed over Hunter's face. *Tori wasn't his wife, but she would be.* She'd divorce that twat as soon as she could and *then* she'd be his wife. He'd marry her in an instant. And very soon he'd also have a child.

Ashley Hunter – with a wife and a child. Who would have thought it? Certainly not him, but he couldn't be happier.

He would see if he could get a few minutes with Tori to tell her the good news. With any luck, her harridan of a mother wouldn't be about. He couldn't afford to risk her seeing him and freaking out. That would put a spanner in the works and he didn't want anything doing that. Not now he was this close.

· · · ·

MATT TRIED HIS best to let the morning's events rise above him, but try as he might, all of that business Jeremy had pulled in an attempt to freak him out, was still gnawing away at him.

He stared at the sheaf of paperwork on his desk aimlessly. He couldn't concentrate. As it was, he'd missed several opportunities during that lunchtime meeting because his mind wasn't focused. It was noted too. He'd seen the furtive glances Bob gave him.

Damn Jeremy for riling him and damn Tori for putting him in this position. It was down to her that people had ammunition to throw at him in the bloody first place! *That was it! He'd made his mind up.* After work he'd get straight on the road and go and see her. Give her a reminder of what she had and jog her memory that he was not to be messed with.

Matt hadn't seen Tori face to face since the incident Carmen felt the need to intrude on, so it was definitely something he needed to do. Clear the air, so to speak – and remind her what she would be doing from now on.

His brows furrowed. If he had time, he'd also swing by Jeremy's and pay his cock-sucking sister a visit. Perhaps slip it into the conversation that he'd left a message for her husband? That would wipe the smile off her face. And when Luca finally got back to him, he would relish bringing the man up to speed.

Matt grinned. It wouldn't be long because now he'd left a very *specific* message with his secretary and thought that this time, she'd deem it important enough to pass on.

He glanced at his desk clock. One more meeting and then he'd get on the road.

• • • •

WITH RISING IRRITATION, Richard replaced the receiver. *Why was no one bloody well answering his calls?*

He hadn't heard from Matthew for a day or so and wanted to check if there were any further updates he should be concerned about regarding the Reapers. He'd called Matthew's work number and the simpering girl who finally answered informed him that he'd already left.

The stupid cow had initially been unwilling to give him any information as to Matthew's whereabouts, even though he'd made it quite clear who he was. The damn cheek of the woman! It had been a long time since he'd had to explain himself. He'd been in virtually *every* one of the bank's nationwide newsletters for the past God knows how many years and she hadn't recognised the name 'Richard Stevens'?

Richard frowned. Matthew never left until, at the earliest, six or seven o'clock, but it was only 5.30. It wasn't good enough. He was never at the rented house either, so how was he supposed to get in touch?

He'd then phoned Bob – again no answer. He'd thought it a good idea to see if Bob had had any further visits, but surely he'd have called if there was anything to report?

Richard chastised himself for being paranoid. It wasn't helping. Besides, everything seemed positive and whatever *had* been going on, appeared to have died down. Matthew was returning for good in a few days and he'd be retired by the end of next week, so life was good.

A tap on Richard's study door made him glance up. He smiled as Susan walked in and placed a cup of tea on his desk.

'Thank you,' he muttered. Personally, he'd have preferred whisky, but tea would suffice.

When Susan hovered in the doorway on her way out, his heart sank. It meant she wanted to discuss something.

'Is there something wrong?' Richard asked, knowing full well that there must be, but Susan's version of something wrong wasn't usually anything remotely ground-breaking.

Susan fidgeted uncomfortably in the doorway. 'Well, th…'

'Come back in then,' Richard snapped, beckoning his wife into the room. He hated people lurking in doorways.

Susan sat in the chair the opposite side of Richard's desk. 'I expect it's nothing… I bumped into Lillian this afternoon and she mentioned Carmen had called round to see Victoria the other day.'

Richard raised his eyebrows. '*Carmen*? I didn't realise she and Victoria got on.'

'That's exactly what Lillian said. She made quite a thing of it,' Susan said. 'Carmen took Victoria out for the afternoon and Lillian said she seemed different…'

'*Different*? What's that supposed to mean?' Why did women insist on speaking in riddles? It was like they enjoyed making men guess what point they were making, rather than just saying it, like a normal person.

'Well, that's just it. I don't know *what* she meant.' Susan paused. 'But she also dropped a couple of hints that she'd heard Carmen was having problems…'

Richard sighed. 'And that's newsworthy, is it?' It was only a matter of time before Lillian heard the jungle drums after Susan had opened her mouth to that group of old gossiping hags she spent time with.

'She'll go around saying that Carmen's marriage is over

and that won't help with wh…'

'Oh, Susan! Those busybodies you socialise with have nothing better to do. They'll find something else to discuss before long.'

'But I've been asked about this several times now and I'm running out of excuses. I really think we should speak to Luca. It's gone on far too long.'

Richard frowned. He couldn't have Susan stepping in. She might even take it upon herself to phone and he couldn't risk that. If Luca felt there was an issue, then something might be mentioned about the arrangement. Susan would go berserk, as would Carmen.

'They'll sort it out. Whatever's gone on is a storm in a teacup, I'm sure. Carmen said something along those lines to Matthew,' he smiled. 'If we interfere, we could ruin that.'

'You never told me she said that!' Susan whined.

Richard studied the deep creases on his wife's forehead and imagined he could quite easily roll a marble along the furrows. She really should consider doing something about them. 'Didn't I?' *That's because it hadn't happened.*

He picked up his diary, hoping Susan would get the hint and leave him be.

'Lillian said something else too which worried me,' Susan continued.

Richard hoped his eyes hadn't really rolled to the back of his head like they felt they must have. 'Oh yes and what's that?' he muttered uninterestedly, flicking through the pages of his diary. *Hadn't he got a golf match coming up?*

'Matthew phoned Lillian this morning. Those bikers have been infiltrating houses in the neighbourhood under the ruse of conducting consumer surveys.

Richard froze. *Matthew had done what?* 'I beg your pardon?'

'Yes, he was most concerned. He wanted to make sure Victoria hadn't been left alone, or answered the door to anyone. It's a bit worrying. Those people are scum, Richard. Utter scum!' Susan pursed her lips.

'Lillian was most put out. She felt Matthew was insinuating that she hadn't been protecting Victoria from possible harm, but bless him, anyone can see that he's worried. And why wouldn't he be? His wife's about to give birth to his first child and he doesn't want some dirty biker frightening her, does he?'

Richard's fingers stuck in the same page of the diary that they had been when Susan had started talking. If Matthew had heard bikers were sniffing around Victoria's house, then what did that mean? Was it connected to him? Were they trying to get to him through Victoria? Furthermore, why the hell hadn't Matthew told him of this?

'Are you alright?' Susan eyed her husband's sudden grey pallor.

Richard frantically pulled himself from his panic. 'Yes, yes, I'm fine. I think I just need something to eat. I was so busy today I didn't have time for lunch.'

Susan raised her hands to her mouth. 'Oh, you poor thing! You should have said. Dinner won't be long, but do you want me to get you something in the interim?'

Richard flapped his hand. 'Don't worry, it's fine. And don't worry about this biker rumour either. Victoria's fine and you're right, Matthew's just over-concerned. Us men do care, you know.'

He forced a smile, sure that the pressure would cause his face to crack. 'He'll be back in a couple of days which will put his mind at rest.'

It didn't put *his* mind at rest though. And the fact that no one was answering his calls made it even worse.

## THIRTY TWO

THROUGH THE OPEN CURTAINS and courtesy of the light being on, Hunter watched Lillian Morgan steadily drinking glass after glass of expensive wine, alternated with glancing at the mantlepiece clock and drumming her fingers on the coffee table. *Would she ever go out? It was already twenty past eight.*

From his previous surveillance, he knew she usually went out at eight, but that was before she'd agreed to help her son-in-law keep Tori prisoner.

Watching Lillian top her glass up yet again, Hunter scowled. If she carried on like this, she'd be too plastered to go anywhere. He itched with impatience. He wanted to tell Tori the good news about the house, but couldn't hang around.

Hearing a car approach, he retreated back into the shadows, ducking behind a bush as the bright headlights of a taxi made its way up the gravelled driveway.

The door of the house slammed and Lillian Morgan's grating voice loudly berated the driver for his lateness and Hunter twitched with anticipation watching the car make its way back down the drive.

Once the taillights had disappeared, he wasted no time entering the house through his usual way – the utility room window.

Racing up the stairs, he banged loudly on Tori's bedroom door and opening it, beamed widely at the sight of the woman he loved easing herself off the chair by her dressing table.

'I thought I heard you,' Tori smiled, padding towards him.

Hunter pulled Tori into his arms, his fingers winding in her silky hair as she pressed herself tightly against him. Lowering his mouth onto hers, he felt drunk with the feel of her lips and the taste of her.

After a few moments he begrudgingly pulled himself away. 'How's my son today?'

'Active!' Tori laughed. 'I've missed you.'

Straightening up, Hunter took Tori's hand and led her to the bed. Sitting her down, he resisted the urge to undress her and run his tongue over every inch. 'I've found us somewhere,' he smiled.

Tori's face lit up with excitement. 'Really? Where? When is it available?'

Hunter pulled the keys from his top pocket and jangled them. 'Now. I've paid six months up front.' His face fell slightly. 'I have to warn you that it's not very big and th...'

'Hunter,' Tori interrupted. 'I'd live in a cardboard box with you. I don't care what it's like, but how will this work? When are we…'

'That prat returns, when? Saturday?' Hunter's fingers trailed circles on the outside of Tori's thighs.

Tori fought the urge to kiss him. 'The house completes on Saturday morning, so he'll probably be back on Friday.'

'Then I suggest we go on Thursday,' Hunter said, his face nuzzling into Tori's neck, his voice vibrating against her throat. 'You won't need much. Just essentials. We'll get everything else we need afterwards.'

'B-But what if he finds me?' *This was real. She really was doing this.*

Raising his head, Hunter stared straight into Tori's eyes. '*If* he does, then he won't get far. You have to trust me. I won't let him take you away from me again.' He realised this sounded rather lame being as he'd been the one to leave, but it wouldn't happen again. *That much was certain.*

He placed his hand on Tori's belly. 'We'll be together this time, Tori. *All* of us. I promise I won't let you down again.'

Tori nodded, tears forming at the back of her eyes.

Hunter could see Tori's fear, but she didn't need to be scared, nor worried. *Not now, not ever.* 'And you're sure he's back Friday or Saturday?' He'd much prefer to tell the prick face to face that he was taking Tori off his hands and if he tried to stop him, or touch a hair on her head, then he'd break his neck. But this wasn't about what *he* wanted. It was what was best for Tori.

'I haven't heard anything different. He called and spoke to my mother only this morning and she said the same.'

Hunter frowned. 'Perhaps we should go tomorrow then, just in case. I don't want him scuppering anything.'

'But I can't get everything together by then!' Tori exclaimed. 'I have to be careful how I do this otherwise it will set the alarm bells off.'

Hunter nodded. *That he most certainly didn't want.* 'Ok. Thursday it is. That's two days.' He'd pack up his tent in the morning and use tomorrow to source a car.

'But where…'

'Invent a doctor appointment. How do you normally get there? Taxi?'

'Yes, but it waits until I come out.'

Hunter scowled. *They really had worked hard to keep her under lock and key, hadn't they?* 'Get there for 2pm. I'll be waiting.'

'What about my stuff? How will I get that out?'

'Like I said, pack light and I mean, *light*. Put a few bits in a large handbag and I'll get you anything you need, plus more the other end.'

'I-I can't get on a bike… not with…'

Hunter laughed. A wonderfully throaty laugh. 'I'd hardly

expect you to clamber on the back of a motorbike like *that*, would I! Although plenty of the Reapers old ladies do exactly that. Maybe if yo…'

'No!' Tori's eyes grew wide in terror. 'I really can't, Hunter, I…'

'Relax! I'm joking! I know you wouldn't get on it even if you weren't pregnant! I'll get a car. No idea what sort, but it'll be a car, ok?'

And if the taxi was hanging around, then he'd also need a set of false plates. He could switch them after he'd collected her. *Damn. All of his plates were stored in the cellar at the Factory.*

His brow furrowed. Not to worry. He'd get some more made up tomorrow. He'd pop into the pub down from where he'd pitched his tent and have a word with Bella. He didn't doubt that she'd know someone who would do it, no questions asked.

Tori eyed Hunter's expression. 'What's the matter? Is something wrong?' she asked, an edge of panic in her voice.

Hunter grasped her face with both hands and kissed her. 'Nothing's wrong, I'm just working out logistics.'

Tori smiled. 'We're really doing this, aren't we?'

'We most certainly are!' Hunter grinned. 'God, I love you, Tori Morgan!'

'And I love you!' she replied, almost unable to believe that in two days' time her life would be vastly different, yet utterly *perfect*.

Hunter suddenly frowned and looked at Tori sternly.

'What?' Tori squeaked, her panic returning.

'You do realise I'm expecting you to honour what you promised some time ago?'

Tori looked confused. 'What I prom…'

'To marry me? I need to make an honest woman out of you.'

Tori laughed excitedly. 'You've no idea how quickly I'm going to get a divorce and yes, I *am* going to marry you. I would love nothing more. And for the record, you can do *anything* you need to do to me…'

Hunter slipped his hand up Tori's dress and traced a line between her legs teasingly. Groaning with frustration, he pulled away. 'Oh, God, don't tempt me! You do realise that by Friday morning you're going to be exhausted after I've kept you up all night.'

Getting to his feet, he pulled Tori with him and nestled her in his arms. 'I'd better go. I don't want anything to mess up our plan and there's stuff I need to do.'

He pressed his lips on hers. 'Two o'clock at the doctors. Be there!' he winked.

Tori grinned widely, watching as Hunter left her room and thundered down the stairs. She wrapped her arms around herself as much as she could and almost did a little dance. *This was really happening. She was going to be with Hunter.*

# THIRTY THREE

MATT WAS AGITATED. Almost ten past bloody nine and he'd only just got back. The one night he was desperate to get anywhere and he'd got snagged up in a rolling roadblock on the motorway, using time he hadn't had to waste.

He scowled. It was probably all down to some idiot changing a tyre on their blasted caravan on the hard shoulder and everyone else, being so desperate to cash in on the potential of seeing something grisly to fuel their morbid curiosity, had brought the motorway to a virtual standstill by rubbernecking. *Bloody pointless bastards.*

The worst thing was, he'd got to return tonight because, as usual, he'd got a meeting first thing, so it wouldn't leave much time to talk to Tori. It certainly meant he wouldn't get chance to go to Jeremy's to see Carmen. *Damn it all.*

Impatiently turning into the long road leading to Lillian Morgan's house, Matt pressed his foot down on the accelerator in the blind hope that by speeding down the tree-lined avenue, it would somehow make up for the hour delay.

Nearing the turning for Tori's road, he slammed his hand down on the horn when a motorbike shot out from the junction, cutting the corner. *Fucking bikers! And they wondered why they got knocked off their stupid death-traps?*

Matt suddenly froze. He stared in the rear view mirror, but the taillight of the large bike had all but faded into the distance. *That was one of them. That was one of the Reapers!*

The noise of their kind of bike wasn't something readily confused with anything else.

He hadn't had a clear glimpse of who was riding it. He'd been more intent on avoiding the massive chrome monstrosity as it roared out in front of him, but it had to be a Reaper. *Fuck.* Had they been to Tori's? Had Jeremy been right all along and what he'd said wasn't a wind-up?

A sick feeling radiated from Matt's insides. *It was that bastard, Hunter, wasn't it?*

Gnashing his teeth, he sped towards Tori's house. Screeching up the driveway, gravel chips flew in all directions and Matt almost fell out of the car in his haste to get in the house. He rushed up the steps. The light in the sitting room was on, but there was no one in there. He banged on the front door loudly with his fist and then pressed the doorbell – one, two, three times. *No answer. Come on, come on.*

Continually hammering on the door, Matt nearly fell onto his face when it suddenly opened. Stumbling, he righted himself and angrily glared at his wife. 'Took your fucking time, didn't you?' he roared.

'M-Matt!' Tori was paralysed with fear. *He wasn't supposed to be here.* 'W-What are y…'

'Ah, so you've remembered you've got a husband?' he screamed, his eyes darting around the hallway. 'What took you so long to answer the door?'

'I-I was upstairs. I can't move too qui…'

'What were you doing upstairs?' Matt was incensed. *He'd been here, hadn't he? That bastard, Hunter, had been here, which meant, if what Jeremy said was right, he'd been round twice this week alone.*

Grabbing Tori's wrist, he dragged her into the sitting room. 'Has he been here?' he spat.

'Matt, you're hurting me!' Tori cried, stumbling as Matt pulled her along too quickly to comfortably keep up.

Matt felt like he would blow a gasket from pure rage. *How dare she take the piss like this!* 'Well? Answer the fucking question!'

Tori leant against the wall, her breaths coming in short, ragged bursts. Had Matt seen Hunter? Had he been outside watching the house and seen him leave? Was the house or her room bugged? Had he heard what was said?

All manner of possibilities raced through her mind. She wouldn't admit anything. *She couldn't.*

Matt lurched forward, gripping Tori's face with both hands. 'Answer the question, you bitch. Has that baboon been here?'

'I-I don't know what you're talking about,' Tori stammered. She'd play for time until she knew for sure whether Matt knew anything.

Matt's face twisted into a sneer as he pushed Tori roughly into a side table. 'I mean, Hunter, that's who. You know, that fucking silverback you planned on jilting me for a long time ago? Remember him?'

'No, of course he hasn't been here. Why wou...'

'I *saw* him, Tori. I just fucking saw him!' He waved his arms around wildly. 'Down the road. Just now! Well, I saw his bike, or what looked like his bike. There aren't many of those sort of machines around, you know?'

'I-I...' Was it possible Matt and Hunter had crossed as he'd left? It could be. *Shit.* Sweat trickled down Tori's back.

Matt glared at Tori as she leant against the side table. 'I wouldn't put too much weight against that table if I were you. Look at the fucking size of you. You'll break it!'

Tori let Matt insult her. It gave her extra time to think of what to do or say. She placed her arms protectively over her belly.

'You're not saying much?' Matt spat.

'It must have been coincidence. No one has been here. I...'

'Weirdly enough, that's what Lillian said, but where the

fuck is she?' Matt screeched. 'She's not here, is she?'

Tori shook her head. Let her mother take some of the shit for once.

Matt's teeth clenched. So, Lillian was lying. She'd blatantly lied, the scabby old hag. That meant she didn't know whether anyone was here the other night or not. Or more importantly, whether *Hunter* had been there.

'You disgusting slag!' Matt roared. 'I only came back tonight to clear the air for when we move into the new house being as you ran away like a child the last time we had a little argument, but I return to find that you've been doing *this*?'

Tori remained silent. She'd hardly left because of a 'little argument'. Matt was an abusive bully and she wouldn't take it anymore.

Should she tell him she was leaving? That they were over? She knew it wasn't part of the plan to do it this way, but neither was what was happening right now. She wanted to, but wouldn't. She couldn't risk anything messing up the plan.

'I didn't believe him, you know?' Matt ranted. 'I thought he was lying when he said Hunter had been round, but I should have listened.' He ran his hand through his hair in agitation.

Tori stared at Matt in complete confusion. 'When *who* was lying? Wh…'

'Jeremy, that's who! *Jeremy*, you stupid cow. I thought he was jealous. He's always been desperate to get one over on me.'

Tori frowned. *How could Jeremy know anything?* 'J-Jeremy? What would he b…'

'Your *mate* dropped you in it,' Matt barked, reading Tori's expression. 'Didn't think of *that*, did you? That Sarah's got a big mouth on her. She was telling all and sundry that Hunter was coming to see you. She'd told him to, see? Oh dear, Tori… I think you fucked up by telling her your secrets!'

Tori's mouth flapped open. 'I haven't even seen Sarah!' But she had. She'd seen her at the doctors that day and they'd talked. She must have contacted Hunter. *Oh God…* Why would Sarah have told anyone about it?

Matt smiled. 'That's rattled you, hasn't it? What a shame,' he sneered. Inwardly he was steaming. *It was true. It was fucking true because he could see it in her face.*

He lurched towards Tori once more. 'How long has this been going on? Weeks? Months?' He suddenly laughed loudly. 'You're actually thinking of leaving me again, aren't you? Oh my God, you stupid bitch! Lover Boy won't want someone else's kid!'

He yanked Tori's dress up. 'Look at you! You're hardly a catch! That's got to put him off, for fucks' sake. It's disgusting!' Poking her belly, he smiled as Tori yelped in shock.

'Although, perhaps he really is stupid, blind and desperate. Let's have a check to see if he's been in my wife tonight, shall we?' Matt pulled at her knickers.

'Matt! Stop this!' Tori sobbed.

Dragging Tori to an armchair, he pushed her down and pressing on her belly, pulled her knickers off.

'Get off me!' Tori screamed, feeling her baby writhe in distress.

Matt held Tori's knickers up to his nose and sniffed deeply. 'Hmm, strange. I expected to smell evidence, unless you've quickly changed them, of course.'

He forced Tori's thighs apart and stuck his head between her legs. 'Nope. That doesn't smell of sex either. Fucking hell, I guess he couldn't cope with screwing a beached whale after all.'

Tears rolling down her face, Tori struggled to her feet. 'You're sick, Matt. SICK!'

Matt laughed nastily. 'Not as sick as you. Well, go on then. If you *really* want to fuck off with that man, then do it! GO ON!'

His eyes narrowed further at Tori's silence. He'd been planning to save his secret weapon, but on retrospect, this situation more than warranted it.

'So, tell me this. You want to fuck off with another man when you're about to give birth to *my* child? You'll never get custody. Not after the court hears you've left your child's father to live with a fucking biker in a squat.'

Tori blanched. *He couldn't take her baby, could he? Could he do that?*

Hunter's words that she was in danger flooded into her mind. *Just keep quiet, Tori,* she told herself. *He'll run out of steam very shortly. He had to.* At least she hoped so because she was terrified. Utterly terrified.

Matt was now comfortably calm. He wanted to enjoy watching Tori's face when he told her the truth.

Walking casually over to the sofa, he leant against the backrest and smiled widely. 'Ok, if you want to do this, then please… walk away.' His hand motioned to the door. 'Although, it's hard to believe you'd choose to be with the man who murdered your father.'

Tori's skin tingled. *Did he really just say what she thought he'd said?*

'You look confused,' Matt continued, walking back towards her. 'Did you not hear? I'm giving you the option of walking away to be with the person who murdered your beloved daddy, or being with me.'

Tori shook her head in bewilderment. 'You're crazy!'

Matt clapped his hands together loudly. 'Wake up! You think I'm lying? You think I'm making this up?' *Oh, this was good.* 'I'm telling you now, that man killed Jack Jacobs – your father. Why exactly do you think he fucked you off the first time?'

Thoughts sped through Tori's mind. *Hunter hadn't done that. He couldn't have done that…*

'Still don't believe me? Ok, your call. Hunter fucked off and left you because he's a fucking coward. Why do you think he didn't expose what me and Noel did?'

Matt let his words sink in before continuing. 'Why would he have done that, then? Hmm… let's see… Wasn't the plan to broadcast what we'd done? You know, the property contracts he'd made sure were void because he'd cleverly spotted a loophole?'

He grinned. 'See, I know all about it, so why would he change his mind? And leave Noel in charge? Surely that would be the *last* thing he'd have wanted to do?' Matt ran his tongue slowly over his bottom lip. 'I'll tell you why, shall I? Because Noel knew what Hunter had done. He was planning to expose *him* and tell *you!*'

He traced his finger down Tori's face, down between her breasts, over her belly and down between her legs, laughing as she shuddered and backed away.

'Recoiling at my touch, but not from his? How very odd. Your father was Hunter's initiation hit, Tori. He was a hit because he raped someone.'

Tori blanched. 'R-Raped someone? What? Who?' *This couldn't be happening. Not her father.*

Matt smiled. *That got her, didn't it?* He didn't actually know who the woman was or the story; Noel hadn't elaborated. In fact, he hadn't said much about it at all, but he hadn't needed to. Jack Jacobs was wrongly targeted by Hunter and that was enough.

'Don't worry, sweetheart. Daddy dearest wasn't the rapist. That's the best bit. Hunter fucked up. *He* decided it was your father and took him out. Not very good at detective work, is he? He killed the wrong fucking bloke and unfortunately for your father, it was him.'

Matt folded his arms and grinned. 'Hunter knew he'd fucked up and has spent ever since trying to hide it. So, there you go. If you don't believe me, ask him yourself. Ask your wonderful Mr Hunter and see if he tries to lie his way out of it!'

Matt snatched his car keys off the table. 'I'm going now. I'm going to go home and get some enjoyment from the woman I fuck. At least I can be assured she hasn't killed one of my parents!' He laughed loudly. 'Give my regards to Lillian. Tell her I hope she had a good evening out.'

Matt walked through the lounge door, then turned and retraced his steps. 'Oh, by the way. Let me know what you decide. If I don't hear from you by close of play tomorrow, I'll be back on Friday to sign the paperwork for the house and then we can get on with things.'

Leaving Tori leaning against the wall, Matt let himself out of the house and got back in his car, confident he had no worries about her going anywhere.

## THIRTY FOUR

COLIN SQUEEZED SARAH'S HAND as they stood behind the bar and smiled. She was happy things were back on track between them. She'd had an awful lot of explaining to do, but they'd spent most of last night and today talking and Colin was now up to speed with everything.

The best thing was, the part of him that had been missing lately which made him 'Colin', was back and she'd never been more grateful.

Sarah felt Colin's body tense as Noel sauntered into the bar. 'Remember what I said,' she hissed. 'You did fine last night and therefore you can do so again.'

Colin eyed Noel strolling in his overly confident way towards him. He'd never felt more like killing someone than he did with this man. He understood the reasoning behind not doing anything about what the scrote had done to Sarah until everything else was finished, but it was easier said than done.

A nerve twitched irritably in his neck. He commended Sarah's resilience and selflessness for putting Tori's welfare before her own, but Tori wasn't his wife, *Sarah* was and it was his duty to protect her from this lowlife.

He gritted his teeth from a combination of suppressed rage

and guilt. Lately, he hadn't been supportive – the opposite, in fact and he'd left her to deal with this wanker on her own. His ego and annoyance had allowed him to fail Sarah. *What sort of husband was he? A bloody shit one, that's what.*

He also felt guilty about blaming Hunter and Tori. He should have known better. He'd always thought Hunter a decent man and Tori, from what he knew, seemed genuine too, yet he'd quickly blamed them both, but worse, overall he'd blamed Sarah. He should have taken his wife's word, rather than mistrust her judgement.

'Smile,' Sarah whispered, squeezing Colin's unclenched hand as Noel approached.

Forcing a smile, which resembled more of a grimace, Colin released Sarah's hand and grabbed a pint glass, quashing the urge to smash it in Noel's face. 'The usual?' he muttered.

'Cheers, Col,' Noel grinned. Turning to Sarah, his eyes slowly trailed over her. 'Evening, Sarah. You look nice tonight.'

Sarah bristled. 'Do I?' She stared him directly in the eyes. Now Colin was on her side again she had a renewed sense of courage.

Noel shrugged. Disappointed that he'd failed to get the desired reaction, he picked up his pint that Colin had placed on the beer towel.

'Your *girlfriend* not in tonight?' Sarah asked.

Colin glanced at Sarah, wondering why she felt the need to try and rile the man but couldn't help smiling at her attitude.

Noel glanced at Sarah suspiciously. 'I don't do 'girlfriends', everyone knows that. I prefer to stay available.' He winked. 'There's too many ladies who'd be sorely disappointed otherwise.'

Colin felt his hand forming into a fist. *How he hated this man.*

'I'm sure the bird you're talking about will be in soon. Can't get enough of me, that one,' Noel grinned. *It was true.* He'd spent another thoroughly enjoyable night with Carmen, this time at Jezza's gaff and it had been good. It had also been pleasant not to sleep on a lumpy mattress for once, not that he'd had much sleep.

'It looks like you're in luck,' Colin growled, 'because here she is now.'

Noel turned to see Carmen, Jeremy and Ginny enter the taproom and grinned widely. 'Told you, didn't I?'

Sarah cringed when the blonde woman approached Noel and slipped her arms around his waist. She eyed the expensively manicured fingernails. This woman certainly wasn't short of money, but then she wouldn't be if she was knocking around with the likes of Jeremy and his dreadful girlfriend.

She glanced at Ginny – still as sour-faced as ever. But this other woman – she was stunning and despite her behaviour with Noel, seemed pleasant. What on earth could she possibly see in a scum-bag like him?

Plastering on a smile, Sarah stepped forward. 'And what can I get you guys?'

Noel pulled out another huge roll of cash. 'They can have whatever they like. I'll get these,' he said. 'And take one for yourselves, too. I'm feeling generous tonight.'

Colin scowled. He'd rather cut out his own tongue than take anything from Noel, but in this instance, he'd have the largest measure of the most expensive brandy they had, piss in it and then serve it back to him later on.

• • • •

TORI LEANT AGAINST the back of the sofa and having finally regulated her breathing, rubbed her belly in the hope it would soothe the nagging, throbbing ache, as well as the relentless burning in her back.

Taking a long deep breath, she exhaled slowly and tried to make sense of what had happened. What Matt said must be a lie. Hunter had already admitted to doing bad things in the past, but *this*?

She'd already described what had happened to her father

and he'd assured her the Reapers had had nothing to do with it. But wait – Matt had said it was to do with a *rape*. Tori felt nauseous with the prospect that her father could ever have been suspected of something so heinous. She'd been told it was over a drug deal. Her mother had never mentioned anything about *rape*.

Didn't that prove Matt was lying? Of course it did. If he couldn't get the details right, then it showed it wasn't true. This was just yet another one of his schemes to manipulate her.

Tori's mind sped and what Matt had said about taking her child seeped into her mind. That would crucify her. He knew she'd never leave her child or risk him winning custody and if it went to court, they'd dig into Hunter's past. Matt wouldn't hesitate enlisting Noel for more details about all the things Hunter had done and Noel was the one who'd know. Hunter would go to jail. But if her instincts were right and this was Hunter's child, Matt couldn't get custody because he'd have no rights at all. *Think clearly, come on!*

Even if it *was* Matt's baby, then they'd find a way to ensure the child stayed with them somehow. Hunter would make sure of it.

Her teeth clenched. Matt was clever, she'd give him that. The way he'd told her all of this had made it seem believable, but looking at it logically, it wasn't. She'd even shown Hunter a photograph of her father and he hadn't said anything. In fact, from what she could recall, he hadn't reacted at all.

But wait a minute. Now she came to think of it, it was *directly* after she'd shown him the photo that he'd said their love wasn't real and then he'd left...

*Tori, you're being ridiculous. Utterly ridiculous. He's explained all that*, she reminded herself. Ok, he hadn't explained the details yet, but he'd said there was a reason. She trusted him, didn't she?

She'd ask him about it on Thursday. She'd tell him straight out what Matt had said and watch his reaction. He'd laugh and reassure her that it was rubbish. She could see it now.

Tori set her chin determinedly. She wouldn't let Matt win. She wouldn't let his manipulating games get to her. *She was leaving with Hunter whether he liked it or not.*

Suddenly an overwhelming pain tore through her, sending her to her knees. The air was knocked from her lungs and she was unable to take a breath as the overwhelming agony escalated.

Tori cried out in both pain and fear, her hands reaching to her belly which had tightened and hardened. She tried to remain calm but it was difficult. Was she in labour? Was this what it felt like or was there something wrong? She didn't know. She hadn't gone to any ante-natal groups and probably should have.

As the pain gradually subsided, Tori began to get to her feet, but was stopped when another debilitating pain crunched through her. She gasped, sweat breaking on her forehead and her breath came in ragged pants.

Without warning, water gushed from between her legs. Terrified, she crawled towards the phone. *There was no doubt about it. She was in labour.*

She'd have to call someone, but who? She couldn't do this on her own. How she wished Hunter was here. How would she meet him on Thursday now? She had no means of getting in contact and if she wasn't there, he'd think she'd changed her mind.

Sobbing with rapidly rising despair, Tori picked up the telephone. She had to get word to him.

*Sarah.* Sarah would know how to reach Hunter even though she said she didn't. The fact that she'd lied about it didn't matter. At this present moment in time, nothing mattered, apart from *this.*

Tori howled as another contraction hit and she was temporarily rendered incapable of moving. *Where was the number for the White Hart? Oh God, it was upstairs in a book in her bureau. Could she manage the stairs?*

Desperately pushing herself to her feet, she fell back to her knees. She'd never be able to do it, but she could call the operator. That was it. She'd call the operator. They would put her through to the pub.

# THIRTY FIVE

JEREMY PRETENDED HE wasn't looking as Noel ran his tongue around the inside of Carmen's ear. This was so bloody awkward and he could do without this like a hole in the head.

It had been a bad day all round. At work, Richard called a meeting for the entire staff, reminding them they had a week and half to ensure their projects were in good order and in tip-top condition ready for the new bank manager.

Inwardly scowling, he'd clocked several of the staff exchanging glances, all questioning why Richard Stevens felt the need to refer to Matt as the 'new bank manager' when there wasn't anyone who didn't know Matt was his own son.

Draining his bottle, he sighed with relief. At least now he had an excuse to go to the bar, meaning he would get a few moments away from this horny pair and his miserable girlfriend. Perhaps if he was clever, he could waste more time on top of that by dawdling or going to the toilet?

Getting up, he conveniently ignored Ginny unsubtly waving her empty wine glass in his direction and headed over to the bar. She needn't worry. It wasn't like he'd forget her drink. *Christ, if he did, he'd never hear the end of it.*

He'd better get Noel and Carmen one too, being as Noel

had bought the last two rounds. In fact, Noel had been overly pleasant tonight and Jeremy didn't know why. Maybe he felt bad about the way he'd acted last night, but realistically, that was doubtful. He was more likely just in a good mood because he was shagging the most beautiful woman here.

Reaching the bar, Jeremy glanced furtively back at the table, quickly turning away noticing Ginny watching him like a hawk.

Sarah finished serving and turned to Jeremy. 'Yes, what can I get you?'

'Same again, please. Carmen and Noel too,' Jeremy said, the words sticking in his throat.

'Noel doesn't fancy a brandy by any chance, does he?' Sarah asked, winking slyly at Colin. She knew what he'd done to the drink Noel had bought him earlier.

Jeremy looked confused. *Was he missing something?* 'I don't think so, no…'

Sarah waved her hand. 'Don't worry. Private joke.' She turned to reach two bottles of beer when the phone rang. 'Col, can you get that?' Seeing Colin busy pouring two pints of lager, plus a pint of Guinness on the go, she smiled. 'Don't worry, I'll get it.'

Placing the bottles on the side, Sarah glanced at Jeremy. 'I won't be a moment.' She picked up the handset. 'Hello?'

Immediately recognising Tori's voice, Sarah concentrated as she listened. She could barely make out the words. 'What's going on?' she cried. 'Are you hurt?' She glanced at Colin who frowned questioningly.

Listening further, Sarah gasped. 'Are you on your own? Ok… Yes… Ok… Yes, I will do.'

Jeremy's ears pricked up. *What was this?* Had somebody got knifed? That sort of thing happened frequently around here. It wasn't an issue – he didn't mind waiting. The longer it took to get served, the longer it was before he had to return to sit with the bloody Addams Family.

'Don't panic, Tori. I'll be there are soon as I can, ok?'

Jeremy frowned. *Tori?* He watched Sarah replace the handset and scribble something on a scrap of paper. She beckoned Colin over and pulled him out of the bar area. They were out of his vision, but he could just about hear what was said.

After Sarah returned, snatched up her handbag and rushed from the White Hart, Colin reappeared and glanced at Jeremy. 'I won't keep you a moment. I just need to make an important private call.'

Jeremy watched Colin disappear upstairs, but it didn't matter. He'd heard enough to know whatever he thought of Matt at the moment, he had to tell him Tori had gone into labour. His child was coming and he should to be here. Furthermore, he also needed to tell him that *someone else* had been informed too.

· · · ·

'DID YOU PHONE HIM?' Tori panted, her hair wet with sweat.

Sarah wasn't the sort to panic when faced with difficult situations, but she'd never delivered a baby before and didn't know where to start. All she knew was that a lot depended on how far apart the contractions were and from what she could tell, it would be a while longer before the baby arrived. She breathed a quiet sigh of relief. At least they had time to get to the hospital.

'Sarah!' Tori wailed, doubling over as another contraction ripped through her.

Sarah rubbed her back. 'Breathe, *breathe*!' She'd heard them say that on the telly, so it must be important, but Tori's insistence on pacing around made her nervous.

'Did you phone Hunter?' Tori wailed again. 'I need him!'

'I left Colin to do it. I told him to tell Hunter to go straight to the hospital.'

'I don't want to go to hospital!' Tori sobbed. 'What if Matt comes? He was here earlier. He was saying all sorts and he'll take my baby!'

Sarah scowled. 'Sod Matt. He won't be taking anybody, besides he won't even know you're there. How will he find out? We do need to get you to hospital though, so I'll run upstairs and get you some things, then we'll get you in the car.'

'But, Hunter…'

'Hunter will come as soon as he can.' Sarah raced upstairs to Tori's room. She hoped Hunter was at that pub – it was the only point of contact she had for him, but all things aside, she needed to get Tori out of here before Lillian returned because she would definitely call Matt.

• • • •

IT WAS TYPICAL that Debs wasn't in. Matt had raced back up the motorway and gone straight to her apartment. He'd made good time and had returned by 11.30pm. He supposed he could have hung around and waited, but she may not come back at all tonight.

An unexpected pang of irritation hit him. Was Debs out with another man? After all, he'd be gone himself in three days. He knew she'd move on to someone else, but she could at least wait until he'd left!

Pulling onto his drive, Matt got out of his car. *What a shit night.* At least he'd put Tori in her place. He couldn't believe the audacity of that overgrown missing link creature to be on the scene again. He smiled inwardly. In retrospect, it had done him a favour. It had granted him another opportunity to drive his point home. At least Tori now knew for certain what she had to lose and what a close escape she'd had. She should be grateful and would be in the end when it sank into her tiny brain. If she *had* been thinking of anything with that ape, she most certainly wasn't now!

Matt smirked. He knew the second he mentioned taking the child, it would stop her in her tracks. That's if the news about her father hadn't. *Her face had been a picture when he'd told her. How he'd wished he'd had a camera.*

Either way it didn't matter because he was the one who'd be coming out of this better off. He'd got his job, his token wife and child and, at the end of the day, he'd have Ginny when he returned too.

On the downside, it meant he owed Jeremy an apology, but he'd call him in the morning. He couldn't be bothered right now.

Letting himself into the house and chucking his jacket on the peg, Matt flicked on the light and scowled, spotting the red light flashing on the answerphone. *Who now?*

Wait, it might be Debs telling him where she was so that he could go and join her.

Matt pressed the play button and listened.

• • • •

HUNTER SMASHED THROUGH the double doors of the hospital and ran up to the reception desk. He'd got here as soon as he could and was just lucky the roads had been quiet. It had also been a good job there wasn't any cops about, otherwise he'd have earned himself several tickets.

'My…' *He'd been about to say, 'wife'.* 'Tori Mor… Tori Stevens is having a baby. I need to see her,' he panted.

The receptionist looked Hunter up and down suspiciously. 'Maternity. Down the corridor, first left.'

Turning on his heels, Hunter raced to where the frosty woman directed him, only to be greeted by an even frostier woman, who resembled a prison guard – except a *lot* wider.

'Where you do think you're going?' she barked, standing in Hunter's way as he reached the doors.

'Get out of my way,' Hunter roared. 'Tori. Tori Stevens? She's having a baby.' *If this old bat didn't let him through, then he'd forcibly throw her out of the way, even if it did his back in.*

'Mrs Stevens?' The Sister frowned, scrutinising Hunter. 'And you are?'

'Family!' Hunter spat. *Well, he would be soon.*

The Sister scowled even harder. *This wasn't the husband.*

*There was no way this was the same man she'd seen in the magazine. This guy was definitely not a bank manager!*

Hunter could see the woman's suspicion. 'Look, she wants me here. She was brought in by Sarah Mathers. Go and ask if you don't believe me.'

Pursing her lips, the Sister disappeared through the doors and entered a side room on the left.

Hunter wasn't going to wait for her to come back and interrogate him further, so he followed and burst in the room, relieved to see Tori on the bed, her hospital gown pulled up to just under her breasts and her naked belly exposed. A nurse was listening to her stomach with a stethoscope.

'Is everything alright?' he cried.

'Hunter!' Tori cried.

'GET OUT!' the Sister screeched. 'You can't barge in here!' She turned to Tori. 'I'm so sorry, Mrs Stevens. I told him to wait. This *person* insists he's family and that you want him here. I'll call security imme...'

'You won't do that,' Tori yelled. 'I *do* want him. He's going to be my husband.' She smiled at Hunter and reached for his hand.

Sarah glanced nervously at Tori. She shouldn't be saying that. This lot looked the sort to go to the press, especially the one with the stethoscope.

'H-Husband?' the Sister spluttered. 'B-But I thought you were already marr...'

'He's family,' Sarah interjected, giving the Sister a quick raise of the eyebrows to lend the impression that Tori didn't quite know what she was saying. She needed to ensure no one had any reason to alert Matt to Tori's whereabouts.

'So, you want this man here?' The Sister asked Tori.

'Yes. Yes, I do!' Tori said, her face screwing up as another contraction hit. 'OWWWW!'

Hunter moved to Tori's side, watching in both fascination and terror. He grasped her hand tightly.

'You made it then?' Sarah smiled. 'She's doing well.

Shouldn't be too many more hours now.'

'Five centimetres dilated,' the nurse said. 'You're halfway there – until the important bit, that is.'

'I'm here now,' Hunter said, wiping Tori's sweaty hair from her forehead and placing his hand on her belly.

The Sister shook her head in confusion. 'I'll leave you to it.'

'Thank you, Sister,' Tori smiled sweetly, grateful the contraction had ebbed away.

The nurse placed the stethoscope on a metal trolley and wrote something down in the folder at the end of the bed. 'I'll come and check on you again in about an hour and see how you're progressing.' She smiled. 'If anything changes, or if you need anything, just press the buzzer.'

Sarah waited until the nurse left the room. 'God, you pair don't half know how to cause unnecessary scandal! We're supposed to be playing it cool here, remember?'

'Easy for you to say when you're not the one who OWWWW!' Tori gritted her teeth as another contraction ripped through her.

Sarah laughed. 'I'll give you some peace. I'll make myself scarce for a while - that's if you want me to hang around?'

Tori grasped Sarah's hand. 'Of course I do.'

'Thanks, Sarah,' Hunter grinned, his large hand stroking Tori's hair. 'See you in a while.'

After Sarah left, Hunter ran his finger down Tori's cheek. 'Now don't you worry about anything. We'll rethink about how we're going to leave. All that matters right now is that you concentrate on wh…'

'I need to ask you something. I know it's ridiculous, but for my own peace of mind, I need to you tell me the truth,' Tori said. *It had to be now. This might be the only chance she got for a while.*

## THIRTY SIX

MATT ROARED DOWN the motorway at the speed of light.
He could not believe he had to go back *again*. It was completely
unfathomable, but he had no reason to doubt Jeremy. Not this
time. Thank God the man had been at the White Hart, otherwise
he'd never have discovered this until it was too late.

He glanced the dashboard clock. *Come on. COME ON!*

Those bastards were in it together. *All of them.* People's
heads would fucking roll over this. Especially Sarah – that sly
two-faced interfering cheap bitch!

When Matt had picked up Jeremy's answerphone message
to hear Tori had gone into labour, he'd been pissed off, but not
unduly concerned. He'd found it amusing more than anything
else because he'd thought that had been the reason for Jeremy's
message the other day, but this time it really was. He'd been
about to let her get on with it – after all, she didn't need *him*
there. That was until he heard the rest of the message…

Matt listened to Jeremy saying he'd overheard that slut of a
landlady telling her manky husband to call Hunter. At least he
presumed it was Hunter they'd been talking about. Something
about getting a message to a pub and to 'let him know as soon
as possible'. It wasn't *him* they'd been talking about because

they weren't exactly going to let him know. Sarah hated his guts, so that only left one other person…

He couldn't believe it. After everything he'd said tonight, Tori was *still* asking for Hunter?

Sweat ran freely down Matt's face as he negotiated the quiet lanes of the motorway at ludicrous speed.

What happened to what he'd said about Hunter killing her father? Had that not even hit the sides of her skull? Did she not believe him? *Oh, this had all gone horribly wrong. More than horribly wrong.*

The only thing he could do was get to the hospital. That bastard would not get away with laughing at him like this.

Matt glanced at the clock once again. And as for Tori – well, he didn't know how he would deal with her just yet, but he had about an hour to work it out and would make sure he'd thought of something by the time he got to the hospital.

· · · ·

'BUT YOU DON'T UNDERSTAND!' Hunter cried, trying to protect Tori from hurting herself as she pounded her fists into his chest, her nails searching for his eyes.

Tears streaming down her face, Tori was at the point of hyperventilation. Despite not thinking she had it in her given the situation, she'd pushed herself out of the hospital bed and launched herself at Hunter.

The moment she'd asked the question, she knew Matt had been speaking the truth. She'd seen from Hunter's eyes that the man she loved beyond anything had been the one to take her father and her heart had shattered into a thousand pieces.

'Tori, *please*!' Hunter yelled, holding Tori's arms. 'Stop this. You're about to have a baby. You cou…'

'Don't tell me what to do!' she screeched. 'You bastard! You lied *all* of this time? How could you do this to me? Were you ever going to tell me, or were you going to let me continue loving you?'

'Please,' Hunter begged, his eyes panicked. 'I only found

out myself recently, th…'

Swinging wildly, Tori caught Hunter's face, her nails ripping a line down his cheekbone.

'Tori, you're going t…'

'AARGH!' Tori doubled over with an agonising contraction.

Rendered incapable by the pain, Hunter took the opportunity to drag Tori back to the bed. 'Lie down,' he said calmly. 'You can't throw yourself around.'

He was terrified. Terrified she would hurt herself or the baby in her mission to rip him to pieces. He knew this would happen at some stage, but he'd wanted to be the one to break it, not for her to find out. And he certainly hadn't wanted her to find out when she was about to give birth.

'Why do you think I left that night?' Hunter took Tori's hand but she pulled it away, sucking heavily on the gas and air to the left of her bed. 'I wanted to tell you,' he continued. 'But I had to find out who I *should* have taken out. *Then* I was going to tell you.'

'And… you… thought… I'd… be… alright… with… that…? Tori's words came out in staccato bursts, her sobbing verging on hysteria.

'Tori, I'm sorry. I truly am. For everything. Our love can transcend this. It can, I *know* it can. I know who really did it now an…'

'I don't fucking care!' Tori screamed. 'You killed my father and condemned me to hell!'

Tears fell openly from Hunter's eyes. 'I know, I know and I'm sorry. You don't know how much. I genuinely had no idea until recently. That night, that night we…'

'The night I showed you the photo, wasn't it? Yes, I know. I… AAAARGH!'

Hunter grabbed Tori's hand. *The contractions were getting close together now.* 'But I love you. I love you so much. We can work this out. Please, Tori. Let me put this right an…'

'How the fuck can you put this right?' Tori wailed, her life crashing down around her. 'How can… how…' *Oh, what was the use?* Putting her face in her hands, she dissolved in loud racking sobs that shook her whole body.

Hunter tried to enfold her in his arms from his position at the side of the bed. 'I'm sorry. I'm *so* sorry, baby. It's haunted me for years. I was trying to do the right thing. It was Noel's mother an…'

'DON'T TOUCH ME!' Tori screamed, pushing Hunter away. She picked up a metal dish and threw it as hard as she could. 'GET AWAY FROM ME!'

Hunter ducked and with an almighty crash the metal dish smashed into other items sitting on the trolley by the door. Wide-eyed he tried to calm her down. 'Tori, please don't do this. We can…'

Tori was pushing herself out of bed again when the door burst open. 'What is God's name is going on?' the Sister roared, her eyes darting around the room, seeing equipment scattered over the floor.

She glared at Hunter, spotting the claw mark down his face. 'You! What have you done? Tell me what's going on in here!'

'Get him away from me!' Tori screamed, her eyes wild.

'I'm not leaving, Tori!' Hunter roared.

Hearing the commotion on her way back down the corridor, Sarah rushed into the room. She looked around in dismay. 'Oh my God! Tori?' She rushed to Tori's side and looked at Hunter, panic evident in his eyes.

'Please, Sarah, get him away from me. I don't want him near me,' Tori sobbed, clutching at her belly.

'What the hell's gone on?' Sarah looked between Tori, Hunter, the Sister and then back again.

'GET HIM AWAY!'

The Sister had heard more than enough. 'Mrs Stevens is clearly very distressed. I don't know what's happened, but you need to leave.' She grabbed Hunter's arm at the elbow.

Hunter wrenched his arm out of the Sister's grip, sending her stumbling into the wall.

'HUNTER!' Sarah cried.

'He killed my father! He killed my fucking father!' Tori screamed, her sobs painful to hear.

'*What*?' Sarah stared at Hunter.

The Sister righted herself, rubbing her sore hip. 'That's it. I'm fetching security,' she mumbled.

Sarah had no idea what was going on, but whatever it was, it wasn't good. She had to do something. She couldn't have Tori saying things like that because the hospital would call the police. 'Sister, Tori clearly doesn't know what she's saying and is distressed. The labour is getting to her.' She grabbed Hunter's arm. 'Come on, let's leave Tori for a moment, yes?'

'I'm not going anywhere,' Hunter hissed, catching his breath. He looked at Tori. *He loved her. How could he leave her?*

'Seriously,' Sarah muttered quietly. 'You need to make yourself scarce before the police get called. That won't help anyone and it certainly isn't helping Tori. Look at her - she's in a right state.' She steered him towards the door.

'Tori! We'll sort this, I promise!' Hunter called as he was led out of the room.

Tori could do nothing anymore. She couldn't even respond. The contractions were coming thick and fast, back to back.

Shaking her head with confusion at what she'd just witnessed, the Sister looked at Tori. 'This baby's coming now, Mrs Stevens.'

Tori sobbed harder. 'I can't... I can't... What am I going to do...? I can't... I...'

The Sister peered between Tori's legs as she let out an ear-splitting wail. 'The head's crowning. That's right, Mrs Stevens. You're doing well.'

Sister had no time to think about what had been occurring in here. This baby took priority, but she'd deal with the problem later. It seemed this woman was a sandwich short of a picnic. Even her friend said she didn't know what she was saying. She'd put a call in to the psych team if the woman didn't calm herself. Her opinion was this one wasn't in any fit state to look after a new-born. And furthermore, where was the father?

• • • •

JEANIE TURNED STONE COLD. That was it. She couldn't wait a moment longer. That was the second time in the last hour the same warning had come through and it was enough to tell her that she needed to act.

Pulling her coat on, she stepped out into the night and hurried across the road to the telephone box down the road from her cottage.

Going inside, she pulled the number for the White Hart out of her handbag and dialled it. Lining up several ten pence pieces on the top of the telephone, she waited for the call to connect. She knew it was late and that the pub would have closed, but what choice did she have? *She had to get this message through.*

'Hello? Sarah, is that you?' Colin was out of breath from running down the stairs.

Hearing the man's voice, Jeanie quickly pushed the money into the phone. 'Colin? It's Jeanie. You might not remember me? We spoke a little while ago and I think you thought I was insane as I…'

'I'm sorry about that,' Colin said. 'Are you with Sarah? What's happened?'

'No, I'm not with Sarah. Why?'

'It's Tori. You know about Tori, don't you? Sarah said y…'

'She's gone into labour, hasn't she? I knew it,' Jeanie interrupted. *She'd been right. Again. She'd seen it in her mind.*

'Yes,' Colin said. 'Tori called Sarah several hours ago. She's with her at the hospital.'

Jeanie's heart beat rapidly. 'Is Hunter there? He needs to be. She mustn't be left alone.'

Colin frowned. 'I left a message, but I don't know whether he got it. I was assured it would be given to him as soon as possible. The barmaid at the pub he drinks at said she knew wh…'

'So, you don't know if he's there or not?' Jeanie's stomach plummeted. *This was not what she wanted to hear.* 'Whatever happens we have to make sure he's there. He needs to remain with Tori.'

The hair on the back of Colin's neck prickled. This was the woman who sensed things, wasn't it? She'd been right about what she said to him. He didn't like the sound of this. 'Jeanie, what's going on?'

Jeanie paused. 'I don't know. Not exactly. But I do know Tori's in danger and mustn't be on her own. However upset she is, she needs to keep Hunter with her.'

*However upset she is?* 'Sarah's with her an…'

'Hunter has to be there. Sarah won't be enough.'

Colin nodded. This woman was freaking him out. There wasn't really anything else for it. 'I'll go there myself now and find out what's going on.'

TORI FELT STRANGELY disassociated and weird. The past few hours seemed unreal and her brain found it impossible to associate anything of what had happened with real life.

She didn't even feel part of herself. The only thing that reminded her that she was still part of the human race was the sheer exhaustion, both physically and mentally. She stared almost trance-like at the tiny creature placed in her arms.

The nurse smiled widely. 'Well done, Mrs Stevens. You have a beautiful baby boy.'

Tori pushed her matted hair away from her face and with trembling fingers, gently pulled at the white blanket her baby was wrapped in.

She stared in awe at the perfect little face with rosebud lips and tightly screwed-shut eyes. The little boy's head was covered with a healthy layer of dark brown wispy hair – the same colour as her own.

Counting the tiny fingers on the starfish-shaped miniature hands moving jerkily towards her, an avalanche of emotion rushed over her.

*She had a son. She was a mother. And this was her baby. Was this real or was she dreaming?* Everything seemed strangely muted, like in an old film or an odd dream.

'I-Is he mine?' she whispered. 'Really mine?'

The nurse smiled. 'Yes, he's most definitely yours. It's a bit overwhelming to start with, isn't it?' Reactions of new mothers were always a joy to watch. That was half the reason she'd wanted to work in such a heart-warming job. She'd heard that this lady had had a bit of an issue during labour, but thankfully, she seemed fine now.

Tori smiled back weakly. She gingerly touched her baby's head and a lone tear rolled down her cheek. *He was beautiful. Perfect.* She'd never ever felt such all-encompassing love for something in her entire life. She didn't think it was even possible, but it was.

Leaning back against the pillow, Tori closed her eyes momentarily and took a deep breath, attempting to mentally compartmentalise that she'd just had a baby. That she'd given birth to this perfect little creature she held in her arms.

'Oh, he's yawning. Are you tired, little one?' the nurse cooed. 'And now he's having a good look around. Fancy seeing the world for the very first time! Magic!'

Tori smiled listening to the nurse speak. Now, she needed to get her head together.

'Wow! Look at his eyes. They're so unusual!' the nurse exclaimed.

'What's wrong with them?' Tori's eyes snapped open, abject panic crashing through her.

'Absolutely *nothing*. They're amazing! I meant the colour. It's most unusual. Most babies' eyes are dark blue at birth and then gradually change into their permanent colour, but I think this little one has already decided what colour his eyes are.'

Tori looked down at her beautiful son and staring back at her was an identical replica of Hunter's eyes. *Gun-metal grey.*

Like a large darning needle shoved into a balloon, Tori's few minutes of ultimate happiness burst as the recollection of the past few hours steamrollered back into her consciousness. A trillion and one thoughts ambushed her all in one go and she felt herself shake uncontrollably.

'Mrs Stevens? Whatever's the matter?' The nurse asked, concern on her face.

'I... I...' Tori stuttered. *She couldn't find the words. What were the words?* This was what she'd wanted. This was what she'd hoped and prayed for every day as her belly had gradually swelled. Every time she'd felt her unborn child move, she'd hoped that the man she loved beyond all else was the one who had fathered the life inside her. *And he had. Hunter was undoubtedly the father of her child.* Tears rolled down her cheeks in a weird combination of relief and despair.

'Mrs Stevens?' the nurse said, worry now clear in her voice. *This lady was displaying worrying signs again, like the Sister mentioned when she'd started her shift.* 'MRS STEVENS!'

Tori could hear the nurse, but was unable to respond and instead remained fixated on the gorgeous little face of her new-born son. The love for him was crushing. The love for his *father* was crushing. It was *still* crushing with its strength even with what she'd discovered. As well as murdering her father, Hunter had murdered his child's grandfather, but she still loved him.

At this moment, Tori hated herself more than she thought possible. It was too much. How could she love the man who'd killed her father? She couldn't, could she?

Panic swirled. Where was Hunter. She needed to see him. She wanted him to meet his son. 'Where... where...'

'Where's your husband, do you mean? I'm sure he'll be here soon.'

Tori swallowed back a scream. *Matt. Was he here? Did he know she'd given birth?* 'No, I... NO!!'

'Mrs Stevens?' The nurse watched Tori's eyes dart around frantically. 'Let me just take the baby for a moment.'

'He killed him. *Killed* him! How can I love him? How can I? It doesn't make sense, but I need to do this... I love him... Please...'

The nurse pressed the buzzer for assistance. She wanted the Sister's take on this, but more importantly, she had to get the baby out of harm's way in case this woman made any sudden movement. It was like she'd suddenly become delirious.

Bending down, the nurse began to lift the baby from Tori's arms.

'NOOOOO!' Tori screeched. 'DON'T TOUCH HIM!' Tears flowed down her face. 'I won't let you take him. I won't let *anyone* take him. Hunter… I need…'

The Sister rushed into the room, took one look at Tori Stevens and locked eyes with the nurse who appeared equally distraught.

This was no good. She didn't like doing this unless there was no other way, but she didn't have any other choices and when Tori Stevens lashed out at the nurse for the second time amid screaming and sobbing hysterically, she hurried from the room to page the Psych team.

• • • •

MATT STOMPED UP to the reception. 'My wife's here. Take me to her now.'

The woman behind the desk continued tapping on her keyboard and scowled inwardly. *Another one with no manners. He could wait.* 'I'll be with you shortly,' she muttered.

'I said, *now*. This is important. She's having my baby.'

'Sir, you ne…' Glancing up, the receptionist immediately recognised the man from the newspaper and the magazines. He was about to become the new bank manager and she and her husband wanted to apply for a mortgage next month. *Shit.*

'Mr Stevens!' she gushed. 'Yes, your wife is here. If you ju…'

'I'll find her myself,' Matt snapped, having spotted the sign for the Maternity department further down the corridor.

Slamming through the double doors, he scanned the myriad rooms leading off. The sound of women howling in the throes of childbirth assaulted his eardrums. *Christ, this was like stepping into purgatory.* 'Tori?' he bellowed.

Hearing a man's voice, the Sister jumped up from her desk

further down the corridor. If this was that massive bloke again, then regardless of what was said, she'd call security this time.

Huffing petulantly, she straightened her blue uniform and stamped around the corner, primed to have a row. She eyed the man peering through the windows of a side room. *Now, this was the husband. It was the man she'd seen in the magazines.*

'Mr Stevens?'

Matt swung around. 'Where's my wife?'

The Sister frowned. This was a delicate subject and she suspected he wouldn't be happy. 'Would you mind coming with me, please?'

Matt scowled. 'Why would I want to come with you? I just want to see my wife. I've been told she's in labour an…'

'Please.' The Sister took hold of Matt's elbow and steered him into a small room not much bigger than a cupboard.

Matt spotted a box of tissues on a small table wedged between four chairs that had somehow, against the laws of physics, been crammed into the tiny space. His mind churned. 'Is there something wrong? Is th…'

The Sister shook her head and gestured for Matt to sit down. 'All's fine with the baby. You have a beautiful son, Mr Stevens. Congratulations.'

Despite himself, Matt found his face breaking into a smile. *He had a son. He was now a fully-fledged member and had everything he needed to succeed.* 'So, what's th…'

'I'm afraid the issue is with your wife.'

Matt stared at the Sister. 'My *wife*? Wh…'

'Does she have any history of mental illness? Any breakdowns? Depression of any kind?' The Sister was not sure how to word what she was about to say. 'It could have been triggered by the shock and pain of labour, but I do have to ask for her and the baby's well-being, I'm afraid.'

Matt was unsure what this woman was getting at. 'I don't really th…'

'Let me explain,' the Sister interrupted. 'In the middle of her labour, your wife had what appeared to be a psychotic episode.' She cleared her throat. 'She was out of control and put herself at risk. She was arguing with a family friend that your wife insisted she wanted with her. I personally didn't think it appropriate, bu…'

'Family friend?' Matt's nerves tingled. *It was him, wasn't it. Hunter. He was here, the bastard.*

His initial reaction was to storm off and find the fucker, but then he quickly reminded himself of what he'd thought of during the final hour of his drive and reined in his anger. What he'd planned for Tori would floor the pair of them. They wouldn't think they were so clever soon. Trying to pull one over on him? Taking the piss? *Not anymore.*

'A very large man. Looked a bit of a brute, if you ask me. I did wonder as to his presence, but Mrs Stevens was adamant th…'

'What happened?' Matt interjected. He wasn't interested in this fat bitch's personal opinion. He needed to know *exactly* what had gone on so he could decide which way to play it.

'Initially, Mrs Stevens was overjoyed to see this man and the other woman knew him too.'

Matt's fist clenched. 'This woman – was this Sarah?'

The Sister glanced towards the ceiling as she recalled the name. 'Yes, I think so. It was the woman who brought your wife in. After a while she left your wife talking to the man. Sometime after this, we were alerted by crashing and shouting coming from the room.'

'And?' Matt was getting impatient. *He wished this old trout would just get to the bloody point.*

The Sister stared at Matt. 'When we got there, we found your wife extremely distressed and the room had been fairly smashed up. The man was agitated, but it was your wife who had done the damage… She was most uncontrollable…'

Matt bit back a smile. *So, the cunt had admitted what he'd done? Bingo. Now he knew exactly how to play this and would have less work to do than expected.* He shook his head sadly. 'Oh dear. She must have had another one of her episodes.'

The sister frowned. 'Episodes?'

Matt nodded. 'Tori's improved the last couple of years, but I guess the stress and hormones of pregnancy must have exacerbated it.'

'Exacerbated *what*, Sir? We can't find any record of mental health issues in Mrs Stevens' medical notes.'

Matt wore a thin, sad smile. 'She's always refused to seek formal help.' He lowered his voice as if people could be listening. 'Being in our position, it wouldn't be something we'd want becoming public knowledge, as I'm sure you can appreciate, so we've always kept it within the family.'

The Sister nodded, warming to this handsome man's genuine sadness and care for his wife. 'I can understand that, Sir. I have seen you myself in the papers quite a few times. But I have to ask – who is the man?'

'Long hair, beard?' Matt asked, just to be one hundred percent sure, even though he already knew the answer.

Seeing the Sister nod, he continued. 'Yes, I know he's a bit rough-looking. A bit eccentric, I think, but it's true he's a family friend,' he said, the words almost choking him. *Stick to the plan, remember? The old goat would swallow every fucking word – he could tell.* 'Well, not a family 'friend', so much as someone who was recommended to help my wife with her issues. A counsellor, you might say. He's been quite helpful in the past, but sh...'

'Your wife was saying some very strange things, Mr Stevens. First of all, she said this man was going to be her husband and then later she accused him of murdering her father!'

Matt shook his head sadly to mask the pure rage he felt over Tori still wanting that thug. 'She's started that again, has she? I thought that was all done and dusted.'

'What do you mean? Started what?'

Matt sighed. 'She did something like this a few weeks ago. She made a pass at another family member, thinking he was me and then accused someone who we'd only just met of killing her father. It was horribly embarrassing. I thought it was a one off…'

He wrung his hands together. *He needed to make this look convincing.* 'My wife's father did die, but it was in a car accident many years ago. I'm surprised she hasn't accused *you* of causing it yet.'

The Sister raised her hands to her mouth in shock. 'Oh, that's dreadful. It must be very difficult to cope with.'

Matt smiled sadly. *Oh, he should have been an actor.* 'It is, but she's my wife and I love her, so all I can do is help her get through these episodes when they occur. I think the pregnancy must have triggered things off again.'

'It sounds like some form of pre-natal depression, although I suspect there is an amount of underlying psychosis too. The woman that brought her in previously pointed out that your wife didn't know what she was saying,' the Sister mused.

Matt smiled. *Well done, Sarah. You've helped my cause without even realising it.* 'Can I count on your support that what I've said will remain between us?' He didn't want this getting out. He wouldn't have anyone thinking he'd married a nut-job.

'I can assure you I won't mention our conversation. However, I must warn you the episode was recorded on your wife's medical notes because after giving birth, she began behaving erratically again and had to be sedated.'

Matt forced himself to look suitably upset. 'Is she going to be ok? I mean, will she be able to cope looking after a new-born?'

The Sister shuffled her paperwork nervously. 'Hopefully, yes, although this does need to be dealt with. The psychiatric team have recommended a voluntary section…'

'What? You mean a *mental hospital*?' Matt cried, looking aghast. He couldn't allow that. It would get out and really wouldn't look good on him.

The Sister shook her head. 'No, nothing like that. It would just be the psychiatric unit in this hospital. It's secure and she would be held there, but only be for a couple of weeks, you understand? Just until we find medication to stabilise her delusions.'

Matt almost had to sit on his hands to stop himself from punching the air. *This was perfect*. He couldn't have asked for anything better. This would get the message home to his cheating bitch of a wife not to fuck with him and it would also remind ape-man that *he* was the one with ultimate control. 'If you think that would be best...' he muttered in a fittingly sad voice.

'You would have to take your child until your wife is released, although if that's not possible, we could always arrange fo...'

'That won't be a problem. I have a wonderful support network in my family.' *Oh, this was getting better and better.*

'And lastly, I know it's difficult, but if your wife doesn't agree to a voluntary section herself, as her spouse and next of kin, you'll have to authorise it on her best interests.'

Matt raked his fingers through his hair in false agitation. 'Oh dear. That is difficult, but if it's the best thing for my wife, then of course.' *Bonus. Bonus, fucking BONUS! Ha Ha! Fuck you, Tori – you lying bitch!* 'Now, can I go and see my son.'

The Sister smiled warmly. 'Of course, Mr Stevens. Please follow me.'

## THIRTY EIGHT

MATT HELD HIS new-born son and stared down at the child's face. He had Tori's hair, but that was about it.

'Make sure you're supporting his head,' the Sister said, moving Matt's arm slightly.

Matt tried not to pull a face. How was he supposed to know what to do? He knew nothing about bloody kids and didn't particularly want to. That was women's stuff. All he knew was that he had to keep this crusty old bag on side.

So far everything was going to plan. He'd signed the paperwork for Tori's enforced incarceration and after further sedation she'd already been moved to the psychiatric unit.

Matt smiled. Tori wasn't mad in any way, shape or form. No, that bitch was perfectly sane and knew *exactly* what she was doing when she made the unfortunate decision to choose that psycho over him for the *second* time. But now it had backfired and he couldn't have timed the delivery of his news better. Her full meltdown in front of all of those witnesses had sealed her fate. She'd only be kept here for a few weeks, which was easy enough to stop from becoming public, but it would be *more* than adequate to drive home who was in control. *And it wasn't her.*

He'd thought she was going to kill someone when the psych team arrived to give her the choice of taking voluntary treatment. Of course, she'd refused and he'd been unable to hide his smirk when her eyes met his. He'd wanted to make sure she knew, without any doubt, that he'd had a large hand in organising this with the hospital, but at the end of the day, she'd also done a percentage of it to herself. What did she expect if she couldn't keep her emotions in check in public?

Oh, he'd played the concerned husband well. He'd stroked Tori's hair and pretended to reason with her. That it was in both her and the baby's best interests to get better and accept help for her problems.

She'd been shouting and screaming – saying things that only backed up what he'd already discussed with the Sister and the team. She'd set herself up beautifully.

It had been when Matt had assured Tori that he'd take good care of their son whilst she got treatment that she'd *really* lost it. She'd lost it so dramatically they'd had to get their needles out again. It had been suffocatingly pleasurable witnessing her eyes dulling as the drugs kicked in and she'd been forced to watch him signing the section paperwork. She'd been able to do nothing about it. *Nothing at all.*

*Pure fucking genius!*

As the baby squirmed in his arms, Matt glanced down once more. Apart from the risk of public stigma falling back on him, he wouldn't have Tori away too long. He wasn't looking after the kid. He had work to do and people to see. Which reminded him, his parents and Lillian would arrive soon. He'd done the expected thing and called them and suspected they wouldn't be happy to hear about the implications over Tori's mental health and what it could mean for the family's reputation, but they'd still be excited that he'd got a heir. He also knew they'd be pushing to do that press release about the quads, but that could wait a few days.

'I'll leave you to it for a while to get acquainted with your son and I'll show your family in when they arrive,' the Sister smiled, patting his arm. 'I'll also find your friends and pass on what you've said.' She smiled. 'Don't worry, I'll explain everything. I know this has been extremely difficult for you.'

'Thank you, Sister,' Matt said, holding his smile in place until her large backside had safely left the room.

In a way, he'd love to be present when the old bat told them the score because he'd had the last laugh, but he'd got to remember that, as far as this old crone was concerned, they were all friends and the news she was delivering wouldn't go down well.

But he'd successfully managed to rub that bastard's face in it. Tori was out of the picture and that was more pleasurable than anything else. Hunter, the overgrown wanker, had nothing, whereas he'd got *everything*.

· · · ·

HUNTER GRITTED HIS teeth as he raced along the corridor. He knew it was a bad idea to leave Tori. He should have overridden Sarah and that hatchet-faced Sister. He should have stood his ground. He'd been gone several hours and had been desperate to return to her side every second of every minute he'd been away. She must have had the baby by now.

And when Colin turned up with a message from Jeanie it was the last straw, instilling fear into the very root of his soul.

*'Not to be left on her own, regardless of how upset she might be,'* Jeanie had said. She'd said before that Tori was in danger, which was why he'd returned before schedule in the first place. And now *he'd* left her on her own. If anything had happened and he hadn't been there...

Sarah struggled to keep up with Hunter. Her mind was still busy processing what he'd told her. After leaving Tori, she'd led him to a quiet spot in the deserted and closed hospital cafeteria and she'd barely been able to believe her ears. Now it made sense why he'd left all those months ago and why he'd been so hell bent on finding out information before getting Tori back.

Her mind was swimming. It was horrific to think what Hunter had done to Tori's father. What an absolutely *dire* situation. No wonder Tori was so distressed. She had no idea how she'd deal with it if she'd been in the same situation.

Hunter had been difficult to control. It had taken all of her power to keep him from returning to Tori's room. It was only by saying that she needed to concentrate on giving birth, rather than what he'd done which finally got through to him and forced him to keep his distance.

But once Colin arrived with Jeanie's message, the bad situation quickly morphed into an even worse one. Maybe she should have let Hunter stay, even if it were just to stand guard outside Tori's room. But to keep guard from *what*?

'They won't let us in, you realise,' Colin panted as he hurried to keep pace with Hunter's long, determined strides.

'They'll *have* to!' Hunter raged. All that mattered first and foremost, was ensuring Tori was not on her own a moment longer.

Rounding the corner, Hunter crashed into the delivery room, then froze seeing the empty bed. Two nurses in the middle of changing the sheets swung around at his unexpected entrance.

'Tori Stevens?' Hunter cried, panic surging. 'Where is she?' He watched the nurses exchange glances. 'TELL ME WHERE SHE IS!' he roared.

Following Hunter into the room, Sarah and Colin stood impotently behind him.

'Remember what I said,' Sarah hissed, gripping Hunter's arm. 'We've got to do this the *right* way.'

'Ah, I thought I heard voices,' the Sister said, entering the room behind them. 'I presume you're looking for Mrs Stevens?'

Sarah controlled her rising panic and glanced at Hunter staring at the Sister, his eyes burning with hatred.

'Where is she?' he growled.

The Sister stood in the doorway, making it nigh on impossible for anyone to leave without causing a scene. She nodded subtly at the two nurses changing the bedding, who quickly squeezed past and scuttled out of the room, shutting the door behind them.

'Will you just tell us what the *fuck* is going on?' Hunter spat through clenched teeth.

'*Hunter!*' Sarah hissed. He must curb his language. They couldn't get thrown out for threatening behaviour. *Not now.* They'd get nowhere if he threw his weight around.

The Sister exhaled impatiently. 'I know that you're family friends and Mr Stevens has requested I bring you up to speed with the situation.'

Sarah frowned. *Situation? Family friends? Mr Stevens? Oh Christ, Matt!*

Hunter moved towards the door. 'That fuc…'

Sarah nudged Hunter none too lightly. They had to be careful. If Matt was here, which he clearly was, then she needed to think how he'd played this. He must have been told about the commotion between Hunter and Tori in the delivery room, so made out they were all friends so not to divulge any socially uncomfortable situation that could portray him in a bad light. *That shit-for-breath snake in the grass.*

'Matt's arrived then?' Sarah hoped she'd said the arsehole's name without showing the utter contempt she felt.

The Sister nodded. 'He is indeed and they have had a beautiful baby boy.'

Sarah felt Hunter go rigid. 'A *son*!' she cried. 'Are they both ok?'

The Sister frowned slightly. 'Baby's fine, but Mrs Stevens...' She paused dramatically. 'Mr Hunter, Mr Stevens has explained your role in being his wife's counsellor and he's also brought me up to speed with Mrs Steven's situation.'

Hunter blinked in confusion. *Counsellor? What was the twat doing?* 'I'm n…'

'Ok, and?' Sarah interrupted. *Shut up, Hunter. Don't say a word.* She glared at him.

'Yes,' the Sister continued. 'He said how much you've

helped Mrs Stevens in the past, so this will probably be something you won't want to hear.'

Hunter stiffened further. 'What have you done with her?'

The Sister's lips set in a fixed line as she regarded him with impatience. 'It's been a difficult few hours an…'

'Is Tori alright?' Sarah interrupted. She could imagine the smug smile on Matt's face. *What had he done?*

'As you know, Mrs Stevens has struggled with episodes of mania since the death of her father,' the Sister continued. 'And from what I understand, as her pregnancy progressed, it started again.'

She looked sadly at Hunter. 'I also know you took the brunt of her wild accusations today and I'm sorry you had to go through that.'

For once in his life, Hunter was rendered speechless. *Was this a joke?* Matt knew full well why Tori had blown her stack at him because he'd been the one to tell her about her father - it was obvious. But Tori wasn't manic. She was the sanest person he knew.

The Sister stepped forward. 'Understandably, Mr Stevens is finding this difficult, hence why I'm explaining this to you. It's knocked him for six, I'm afraid.'

Sarah clenched her teeth. She had to admit it, Matt was fucking good at playing the doting husband and the Sister had clearly fallen for his bullshit, hook, line and sinker, which wasn't a good sign.

The Sister placed her hand reassuringly on Hunter's arm. 'Mr Stevens made the unenviable decision to authorise a section on his wife for her own safety.'

Sarah's mouth fell open. *He'd got Tori locked up in the loony bin? Oh God!*

Hunter blinked rapidly, trying to make sense of what he was hearing. He felt like he was underwater, his chest visibly rising with pent up anger and emotion.

'Hopefully it will only be for the short term,' the Sister continued. 'Once Mrs Stevens has undergone full psychiatric evaluation, suitable medication can then be prescribed to control the manic episodes, depression and delusions. Once they are under control th…'

'*What*?' Sarah found this unthinkable.

The Sister casually ignored Sarah's interruption and carried on. 'Meanwhile, Mr Stevens will need to singlehandedly care for his son until his wife is well enough. I'm sure you will all help him wit…'

'You've taken Tori away from her baby?' Sarah cried, aghast. Knowing Matt had been given the child would destroy her.

Hunter's rage hit boiling point. *He knew what Sarah had said, but he couldn't take this. Enough was enough.* 'You're fucking joking, right? Where is she? I want to see her and I want to see the baby.'

The Sister shook her head. 'That won't be possible, I'm afraid. Mrs Stevens is heavily sedated and after she's recovered, she'll be undergoing psychiatric observation. Our policy is *strictly* no visitors, except immediate family.'

'And the baby? Can we see the baby?' Sarah added. She could see Hunter was desperate to see what could be his child and her heart broke for him.

'Due to the distressing time that has occurred tonight, Mr Stevens has asked that no one apart from *direct* family are admitted. His parents are due anytime now. He said you'd understand.'

Hunter's voice was icy cold. 'Oh, we understand alright.' *The question was, what was he going to do about it?*

· · · ·

MATT MADE A big show of proudly holding the baby, wanting everyone to concentrate on something other than where Tori was. He had to play it the opposite way with his parents than how he'd played it with the Sister and the psych team, otherwise it would be a constant round of how much it could affect the family status, or worse, affect him taking the manager position which was only a week and a half away.

He also couldn't risk it being mentioned that Hunter, Sarah and that dolt husband of hers was here. If that arose, then he'd be in a position he very much didn't want to be and have to explain to his parents or Lillian.

He shuddered, imagining just how wonderfully well all of that would go down. Still, with any luck, the bunch of pricks would most likely have buggered off with their tails between their legs by now.

The Sister would have told them about Tori, like he'd asked. They'd be spitting chips, but would know enough to realise they could do jack shit. He'd won and they could stick it up their arse.

Matt smiled. He'd have loved to see the expression on that fucking thug's face when he found out his bonfire had been well and truly pissed on. *Yes, Hunter's plans were fucked.*

He smiled at his parents again. He even smiled at Lillian and it was, for once, genuine. He was in such a good mood that even her sour trout-like face was not enough to irritate him.

'It's a classic case of *pre*-natal depression apparently, 'Matt said. 'To be honest, it makes sense. Tori was very down, which was why I thought it a good idea for her to stay with you for a while, Lillian.'

Lillian narrowed her eyes. 'You never said that she was… that she was having some kind of *breakdown* when you asked me to keep an eye on her.'

'She *wasn't*, Lillian, that's why. It's not like that. The Sister has explained that pregnancy hormones can cause a temporary imbalance, which more frequently occurs *after* the birth and is known as post-natal depression, bu…'

'I've heard of that!' Richard added, pleased that he sounded knowledgeable about women's things.

'But,' Matt continued, 'it can sometimes also occur *before* the birth and that is *pre*-natal depression.'

'But she's locked in a psychiatric ward,' Susan wailed. 'What will people think?'

Matt swallowed his fast-burgeoning irritation. 'She's not locked anywhere and no one will know. On the slim chance anyone *does* happen to ask, it's easy. We say complications after the birth – loads of stitches or something. That would require a few days in hospital, I expect.'

He sighed, noticing the expression on Lillian's face was far from convinced. 'Besides, something had to be done because of this *pre*-natal thing. It's more likely it could develop into *post*-natal depression and we don't want that,' Matt said. He didn't know whether that was true or not, but didn't care. It sounded plausible, so it would do. 'She'll only be in for a few days.'

'I always thought there was something wrong with that girl,' Richard muttered. *This was typical.* He knew what it meant, even though no one had said it. It meant they'd be lumbered with the baby at *their* home until Victoria got out. It also meant he'd have to listen to it wailing, whilst Susan flapped about like Mother Hen. He'd put up with it twice himself and didn't want it again. He was done with all that stuff and would *not* have this screw up his retirement.

'There's *nothing* wrong with my daughter, thank you, Richard,' Lillian snapped, not appreciating his insinuations. She slapped her handbag down on the table. 'I'm going to find that Sister and demand to be told *exactly* what they're proposing to do about it.'

'NO!' Matt cried, making the baby in his arms, jump. She couldn't do that. As Tori's mother, the Sister would be obligated to tell her everything and he'd given her a thoroughly different story. 'I-I mean, I'd rather not keep going over and over it.'

He wiped his hand across his forehead in the hope it would portray his distress. 'It's just been such an emotional time...' He smiled widely, determined to veer the subject on to something else. 'I'm a father! I can't believe it! Look at my son.'

Susan rushed over. 'I know, darling and he's gorgeous!' She stroked the baby's tiny cheek. 'Look at his little face.

Adorable!'

'Yes, he is, isn't he?' Matt beamed proudly. 'Just like his dad, naturally.'

Susan smiled. 'Has he been asleep this whole time?'

'Yes, I haven't heard him cry or seen him open his eyes yet.'

'Amazing,' Susan cooed. 'You're going to be a good baby then, aren't you, darling?'

Richard squirmed. He hated gooey baby talk. It never failed to make him feel nauseous. He didn't care what Matt said. He'd find that Sister and get out of her exactly how long Victoria would be here. He couldn't have anything impede the bank handover, or more importantly, his sleep.

'Would you like to hold him?' Matt asked, knowing his mother was desperate to.

'Oh, I'd love to!' Susan gushed, holding out her arms.

Matt rearranged himself to let his mother take the child, when the baby opened his eyes and let out a loud wail.

'You were saying, Susan?' Richard scoffed. *See. It was going to cry all the time. They always bloody did.*

'What unusual eyes!' Susan remarked. 'Very striking.'

Matt stared at the baby as he handed him over and froze. He'd seen those bright grey eyes before and they weren't his. Neither were they Tori's…

*Hunter…*

A wave of cold rushed through Matt's body and he staggered slightly. *The kid was Hunter's. There was no doubt about it.* He felt like screaming. That was why Hunter was here. He knew the kid was his, as did the rest of them.

That arsehole had impregnated his wife, meaning the bitch had blatantly lied about using protection the times she'd slept with him. She hadn't used protection at all, that much was obvious.

Sweat ran freely down Matt's face. Would anyone else be able to tell? He had a reputation to uphold and if it got out that his wife had given birth to another man's child, where would that leave him? *In tatters, that's where.* Or worse, what if it became known that he, himself, had asked Tori to sleep with the ape, and why? He'd be a bloody laughing stock and the subject of ridicule for ever.

Susan quickly handed the baby to Lillian and grasped Matt's arm. Helping him into a chair, she stroked his hair. 'Whatever's the matter, Matthew? You've turned as white as a sheet. Are you alright?'

Matt stared at his mother vacantly. *No, he wasn't alright. He was far from alright. What was he going to do? If he could see this kid wasn't his, then surely, so would everyone else?*

'Matthew?'

Matt tried to unscramble his brain. 'Yes, I'm ok. I just went a bit shaky.'

'Do you need me to call a nurse?' Susan flapped.

Richard rolled his eyes. *That would be typical.* Susan insisting that Matthew should be the only man in the history of mankind to need a hospital bed in a maternity wing. 'Leave him alone, Susan. He's just exhausted.'

Lillian edged towards Susan, hoping she'd take the baby from her. 'You'd better give him back to Matthew.'

Susan took the baby from Lillian's arms. 'Are you missing your father, my little darling?'

As his mother went to place the baby back in his arms, Matt jumped from the chair. 'NO!' he cried. *He wasn't the father. It wasn't his fucking kid! That bitch had turned him over.*

Matt staggered towards the door. 'I need a breath of fresh air,' he muttered, stumbling from the room.

## Thirty Nine

IT HAD TAKEN Susan ages to settle the baby. She hadn't counted on dealing with this so soon and had only previously purchased a few essentials in preparation for when Matthew and Tori brought the child to visit. She had nowhere near the amount of things required and, if she was honest, was quietly slipping into panic mode. Luckily, Matthew's baby things were still in the attic which was a good job.

As the baby was born in the early hours of the morning and they hadn't arrived until several hours later, it was late afternoon by the time the hospital said the baby could come home. Matthew and Richard had disappeared somewhere and Lillian, insisting on accompanying them back to the house, made herself comfortable on the sofa with a bottle of wine, whilst *she* was left sorting everything out.

Susan pursed her mouth in silent irritation. Lillian showed little interest in the child, but she'd expected nothing else. How that woman had ever raised a child at all with the distinct lack of interest she showed to anyone other than herself was beyond her, but somehow, Victoria had made it to adulthood.

She hadn't expected Richard to be any help. He'd been one hundred percent hands-off with his own children, so the lack of attention to his grandson was no surprise. Susan, however, loved children. She'd have liked more herself, but Richard was insistent that two was the ideal number and wouldn't entertain any more. The subject was then closed and so she'd had to accept it. Besides, it was hardly relevant now, being as that time for her had long since passed.

Susan stared at the baby in the crib and a pang of sadness engulfed her. New-borns should be with their mothers and poor Victoria... well...

She'd been shocked to hear her daughter-in-law had been struggling. Victoria hadn't come across that way when she'd last seen her, but from what Matthew had said...

Susan frowned, prickling fear creeping up her spine. Matthew was behaving most strangely. Again, he'd been fine when they'd arrived at the hospital. He'd been proud as punch, but then all of a sudden he'd started acting very oddly.

She glanced back at the baby, now sleeping soundly. Since returning home, Matthew hadn't spent a second with the child. It was like he couldn't bear being around his son. Maybe it was the shock of the day catching up with him? It must have been difficult. Certainly nothing like he'd planned or expected, she supposed.

$$\bullet \ \bullet \ \bullet \ \bullet$$

RICHARD SAT FOR ten minutes waiting for Matthew to speak, but he still hadn't uttered a word, short of grunting when he was handed a whisky.

He wanted to give Matthew the opportunity of telling him what was going on, but it was clear he wasn't willingly divulging anything, so it looked like he'd have to ask directly.

Richard was surprised he'd held his tongue so long. Perhaps it was due to the thousand and one questions ricocheting around his brain since he'd spoken to the Sister, or pure, unadulterated fear. Either way, he needed to find out.

Pouring himself a top up, Richard folded his hands together, assuming a picture of authority, even though inside his nerves were jangling. He watched Matthew stare vacantly into his glass. 'Do you want to tell me why that man was at the hospital with Tori tonight?'

Matt's head snapped up at his father's words. *Oh, shit!*

'And why the Sister was under the impression this man is a family friend? This, I might add, apparently came from *you*.' Richard knew his voice was rising and fought to control it. The last thing he wanted was Susan or Lillian overhearing this conversation.

'F-Family friend?' Matt stumbled over his words. *What could he say? Think. THINK!*

'Don't bullshit me, Matthew! She said you told her he was Tori's *counsellor*? To help her 'manic episodes'? What the hell were you thinking?' Richard yelled, his jaw clenched. 'Was it a Reaper?'

Richard's heart plummeted into his feet watching Matthew nod. 'Why in God's name was a Reaper with your wife at the hospital?' *The prospect was ludicrous.* 'And what is all this about manic episodes?'

'I-I had to say something. You don't understand.' Matt felt deflated. Completely and utterly deflated. His anger had diminished into a hollow void.

'No, I don't understand, that's why I'm asking.' A nerve in Richard's neck twitched. He'd told Matthew he needed those people as far away as possible, especially as they'd started digging around again and he couldn't have been clearer in his wishes.

'Are you telling me that you, despite everything I said, are maintaining contact with them?' he spat.

Matt's eyes flashed momentarily. He might have known it would be assumed that he had orchestrated this. *Well, in a way he supposed he had.*

'Oh my God!' Richard exclaimed. 'You're not *friends* with one of those scum, are you? I wouldn't have thought in a million years that you'd be so stup…'

'Of *course* I'm not friends with him!' Matt raged, suddenly regaining his anger.

'Then wh…'

'I fucking *hate* the man!' Matt raged. *Friends with him? He despised the cunt!*

Richard frowned. A creeping sense of waiting for something he knew he wouldn't like crawled over him. It was so strong it almost overtook his personal fear that he'd been discovered. But only almost.

Throwing whisky into his mouth, he locked eyes with his son. 'Then would you mind telling me what he was doing there? And why you told the godforsaken old cow that he's a friend?'

Matt slammed his glass onto the desk and stared at his father. *He wanted to know, did he? Really wanted to know?* 'Because Tori is in love with him and him, her.'

Richard stared at Matthew in silence for a few seconds, before bursting into laughter. He slapped his hand on the table 'Oh, you almost had me there!'

Watching Matthew's expression, he stopped abruptly and his eyes narrowed. 'Wait! You're serious?' For God's sake, tell me you're not serious?' This would embarrass the family for centuries. *Victoria? The deceitful little bitch.*

'Oh, I'm serious, alright. And before you ask, I told that woman that stuff to avoid questions like, *'what's this long-haired psycho doing here?'* She was suspicious enough as it was.'

'At least you had *some* sense,' Richard spat. 'I heard Victoria was accusing people of all sorts, so I presume her being in the psychiatric unit was your way of dealing with this 'other man' situation?'

Matt nodded. 'Sort of, yes.'

'What you do mean, *sort of*? Can you not control the stupid girl? I warned you if you weren't up to doing this, then y…'

'It's worse than that…' Matt muttered. *He would have to tell him. There was no other option.*

Richard threw his hands in the air. 'How can it be worse? You can't allow your wife to converse with Reapers, let alone have *feelings* for one of them?' The word 'Reapers' cut his throat like broken glass. 'I don't want you or *anyone* associated with this family to be within ten yards of them. How many more times do you have to be told?'

'Tori had a meltdown tonight because earlier I told her who had killed her father.' Matt's voice was quiet, subdued.

Richard was angrily pouring himself yet another top up of whisky, but the spirit sloshed over his desk. *Her father?* 'What did you say?' *How did Matthew know any details about that?*

'I said, I told her who killed her father,' Matt repeated. 'And it was *him*.'

'It was *who*?' Richard spluttered.

'Jack Jacobs was the target for a Reaper. Except he was the wrong target.'

Richard's mind swam and his heart beat dangerously fast. Sweat dripped between his shoulder blades.

'Jacobs was killed by mistake. By *Hunter* - the man Tori's in love with. He's also the man I asked her to bed to get information on those property deals all that time ago.'

Richard was convinced he would pass out. '*You* asked Victoria to sleep with a *Reaper*? The Reaper that killed Jack Jacobs?'

'I didn't know about that part at the time,' Matt barked. 'I only found out myself a few months ago, but what does it matter? It's certainly pissed on her plans to run off with him.'

Richard struggled to take this in. The man in his daughter-in-law's hospital room was Jack Jacob's killer? This *Hunter* person? And Victoria had been planning to leave Matthew for him? 'What does this man look like?'

Matt didn't even want to picture Hunter. Every time he thought of that man, all he could see was the eyes of that baby upstairs. *The baby who was supposed to be his son.*

'Tell me what he looks like, Matthew!' Richard roared. He needed to know if it was the same man asking questions of Bob Greaves. The same man who could, by now, be looking for *him*.

'Massive bloke, about six feet-four. Long blond scruffy

hair. Dark blond, not light. A beard. Looks like an ape,' Matt said, through gritted teeth. 'Grey eyes…'

Richard felt thoroughly sick. *That was who Bob Greaves described.* He dug his teeth into his bottom lip to stop himself from screaming.

He didn't have time for this. He hadn't time for it at all. He wasn't explaining the ins and outs why this man could not be here. It should be obvious for Matthew to have his own reasons, so he didn't need to know his, did he? But this Hunter person had a photograph. *A photograph of him with Leila Cooper…*

'We have to make sure this man *never* comes here, Matthew. That he has nothing to do with you, Victoria or any of our family *ever*,' Richard ranted. 'It's *imperative*, do you understand?'

Matt felt strangely relieved from unburdening himself, but there was one more small point he hadn't yet mentioned. 'That might not be quite so simple.'

'Of course it's simple! What the hell are you talking about? What's the matter with you, boy?'

Matt looked his father straight in the eyes. 'The kid upstairs? Hunter's the father…'

As the bottle of whisky slipped from Richard's hand to smash loudly on the floor, he cringed. He'd have to do something about this situation - and quickly. He could only hope Susan hadn't heard the bottle smashing because then she'd come in to see what had happened and he needed to think.

# FORTY

THE BEST IDEA they'd come up with after leaving the hospital in confusion and defeat, was to return to where Hunter pitched his tent and go to that pub, The Ragged Staff. They could hardly take him to the White Hart, not with the rest of the Reapers there, but it wasn't a comfortable situation here either.

Sarah glanced at the woman behind the bar – the same woman shooting daggers at her that time she'd come to see Hunter here before.

Sarah looked at Hunter. She was unsure what he would do now, but whatever happened, her and Colin needed to return home. It was already noon and if the pub was late opening, it would raise eyebrows.

'Hunter, we've got to remain rational,' Sarah cried, watching him pace up and down. 'You're drawing attention to yourself.'

'How am I supposed to be rational? What the fuck am I going to do?' Hunter growled, raking his hands through his hair. 'I need to see Tori. I need to explain what happened with her... with her father.'

'And you think that will change anything?' Colin said. 'I think you've got to accept the inevitable.'

'NO!' Hunter slammed his fist on the table. 'I know I can't take it back – fuck knows I wish I could, but she might understand if I could just explain.'

Colin looked at Sarah. *He wasn't so sure*. It was a pretty big deal butchering someone's father, then expecting them to be ok with it. Although, from what he'd learnt there were extenuating circumstances and Tori and Hunter loved each other deeply, but it still didn't make the situation any better.

Hunter's jaw set in a straight line. 'That baby might be mine and I haven't even seen him,' he said quietly. He wanted to see the baby. He'd know if he was the father. He'd feel a connection and the prospect of Matt touching his child was too much to think about for any great length of time.

'That wanker will make sure we won't be allowed to see Tori. Christ, he's done her up like a kipper. He may have made out that we're friends and all that bullshit to save his own skin, but you can rest assured he'll have said something to ensure we won't have access,' Sarah spat.

'I can't believe he's done this!' Hunter cried. 'This is all my bloody fault! He told Tori about what I'd done and it sent her into labour. For fuck's sake, what sort of bastard does that to score points? Why else would he have told her so close to her due date if he hadn't meant to cause damage?'

'He must have discovered she was planning to leave,' Colin suggested. 'Either that, or you were seen.'

Hunter put his head in his hands, exhausted. 'I was really careful, but yes, he may have seen me. Or *someone* might, but aside from that, I have no idea how he knew about Jack Jacobs.'

'Think about it, there's no guessing as to who enlightened him, is there?' Sarah spat. *This was Noel all over*.

'But if I hadn't fucked up, then none of this would have happened,' Hunter growled. *It was his fault. All of it.*

'But you did fuck up and you can't do anything about that. Hindsight's a wonderful thing but changes nothing,' Colin mused.

Hunter struggled to keep his composure. He wanted to tear

Matt to pieces, rip his head from his neck, peel him and leave him out to dry. If it was up to him, he'd floor the twat and anyone else getting in his way. He'd snatch Tori and the baby and get them away from those people.

He wasn't sure how Sarah had talked him down. He didn't feel rational and furthermore, listening to her had got him nowhere. If anything, it had pushed him further away from rectifying this mess. Meanwhile, Tori was at the mercy of Matt and the hospital, as well as being without her child.

'Matt will use Tori's 'mental instability' to keep her with him and in turn, keep the child,' Hunter raged.

'Tori's far from crazy, Hunter.' Sarah placed her hand on his arm. 'The hospital will eventually see that.'

'But how long will that take? Don't you see? That's why he's done it! To set her up and make her look unstable. Even if they say she's ok, it will always be used against her.' Hunter was exasperated. 'I need to do something, I can't just sit here. I...'

'Firstly, someone needs to see her and explain. Aside from anything else, she needs to know the whole story. It will help her rationalise things, then perhaps you *might* be able to make it work. But even if not, you owe her that at the very least,' Sarah said. 'Then we have to work out how to override the bullshit with this psych stuff.'

Hunter clenched his jaw. That's what he'd wanted to do, but all he'd achieved was to make it look like he'd been hiding it for his own sake.

'No one else knows enough about the situation, apart from me and like you said, they won't let me in!' Hunter snatched his cigarettes from his pocket and lit one, the adrenalin pumping through his veins making his fingers shake. 'I'll break in if I have to. I'll do whatever it takes to get through to her.'

Colin looked thoughtful. He glanced at Sarah, then fixed his eyes on Hunter. 'You're right, they won't let you in, and you don't want to break in – that's a sure fire way to get nicked and then you'd be in an even *worse* position, but I think I know who could do the job.' He raised an eyebrow. 'From what I've gathered, she knows enough to tell Tori what you need her to hear.'

Hunter paused, his cigarette dangling from his mouth. 'I'm listening.'

Colin smiled. 'Your friend Jeanie, of course!'

. . . .

JEANIE KNEW SOMETHING had happened the moment she received the message. Although from what the barmaid at the Mackerel and Hook relayed, there wasn't much to go on, but enough to realise she had to do what was needed.

She also knew whatever had happened, the danger to that woman of Ashley's was not yet over. Far from it. The warnings were consistently landing in her head and getting stronger every minute that passed.

It was bothering her deeply as to what had occurred and worse, what was *yet* to occur. She knew the signs only too well and she only hoped it wouldn't be too late.

Jeanie smiled at Joe concentrating on the seemingly never-ending stretch of motorway. It was a big ask expecting him to drive her so far, but time was of the essence and to go by train, with all the changes required, would take a lot longer.

However, she was well aware that any time away from his fishing boat knocked a huge dent in his livelihood and she didn't know how long all of this would take. She had no idea where they would even stay.

'I really am grateful to you for this, Joe,' Jeanie said, touching his arm.

Joe momentarily took his eyes off the road and smiled. 'It's my pleasure. You know I'd do anything for you.'

Jeanie's face fell slightly. Was she taking advantage of Joe's generosity? It hadn't gone unnoticed that he hadn't questioned why she needed to make the trip so urgently. He'd accepted it without knowing a thing. She should tell him. She should tell him *everything*, but where would she start? He hadn't even asked how Ashley had come to be in her life after he'd turned up at the Mackerel and Hook and neither had she volunteered any information. She frowned. She wasn't being fair to the man.

Quickly realising what Jeanie must be thinking, Joe squeezed her hand. 'You know how I feel about you, it's hardly a secret, but this isn't about that. First and foremost, you're my friend. A *very* important one and I'm doing it for that reason alone, ok?'

'Thank you,' Jeanie whispered gratefully, again wondering why she lacked the courage to take a chance on this lovely man who had only ever been amazing to her.

Lost in her thoughts, she stared out of the passenger window and rested her head lightly against the rattling glass. It was nerve-wracking returning to her hometown. She hadn't stepped foot back within the city limits for such a long time. She hadn't been there since Leila…

She also knew that subject would arise and her body thrummed with nerves, but she mustn't forget, she was doing this for Ashley. The son she'd never had and the one she loved dearly.

The Reapers had a lot to answer for. Because of them, Ashley's life, as well as others had been ruined and she wanted to break the cycle, even if only in a small way. Leila wouldn't want this dear boy to pay any more for her retribution. It had already cost everyone enough. Ashley deserved to be happy and for that and that alone, she'd deal with whatever came her way.

• • • •

RICHARD KNEW WHAT he had to do. He'd been up all night thinking about it. That and being kept awake by crying babies. Just one night the kid had been here and it was already affecting his life. A nerve twitched in his neck. The bloody thing wasn't even a relation, so why was it even here? Well, he knew why - to keep up appearances.

It wasn't just the baby's crying though, was it? What

Matthew had told him last night had blown his mind. He would never have guessed his son would be so stupid in what he'd engineered for his deals. That alone was incomprehensible, but now they'd got a lasting reminder of his idiocy.

Richard trudged along the landing, planning to get a cup of coffee. God knows what time it was, but it was early. Susan normally got his morning coffee, but she was still fast asleep. She'd been up most of the night dealing with the kid, so he'd let her sleep. At least that way she couldn't moan or ask questions.

His nose wrinkled up with distaste as he passed one of the guest bedrooms, hearing Lillian snoring like a foghorn. After making quick work of several bottles of wine last night, she'd fallen asleep in the chair, her mouth hanging open and dribbling on herself, so they'd had little option but to allow her to stay.

His initial instinct had been to find his camera and take a photograph of her to post to the Women's Institute, or wherever she spent half her life gossiping, but he hadn't. *Damn the woman*. If she hadn't blackmailed him into having Victoria as a daughter-in-law, then he wouldn't be in this position.

This whole situation was dire. Victoria now held the power and also the *proof* to ruin his entire family. She'd slur her own name in the process, but he suspected she wouldn't much care. Worst of all, the offspring of the man who was now looking to murder him was lying in his son's old crib.

Richard shook his head in despair. He had to do something to stop this. It wasn't anywhere near the top of his list of things he *wanted* to do, but it was the only option.

Continuing along the landing, he pushed the already ajar door of another spare room open. He could hear the snuffles of the new-born, now finally asleep. He thought he should talk to Matthew about it, but decided that was unwise. Matthew had disappointingly proved not the best when it came to decision-making abilities and the less said to anyone, the better.

Richard had spent considerable time last night bolstering his son's sagging ego. If it looked to the outside world that everything was as it should be, then it *would* be. For a start, he couldn't work out what difference it made anyway. All that was important was that Matthew believed the situation was saveable.

Walking over to the crib, Richard looked down upon the sleeping child. Reaching in, his fingers pulled at the blanket and stared at the baby's face.

The situation was far from saveable, but as long as he didn't voice that to anyone, then no one would be any the wiser.

## FORTY ONE

THE LAST TWO DAYS had passed in a strange drug-induced blur. During the small amount of time Tori had been awake, her brain was fogged and she couldn't think clearly. Every time a lucid thought presented itself, it was accompanied by a crushing sense of panic, desolation and awareness that a big part of her was missing.

Each time this distress had set the cycle in motion again. Nurses appeared with more loaded needles and Tori had quickly drifted off into the world of no memory or pain – just *nothing*.

This time she would break the cycle. She *had* to. Regardless of how distressing it was, she would force herself to piece together what had occurred so she could plan exactly what she needed to do. If she didn't, then she'd be here for a very long time. And that wasn't an option.

With trembling hands, Tori pushed herself up in the bed and a wave of dizziness engulfed her. She pushed through it, needing to get her head straight enough to process everything. She braced herself, waiting for the realisations to flood her once again and dug her fingernails into the palms of her hands as the memories swamped her consciousness. Whatever happened she wouldn't start screaming, shouting or threatening anyone this time. She needed to play the game if she wanted to get out of here and get her child back.

Her entire body ached with the pain of not having her baby beside her. The huge empty void threatened to swallow her and she took deep breaths to stabilise herself.

Her throat constricted tightly, the hatred for the man masquerading as her husband, crushing her. She had to get herself and her child away. Once she'd done that, she'd prove he wasn't the child's father and then he could do nothing.

'Mrs Stevens?' A nurse bustled into the room. 'You're awake! How are you feeling today?'

Tori maintained a neutral expression. She couldn't react in the way she'd done the past two days. All it achieved was to add more fuel to the fire and back up Matt's lies. No, she'd do it the required way, even if it killed her.

She forced a smile, aware a nerve was twitching incessantly around her eye. 'I'm feeling a lot better.'

'That's good to hear. These pills must be starting to do the trick.' The nurse handed Tori a paper cup containing a small round tablet and poured a glass of tepid water from the plastic jug on the side cabinet. 'Let's have today's dose, shall we and let it continue getting you back to normal?'

Smiling weakly, Tori picked up the paper cup and stared at the little white pill. She didn't need it. No amount of pills could cure her problems or remove the knowledge she had learnt, but she'd play the game. 'Thanks,' she muttered, tipping the pill into her mouth and taking the glass of water from the nurse's hand.

The nurse watched her swallow the tablet and ticked her clipboard. 'I expect the doctors will be around to see you again shortly,' she said. 'Is there anything else I can get you in the meantime?'

Tori shook her head and forced herself to smile. She watched the nurse leave and then retrieved the tablet concealed under her tongue. *Phase one complete.*

The door opened again and Tori looked up, expecting to see

the doctors, but it was the same nurse.

'I know you're not supposed to have visitors, but being as you're clearly so much better today, I don't see why we can't bend the rules a little,' the nurse smiled.

Tori's heart raced. *She had a visitor? Was it Matt? Had he brought the baby to see her?*

'I must say, it also helped your case that your mother's so insistent,' the nurse winked. 'She's in here, Mrs Morgan.'

Tori's stomach plummeted. She didn't want her mother here. Feeling the first signs of panic brewing she fought against it. *Control, Tori, control*, she chanted. *Stick to the plan.*

Glancing up as the nurse ushered in her visitor, Tori gulped. *This wasn't her mother, so who was it?*

· · · ·

JEANIE WAS STILL trembling by the time Joe had driven her to the White Hart. She'd expected her role in this to include Leila, but hadn't quite envisaged it including telling a complete stranger the entire story. When she'd met with Hunter at the Ragged Staff, he'd filled her in with what had happened and she knew she had no choice.

She had to do it for him. He'd been in an utter state. The last thing she wanted was to worry him further by telling him the danger warnings were stronger than ever. All she knew was that there was no time to waste.

Her initial hurdle after that was to gain access to Tori Stevens, but following Hunter's instructions and posing as the girl's overbearing mother, she'd bullied her way in surprisingly easily.

Once she'd been ushered into the small side room what really bowled her over were the first impressions of the woman sitting in the bed looking little more than a hollow shell. The pain radiating from her was thick, but she could also read the burning love surrounding her for Ashley and her child.

A faint glimmer of hope burnt in Jeanie's soul and wasting no time, she'd ignored the confusion on Tori's face and launched straight in with introducing herself.

Jeanie had immediately liked Tori. She'd liked her very much. She was a genuine person and one who she felt in her heart would somehow move past this as things stood.

She'd studied Tori's face as she told her story, the whole cycle of emotions: disbelief, anger, betrayal, passion and hurt morphing across her face. It was difficult and there were a lot of tears from both sides.

What moved her most of all was when Tori had clasped her hand. 'How can I get my baby back?' she'd asked, her eyes brimming with tears.

Unfortunately, Jeanie hadn't an answer for that and even though she'd put the question out to the ether, she'd received a worrying silence which had bothered her immensely, but this she had wisely chosen to keep to herself. Voicing her concerns would have, in any way, helped this already fragile woman.

What she could sense was that Tori would get out of there and very soon. She couldn't say how or why and at face value, given the circumstances, it looked unlikely, but Jeanie had detected that most clearly and that she *had* voiced.

'Hunter's the father,' Tori had added.

'I know, dear,' Jeanie had replied. 'I've always known.' She could read what was going through Tori's mind and grasped her hand. 'Nothing will bring your father back, sweetheart,' she'd said, swallowing hard as silent tears coursed down Tori's cheeks. 'But he'd want you to be happy.'

She'd smiled at the woman in the bed, clearly fighting her conflicting emotions. 'I should add that it won't betray your father if you choose to be with Ashley, even knowing what you know. Ashley's a good man, regardless of the dreadful mistakes he's made. Life moves in mysterious ways, my dear.'

Tori hadn't said much after that. She'd been deep in thought.

Jeanie pushed a strand of Tori's wavy hair behind her ear and placed a hand on her pale cheek. 'You will get out of here, love, but whatever you decide, you need to promise to leave

Matthew and his family,' she'd said. 'They're toxic, do you understand?'

She knew Tori had first-hand experience of how poisonous that family were, but just as to *how* toxic, she was unsure. Yet again, she felt unable to state the danger, but was confident she'd seen a glimmer of fighting spirit flash behind the dulled cornflower blue of the young woman's eyes, so there was hope yet.

• • • •

SARAH NUDGED COLIN as a couple hovered uncomfortably in the White Hart doorway. 'This must be them.'

Rushing over, she looked into the bright green eyes of the woman. 'Jeanie?'

Seeing the woman nod, Sarah hugged her tightly. 'I'm Sarah. Thank you so much for coming. Please come in.'

Kissing Joe on the cheek, Sarah led them over to the bar and after introducing the couple to Colin, she smiled. 'Would you like to stay down here for a drink, or would you prefer to go upstairs to the flat?'

'I think we'll stay down here for a while. Are you sure you don't mind us staying tonight?'

'Of course not. It's the least we can do. You've come such a long way. Now, let me get you both a drink and then I'll come and join you and you can tell me how it went at the hospital. As long as we keep our voices down it won't be a problem.'

Joe led Jeanie over to a table and pulled her chair out so that she could sit down. He glanced around the pub. Seemed like his sort of place – down to earth and non-pretentious. 'Nice girl,' he said, nodding towards Sarah busy pouring their drinks.

Jeanie nodded. 'She is.' She could tell Sarah was a good person. She'd already picked that up the first time they'd spoken and was warmed to see that the woman's marriage seemed to be back on track like she'd predicted.

She smiled at Joe. Poor man. He'd been waiting for her in the hospital carpark whilst she was in with Tori. She'd been in there at the very least, three hours and again, not one question or complaint had come from him.

Jeanie was thoroughly exhausted from both the travelling and the wrench of the afternoon's conversation. Her nerves were frayed and she was on edge. Her senses were bristling and alert, waiting for something to happen and this constant state of angst weighed heavily.

Bringing the drinks over, Sarah set them down on the table. 'I don't expect you to give me a word for word account of what was said to Tori, but if you could just let me know how it went, then I'll let Hunter know.'

Jeanie nodded, aware Sarah was whispering and glancing around the pub out of the corner of her eye. She already knew this was the Reapers' choice of pub and although there weren't any present at the moment, she knew the chance of getting through the evening without seeing any was slim.

Another thing which wasn't helping her general unease wasn't so much that any of them would recognise her, not these younger ones anyway, but that she'd come face to face with Noel. *Leila's son. Her best friend's son.* And she was dreading it.

Jeanie realised Sarah was still looking at her expectantly, waiting for her to talk and she glanced at Joe.

'Sorry,' he said, quickly rising from his chair. 'I'll make myself scarce.'

Jeanie grabbed Joe's shirt sleeve; her fingers surprisingly strong. It was about time she gave him the respect he deserved. 'No, please. You don't need to,' she said softly.

Surprised, Joe slowly sat down and listened as Jeanie began to talk.

## FORTY TWO

RICHARD COULD BARELY hide his distaste. It was Sunday. A goddamn Sunday. He knew the chances were slim, but he had the bizarre notion of escaping for a game of golf or *anything* rather than be stuck in this house with his cooing wife and the usurper child. That was until Susan pointed out he couldn't disappear off out to socialise.

What if someone asked about Victoria and how she was doing with her 'multiple pregnancy', she'd said. Had he stopped to think about that?

That was easy. No, he hadn't. Funnily enough, he'd had other things on his mind, but that was yet another problem he'd have to deal with and he hadn't even dealt with the first one yet.

He glanced at Matthew slumped in an armchair, staring vacantly through the patio doors overlooking the immense garden. *Was he going to pull himself together? People would start asking questions if he didn't start acting bloody normal.*

'Matthew?' Richard barked. 'Come and take your son and give your mother a break.' He watched Matthew flinch at the use of the word 'son'. For Christ's sake, he needed to do better than this. '*Matthew!*'

'It's fine, Richard. I really don't mind.' Cradling the baby in her arms, Susan rocked him gently.

'No, it's not fine, Susan,' Richard said. 'You've been on the go for over forty-eight hours and it's not acceptable. Matthew, come and take your child.'

Matt glared at his father as he heaved himself out of the chair. *Was he taking the piss? Purposefully rubbing his face in it?*

Susan smiled when Matt took the baby out of her arms. 'That's right, you go to Daddy. Oh, Matthew, he's *so* adorable!'

Holding the baby at arms' length, Matt shuffled back to the armchair, his anger simmering quietly underneath the surface.

When the baby opened his eyes revealing their traitorous colour, Matt felt like putting him on the floor and locking himself in his old bedroom, anything to get away from this, but instead remained where he was and purposefully looked somewhere else other than at the child.

He knew what his father said last night – that he should act normally, but he was struggling to do that. It was a lot more difficult than it should be. Usually it was easy overriding things if something needed achieving, but he felt horribly resentful and couldn't quite comprehend why he couldn't rise above his festering thoughts.

'I'll get you a bottle, Matthew. It's almost time for his feed,' Susan said, gliding past him towards the kitchen.

Matt scowled inwardly. Now he'd got to feed the bloody thing and wondered if he could get away with choking it.

Whilst Susan was out of the room, Richard moved towards Matt. 'For Christ's sake!' he hissed. 'Sort yourself out!'

'I'm trying my best, I…'

'I, *nothing*!' Richard spat. 'Damn well get on with it. It won't be for long.'

Matt stared at the floor. 'That's the problem. It will.'

'I meant Victoria will be back soon and then you'll be at work. You'll barely have anything to do with the kid.'

At the sound of the doorbell, Richard glanced up and sighed. *Who now?*

Hearing an unmistakeable voice when Susan answered the door, Richard groaned. *Seriously? Again?* That woman wasn't staying here again tonight, regardless of how much wine she drank. He'd tell Susan to limit the bloody woman to one glass.

As the lounge door pushed open, Richard was just in time to replace his scowl with a plastered-on smile. 'Lillian! How nice to see you!' he lied.

Lillian breezed into the sitting room, smiled at Matthew but strategically ignored her grandchild. 'I've come about the press release. We need to think about what and when we're going to say ab…'

'We can hardly do that whilst Victoria is still in *that* place!' Richard cried. *Was the woman completely bereft of all sense?*

Lillian pursed her lips. 'We can't leave it indefinitely, Richard,' she said caustically. 'Besides, do you *really* think they'd be so callous to expect a photo opportunity, given the circumstances they'll be told?'

'What do you mean 'circumstances?'' Richard said, a little too hastily. *Did Lillian know about this other man? Had she always known?*

Lillian rolled her eyes. 'Are you going senile, dear?' she tittered. 'Surely you haven't forgotten that as far as the press are concerned, three of the four babies will sadly not have made it.'

Richard stared at Lillian. *How he'd love to smash her head into the lid of his grand piano. He could just imagine the cacophony of sound as her skull hit a mish-mash of strings.*

'I agree with my father,' Matt piped up. 'We need to wait until Tori's been discharged. If we release a story such as that, it's only natural the press will start digging and *none* of us want that.' He stared at his father pointedly.

'Like I said,' Richard continued, pleased that he'd got some backing against the conceited old bitch. 'It's not a good idea.'

Lillian threw her hands up in the air. 'Fine, but what will I say to the ladies at drinks evening on Tuesday?'

'Say nothing, that's what!' Richard scoffed. *If you're capable of ever keeping your mouth closed, that is.*

Susan entered the lounge with a bottle of wine and a glass. 'Here we are, Lillian. Your favourite.'

Lillian made herself comfortable in an armchair and took the wine and glass from Susan's hands. 'Oh, I wasn't planning on staying, but being as you've opened it…'

Richard gnashed his teeth. *Great. Now she was here for the evening, no doubt.* He'd make an excuse to retreat somewhere. He needed to think about when he could pull off what was required so it came together in time and he couldn't think about that whilst all he could hear was Lillian.

· · · ·

ALL THINGS CONSIDERED, Jeanie was enjoying herself now she'd said all she had to say about Tori and her thoughts as to how her visit had been received.

Sarah had made her excuses to put a call in to Hunter as arranged and even though she was now back downstairs and had popped over several times to bring more drinks, the pub was too busy for her to sit with them and she was tied up with helping Colin serve behind the bar.

Glancing over, Jeanie smiled to herself. Such as nice couple. Sarah had made it clear they could retire upstairs any time they wished and not to feel like they had to wait for her and Colin to close up because it was usually late by the time everyone had gone. Jeanie was quietly relieved. She was extremely tired.

She glanced at Joe who had been very quiet since the conversation she'd had with Sarah and hoped what she'd said hadn't worried him too much. She realised he must have a thousand and one questions. She knew she would if it was the other way around, but Joe being Joe, as thoughtful as ever, knew it had been a particularly trying day, so he'd had the sense not to press for additional information. Again, something she was grateful for.

She'd made a decision though. From now on she'd open herself up to him more. Let him into her life a little. She smiled shyly. Perhaps and only *perhaps*, in time she could take things to the next stage.

Blushing from her own thoughts, Jeanie castigated herself for running before she could walk. But it was a positive sign that she was at least willing to entertain the thought, wasn't it?

She touched Joe's arm lightly. 'Thank you for being so patient,' she said quietly. 'I'll explain all of this properly soon, I promise.'

'You don't have to do that, but if you'd like to, then you know I'm here,' Joe smiled, before his face became serious. 'Obviously, I don't know much about what's gone on, but I know you've been through a very hard time over the years. I'm not going to hurt you, ok?'

Jeanie nodded. 'I escaped lightly compared to some.' She looked down at the table, unable to meet his eyes. 'I suppose things affected my ability to trust and I became insular.' She took his hand. 'But I'm trying to rectify that now.'

Joe smiled happily. If she was hinting at what he thought she might be hinting at, then that would make him the happiest man in the world.

Suddenly startled by the main door to the pub crashing open and a group of people making their way into the tap room, Jeanie tensed. Her eyes homed in on the rough-looking dark-haired man strutting through the room in front of the others. Her skin tightened across her face and she knew Joe's eyes were on her.

She stared at the man, now with his back to her as he leant up against the bar. *That* was Leila's son. That without any shadow of a doubt was Noel Cooper.

Jeanie felt a distinct lightness in her brain. She could sense her friend so strongly, she shook her head to rid it of this sudden and overwhelming deluge of information.

'Jeanie? Are you alright?' Joe had seen her react like this once before. That night when Ashley Hunter had come into the Mackerel and Hook like a blast from the past. But this man wasn't Ashley Hunter.

He followed Jeanie's line of vision, her gaze locked onto a man's back and watched a blonde girl approach the man from behind and wrap her arms around his waist.

Hearing Jeanie's sharp intake of breath, he swung back to see she'd turned an even whiter shade of pale. 'Tell me what's going on. Do you know those people?'

Jeanie's mouth opened and closed without uttering a word. She couldn't formulate them. The pressure in her head was so strong, she found herself placing her fingers on her temples, gently rubbing them to rid herself of the crushing feeling.

How could she explain this to Joe? It was difficult explaining her rushing senses to *herself*. She knew the man must be Noel Cooper. That was an almost certainty. She'd last seen him as a babe in arms, but there was no doubt in her mind that this man was her friend's son. She could see Leila's striking features clearly within his face, that thankfully, from the short glimpse she'd had of him, he bore no resemblance to the bastard who had fathered him, but the girl. *The girl...*

She concentrated harder. She knew Joe was speaking, but she couldn't answer. Apart from not knowing how to, she didn't want to break her connection.

Without moving her eyes, Jeanie reached for her glass of wine with trembling fingers and as if on cue, the blonde woman turned around, briefly meeting Jeanie's eyes as she scanned the room looking for a free table.

Jeanie flinched. She didn't know that woman. Didn't know her at all. In fact, she'd never seen her before. It was just... How could she describe it? There was a link... A connection... A bad connection with danger.

*This woman was somehow linked to Tori and the danger she was in.*

She had to speak to Sarah and find out who the girl was. She had *something* to do with bad things. Bad things that she couldn't name, but desperately wished she could pinpoint.

Joe took Jeanie's hand. 'I think it's time you got some rest.' Getting to his feet, he waited for her to join him.

# FORTY THREE

'WHAT DO YOU MEAN she's in the psychiatric ward?' Carmen cried. She hadn't planned on speaking to Matt for the foreseeable future, if ever – but she'd had to make an exception.

Already hurt that no one, not even her parents, had let her know Matt's son had been born. She'd only heard that Tori was in labour from Jeremy, but now to find that she'd been detained in the hospital was even worse.

Carmen had been looking forward to a good evening with Noel last night. Despite herself, she'd begun developing feelings for the man, but when Jeremy and the miserable bitch, Ginny had rolled up at the White Hart near to closing and asked if she'd heard any more how Matt, Tori and the baby were getting on, she'd been shocked.

No one had said a thing to her. It was most embarrassing admitting she hadn't been told the child had even been born. If she'd been at the flat the past few days, no doubt she'd have found out sooner, but she'd been holed up with Noel the last couple of days and nights.

It had been too late to go to her parents' house by that time last night, plus, she'd been too angry. Things were strained enough between them as it was and she'd been studiously avoiding them for ages, but she'd no choice but to make the visit this morning.

Now Tori had given birth, it meant she'd be dragged back to Matt and after what Carmen had previously witnessed, she'd hoped to get the chance to talk Tori out of that before it happened.

'There was no choice about it, Carmen. Victoria's quite unwell.' Richard eyed his daughter. The last thing he wanted was her sticking a spanner in the works. He was already playing up the situation. At least Lillian wasn't around to get her knickers in a twist over her daughter's mental health and drinking his wine.

Susan glanced at Richard. 'Has something else happened that I don't know about?'

'No, of course not. It's exactly as you've been told. Victoria will be fine in a few days.' Richard smiled in what he hoped was a reassuring way. *Damn.* He hadn't taken on board that the more he bigged it up, the more Susan would fret. Also, he had to be careful. Whatever else had happened, he didn't want it getting out that Matthew's wife was in *there*.

The child was that... that *person's* and Victoria might say something. Actually, it was likely she would. At least Matthew had the foresight to manufacture it so that *anything* she said from now on could be passed off as delusional. He'd also made sure there was no chance of anyone other than direct family getting in to see her.

This whole charade must be stopped. *And soon.* Matthew wasn't holding things together very well, but Victoria couldn't return here until what was needed had been done and it was proving harder than he'd expected.

Hearing a high-pitched wail from upstairs, Richard cringed. The bloody kid had kept him up for the last couple of nights and then there was the other problem. He may be able to pass off anything Victoria said as delusional, but whether he liked it or not, the proof was upstairs in the crib. It was imperative that no one found out.

Carmen watched her mother rise from her chair. 'Don't you think Matt should do that? You look exhausted.' She'd bet any amount of money that her brother had yet to change a nappy.

Susan hesitated and watched Matt reach for his jacket. 'Matthew, do y…'

Matt shrugged his blazer on. 'No can do. I've got to go to the solicitors. Have you forgotten the house completes today?'

Carmen frowned. 'You're doing that now? I would have thought you might have put that back what wi…'

'We'll need the house, especially when Tori gets out of hospital,' Matt snapped. 'I won't delay it.' He knew what his father had said. *Act normal.*

He was trying to, but wasn't touching that child. He couldn't. he just *couldn't*. He didn't know how he would deal with this as time went on, but deal with it, he must. He just needed a bit longer to get his head around it.

His father had been surprisingly good about it, promising that the situation was rectifiable, which was a relief. As far as anyone else knew, the baby was *his* and unless he said anything, that would not change. It would be made clear to Tori that if she wanted anything to do with her child then she'd happily return to the family and damn well get on with it.

But Matt was still angry. Very angry, but also hurt. Feeling this emotion had come as a bit of a shock. He'd felt a huge amount of pride when he'd been handed what he'd believed to be his son and when he'd realised the child wasn't his, it had… it had… hurt. *It had really fucking hurt.*

'Is anyone going to deal with that child?' Richard barked, glancing towards the ceiling, through which the baby's cries could be heard distinctly growing louder.

'I'll go,' Susan muttered.

'And I'll come with you,' Carmen added, rising from her seat. Matt and her father were such selfish pigs, however, at least it gave her an excuse to see her nephew, hopefully without being grilled about her marriage.

She needed to visit Tori. The woman was fine the last time

she'd seen her, but she'd clocked the glances Matt and her father exchanged. Something was going on and knowing what she now knew about them, this didn't instil a huge amount of confidence.

Carmen wanted to see what Tori's plans were. She had to at least try and make her see sense and talk her out of returning to be kept in a cage for the rest of her life.

And she'd do whatever was needed to help her achieve just that.

## FORTY FOUR

'ANY EXCUSE TO LIE DOWN!' Carmen grinned as she was ushered into Tori's room, hiding her shock at the sight of her sister-in-law's pale and hollow face. It was important to maintain an upbeat attitude if she was to get anywhere with helping.

Carmen knew the family needed Tori discharged sooner rather than later to avoid scandal, but then she'd be well and truly trapped. She had to get her out before they did and put her in touch with several friends of hers who were good and who would be able to legally secure the baby's custody.

'Carmen?' Tori said, hardly able to believe her eyes.

'It's funny what a bit of name-dropping can achieve, isn't it?' *That and a generous donation to the hospital.* Her situation may have altered dramatically over the past few weeks, but that didn't mean she'd lost the ability to use things to her own advantage. Not that this was for her. *She was doing this for Tori.*

Carmen sat down in an uncomfortable plastic chair closest to the bed and grasped Tori's hand. 'Stupid question, but how are you?' She had to take this steady, not wanting to steam straight in.

Despite what she'd previously promised, Tori burst into a

flood of tears. 'How is he? How's my baby?'

Carmen squeezed her hand. 'Beautiful, fine and adorable! Don't worry, my mother's looking after him. He's in good hands.' Whatever her gripe with her parents, she couldn't deny her mother loved children dearly and doted on her new grandson.

Feeling immediate relief that her baby was not with Matt or her own mother, Tori dabbed her eyes, before a rush of unexpected guilt washed over her. Her baby wasn't Susan's grandchild, nor Carmen's nephew. They had no link to him whatsoever.

'Listen,' Carmen said, seeing Tori's expression. 'You'll be out of here soon. Dry your eyes and give them no more reasons to think you're dotty!'

Tori took some deep breaths to calm herself. *She didn't even want to utter his name.* 'And Matt?'

'Weird. I think it's all been too much for him or it could be a case of karma!' Carmen raised an eyebrow.

Tori stiffened. Was Matt setting things in motion to make sure she never got out of here?

'I'm going to cut to the chase. What did he do to get you put in here?'

Tori fidgeted uncomfortably. 'He told me something he knew would upset me and it did. I lost it. He also found out I was planning on leaving…'

Carmen's eyes widened. 'So, you were going to do it? I hoped you would.' She clasped her hands together in excitement. 'Oh, that's fantastic!' She paused and studied Tori. 'Which brings me on to what I want to say. I hope you're going to stick to that? You need to get out of here before *they* get you out. Once you're back there you'll be stuck an…'

'But Matt's got my child. I…'

'Divorce him, Tori. Just do it! I know good lawyers. You can have Matt on abuse, irretrievable breakdown etc. Apply for sole custody, using what he did to you when you were pregnant, for one. I'll second that in court if I have to. Besides, I wouldn't trust him not to snatch the baby during the time he has him and…'

Seeing Tori's face whiten, Carmen realised what a thoughtless comment that was, considering her brother had possession of the child at this very moment. 'I'm so sorry. That was stupid of me,' she spluttered.

Tori stared at the wall. She was still unsure whether to tell Carmen, but at this point in time she didn't have much to lose. Besides, it would all come out eventually and she'd rather Carmen heard it from her first.

'By the way, they've decided to call the baby Matthew Augustus,' Carmen continued. 'Just thought I'd warn you.'

Tori blinked. *They'd decided? Her child was not called Matthew Augustus and neither would he be.* 'He's called Andrew,' she said quietly.

'That's a lovely name, much better than Matthew Augustus, but you know what they're like. They'll want to register the birth soon, but they can't until they've made the birth public and you know they won't dream of doing that whilst it risks exposing you being in here.' Carmen put on a conspiring face and winked. 'Imagine their shame?'

Tori didn't smile. She hadn't forgotten about her mother's disgusting story about the 'quads'. If that was printed, she'd go to the press herself and expose their lies. Expose the lot of them for what they were.

Carmen watched the silent emotions passing across Tori's face and sensed she was at the point where she felt she had nothing to lose. 'Whatever you think, I'd advise against pushing them too far. Leaving Matt is one thing – at least you can claim for money, what with the child and everything, but you've got to remember you can't live on thin air. You still need to keep them on side to some extent and you need your child back.'

'Once you've left and they've calmed down, you'll get a reasonable settlement if you play ball. Let them name your son, for instance,' Carmen smiled. 'It's always been a family tradition to name the first born son after the father.

Tori raised her eyes and looked at Carmen. 'Matt's not Andrew's father...'

Carmen's glossy mouth formed an 'O' shape. 'He's not... *What?* He's not the father?'

Tori felt sad. She'd hurt Carmen too. 'No, he's not.'

'W-Who...'

'Andrew's father is the man who Matt wanted me to sleep with to get information for his property deals. The thing is, we fell in love.' Tori smiled. 'His name's Ashley Hunter.'

'I don't believe this,' Carmen cried, trying to take the news onboard. 'Matt made you sleep wi... Who the fuck is Ashley Hunter?'

Tori couldn't keep the smile off her face. 'He used to be the President of the Reapers. You know, the motorbike group?' *He also killed my father, but that was a mistake.* It would be difficult, but she loved Hunter and what that lady, Jeanie, had said yesterday, a lot of things were now clear. She couldn't get her father back, but she *could* get her child's father back.

Carmen's mouth flapped open and closed. 'Yes, I know the Reapers.' *Especially one of them, but now was not the time to get on to that subject.* Was this Hunter the one Noel had superseded? He'd mentioned there was a lot of bad blood between him and the previous president, but either way, this was great! Without being able to help it, she burst out laughing.

Tori stared at Carmen in confusion. 'Are you not angry with me?'

Composing herself, Carmen shook her head. 'Of course not. It serves Matt right. He did it to himself. Does he know?'

'Not yet, unless he's worked it out. I knew as soon as Andrew opened his eyes. They're identical to Hunter's.'

'I'm looking forward to seeing Matt's face when he finds out. I told you, it's karma!' Carmen's face then became serious. 'You do need to get out of here as soon as possible, especially now. He can't discover this until you've got Andrew back. I know he's my brother, but I don't trust him. If he finds out this child isn't his, well...'

Tori went cold. *She didn't trust him either.*

Carmen frowned. 'I need to speak to this Ashley Hunter of yours. I'll need him to help me with this. Where can I find him?'

'I don't know. Speak to Sarah. She runs the White Hart and she kn…'

'I know Sarah.'

'How you do know Sarah?'

'I go out with Jeremy for drinks, remember?'

Tori bit her lip. 'Just don't let anyone else know about this, Carmen. *No one* – including Jeremy. It's really important, because there's people in there… People that mustn't find out about this under *any* circumstances.'

'Ok,' she said. 'I'll be careful.' She had no intention of doing anything to jeopardise Tori's chance of happiness. She squeezed her hand once again. 'And who's the guy in control of your treatment here?'

'Doctor Sterling, I think. Yes, that's his name.'

'Let me see if I can find him.' Carmen stood up. 'I'll have a little chat.'

'What are you going to say? Don't say anyth…'

'Relax, I won't spill any secrets. I'll see if I can persuade him that you don't need to be here.'

• • • •

HUNTER GRATEFULLY DRANK his pint in a quiet corner of the bar. He'd been pleased when Sarah had called last night to say Jeanie had successfully seen Tori. Tori had confirmed there was no doubt he was the father of the baby and that she'd managed to explain everything he'd wanted her to. He knew she'd be able to do it.

His heart swelled. He had a son and Tori still wanted to be with him, despite everything. He was under no illusion that it would be an easy road – murdering someone's father was hardly something that could be swept under the carpet, but the fact that she was willing to try spoke volumes.

Hunter couldn't thank Jeanie enough. He knew how hard it

would be for her to dredge all of that up again and he also accepted there was a part of her which blamed herself for not speaking up a long time ago. She'd already said if she'd have made Leila's rapist's identity known at the time, then Jack Jacobs wouldn't have been wrongly targeted in the first place. That might be so, but it wasn't Jeanie's fault. *It was his and his alone.*

As he'd sat deep in thought most of the night his main priority was how to get Tori out of the hospital and his child away from Matt Stevens without getting locked up in the process. In all truthfulness, he'd be happy to kill the lot of them, but as always, Sarah had pointed out he wouldn't be much use to anyone if he was locked up, rather than being with his family.

*His family.*

Hunter's face broke into a wide smile. Whatever happened he'd take his family out of harm's way as soon as possible.

From her place behind the bar, Bella elbowed Hunter none too gently. 'Don't know who this one is, but considering any women coming in here are invariably looking for you, I can only presume this one is too,' she said sarcastically.

Hunter huffed good-naturedly even though he was hardly in the mood for jokes.

Bella nudged him again. 'No, I'm serious. There really is a woman. A gorgeous one at that!'

Sighing, Hunter turned around, expecting there either to be no one there or a black-toothed sixty-year-old dressed in a lycra mini-skirt, so he was surprised to see a slim blonde glancing around the room. The woman's eyes rested on his and smiling, she confidently walked towards him.

'Told you,' Bella muttered. 'Who is it?'

'No idea,' Hunter said, confused.

'Ashley Hunter?' Carmen asked, her voice clear. She rested her handbag on the bar and glanced at Bella. 'Gin and tonic, please.'

'And you are?' Hunter asked, on alert. Very few people used his first name.

'I'm a friend of Tori's and I need to spe…'

Hunter sat up. 'A friend of *Tori's*?' He hadn't seen this woman before. *Was this a set up?*

Seeing Hunter's immediate unease, Carmen smiled and sipped at her drink. 'Relax. I'm on your side.' She glanced over to the back corner of the room. 'Can we go somewhere a little more private?' She gave Bella a pointed glance, making it obvious that she didn't want anyone else listening to their conversation.

Unable to hide her irritation, Bella slammed a drip tray down and flounced off to the other side of the bar.

'Whoops!' Carmen laughed and walked towards a deserted corner of the room, knowing Hunter would follow.

'How did you find me and how do you know Tori?' Hunter asked once they'd sat at a table, his eyes intently studying the woman in front of him.

Carmen smiled. This man certainly was a looker. She could see why Tori had fallen for him. 'I'm Matt's sister.' She held her hand up when Hunter stiffened and made to get up from the chair. 'Wait! I'm on your side. Please listen to me. Sarah told me where you were. Tori told me to ask her. I know you're the baby's father and I've been hoping for some time Tori would leave my brother. I saw what he di…'

Hunter's eyes narrowed. If Tori had asked Sarah to tell this woman where to find him then she must be on the level, but he needed to be sure. 'And what else has that piece of shit done that I don't know about?'

Carmen bit her lip, feeling suddenly out of her depth. 'Let's not go into that now. You may know everything, but we haven't got time to waste.'

Leaning back in the chair, Hunter folded his arms across his chest. 'What makes you think I'd trust you? This could be a set up for all I know and knowing your brother, it probably is.'

Carmen smiled. 'I appreciate that, but it's not. My brother's a wanker and so is my father. Added to that list is my husband, who I might add, I've left because I'm not putting up with liars and bastards any longer, but that's a different story.'

She flapped her hand as if swatting flies. 'I saw Tori this morning and told her she's got to get out of there before *they* get her out.

'Who's *they*?' Hunter growled. He didn't trust her. He didn't trust any of them.

'Matt and my family, of course!' Carmen said as if he was a bit slow on the uptake. 'They'll want to get her out before it becomes public knowledge that dear Matthew's wife is in a nuthouse. You must know what they're like. What a dreadful *scandal* it would be!'

Hunter couldn't help but smile at the way Carmen had rolled her eyes and put on a voice that sounded uncannily like Lillian Morgan's.

'You know as well as I do that Matt set her up after he found out she wanted to be with you. He had to make her out to be delusional.' Seeing Hunter nod, Carmen continued. 'But, like I said, they can't keep her in too long and when they get her out, she'll be back to square one. Trapped!'

Hunter nodded again. *That much was true.*

'I bullied my way in this morning, along wi…'

'How?' Hunter asked. 'They've got a strict cap on who visits her.'

Carmen flapped her hand dismissively. 'The difference is I can talk posh, act posh, look posh and I'm 'family'. She raised an eyebrow. 'It's also uncanny what a generous donation to the hospital research fund does.'

Hunter found himself smiling again, despite himself.

'I've got good lawyers and I've done a bit of groundwork. Tori should get sole custody once she's out and files for divorce.'

Hunter's smile dropped and a frown furrowed his brow. 'If you think I'm leaving my kid for any length of time in *their* hands you're sadly mistaken, lady.'

'Well, I don't see any other way of doing it legally.'

'Who said anything about *legally*? I'll be doing *something* to get my kid, believe you me.'

Carmen eyed the determination in the steely eyes of the man opposite and didn't doubt that he'd stop at nothing to get his child and the woman he loved away from her brother. She had to keep this calm. 'In the meantime, I'll rent a flat that Tori can live an...'

'It's already done,' Hunter growled. 'A house actually. I rented it last week. We'd planned to leave on Thursday, but th...'

'Hmm, unfortunate timing, no doubt helped by my brother choosing that time to upset her.'

Hunter bristled. Had Tori told this woman about her father and his part in it? He hoped not.

'Of course he guessed she was leaving him for you. I bet that pissed him off. Imagine his face. A bank manager being jilted for a biker!' Carmen laughed loudly. 'Brilliant!'

Hunter didn't laugh. He didn't even smile. This wasn't about status, or lack of it. It was a hell of a lot more important than that.

'I can see you don't trust me and I don't blame you, but I'm not like them. I want to get Tori away.'

Hunter softened slightly and sat forward in the chair. 'And just how do you propose to do that?'

Carmen smiled conspiringly. 'That's what I'm trying to get to. I spoke to the doctor this morning as well; the one in charge of Tori's case. He was *very* understanding of how this could affect her new role as wife of the bank manager and he agreed it was detrimental for her to remain any longer.'

'How di...'

'Turns out I went to school with the man and another cheque happened to slip out of my bag into his hand,' Carmen winked.

'But...'

'Tori's being discharged tomorrow morning at 8 o'clock into my care - her charming sister-in-law.'

Hunter sat upright. 'Are you serious?'

Carmen nodded. 'Always. Oh and I should also mention that unfortunately it slipped my mind to update my brother or parents, so providing they don't turn up to see her tonight – which they won't, then she'll be leaving with me.'

'But what about the baby?' Hunter said. 'What about my son?'

'Once Tori's out, I'll arrange for a private DNA test which will prove he's your son and then they won't have a leg to stand on.'

'Does Matt suspect he's not the father? Tori's never trusted him and if he discovers th…'

'Not as far as I can tell. He'd have gone berserk by now if he did. His ego couldn't stand it. He's acting weird, but that's about the extent of it.'

Hunter exhaled loudly. So this time tomorrow Tori would be out and he'd be with her at the house he'd rented. *Away from them.*

'I'm going back to my parents now to put up with them moaning at me about daring to leave my husband. It means I can keep an eye on them and make sure they'd don't start making noises about going to the hospital.'

She put her hand lightly on Hunter's arm. 'I'll get a swab from the baby too.'

'A swab?'

'For testing. It will be even quicker that way. Just from his cheek. Don't worry, it won't hurt him. I'll need some from you too, but we can do that later.'

Hunter frowned. 'You should just take him.'

'Take him?' Carmen stared at Hunter. 'You mean snatch him?'

'That's exactly what I mean.'

Carmen ran her tongue across her teeth and frowned. *Maybe she should.*

## FORTY FIVE

JEANIE WOKE IN in a state of panic. She hadn't planned on falling asleep. She'd wanted to speak to Sarah and ask who the blonde woman in the bar with Noel was, but she must have been so exhausted she'd failed to stay awake and now it was morning.

Quickly getting out of bed, she moved into the lounge, seeing Joe still asleep on the sofa. *Where was Sarah? Or Colin?* Shaking Joe, her eyes darted around. 'Joe. *Joe*! Wake up! What time is it?'

Joe blearily opened his eyes. Seeing Jeanie leaning over him, he smiled. 'Good morning. Did you sleep well?'

'Too well!' Jeanie snapped. 'Please, what's the time?'

Frowning, Joe pushed himself up onto his elbows and peered at his watch. 'It's 9.20. Blimey! I think this is the first time I've had a lie-in for years, if not ever!' He watched Jeanie dart towards the stairwell. 'What's the matter? Where are you going?'

'I've got to find Sarah,' Jeanie muttered, rushing down the stairs.

Entering the tap room, she looked around for any trace of Sarah. The room was empty. 'Sarah?' she shouted. 'Colin?'

Colin's footsteps echoed loudly on the stone steps of the cellar as he rushed back up into the bar. 'Jeanie? Whatever's the matter? I was setting the barrels up.'

'Where's Sarah?' Jeanie gasped.

Colin frowned. 'She's gone to work. We didn't want to disturb you. Are you alright?'

Jeanie rested against the bar, trying to quell the distinct rising fear surfacing again four-fold. 'That's just it. I'm not sure... Maybe you could help?'

Colin placed down the cloth he was holding. 'I'll try.'

'There was a man in here last night. Tall, dark hair, tied in a ponytail. A biker.'

Colin grimaced. 'Yeah, Noel,' he spat. 'Horrible piece of work. He hasn't upset you, has he? If he's said or done anything out of order, I'll...'

Jeanie shook her head. 'No, nothing like that.' *So she'd been correct in her assumptions. That man was Noel.* 'It's the woman.'

Colin raised his eyebrows. 'The woman?'

'Yes, the blonde one. A girlfriend, I presume. Who is she?' *It was her who'd triggered her senses. It was her who'd flagged up a link.*

'Noel doesn't exactly do 'girlfriends',' Colin muttered. 'But the girl, yes – a bit of a strange situation. She's very well to do. Not sure what's goi...'

'But who *is* she?' Jeanie pressed. *Come on. Come on!*

Colin frowned. 'I don't know much about her. All I know is she's Carmen - Tori's husband's sister. You must have heard all about *Matt*.' He spat the man's name. 'Admittedly, Carmen's much nicer than her brother, but that's not difficult. She must be crazy getting involved with Noel. That man is... You know what he did to us and his part wi...'

'Wait! You say Carmen is Matt's *sister*?' Jeanie felt faint. *So, she is connected.*

'We were all surprised when Tori told Sarah that Carmen had become an unexpected ally where Matt was concerned.

That sort normally stick together. This Carmen woman ran off from her husband - a mega-rich French tycoon, so the story goes. Then she came back over here, rented a room from Jeremy - one of Matt's friends and then suddenly she's hopping in the sack with Noel.'

'I must see Tori,' Jeanie gasped. She had to warn her to have nothing to do with that woman. That Carmen. There was something there. Something wrong. She must be the danger. She'd felt a link. A link to something…

'What? Now? You want to go *now*?' Colin said surprised.

'Yes. Now. I *have* to,' Jeanie cried.

•   •   •   •

CARMEN PULLED UP in the hospital carpark and yanked her handbrake on. These rental cars were getting irritating. She kept meaning to go and buy a car of her own now she was here to stay, but what with everything, she hadn't got around to it.

Walking into the hospital just before 8 o'clock, she made her way towards the psychiatric unit, having no intention of hanging around. She wanted Tori out of there as soon as possible and, as arranged, Hunter was waiting at the rented house ready for when they arrived.

Carmen touched her handbag where she'd put the piece of paper containing the address. Once she'd dropped Tori off, she'd return to her parents as quickly as possible.

She'd left this morning, making the excuse for her unusually early start as wanting to go for a swim. In fact, it had all gone well. Her father was the only one up and he hadn't uttered anything further about her presence.

Although she expected him to make noises about being there rather than sorting her marriage out, it seemed all of that had taken a back seat since Andrew's early arrival and Tori's hospitalisation, not to mention Matt's rather strange behaviour.

Her father had never made any secret of not particularly liking children, especially babies, so last night when she'd made a big deal of commenting about how exhausted her mother looked and that she'd be happy to stay on for a while to help look after the baby, the relief on her mother's face made it difficult for her father to put up any resistance.

Of course, Carmen was genuinely happy to help, but it wasn't so much to assist her mother. She was planning to get the swab from the baby's cheek, but it hadn't panned out.

Carmen continued down the hospital corridor, anxiously hoping nothing had occurred since she'd last been here to hinder Tori's departure.

No, last night had not gone to plan. Getting up at 2am, she'd padded down the landing to Andrew's room, but her mother was in there feeding him. She'd offered to take over, but her mother had steadfastly refused.

A pang of guilt flushed through Carmen. Her mother would be broken-hearted when she'd taken Andrew to be with his *parents*. She'd also be broken-hearted to learn the baby wasn't Matt's and she was not a grandmother after all.

Carmen knew the baby's arrival, although exhausting, had given her mother a fresh lease of life. She knew that despite all her social airs and graces, her mother was unhappy and had been for years. Maybe she was more like her than she thought. The difference between them was that she refused to spend any more time married to a liar and a fake. She wouldn't end up like her mother in twenty years. *No thank you.*

Carmen made a second attempt around 4am, surprised to find Matt in Andrew's room. He'd shown little interest in the child and acted almost like he *resented* him. Not that that was a shock. Matt always had been selfish. Anyone getting more attention would always cause problems. Anyone would still think the man was six years old the way he behaved.

She'd been about to make her presence known, but something made her stop and watch her brother intently. He wasn't feeding Andrew. In fact, he wasn't doing *anything* apart from standing motionless, staring down into the crib.

Carmen had remained partially concealed behind the doorframe, a glimmer of worry fizzing through her. Had Matt worked out Andrew wasn't his?

Since Tori's revelation, Carmen had studied the baby and could clearly see the eyes were a giveaway, but would Matt have noticed? She doubted it. He didn't take much notice of anything unless it stood to gain him something.

In the end she'd had little choice but to leave him to it, thinking she'd get another chance first thing in the morning. She'd returned to her room and before she knew it, it was time to get up.

She'd quickly showered and changed and made her way across the landing, planning to go back into Andrew's room, but hearing someone moving around downstairs, she decided it wasn't worth the risk attempting it. It didn't really matter about the swab now because she'd decided on a plan. One of which, with any luck, would work well.

Last night she'd discovered Matt was overseeing the firm moving the contents into the new house today and her father had a business lunch booked. One of those lunches where it was expected for the wives to join their husbands. Her mother had of course refused. How could she possibly go? Who would look after Andrew?

Well, *she* would, of course, Carmen had said. It was only for a few hours and she'd be fine. With her father's pushing, her mother had reluctantly agreed.

Carmen smiled to herself. At that point she'd known that it would be the ideal time to get Andrew away from her poisonous brother and take him to Tori. *It was perfect.*

She knew the shit would hit the fan and that no one would ever forgive her, but that was ok. It was the right thing to do. Even in the worst case scenario - if her mother changed her mind and insisted on staying home to look after Andrew herself, then it wasn't the end of the world. She'd just revert to her plan of taking him during the night. Either way, she would get the child away.

Finally reaching the reception desk of the psychiatric unit, Carmen smiled at the nurse. 'Carmen LeVere. I'm here to collect Victoria Stevens. She's being discharged this morning.'

The nurse picked up a folder from the desk and glanced over the top sheet of paper. 'Yes, that's right. Doctor Sterling is in with Mrs Stevens at the moment, so she'll be ready shortly.'

Smiling, Carmen followed the nurse to Tori's room. *So far, so good.*

· · · ·

AGAIN, WITHOUT EXPECTING an explanation, Joe had driven Jeanie to the Ragged Staff where they'd met Hunter just two nights before. She'd barely said two words during the journey, her knuckles white from gripping her handbag. And now he was banging on the door of a pub that wasn't even open.

After what seemed like an indeterminable amount of time, the door opened.

'We're not open yet,' Bella said, eyeing the older couple whom she recognised being with Hunter in here the other night.

'I need to see Ashley,' Jeanie cried. 'Ashley Hunter. Can you tell me where I can find him? *Please*? It's important.'

Bella frowned. 'I can, but I know he's not there.'

'N-Not there?'

'His bike roared past at the crack of dawn this morning. It's difficult *not* to hear it, so I knew it was him. I also know when he goes off early like that, he's usually gone for the whole day, although he mi…'

'Was he here last night?' Jeanie interrupted.

'Ah, that might be it. He might have buggered off out with that blonde who turned up last night. Very cosy they were,' Bella griped. 'Ensconced themselves at the back of the room, thick as thieves.'

'Do you know her name?' Jeanie asked, already fearing the worst. It had to be Carmen. She was planning something. Planning something to hurt Ashley and Tori. She'd sensed her link with evil.

Bella shrugged. 'Haven't a clue. Posh and irritatingly beautiful. Hunter didn't know her either, but that didn't stop him from being dragged off into the corner – all cloak and daggers. *Men!*'

Jeanie couldn't even rustle up a smile. Ashley wouldn't be interested in that woman, regardless of how beautiful she was. He was only interested in Tori.

'Do you know what they spoke about?' Jeanie pressed. *Please let this girl have overheard something.*

'No chance! She made it crystal clear she didn't want the likes of me eavesdropping!'

Jeanie's heart raced. They had to get to the hospital. Get there and warn Tori. Warn her not to trust this woman.

• • • •

TORI'S HEART BEAT like a drum as Carmen pulled up outside a row of terraced houses. She looked up at the row of small buildings, her nerves jangling.

She was unsure how to react or deal with Hunter. It was all very well telling herself she would deal with what he had done, but it could be different in reality. What if she couldn't? What if she resented him? She didn't want her love turning to hate.

She couldn't think clearly. All that she could concentrate on was the gnawing need for her son and that overshadowed everything else.

Carmen broke Tori from her thoughts by gently putting her hand on her arm. 'Are you getting out?'

Nodding slowly, Tori reached for the door handle, only to freeze when the front door of the terrace directly in front of her opened, revealing Hunter. Her mouth quivered, watching him forcing himself to walk down the path at a normal rate, rather than run. She could tell by his face that he was unsure how she'd react to him and how to play it.

Opening the passenger door, Hunter took Tori's hand and helped her to her feet. He silently stared at her for a few moments. 'Welcome home,' he whispered.

Defying logic, Tori fell into his arms, resting against his chest and letting him enfold her in his arms.

Carmen hovered uncomfortably by the car. Retrieving Tori's bag from the back seat, she slammed the door to jolt Tori and Hunter from their silent embrace.

As they walked into the tiny house, Tori looked about her, her mind already picturing what it would look like when Andrew was with them. *When they were a family.*

Hunter watched her intensely. 'I-It's not much, I know, but…'

'It's perfect,' Tori said, her voice barely more than a whisper. Her emotions span like a wooden top; a combination of wanting to fold herself back into this man, to feel his mouth on hers, merged with betrayal for her father – for loving the man who had ended his life, combined with the nagging ache deep in her heart for her baby. Her baby who right now was in the hands of the one man that she hated above all others.

Despite her need to remain together, focused and calm, Tori began to tremble.

Carmen glanced at Hunter seeing his concern. They both knew this would be difficult. She felt like she should stay – if only for a little while, unsure if Tori could handle being alone with Hunter. So much had happened over the last week and her emotions were understandably clashing like an avalanche, that much was obvious. But she also needed to get back to her parents' house. It was already almost 10 o'clock and it would take nearly an hour to get back. They'd need to leave by 11 to get to the lunch date.

Carmen wanted nothing impeding the chance of taking Andrew. The longer it went before she got him, the higher the risk of them finding out Tori had already been discharged.

Moving forwards, Carmen gently touched Tori's arm. 'I'm going to have to go. Will you be ok?'

Tears brimming, Tori nodded, 'Y-Yes, yes, I'll be fine.'

'We'll be ok,' Hunter added. He'd give Tori as much space as she needed, despite his intense urge to be around her. 'And thank you, Carmen… for… everything.'

Carmen smiled. 'Think nothing of it. I've yet to do the most important thing yet, so thank me once I've done that!'

'And you'll really bring Andrew here later?' Tori whispered, barely able to believe the plan Carmen had told her on the way back from the hospital.

Carmen smiled. 'I'll try my best.'

Tori's eyes widened. 'Do you think you won't be able to?'

Carmen hugged her. 'I'll be doing everything I can. If I can't get him this afternoon, it will be tonight. Either way, I'll be getting your son to you before this day is out, I promise.'

Tori nodded, a lone tear escaping. Even though she knew things needed to be right for Carmen to be able to do this, it didn't stop the uncontrollable yearning. Every minute away from her son was torture. She'd only had an hour with him since his birth and that was six days ago.

'I'll be back as soon as I can.' Carmen slipped away from Tori's grasp and out of the door.

Tori watched Carmen leave and slowly turned to Hunter. He looked as helpless and on edge as she felt.

## FORTY SIX

MATT STARED AT the papers on his desk. He wasn't due to start his new position at the bank for another few days, but he'd had to get out of the house. Last night he'd barely slept a wink and at 6am this morning he'd made the decision to get some solace in his new office.

His plan was to stay here until the removal men unloaded the house at 9 and then he'd get on with overseeing them, making sure everything went to plan with no breakages. There was no way he could remain at his parents' house whilst everyone bustled around playing 'happy families'. *Not now he knew the truth.*

He'd left pretty damn sharpish when he'd heard someone moving around and hadn't bothered stopping to find out who it was. He hadn't wanted to see *any* of them. None of them at all. His father would have made another 'pulling yourself together' comment, his mother would have smiled dotingly, whilst encouraging him to take more of a hands-on approach with his 'son' and Carmen – well, Carmen – that bitch, would have just been *Carmen*.

They could think what they liked. They weren't the ones dealing with this, were they?

Matt glared around his office. His personal items had been transferred and irritatingly placed by his new personal assistant or secretary – whoever that was – in his absence. His magnetic paperclip holder was next to his desk organiser. And it was upside-down.

He angrily turned it up the right way. God damn. If the woman couldn't work out which way up it went that didn't bode well because it was fucking obvious.

Matt then glared at the silver picture frame on his desk displaying a photograph of him and Tori. It was one of the official photographs from his wedding. His father had told him it was fitting to place family pictures on his desk, so he had, but he didn't want it. He didn't want to look at it.

It was one of those photos where they had been instructed to gaze into each other's eyes adoringly. He remembered it well because he'd been more interested in the petite redhead he'd spotted in the grounds of the country house where they'd held the reception, than looking into the eyes of his brand new wife. Of course, he'd done what was expected and to anyone else his expression was convincing. Even Tori looked marginally happy, but she didn't fool him. She'd been anything *but* happy. He knew it then and he certainly knew it now. Even then she'd probably been busy making plans. Plans that didn't involve *him*.

Matt's teeth grated harder, his jaw aching. His eyes moved along to another photograph in a similar frame further along the desk. That one had been taken by a magazine covering his return to the area. His eyes ran over his posed stance, one arm resting around Tori's shoulders, his other hand on her bump showcased to maximum effect in the tight cream dress the photographer advised she wore.

He stared at his hand touching her belly. No wonder he hated touching it. The treacherous bitch. That thing growing inside her hadn't been put there by him and she'd known it all along.

Matt's fury ascended further. Well, she'd pay now. She'd more than pay for what she'd done. He'd make sure of it. And as for Carmen. She must have known about this for ages. That's why she was so pally with Tori and why she'd pushed her to Lillian's. When she'd threatened to tell their mother all that bollocks it was just a fucking smoke screen giving Tori an excuse to run off with that ape. Well, no more. Tori was going *nowhere*.

Matt glanced at the clock. 8.30. He couldn't stay here much longer. People were arriving for the day and he'd already shooed away several who felt the need to introduce themselves. Like he cared?

Right now he didn't much care about who any of these people were, but that wasn't the way he'd wanted to start the most important phase of his career. It wasn't the way it should be at all. His slut of a wife had ruined everything and his lying sister had done nothing but encourage her.

When his desk phone suddenly rang, Matt's head snapped up. *Who the hell was ringing him here*? He hadn't even officially started yet.

He snatched up the receiver. 'Yes? What?'

'M-Mr Stevens?' a timid female voice uttered.

'Yes, this is Matthew Stevens.'

'I'm Belinda, your new secretary an...'

Matt's eyebrows knitted together. *Did people understand nothing?* 'Yes, very nice, Belinda, but I haven't officially started this position yet. I only popped in fo...'

'I realise that, Sir, but I have a gentleman who is most insistent on speaking with you. A Mr LeVere who sa...'

'I'm far too bu...' Matt stopped in his tracks. *Did she say LeVere? As in, Luca LeVere? He'd finally returned his call, had he?*

A slight smile worked its way across Matt's mouth. *Carmen thought she could fuck with him, did she?* 'Wait, Belinda! Please put Mr LeVere through.'

'Yes Sir,' Belinda simpered.

Matt waited as the line connected. 'Luca?'

'Matthew?' 'You've been trying to get hold of me?'

'Yes,' Matt said, barely able to contain his glee. 'Thanks for getting back to me. I wanted to talk to you. There's some things I thought you should be made aware of...'

· · · ·

SUSAN WAS NIGH ON hysterical and her wailing assaulted every single one of Richard's nerve endings. He knew she'd take the news badly, but it was getting to the point where he would have to slap her – more for his own sake than hers.

'Susan,' he said, placing his hands on her shoulders as she rocked disturbingly back and forwards in the dining room chair.

'*Susan*!' he repeated, giving her a slight, but firm shake. She'd break the chair if she carried on like this. 'You need to stop this! It isn't helping.'

'NOOOOOO! OH NOOOO!' Susan wailed, rivers of tears running thick grooves down her overly made-up face.

Richard reluctantly pulled his wife's head against him, feeling her shaking uncontrollably. He swallowed a sigh, betting her thick foundation was now smeared all over the front of his suit. He'd never get it out. Even dry cleaning wouldn't remove it. What a nuisance.

She'd always worn too much makeup and on top of that, they'd miss that lunch date now. Irritating, but there was no way around it.

Richard forced himself to think about what he should say and stroked his wife's hair. 'Susan? *Susan*! Listen to me. You need to calm down.' He kept his voice level even though all he really wanted to do was scream at her to shut the hell up.

'*Please*, sweetheart. You'll give yourself a heart attack if you carry on like this and things are bad enough already.' He continued gently stroking his wife's hair, noticing she hadn't touched up her roots recently. That would never do.

Richard had thought when Carmen appeared first thing that his plans were somewhat thwarted, but thankfully his daughter was as eager to leave as he had been for her to go.

He hung around in the kitchen for ages waiting for Susan to

finish her shower and come downstairs for breakfast before he'd broken the news. He'd allowed her to sleep so late because he'd needed as much time as possible to work out what to say.

He surreptitiously glanced at his watch. It had just gone 10.30. He continued stroking Susan's head. It was having a calming effect and he didn't want that to change.

'I just can't believe it,' Susan said, her sobs reducing to hiccupping gulps.

'I know,' Richard soothed. 'Dreadful.' *God, he could do with a drink. A large one. But that would have to wait.* 'These things happen, I'm afraid.'

Susan wrenched her head up, her eyes bright red from crying. 'What do you mean, these things happen? They *shouldn't* happen. Not to us. Not to *anyone!*'

'I know,' Richard said blindly. 'No, you're right. They shouldn't.'

'Why us? *Why*? He was our grandson, Richard. Our *grandson.*' Susan broke into a fresh round of loud sobs. 'That beautiful little boy…'

Richard scowled. The kid wasn't their grandson at all, but now was not the time to mention that. 'I know, I know,' he repeated yet again, beginning to feel like a cracked record. *How long would this take? Surely she couldn't cry all damn day?*

Susan's head snapped up again. 'Oh my God! Have you got hold of Matthew yet?' she cried. 'My poor boy. He'll be devastated.'

*Doubtful*, Richard thought. 'No, I haven't had ch…'

'You *must* get hold of him!' Susan clutched at Richard's arm, her nails digging through the thick material of his suit jacket. 'He needs to know. It's his *son.*'

'He's with the removal company this morning.'

'Oh no and Victoria!' Susan buried her face in her hands. 'That poor girl! This will finish her. She'll be in hospital for ever after this.'

Richard rolled his eyes, grateful Susan was too busy crying to notice. Victoria *wouldn't* be in hospital for much longer at all. She'd be back with Matthew doing what she should have been doing in the first place. If Matthew had any sense, he'd waste no time impregnating her. But this time, making sure it was *him* who did the job. That would give the girl something to focus on rather than dwell on this unfortunate incident.

He'd been beginning to wonder whether he'd even get the chance to do what he'd needed to do. Last night the kid's bedroom and landing area was like the bloody M25 what with people coming and going left, right and centre. It was daylight when he'd finally got his chance and even then he'd heard someone starting to stir.

Luckily it hadn't taken long and he'd been safely ensconced at the breakfast table by the time Carmen had shown her face.

Richard sighed deeply. Matthew had better be grateful for this. Despite everything, it hadn't been a particularly pleasant thing to do, but it had to be done nevertheless. Matthew should have been the one to deal with it, but as usual it was *him* who had to step up and take control. He really was finally doubting his son's ability and it was all getting rather disappointing.

'What are we going to do?' Susan said, her sobs reducing back to muffled hiccups.

'First things first, we need to contact the Doctor.'

'The *Doctor*?' Susan cried. 'He can't do anything to make things better!'

Richard sighed again. This time loudly. 'I know that, but a doctor is called in these circumstances to arrange things.'

'But wh…'

'I won't be able to get in touch with Matthew until he returns later. We have no choice in that,' Richard interrupted.

'Oh, poor Matthew. All day he'll think things are fine and then when he comes back he'll…'

'I can't do much about that if he's not reachable,' Richard snapped.

'Go over to the house. His new house? Why didn't you think of that? He'll be there, won't he?' Susan griped.

Richard let Susan's comment go over his head and resisted

the urge to punch her in the face for her rudeness. Under the circumstances he'd let that one go this time.

'Oh, the house they were supposed to be taking their son to. That home the baby will never see...' Susan burst into another round of sobbing. 'Matthew had done the nursery up and...'

'I'll go straight there after I've been to see Victoria,' Richard mumbled. 'But I'm not leaving you on your own.' He wanted to though. He wanted to get away from her whining voice before he lost it.

'What about Lillian?' Susan asked.

'Fuck Lillian!' Richard barked. 'I'll get around to her later. Our family comes first.' *And it was about time people realised that. Perhaps if they had, then he wouldn't have been forced to take matters into his own bloody hands. Again.*

The door suddenly slamming made both Susan and Richard glance up.

'I'm back! You'd best get a move on for your lunch date if yo...' Seeing the state of her mother's face, Carmen stopped mid-sentence, icy tendrils of fear inching up her spine. 'W-What's happened?'

Getting no response, Carmen rushed over. Had they discovered Tori had been discharged or that Matt wasn't the baby's father? 'Mum?' Her mother looked like... well...nothing she'd ever seen her look like before. '*Mum*? What's happened? Please tell me?'

Susan looked pleadingly at Richard before breaking into a fresh round of tears.

'I'm afraid it's not good news, Carmen,' Richard said, forcing himself to place a hand on his daughter's shoulder. *His conniving daughter who had let him down.*

Carmen's eyes darted between her parents, knowing whatever she was about to hear, without a doubt wasn't good.

'The baby... I'm sorry to say... he's died...' Richard said solemnly.

'H-He's... *what*?' Carmen's words stuck in her throat. They felt they weren't even coming from her mouth. *Was she hearing correctly?*

'Terrible thing. I found him when I went to check on him whilst your mother was in the shower... He wasn't breathing... There wasn't anything I could do...' Richard said.

Carmen didn't hear if anything else was said as she slumped to the ground in shock. *This was Matthew. He'd done this. That's what he'd been doing last night. It must have been. He'd killed the baby.*

## FORTY SEVEN

JEANIE ALMOST FELL against the reception desk, leaning against it unsteadily as she caught her breath.

The receptionist eyed the woman slumped in front of her disapprovingly. 'Can I help you, Madam?'

'Yes,' Jeanie panted. 'I need to see Victoria Stevens.'

'I'm sorry, Madam. That won't be possible.' The receptionist's eyes had already averted from Jeanie back to her screen.

'It *has* to be!' Jeanie exclaimed, aware her voice was loud and desperate and she fought to regain control and remember who she was supposed to be.

'Madam, this is a *psychiatric* unit.' The receptionist looked pointedly towards the large notice on the wall reading: *'QUIET PLEASE.'*

'I'm sorry, it's just very important that I see my daughter.'

The receptionist smiled sweetly. 'Oh, Mrs Morgan, I didn't realise.'

Jeanie breathed a sigh of relief and moved as if to walk through the double doors. 'I presume Victoria's in the same room as sh…'

'Mrs Morgan, you must be confused. Your daughter was

discharged earlier this morning.'

Jeanie froze. *Discharged? Oh no. Not to Matt?*

Sensing the bewilderment on the older woman's face, the receptionist stood up. 'Are you alright?' *Madness must run in their family*, she thought, eyeing the woman's darting eyes.

'Yes, yes, I'm fine,' Jeanie blathered, realising the woman was scrutinising her. 'I must have misheard what time this was arranged for.'

Visibly placated, the receptionist sat back down. 'You've most likely crossed over during the journey. Mrs Stevens and her sister only left an hour or so ago.'

'Her *sister*?' Jeanie spluttered, unable to help herself.

'Sorry,' the receptionist smiled. 'I meant, her *sister-in-law*, Mrs LeVere.'

Jeanie forced a smile, her throat constricting. *Carmen.* That woman had Tori. Where had she taken her? 'Was Mr Stevens also present?'

The receptionist shook her head. 'No, just Mrs LeVere. She said she was taking Mrs Stevens straight home. She must be so excited to see her son again when sh…'

'Yes, thanks,' Jeanie muttered, quickly spinning on her heels. 'Must dash.'

Jeanie stumbled into the waiting room toilet and locking the door, leant up against the washbasin unit and stared at her reflection in the mirror.

She had to find where Carmen had taken Tori. The sense of badness she'd felt rising off that woman was like a miasma. Something was going to happen and that woman was behind it. There was no other explanation for that feeling otherwise.

Who would know where Carmen was? Where did Matt's parent's live? Was that where she was taking her?

Hunter would know, but he wasn't anywhere to be found. He'd met with someone she could only presume was Carmen last night. Had he fallen for whatever had been said? Had Carmen done something to Hunter and then gone for Tori?

*Sarah*! Sarah would know where Matt's family lived,

surely? She'd get Colin to take her to Sarah's workplace. She couldn't afford to wait until she got home tonight. Not when Tori was in danger.

Suddenly receiving a searing pain to her temples, Jeanie staggered forward against the washbasin. The pain was crushing. And that feeling... It was that feeling again... Stronger than ever. It was so intense it was debilitating.

Gasping for air as the strangulating pain increased, Jeanie focused on the voices from the reception that she could hear through the door. Could she call for help? This pain was getting worse.

Suddenly hearing Victoria Stevens' name, Jeanie remained rigid, her whole being centred on breathing through the overriding pain in her head.

*That voice.* She knew that voice. She'd never forget it. It had been years, but the recollection steamrollered through her as if it were yesterday. The foreboding feeling enveloping her was suffocating. *Concentrate, Jeanie, concentrate.*

She stumbled closer to the door and strained her ears to listen to the conversation going on at the reception desk.

The man's voice she'd just heard was getting louder, more hostile. *Irate.* It ripped through her brain like barbed wire.

'What do you mean, *discharged*?' the voice roared. 'How can that be possible?'

Jeanie pressed closer against the door, nausea overwhelming her. She couldn't hear the receptionist's response – just the man's nasally voice. *That* man's voice...

It couldn't be, could it? The overpowering feeling of danger was so strong it left little room for manoeuvre on finding alternative reasons. It *had* to be him. *Oh God...*

'You're telling me my daughter collected Victoria? She was discharged into Carmen's care?' the voice continued.

*Carmen? That woman?* Carmen was that man's daughter? Jeanie felt cold sweat break across her brow as everything suddenly dropped into place. It wasn't *Carmen* who was the danger. It was her link to that man. That man was Carmen's *father*, which meant that Tori was married to…

Bile rose in Jeanie's throat and her nails raked against the shiny door in an attempt to steady herself. She had to get out of here, but couldn't. She couldn't come face to face with that… that *man*.

'You won't be hearing the last of this!' the voice roared. 'I'll take this further, mark my words. And this Doctor Sterling, who you say deemed it acceptable to release my daughter-in-law to someone's care other than her own husband? His head will be on the chopping block for this! I'll make sure of it!'

Jeanie held her breath as the man's footsteps retreated down the corridor then exhaled slowly with relief. She'd leave it five minutes before leaving. Aside from anything else, she doubted whether her legs would hold her up enough to walk just yet.

She had to find Tori and she had to find Hunter. Tori was married to the son of the man who had raped Leila Cooper. It was him without any shred of doubt and knowing that, it was more imperative now than ever that she got Tori and the baby away from that man.

· · · ·

RICHARD STORMED DOWN the corridor. How dare Carmen take it upon herself to organise Victoria's release. That was why she'd been so eager to leave this morning.

What the hell was she doing? How *dare* she overstep the mark like this, the conceited little cow. Daughter or not, he'd had enough of her games. First of all, this charade of rocking the boat with Luca which would drop him right in it, not to mention embarrassment and talk in their circles about marriage breakdown. Not content with that, she'd caused a stir with Matthew by interfering with his marriage and now she'd taken it upon herself to run off with Victoria.

What was she doing? Poisoning Victoria's mind? Trying to split her and Matthew up again? She'd always been a jealous bitch, trying to get one-upmanship over her brother. Well, she wouldn't be quite so cocky if she realised her own marriage had been orchestrated and that she didn't know her own husband, would she?

Richard jutted out his jaw. He didn't care what Susan said, Carmen had gone too far this time. Much too far. And as for that doctor – he'd personally ensure the man lost his position. Oh yes, he played golf with one of the most influential members of the hospital management board of chair and he'd see fit Doctor-bloody-Sterling, or whoever he was, lost his place.

Richard gnashed his teeth. As if today wasn't bad enough. Now he'd got to track down Victoria as well as tell her what had happened to her baby. And where was she? Running around somewhere with his bloody conniving daughter.

Carmen *must* have been influential in this. Richard fumed, betting his life that his daughter knew all about Victoria's dalliance with that bloody Reaper and, God forbid, may even know Matthew wasn't the father of the kid. Well, he'd washed his hands of her now. That was it. She was out of his life and out of his bloody will.

Richard stopped suddenly in the corridor. He wasn't having this. Wasn't having it at all. He'd demand to see one of the hospital managers immediately. He would set an official complaint in motion right this very minute.

Turning on his heels he spun around, rapidly making his way back the way he'd came. He'd start with that slapped-face receptionist. She'd been as helpful as a manhole cover, but she could damn well find *her* manager for him to discuss this with in the first instance, couldn't she?

Rounding the corner, Richard strode along the shiny tiles, his shoes making a teeth-curling squeaking noise each time they touched the floor and scowled as he stomped past piles of rubbish stacked up against the wall. This place was a goddamn dump. Why didn't they get extra staff to get rid of this mess? All they had to do was to push it down the chute, but instead, no one was bothered. They just left it piled up until someone finally made the effort to get round to it. That was something else he'd complain about whilst he was at it. Health and safety and basic lack of hygiene. *There could be anything in those bags for Christ's sake. And this was a bloody hospital!*

Now, where was the damn psychiatric unit again? It was around here somewhere, but the place was like a blasted rabbit warren.

Turning down another corridor, Richard eyed a woman further along who, as he'd rounded the corner, froze like a statue, staring at him. Clearly someone with a sandwich short of a picnic who'd wandered off from that unit, he didn't doubt.

Irritated, he continued. Why did they bother having so-called 'secure units' in these places if they let the nutters come and go as they pleased willy-nilly?

Glancing at the woman again, he faltered. *No. It couldn't be.* It had been a bloody long time, but those eyes! *Those green eyes...* He'd seen them before. They were so bright green they weren't something easily forgotten or seen very often.

His mind working overtime, Richard scrutinised the woman. Her hair was no longer completely dark and it was fixed in a bun instead of long and loose, but those eyes... Those *gypsy* eyes...

*Oh shit! This woman... It was that woman... Leila Cooper's friend... He was sure of it. How on earth...?*

Why was she here? Was she something to do with the Reapers and whoever was trying to keep tabs on him or locate him? Did she know about... Did she know what he'd...

She was Leila's best friend. He'd seen them together many times. All the times he'd watched Leila on the quiet as she'd gone about her business or when she'd been with Jack. They'd never seen him of course. This woman... He thought he'd only officially met her a couple of times, but he'd seen her. She'd always been around somewhere.

Was she there that day? That day when... No. She hadn't, but why was she here now? This was too much of a coincidence, surely? Was she here to ruin everything? To ruin his life after all this time?

*A gypsy's word over a bank manager? No, it was*

*laughable.*

*Or was it?*

Beads of sweat formed and trickled down Richard's collar. He glanced behind him before continuing towards the woman still stationary against the wall. Maybe she hadn't recognised him? It had been years. Could he risk it and walk past? Pretend this hadn't happened?

'Stay away from me!' Jeanie hissed as Richard approached. It *was* him. Even though he'd put on lots of weight and lost most of his hair, she'd recognise his horrible, evil eyes anywhere, even without hearing his nasally voice. He'd radiated badness then and still did. His evil came from within - running through his veins like poison.

Watching him closely, Jeanie stiffened, the crushing sense in her brain paralysing her both with fear and the weight of the oppressive feeling. 'I *said*, stay away from me!' she cried.

Richard smiled. It was more of a sneer. No doubt about it then. He was right. It *was* her and furthermore, she *had* recognised him after, what, how many years? He couldn't have lost his looks as much as Susan always liked to tease him about. However, it didn't give him many options on how to deal with this unexpected development.

'Do I know you?' Richard asked.

'Don't give me that!' Jeanie spat. 'I know who you are and what you did!'

Richard laughed, attempting to make light of the bizarre situation. He'd play it this way first. 'What are you talking about, Madam? Do you have a crystal ball or something?' he joked.

Jeanie's eyes narrowed, overpowering hatred for the man who had ruined her friend's life flooding her. The man who had been the cause of Leila's demise. The man who had also, by proxy, ruined Ashley's life with the Reapers' damn need for revenge. On top of that, the domino effect of all the other lives ruined after that.

And Tori? Tori was married to this beast's son. Hardly

surprising he was such an awful person if he had this monster's blood powering him.

Richard smiled again. 'What do you believe I'm alleged to have done, may I ask? Would you like me to help you back to the unit? It's just down that way.' He pointed down the corridor. 'I presume that's where you've come from?'

'I'm not mad, you piece of filth!' Jeanie yelled and before she could stop herself, flew at him, her nails raking wildly for his eyes. 'You raped my friend! Remember Leila, do you? Remember what you did, you bastard?' she screamed. 'You're evil!'

Richard jolted back in shock, narrowly avoiding having his eyes gouged out. He hadn't expected that, but this woman unexpectedly launching at him had proved one thing; she knew everything and that could not be allowed.

Furthermore, judging by what she'd just done she wasn't likely to keep quiet about it either. This had to be stopped. 'Shut up!' he growled, roughly clamping his hand over Jeanie's mouth and pulling her towards him.

Jeanie flailed, her eyes wide in a combination of fear and rage. She writhed and twisted in Richard's arms like a banshee crossed with a caged animal.

Richard struggled to control the woman. Damn, she was a feisty one and he was hardly the fittest or strongest out there these days. He glanced around again. There was no other way around this. Not one enabling him to come out of this acceptably anyway. No, he had no choice. Besides, it would hardly weigh on his conscience, based on what he'd already done today.

Richard quickly placed one hand around Jeanie's slim neck, whilst the other, firmly grasped the top of her head. With minimal effort he made a rapid movement and heard a snap.

So, it actually worked? He'd read about it many moons ago and it was a lot easier than he'd imagined, too.

Aware of Jeanie's limp body in his arms and that someone could appear along the corridor at any given moment, Richard had no time to waste and rapidly dragged her around the corner towards the rubbish chute.

## FORTY EIGHT

'I JUST DON'T KNOW,' Colin repeated. He turned to Joe sitting at the bar with his head in his hands, looking utterly bewildered and consumed with worry, before turning back to the receiver. 'I waited *ages*, Sarah, I told you. When Jeanie didn't come out, I looked for her. I looked *everywhere*, but there was no trace.'

Sarah eyed the people around the office cutting her furtive glances as they listened to her telephone call. Everyone knew personal calls weren't allowed unless it was an emergency, but this *was* an emergency. *How could Jeanie have disappeared off the face of the earth?*

If Colin had bothered to check before he'd rushed Jeanie back to the hospital on this wild goose chase about Carmen, then she'd have told him there was nothing to worry about. She'd have told him herself, but she'd been late for work and now she very much wished she'd stayed a few minutes longer to explain.

At Tori's request, she'd given Carmen Hunter's whereabouts - she knew they'd planned something and first thing this morning she'd had a call from an excited Tori about Carmen's plan to bring her baby to her.

Carmen had come good and wasn't the enemy by any stretch of the imagination - even if she was silly enough to sleep with Noel.

Tori explained she was with Hunter at a rented house and they were waiting for Carmen. Everything was going to plan. That was until this happened.

Sarah turned her back against the man eyeing her suspiciously from the next desk. 'And you checked the unit?' she asked Colin. 'That's where Jeanie was going, wasn't it?'

'Of *course*!' Colin barked. 'I'm not stupid, Sarah. Like I said, that was the *first* place I looked. The snotty cow on reception said 'Mrs Morgan' had left over half an hour ago after getting confused over her daughter's release time.'

'Did she say anything else?'

'No, just that the woman was agitated. Apparently, Jeanie came out of the toilets muttering something about 'that man, that man',' Colin explained.

Sarah was now even more confused. 'What man?'

'No idea. There was no man in sight. The receptionist gave me the impression she thought Jeanie a bit dolally.'

'Then where the hell is she?' Sarah cried.

'I just don't know.'

'How's Joe?'

'Worried, but he's here with me.'

Sarah frowned. She'd have to tell Hunter. He'd be gutted and could do without anything else on his plate but what else could she do?

'Colin? I'm coming back,' she said, knowing she'd have to help sort this mess out.

'But what about work? You can't just leave. You'll ge…'

'Stuff that. This is more important. I'll be back as soon as I can. Stay with Joe at the pub in case Jeanie returns and I'll go to Hunter's and let him know what's happened.'

Replacing the receiver, Sarah grabbed her handbag and stood up. She turned to the man blatantly eavesdropping her conversation. 'I need to go. It's an emergency.' Without waiting for a response, she left the office and quickly made her way to the car.

. . . .

SITTING IN THE ARMCHAIR, Tori ignored Hunter's thick fingers gently caressing her hand whilst she gazed out of the window, waiting with ill-concealed impatience for Carmen to return with Andrew. *Andrew – her beautiful boy.*

Tori knew Hunter wanted to talk. He wanted to resolve all of what had gone on, but now wasn't the time.

Once Carmen had left and after an initial awkward period between them, he'd begun explaining how he couldn't get retribution for her father now he'd discovered the real culprit had died six months ago.

Tori had stopped him. She didn't want to discuss it. It hardly mattered now. Jeanie had already told her how he'd been hunting the man down and how important it was for him to get her the truth. She believed it, but getting her head around everything wasn't something that could be sorted out overnight. She didn't know how she felt about anything. Not really. The only thing she could think about was Andrew.

Nothing would change the man she loved had wrongly killed her father, but all she cared about at this present moment in time was getting their baby back. She'd eventually somehow find the strength to get past the rest of this once she'd got Andrew back, safe and sound. She had no idea how, but she would. She loved Hunter. She'd loved him from the beginning and once she was free from Matt and they had their child, they could make a fresh start.

A film of sweat broke across Tori's brow. What if Carmen couldn't get to Andrew first? If she couldn't, then it would take years of legal wrangling.

Where was she? How long would it take? She'd been gone *ages* and every minute felt like a century. Despite not wanting to, Tori found herself glancing at the clock on the mantlepiece yet again.

When a car came into view at the corner of the road, Tori tensed, then slumped defeatedly. It wasn't Carmen.

She had no idea how things would pan out once Matt realised she'd got Andrew and that Carmen had organised it, nor what Richard and Susan would do for her walking out on their beloved son. As for her mother – well, God knows what she'd say about it all, but Tori didn't care anymore.

She'd do whatever she had to do to sever herself from that family and had come too far to worry about repercussions.

'Tori,' Hunter said, his voice low. 'It will be ok.' He could see the worry etched over her face like a neon sign. He felt the same, but was trying not to let it show and keep his mind from running away from him. He would prefer to do things the way he knew how and would quite happily steam into the Stevens' house, remove anyone in his way and then taken his son, but for Tori's sake he'd forced himself to do it the 'right' way. Not that Carmen snatching the child was particularly the right way, but it was more palatable where the law was concerned that what he'd got in mind.

Suddenly feeling Tori's hand grip his, Hunter glanced up. A car had pulled up outside. It wasn't Carmen. He squinted against the sun. *It was Sarah.*

Getting to his feet, he rushed to the door, opening it as Sarah reached it. 'Sarah? What are you doing he…'

'Jeanie's missing!' Sarah panted, her face flushed with exertion.

Hunter's rugged face creased into a frown. 'Missing from where? Wh…'

'She got it into her head that Carmen couldn't be trusted and went to the hospital to warn Tori, but she'd already gone. Colin waited for ages and searched for her, but there's no sign.'

Tori appeared at Hunter's side. Her fingers clutched at his sleeve as Sarah explained further. Her mind worked overtime as she thought of plausible explanations why Jeanie would disappear and her heart sank hearing that she'd rushed there under the belief that Carmen was up to no good.

A rush of fear ran though her. Jeanie had sixth sense, didn't she? Hadn't Hunter said that many times? If she'd believed Carmen to be dangerous, then what if she were right?

Sensing Tori's panic, Hunter looked into her eyes. 'Baby, Carmen's *helping* us, you know that. Jeanie's wrong on this one.'

'I agree,' Sarah added. 'Carmen's genuine. I don't know why Jeanie thought otherwise, but she misread this one.'

'So where's Carmen then?' Tori cried, tears forming.

'She'll be here,' Hunter soothed. 'Listen, she got you out, didn't she? If she was setting us up, she'd have taken you back to Matt. Think about it.' He brushed a strand of Tori's hair off her face. 'As much as it surprised me, the woman is on the level. I could see the contempt in her face for Matt and her father. Besides, we don't have any choice but to trust her. She's the only chance we have of getting Andrew.'

Tori nodded. Carmen had also helped her to get away from Matt in the first place. Something she wouldn't have done if she wasn't on the level.

'Don't forget, Carmen will get untold grief from her family when they find out she got you released from the hospital. She wouldn't do that if she was on their side,' Sarah rationalised. *It was true*. Carmen had stuck her neck out for Tori. The only fly in the ointment was her association with Noel.

Sarah frowned, wondering how Tori and Hunter would feel about that. She'd have to tell them, but not whilst everything else was in such a state of upheaval. She didn't want Tori skittering off into even more of a blind panic.

'I would have told Jeanie your plans earlier, but she was fast asleep when I left this morning,' Sarah continued. 'I'm sorry. I had no idea she'd go to the hospital.'

'Oh, Sarah!' Tori exclaimed. 'You'll get sacked for leaving halfway through the day.'

Sarah flapped her hand. 'This is way more important. That bald twat can say what he likes!'

Tori managed a weak smile, but it wasn't funny. She'd

caused so many problems. If only she'd left Matt in the first place, then *none* of this would have happened. If it wasn't for her, Sarah wouldn't be risking losing her job, Carmen wouldn't be about to be ostracised from her family and Jeanie – the lady who had been so kind and helpful and who Hunter loved dearly, wouldn't be missing over a mistaken belief to protect her.

'And Jeanie?' Tori whispered, feeling weak with worry. 'What should we do?'

'Maybe she was ill?' Sarah suggested, even though she felt it unlikely. It was even more unlikely that Jeanie had decided she wanted nothing more to do with this mess and made her own way back to St Ives. That woman thought the world of Hunter and she wouldn't disappear without a word.

'She'll be back. She may even be at the White Hart by now,' Hunter said, wrapping his arms tighter around Tori and exchanging a worried glance with Sarah. He had no idea what had happened to Jeanie, but didn't want to voice his concern.

Hunter frowned. Jeanie had got a sense that Carmen was bad news. She only got that when a person *was* bad news, or they were *attached* to someone who was. Had she picked up the vibes from Matt? He kind of understood how this stuff worked. Carmen was related to Matt, so had that set the alarm bells ringing?

Hearing another car pull up, Tori craned her neck towards the window. All that talk about Jeanie had given her a momentary respite from the desperate and never-ending watch for the car containing her son to arrive, but now she was here. *She'd come.* 'It's Carmen!' she yelled, pulling away from Hunter and rushing towards the door.

Hunter reached the door before Tori and yanked it open.

'Has she got him? Has Carmen got Andrew?' Tori cried, desperation in her voice as she tried to push past Hunter to spot a glimpse of her son.

The lack of response from Hunter made Tori's heart beat faster. 'Has she got him? Yes? Please tell me she's got him.'

Hunter felt unable to say anything as Carmen walked up the

path towards him. That her arms were empty was bad enough, but nowhere near as bad as her bright red, puffy eyes, swollen from crying. His heart sank at the rate of knots. Her attempt at getting Andrew had clearly failed.

· · · ·

CARMEN HADN'T WANTED to leave her mother. It was difficult leaving her on her own, consumed with grief. It was also heart-rending watching her gasp and sob against the dining room table, but what choice did she have? She felt bad her mother was left to deal with the doctor on her own, but felt even worse to be personally faced with delivering such hideous news.

The minute she'd learnt the awful truth, her father disappeared - heading to the hospital to break the news to Tori, so she knew she must act fast. Within the hour, he'd discover Tori had gone and that *she'd* organised it.

Although her father wouldn't know where Tori was, she had to reach her first. She *had* to tell Tori and Hunter. She had no idea how she'd break the news and genuinely didn't even know how she'd driven over to the house. It must have been on automatic pilot because she had no recollection of getting here. Her mind had been drowning in possible ways she could look Tori and Hunter in the eyes and tell them that their child was dead.

The truth was there *was* no way she could make what she was about to tell them any less dreadful and only wished that there was.

As Carmen continued up the path and saw Hunter and Tori rush to the door in anticipation, then disappointment seeing her empty arms, her body trembled. They thought she hadn't got Andrew as planned, but it was a lot worse than that. *A hell of a lot worse.*

'Carmen?' Hunter said, his voice raw.

Slipping into the small terrace, Carmen shut the door behind her. She was dreading this.

'Carmen?' Tori cried. 'Where's Andrew? Where's my baby?'

Hunter put his arm lightly around Tori's shoulders, pulling her back. *Had Matt discovered what they'd planned?* He spoke quietly, his voice betraying the slight tremor he didn't want Tori picking up on. *Something was wrong. Very wrong.* 'What happened, Carmen?' he asked hesitantly.

'I-I'm sorry…' Carmen said shakily, the words catching in her throat. 'I'm so, *so* sorry…'

Tori burst out crying with renewed disappointment. 'Can you get him later? Will you still be able to get him tonight? Oh my God, has Matt found out? Is that it?'

'You don't understand…' Carmen interrupted. 'I-I can't… He's… A-Andrew… He's….'

Even though she'd steeled herself not to break down again until after she'd said what she had to say, it was no use. She dissolved into tears. *It was too awful. Too bloody awful…*

'Carmen? What the fuck is going on?' Hunter roared, sensing Sarah behind him, bristling with the same fear he felt loud and clear.

Carmen raised her head, forcing herself to meet Hunter's metal grey eyes. 'H-He's dead… Andrew's dead…'

Hunter stood stock still, unable to process what he'd just heard. He'd seen Carmen's mouth move and heard the words coming from between her lips, but they couldn't be right. *Had Carmen had just said his son was dead?*

Somewhere behind him, Hunter heard Sarah gasp. He increased his grip on Tori. She hadn't reacted at all. She hadn't said a word. *Nothing.*

'H-He's what?' Hunter whispered.

'When my father went in this morning, Andrew wasn't breathing… Hadn't been for some time… I-I got back… he told me and…'

'Not *breathing*?' Hunter's remained motionless, his voice stony and monotonous. *This wasn't happening. Not his son.*

'I-It wasn't…' Carmen spat, her anger surfacing. 'I-I don't

know…'

She wanted to voice her suspicions. She wanted to say that she believed Matt was responsible. All the way over in the car it had gone through her head, but as much as she despised her brother, she struggled to take on board what she suspected. She'd seen him last night, standing there over the cot. Was that when he'd done it? If she'd gone in, rather than leaving him to it, could she have changed anything?

Carmen wanted to tell Tori and Hunter what she'd seen and what she believed, but she couldn't. Not yet. This wasn't to protect Matt. By Christ, she wouldn't protect *anyone* over something so despicable. It was because being told that would make everything worse.

She looked at Hunter, the pain and shock clear on his handsome face. 'I-I'm so sorry… I…'

The room was quiet, save the loud ticking of the clock on the mantlepiece, the ticking amplified by the icy silence of the room.

The silence was only broken by guttural howling that came from Tori's mouth. A guttural howling that didn't stop.

# FORTY NINE

'What do you mean, *leaving*?' Jeremy spluttered, his wine glass frozen in his hand halfway towards his mouth.

Carmen picked up a few more of her things she'd spotted lying around Jeremy's lounge and put them into the large holdall, along with the rest of her possessions. 'It's time I got out of your hair. I've relied on your hospitality for too long as it is.'

It wasn't that at all. She'd enjoyed staying at Jeremy's – apart from Ginny's sour face and the constant thinly veiled nasty comments, but now her family was aware it was her who had instigated Tori's escape and taken her somewhere she wouldn't disclose, everyone involved with her would suffer via association. Jeremy was a decent enough man and her father would have no compunction in causing problems at the bank for him for *daring* to have anything to with her and she didn't want to be responsible for that.

On retrospect she should perhaps be upset over her situation, but she wasn't. She didn't want anything to do with any of her family – with the exception of her mother.

'Carmen, you really don't have to leave,' Jeremy said, his voice taking on a pleading tone. 'You can stay here as long as you like.' It was nice having someone to talk to aside from Ginny, who he never talked *to* – he got talked *at*. Admittedly he hadn't seen as much of Carmen as he'd have liked since she'd become involved with Noel – another thing he'd never understand, but either way, he didn't want her to go.

And then there was Matt. When Carmen had told him the awful news about the baby, he hadn't known what to do. Matt was late in starting his new position at the bank, but that was hardly surprising, given what had happened, but he hadn't been to see him and thought he should have done by now. Matt was his friend, after all.

'Seriously, Carmen,' Jeremy continued. 'Please stay.'

Carmen turned and smiled sadly, 'I can't. I really can't. It would cause too many problems.'

Jeremy frowned. 'What do you mean? Has something else happened? Something I don't know about?'

Carmen shook her head resignedly. 'I've really got to go.' She hadn't told Jeremy anything about Tori, Hunter or the family. Neither had she mentioned about Matt not being the father or that she suspected he'd had a hand in killing the poor child. She wasn't going to either.

She'd have loved to be able to talk to Jeremy about it, but how could she? In fact, she'd talk to *anybody* about it if it would stop the suspicion weighing her down like a lead weight.

'I really should go and see Matt,' Jeremy said. 'I just don't know when the right time is without making things worse. How is he?'

'Taking things one day at a time.' Carmen lied. She didn't know how Matt was - she hadn't seen him, but she *intended* to. She wanted to look him in the eyes and see if guilt was present or not.

'I think I'll go around later.'

'I wouldn't,' Carmen said rapidly. If Jeremy went round, he'd discover at least some of what she was hiding and that would only bring more questions. Ones she didn't want to answer.

'But he'll think that I don't care if I d…'

'Leave it a bit longer.' Carmen forced a smile. 'Right, I'd best be off. Thanks again for letting me stay.'

Jeremy stood up. 'And I can't convince you not to go?'

Carmen shook her head. 'No. It's the right time.'

'Where are you going?'

Carmen hoped she might leave without that question arising. If Jeremy figured she wasn't sure where she was going, then he'd make it impossible.

Short of a hotel, she didn't have many options, but with everything that had happened and with the load on her mind, she didn't want to be on her own. She'd thought about asking Sarah, but that guy – the one with that Jeanie woman who still hadn't turned up, was still there. It only really left one place…

'Carmen,' Jeremy frowned. 'You *do* have somewhere else to go, don't you?'

'Yes, of course!' Carmen laughed. 'You really think I'd go otherwise? I'm moving in with Noel.' *He just doesn't know it yet.*

'*Noel?*' Jeremy spluttered. 'Are you sure about that? Is that what you really want?'

'Yep,' Carmen said, not having any idea of what she really wanted. She edged towards the front door, eager to leave before she was asked any more awkward questions. As she reached for the handle, the door opened.

'Carmen!' Ginny beamed, all fake smile and white teeth. Her eyes dropped to the large holdall in Carmen's hands. 'Oh, you're not leaving us, are you?'

'Yes. Bye both. See you around, I expect,' Carmen said, quickly walking through the door and pulling it closed behind her, but not before she'd registered the look of pure pleasure etched across Ginny's face.

• • • •

'What's the matter with her?' Noel asked Grin, nodding towards Sarah.

Grin shrugged dismissively. He felt sorry for Sarah. The way the White Hart had gone downhill since Hunter's departure had affected a lot of people, but he also knew she knew more than what she told him. She knew where Hunter was, he was sure of it.

Personally, he thought he had a right to know being as he'd been expected to let Noel get on with everything in the exact opposite way of what he agreed with, whilst keeping the rest of the Reapers in the dark over what Noel and Matt had done.

It was getting harder and harder to justify Sarah's explanation of *'it will all make sense in the end'*. Was Hunter coming back or not? That's what he wanted to know.

Noel nudged Grin none too gently in the ribs. 'Did you hear me? I asked what's wrong with Sarah.' No doubt more scheming. Hunter was back and he was constantly on edge waiting for it to kick off when he least expected it. He knew it would happen eventually.

'Something to do with that Tori from what I've gathered,' Grin muttered. He'd heard Sarah sobbing to Colin about it.

'That silly bitch? What's she done now?' Noel sneered.

'Her kid died apparently,' Grin said, glaring at Noel. He'd actually liked Tori. He'd thought her and Hunter had something at one point, but it seemed not. No matter. He didn't want to get involved.

'Really?' Noel said. 'Thought she was having four? What happened to the other three?'

Grin shrugged once more. 'How do I know?'

Noel's eyes narrowed. He was about to pull Grin up on his attitude when Carmen pushed her way through the heavy doors, a large bag in her hand.

Noel stood up as Carmen approached. *She'd be bound to be upset - the kid had been her niece or nephew, hadn't it?* 'Hey babe. What can I get you?' He leant in to kiss her, but she instead slumped into the chair, pulling her heavy bag underneath the table.

Noel glanced at the other Reapers, hoping none of them had

noticed Carmen spurning his greeting. Shrugging his big shoulders as if nothing mattered, he slouched back in his chair and eyed her bag under the table. 'Going somewhere?'

'I need a word.' Carmen pulled a cigarette from her packet and lit it, her fingers trembling. She had no idea what she would do if Noel said no.

Noel frowned. He hoped she wouldn't publicly announce she was choosing her ponce of a husband over him. The unwelcome thought she might be considering returning to that man had crossed his mind because he felt Carmen was tiring of him. She'd been distant and preoccupied for the last couple of weeks and kept disappearing, giving no information where she'd been or who with. It shocked him that this should bother him, but it did. Even more so if she did it in front of this lot.

He was sure all the other Reapers were laughing behind his back over her ability to tame him and at this very moment they were all looking at him expectantly, waiting to see what his take on her demanding a 'private word' would be.

Noel felt something for Carmen. He was unsure what that 'something' was, but he knew one thing – he wanted her to himself. He couldn't say he was comfortable about that and tried to make out the opposite by the comments he made, especially in public, but there was something about this woman that gelled with him and he couldn't explain why.

Noel gave Carmen one of his half-smiles. 'Anything you've got to say, you can say it in front of the boys.' That would remind both her and the Reapers he wasn't going soft and wouldn't have her speak to him like he'd got a thumbprint on his forehead.

Carmen glanced at her bag under the table. 'I'm going to have to move in with you for a bit.

Noel spat his beer out all over himself, accentuating the stunned silence which had descended around the Reapers' table. 'You *what*?'

RICHARD COULDN'T STAND MUCH MORE. Matthew was being ludicrous. Completely and utterly bloody ludicrous. The stupid boy had missed the first week of his new position at the bank.

He chewed his bottom lip. Although it was the best thing to do under the circumstances, at least as far as everyone else was concerned, his son was now going over the top with this grieving business. For God's sake, he didn't have to put it on to *this* extent!

It was bad enough Susan moping around like a bloody inpatient. She'd barely left the bedroom and made no effort whatsoever with her appearance. She hadn't even got dressed for the first two days. It was disgusting.

He'd been on the verge of saying that her tears were wasted because the damn child had nothing to do with them, but he'd thought better of it for several reasons. One of which was that she was behaving in such an erratic manner there was a real possibility that she may feel the need to unburden herself and that would be a disaster. For a start, the embarrassment of it becoming public knowledge that Victoria, the little slut, had given birth to another man's child would do nothing for their social standing. It would also raise a lot of questions and he didn't want ant suspicion raised over involvement from *his* side.

No, it was *far* better letting Susan carry on believing what she did - along with everyone else.

Richard ran his hand across his chin in irritation. Dear God, this pretence of being suitably upset over the tragic loss of their 'grandchild' was wearing thin and he didn't know how long he could keep it up. At least the stiff upper lip persona – all in aid of easing things for his wife and son earnt him kudos in the sympathy stakes. *Apparently.* Not that he'd had the chance to socialise since because it wouldn't be considered fitting, but his patience was waning. He'd now officially retired and had even been forced to miss his own bloody party because of this.

Richard sighed. Still, at least it was done now so there was no reason why the family couldn't move on and get back to normal.

He poured whisky into his tumbler and then did the same for Matthew, sitting immobile in the opposite chair. Richard resisted the urge to punch some sense into him by concentrating on punching his daughter, the treacherous bitch, instead.

His jaw clenched with barely concealed anger. That girl was finished as far as he was concerned. Whatever had possessed her to take Victoria's side over her own brother's? And then to have the goddamn cheek to show up, presuming no one would notice? She'd caused more problems than the blasted IRA!

And as a further insult when he'd demanded Carmen tell him Victoria's whereabouts, she'd completely refused, which underlined *exactly* where her loyalties lay. She knew though. Carmen knew where Victoria was and he'd find out as soon as he could plausibly extract himself from this bloody house.

He'd told his daughter in no uncertain terms that she was now dead to him and wasn't welcome here ever again. Furthermore, she'd better get her arse back to her husband. He didn't want to think about the can of worms it would open if she didn't.

Of course, when Susan learnt of Carmen's dismissal it had upset her even further. She didn't believe their daughter should be banished, whatever she'd done. Well, *he* did. His brain couldn't take any more.

If Victoria thought she wouldn't be returning to Matthew to do her bloody duty, then she'd need to think again. The stupid little bitch *owed* this family. Even more so now with the position she'd put them in.

And then Lillian was stupid enough to go to the press with that bloody story about the quads. He'd *told* her to wait, but she couldn't help herself. Anything for a bit of attention, that woman. Meanwhile, he'd been left fending off awkward questions by reporters.

If all of this combined wasn't stressful enough, there was that lunatic gypsy manifesting out of nowhere at the hospital.

Richard admitted for a while he'd been on tenterhooks that someone had seen something, but he was being paranoid. No one had seen a thing and he knew full well the chute led straight to the incinerator, so she'd be long gone by now. A pile of ashes, along with all the other offloaded hospital waste.

• • • •

CARMEN STARED IN DISBELIEF at the newspaper Sarah handed her. Some time ago when Tori had previously mentioned what her mother planned with the quads story, she was as disgusted as anyone about the sickening idea, but no one actually realised the story would turn out closer to the truth than it ever should have been. And no one was more disgusted with Lillian for going ahead with it now than Carmen.

Carmen's brow furrowed. She wondered how much of a hand her father had had in it. Not that she'd seen him since last week. She'd expected once it was discovered she'd been instrumental in removing Tori from the hospital then she'd no longer be welcome, but it hadn't stopped her from wanting to see her mother. She was distraught with grief the last time she'd seen her and Carmen was worried.

It wasn't particularly easy at Noel's either. Carmen frowned. She knew she'd dumped the living situation on him. She'd seen his expression, but she hadn't had a lot of choice under the circumstances.

Personally, she didn't understand why there was an unspoken 'reputation' to be maintained in front of the Reapers. Lots of the others lived with women, so what was the big deal if Noel lived with her?

Carmen had seen the shock plastered across the other Reapers' faces when Noel nodded to her request and picked up her bag. Well, it hadn't been much of a request – she'd *told* him that she was moving in, but she hadn't time to mess about.

Noel clearly hadn't lived with a woman before – that much was obvious, but he more than made up for his shortfall in politeness and tidiness, with his ability between the sheets. The downside was he'd become rather demanding in his questioning - asking where she'd been going and who with. If she was frank, it got on her nerves. After Luca she wouldn't kowtow to a man again.

The problem was, regardless of how it had started out between her and Noel, she liked him. *Really* liked him, but sometimes she saw things behind his eyes which she couldn't put her finger on. Coupled with what everyone said about him she wondered if she'd made a horrible mistake by allowing herself to develop feelings for him. But he'd always been decent to *her* and regardless of what anyone said, he lit her fire and she sure as hell needed that after the lack of passion in her marriage.

Carmen sighed. She couldn't concentrate on that right now. Matt was first and foremost in her mind even though she didn't want him to be. She couldn't rest until she knew if he'd done something to contribute or cause Andrew's death, but how could she get inside his head when she wasn't allowed within thirty yards of the house. Unless she could think of something good, she'd have to wait until Matt moved to his new house and that might be ages yet. She couldn't wait that long.

'Unbelievable, isn't it?' Sarah jolted Carmen from her

thoughts. 'How could the old bitch do this? How unfeeling *is* she?' she ranted as Carmen glanced back down at the newspaper article. 'We'll have to hope Tori and Hunter haven't seen it before one of us breaks it to them.'

Carmen nodded absently. She hoped so too. They'd got enough to deal with without this extra twist of the knife.

Sarah studied Carmen. The woman looked like she'd got the weight of the world on her shoulders. She hoped Noel was behaving himself. She was surprised Noel had allowed it, knowing what she knew about his attitude to commitment. Even so, she'd have much preferred Carmen to be staying at the White Hart, but they didn't have anywhere to put her. She could hardly share the sofa with Joe and he couldn't go anywhere – not with Jeanie still missing. What else could he do, the poor man? Apart from cling on to the vague hope that she'd show up, confused and suffering with amnesia. He'd religiously called all the hospitals within a fifty mile radius with no luck and the rest of the time he scoured through newspapers looking for a lead – even one that he least wanted, but that had drawn a blank so far too.

He'd even reported Jeanie missing to the police, but being as Jeanie was a grown woman and there was no hint of foul play, it had taken a backburner as far as any investigation was concerned. At least until something dictated otherwise.

Joe could have given the police the surrounding details if he'd known enough, but thankfully he didn't. That was a relief, but Joe wouldn't want to put any more angst and pressure on Hunter and Tori after what they'd been through. Besides, the police being informed of everyone's dirty laundry wouldn't make Jeanie return, would it?

Sarah sighed. *What a bloody mess.* 'You haven't mentioned any of this to Noel, have you?' she asked Carmen. 'I mean, about Hunter being the father of the baby?'

Carmen shook her head. 'No, of course not.' Admittedly, various people had mentioned the hatred between Hunter and Noel and she figured there was a lot more to that story, but no one had embellished further about the supposed bad blood - not even Sarah, so she hadn't pressed for it. In all truthfulness, she didn't want to know. She wasn't sure how much more she could deal with.

Sarah pushed a freshly topped up glass of wine towards Carmen. 'I'm sorry, I didn't mean to make you feel like you'd gone back on your word. It's just… well, this hasn't been easy on you either, has it?' Despite what she thought about Carmen's family, they were still her *family*.

Carmen stared dully at the glass. *It wasn't that. It was Matt.* Her nagging suspicions were steadily gaining pace. Being unable to voice her concerns was burning a hole in her brain. It was no good. She'd have to go and see him. She didn't want to, but she had to. She needed to see his face and see if she was right.

And if she was, then God help him.

## FIFTY ONE

MATT KNEW HIS father was irritated. He could feel him staring, but it made no difference because he was unable to stop everything replaying in his head.

That day the first lorry load was safely offloaded into his new house was when his father had unexpectedly arrived and Matt knew something was wrong the minute he'd clapped eyes on him.

At first he'd been unable to believe it, hearing that Carmen, his own *sister*, had swung Tori's release and taken her 'somewhere' – of which no one had a clue, but it was when his father continued with, *'Now the kid's dead, that particular bargaining chip to help get Victoria back has gone, but at least we've got one less thing to deal with...'*, that he'd been shocked. Like *really* shocked.

Only the night before he'd spent hours in the baby's room – staring at the child with a mixture of both resentment and hurt. He hadn't expected not being the father to bother him so much.

Ok, so he'd be lying if he hadn't thought about something unfortunate befalling the kid to rid him of living with the insult of the whole fatherhood thing for the rest of time, but he couldn't quite believe that it had actually happened.

Matt took the tumbler his father pushed over his study desk and gulped at it greedily.

The trouble now was his escalating resentment. The issue with the kid being out of the way was one thing, but his rage was at an all-time high where everything else was concerned. It had gradually gained traction, reaching a level where it was increasingly difficult to function. How *dare* they do this to him.

Tori had left him. *She'd fucking left him.* After everything he'd told her, she'd actually done it and chosen to be with that ape. And Carmen had arranged it.

Matt raked his hand through his floppy blond fringe, shaking with fury.

Richard slammed his fist on the table. 'For God's sake, Matthew! Enough is enough!' He stabbed his letter opener into a notebook. 'Channel your anger into putting this mess with Victoria right! I know sooner rather than later you'll make sure she returns where she belongs,' he barked. 'Sympathy is high for you at the moment, so it'll go down a treat at the bank. Nice timing, even if I do say so myself, but you need to get yourself out there. I trust your ability to sort this.'

Matt nodded. It *was* exceptionally good timing and would put him in good stead with laying down the law at work, but how could he get Tori back without everyone discovering what she'd done? He couldn't spend weeks or, God forbid, *months*, fending off questions about his wife's absence. It wouldn't take long for the hideous toe-curling truth to come out and there was *no way* he was having that. There had to be a better way. *An easier way.*

His father was right, but how should he play it? His behaviour was seen as being upset over the child, so maybe use that? Perhaps if he convinced Tori how 'sorry' he was for everything he'd done to upset her, then she'd return?

Matt scowled. He'd be damned if he'd let her make his life a bloody laughing stock. If he could convince Carmen he was genuine, then *she'd* talk Tori into it. After all, judging by everything else, his sister's opinion was clearly what his stupid wife went by.

'Where's Carmen?' Matt asked, his teeth jarring purely from speaking her name.

'Carmen's ostracised from this family,' Richard snapped. 'Of course, it goes without saying that you'll be receiving her portion of the estate as well as your own. She stepped over the line and will be be running back to Luca, if she hasn't already.'

Matt smiled to himself. *Yeah, Luca...* That surprise was just around the corner for his bitch of a sister and that fucking ape, Hunter. Two birds with one stone and all that. He couldn't wait. However, he needed Carmen to do this one last thing for him before her world imploded.

'Luca won't want her,' he laughed. 'Not now he knows.'

Richard stopped fiddling with the letter opener and stared at his son. 'Knows what?'

'Carmen stuck her nose in long before all of this,' he spat. 'She found out what we'd done with Tori's contraception and had me over a bloody barrel, so I had to do things her way for a while.'

Richard stared at his son suspiciously. *Matthew hadn't mentioned anything about this before.* The creeping sense he wouldn't like whatever he was about to hear increased.

Matt grinned. 'I got my own back and called him. Luca, I mean. I called Luca and told him his wife's sleeping with someone else.'

Richard froze. 'You told him *what*? When?' *Was his son insane?*

'The other week, just before all of this kicked off,' Matt said, missing the horror sliding across his father's face. 'Yeah, according to Jeremy, Carmen's shagging one of those Reapers. I couldn't believe it myself at first.'

Richard's hair prickled along his neck, along his arms and across his scalp. 'She's been doing *what*?'

'You know Noel, the...

'I know who he is!' Richard screamed, starting to shake. *This couldn't be happening.* 'And you told Luca that?' *Jesus*

*Christ. He was finished. They all were.*

'Not entirely.' A sly smile spread across Matt's face. His father would love this double whammy. 'I told him she's been sleeping with *Hunter*. You know, the one who fathered the child that was supposed to be mine?'

Richard turned a horrible grey colour. 'You stupid bastard!' he yelled. Luca would come over here, if he hadn't already and everything would hit the fan. 'I rid you of the damn kid only to find you've done something like this!'

'What do you mean, *you* rid me of the kid?'

'Someone had to do something,' Richard scoffed. 'Don't pretend you didn't expect it.'

'But you said the situation was rectifiable,' Matt gibbered.

Richard rolled his eyes. 'Don't be absurd! I had to say something. You weren't rational. Ok, it wasn't your kid, but you were making such a bloody big deal about it. You were being pathetic and it was going to get out and become public knowledge.'

Matt stared at his father in horror. 'Y-You mean… you mean you…'

'Business, Matthew, just business. Unpleasant things happen occasionally to ensure everything flows smoothly. You for one know that, but whatever you do, don't tell your bloody mother!'

As his father's words sank in and Matt realised why the baby had really died, he felt like he might be sick. He didn't know whether to be shocked or not. It had certainly made things easier, but his father had killed a child?

Matt watched Richard move toward the study door. 'Where are you going?'

Richard's face was a mask of fury. 'To the club. I need some space.'

'I don't understand? What have I done wrong?'

'Don't worry about it, Matthew. You don't usually. I'll find a way to sort out the latest mess you've caused, like I always do.'

Matt scowled. Christ, it seemed that nothing he did was ever good enough in his father's eyes.

## FIFTY TWO

HUNTER WAS RUNNING out of things to do with himself. He twisted his large hands together mechanically. He was driving himself stir-crazy with the urge to keep moving – even if only slightly, but he had no choice. It was the only thing he could do.

He ran his hand through his unkempt hair, his eyes tracking over to Tori sitting in a catatonic state like she had for the past few days.

He felt utterly powerless and if he was honest, it was scaring him. What could he say or do to make this better?

*That was easy. Nothing.*

There was nothing which would *ever* make this better for either of them, but he wished with every fibre of his being that there was.

He'd been through every emotion possible to man, albeit silently. After the initial shock faded to a level rendering at constant white noise, the first overwhelming feeling was to smash the world up. Smash the whole fucking world up. Smash *someone* up. *Anyone and everything.*

His child – the child from the woman he loved and whom he'd never even *seen*, had gone. And there was no turning back.

Andrew should be with his rightful parents, but he'd never got the chance, had he? They'd have been a little family and would have been happy. Andrew would have wanted for nothing, he'd have made sure of that. It would have been *perfect*.

Hunter clenched his jaw. He hadn't shed a single tear - he hadn't dared. If he'd let that happen, he was terrified it would never stop. Besides, he had to be strong. Tori needed him now more than *ever* and he was damned if he'd let her down again. If he hadn't let her down in the first place, then this wouldn't have happened...

Hunter's anger and raw pain throbbed. If he hadn't left on that crusade he'd have been there as Tori's belly swelled and he'd have been at the birth of his child. *He'd have seen and held his son. Andrew might still be alive if it wasn't for him...*

Hunter grabbed a bottle of beer, ripped the cap off with his teeth and spat it onto the floor.

When Sarah had come round to check on them the other day, she'd said over and over that these things happened sometimes and there was nothing anyone could have done to prevent it. It was *no one's* fault.

But Hunter needed to blame someone and with the lack of anyone else fitting the bill better, it was him. *It didn't bring Andrew back though.*

He tipped the bottle into his mouth, not much caring that it was warm. Nothing mattered - apart from getting Tori through this.

The question was, would they even be able to bury Andrew or had that already been done? Any other time he'd be banging on the Stevens' door demanding to know what was going on and insisting they were part of it, but for once in his life he felt defeated.

Like a little child, Tori went through the motions – robotically doing what he coaxed her to do. She didn't resist when he carried her upstairs and gently lowered her into the bath, or when he washed and dried her, or combed her hair. She didn't resist when he undressed her and put her to bed, sleeping on the floor himself - awake and ready, should she need him. She'd even managed half a slice of toast this morning when he'd insisted she eat *something*.

Hunter swallowed the remains of his beer. He could do with another thirty, but wouldn't. He couldn't get drunk, however much he wanted to. He needed to remain alert.

Sensing movement, Hunter glanced up at the window as Sarah's car pulled up outside. Wearily, he dragged himself to his feet to open the door.

· · · ·

SARAH WAS SUPRPRISED by Hunter's reaction to learning Carmen had moved in with Noel. She'd expected him to freak out that she was involved with his nemesis, let alone had *moved in* with the man, but he'd just shrugged dismissively. She'd thought it might have garnered some sort of reaction. Maybe he was coping with this a lot worse than she'd initially believed?

She was more concerned about Hunter than she had been the other day. He looked like a wild man, his hair knotted and his beard long and scruffy, but Tori was even *more* of a concern. At least Hunter was still part of the human race, whereas Tori was locked inside herself, acting more like a candidate for that psych unit than she ever had when she'd actually been there. She hadn't spoken a word since Carmen had delivered the news.

Sarah knew every breath Hunter took was for Tori, but he needed to grieve too and if Tori didn't improve, or at least *respond* soon, they'd have no choice but to get outside help.

She watched Hunter pulling deeply from his cigarette. 'Carmen's promised she won't say anything to Noel about any of this.'

Hunter shrugged, slowly rolling his large shoulders to release a small amount of pent up tension. 'I don't really give a flying fuck about Noel,' he muttered, a twisted scowl across his face. 'Whatever he's done in the past is of little consequence compared to what's happened.'

'How is she today?' Sarah nodded towards Tori staring sightlessly out of the window, her fingers picking at the hem of her top.

Hunter's shoulders slumped despondently. 'The same. I just don't know what to do…'

Sarah swallowed the urge to cry. *This was awful.* They had degenerated into talking about Tori in front of her like people spoke around dementia or coma patients and she'd always thought that disrespectful. 'And what about you?'

'Me?' Hunter spat. 'What about me?'

'I meant, how are you coping?' Sarah said softly. 'Have you been eating?' Even in the space of a week, Hunter's brawn was not quite as pumped, his cheeks sunken and his eyes hollow. *Dead.*

'I'm not hungry,' he mumbled. 'How's Carmen?'

Sarah frowned. 'Certainly not herself. Not that anything she's going through compares with what you two are. There's also still no sign of Jeanie.'

Hunter's brows furrowed further. There was no way, had she been able, that Jeanie would choose to up sticks and leave - even more so at a time like this. *Never.* Something had happened and he'd find out what, but not now. Not until Tori was alright again.

'Have you been out, Hunter? I mean, to get food or have you se…'

'I haven't dared leave. We've still got some food left that you brought the other day.' Hunter studied Sarah. 'Why?'

Sarah wasn't sure whether to mention it. She'd initially thought it best not to, but it was only right to warn them. It was only a matter of time before they saw it themselves and that would be worse. 'The paper… Lillian went to press about the… about the quads.'

Hunter's face twisted into a ferocious snarl. 'The callous, evil cow! How could she do th…'

'Because she's a fucking sick *bitch*, that's why!'

Hearing Tori speak for the first time in a week Hunter

rushed over and pulled her towards him. 'Babe, we're going to get through this... somehow... I promise.'

Stiffening, Tori pushed away and resumed looking through the window. Hunter glanced anxiously at Sarah who shifted awkwardly in her chair.

'Tori,' Sarah said softly. 'Hunter's right. You *will* get through this. I don't know how, but Andrew... he wouldn't want... Look, you need to eat and talk, not keep it all bottled up.'

Despite Tori's resistance, Hunter took her hand. Did she blame him? He couldn't tell, but refrained from asking. That question would be to make himself feel better, rather than her.

'You need to talk about how you feel,' Sarah continued, desperate to get Tori to release some grief. She wanted it for Hunter too, but getting him to talk about his feelings was equivalent to getting blood out of a stone – it always had been.

'How do you *think* I feel?' Tori spat, her eyes bright.

Sarah bit her lip. That was the point. She didn't know. She'd never been through something like this and could only imagine how it would feel. Was there *anything* she could say? Anything at all?

'I don't, I know that. I...' Sarah floundered. She didn't want anything she said to sound like she was trivialising the situation. That was the furthest thing from her mind. She didn't think there could possibly be anything worse than losing a child.

She glanced at Hunter, but his eyes were fixed on a point somewhere far away. 'I don't know what to do. I love you both and want to help, but I don't know how,' Sarah continued. 'All I know is that there's been stuff in the news about this over the last few years, you know... when babies... when there's no explanation why they...'

God, she didn't even want to have to utter the word 'die' in conjunction with a child. In a decent world those two words wouldn't co-exist.

'What happened to Andrew wasn't anything like that!' Tori barked.

Sarah blinked. Carmen had said when Andrew was found he hadn't been breathing for some time and the doctor had said there was no explanation. 'But the doctor confir…'

'The doctor might have *said* that…'

Hunter broke from his sightless gazing and glanced at Sarah. *Was Tori really losing it this time?* 'Tori, you know wh…'

'Don't you see?' Tori shouted. 'This is *him*. Matt!'

'What?' Sarah spluttered. *That wanker was a lot of things, but killing a baby?*

Tori looked between Hunter and Sarah, her eyes wild. 'He must have worked out that Andrew wasn't his… It was *him* who did this, it has to be!'

Hunter paled. That thought hadn't even occurred to him. Jeanie had said Tori and the baby were in danger from 'that man'. *Holy fuck.* His palms felt hot and clammy. *Had Matt Stevens killed his son?*

Sarah watched Hunter's face change from ghostly pale to livid with unbridled rage. 'Now, wait a minute. We can't be sure th…'

'It's too much of a coincidence. No one else had the incentive to do this, but *he* did!' Tori cried. 'Matt wanted to repay me for everything.'

Sarah looked at Tori and then back to Hunter. If there was any truth in this then it made everything a thousand times worse - if that was possible.

Tori stood up, her face contorted with a combination of rage and despair. 'I think Matt has killed our baby, Hunter.'

Sarah clocked the expression on Hunter's face and knew she had to do something to bring this down. 'Whatever happens, we can't do anything about this just now,' she said, asserting authority she didn't feel she had the right to voice. 'We need to discuss it *properly* first.'

## FIFTY THREE

'YOU KNOW THAT your father will be furious if he finds out I'm here,' Susan said, sitting in the passenger seat of Carmen's car, her handbag perched on her lap uncomfortably.

'Don't tell him then,' Carmen said abruptly. She didn't care what her father's opinion was. Not anymore. 'I want to see how *you* are, Mum – not him.'

Susan patted her hair nervously. She'd heard Richard and Matthew's raised voices from the study. She couldn't distinguish what was said, but following that, Matthew disappeared up to his bedroom and Richard stomped out muttering about going to the Conservative Club.

When Carmen called shortly afterwards, she knew it was probably one of the few times she'd get to see her daughter if Richard had anything to do with it, so she'd grasped the opportunity with both hands.

She realised Richard was sick of her moping, but she couldn't help it. Everything seemed surreal. Two weeks ago her son was happily married – or so she'd *thought* – about to start the position he'd spent his whole life waiting for. Her first grandchild was soon to be born and Richard was retiring. The only fly in the ointment was the uncertainty of Carmen's marriage, but even that – from what Richard had said, she'd high hopes of the problems blowing over. And then, what seemed literally overnight, her entire world was reduced to a pile of rubble.

Susan blinked back the burning tears. Now she didn't know her right side from her left and was so shell-shocked with the turn of events and the dreadful – oh, that dreadful thing concerning that darling baby.

Carmen watched her mother's hands twist in her lap, the pink nail varnish chipped and her usually perfectly coiffured hair messily pinned, clearly not having been styled or washed in days.

'What does Jeremy think about everything you've done? He's Matthew's his best friend. I presume you're still living there? That's not right either, Carmen. A married woman living like a… like a *student*!' Susan cried. She hated that Carmen refused to discuss what had happened with Luca and when, or even *if* it would resolve. And she hated even more that Richard had banished her from the family. What Carmen had done to Matthew was wrong, but she was their *daughter*.

Carmen gently laid her hand over her mother's, dismayed to feel her flinch. 'I didn't come to talk about myself, Mum. I came to see *you*. I'm worried about you.' Now was not the time to slip into the conversation that she was living in sin with one of the bikers from the motorbike club that everyone feared so much.

Susan turned and looked at Carmen. 'How exactly do you *think* I am?'

Carmen smiled sadly. 'I understand.'

Susan's eyes narrowed. 'No, you *don't*! What on earth were you thinking of?' she spat, struggling to reconcile Carmen's actions.

Carmen sat back in the seat. 'What do you mean?'

'What do I mean? I mean, *interfering*. Taking Victoria away like that. Why would you do that? Have you any idea how much you've hurt your brother? Or how many problems you've caused?'

Carmen sighed. How could she explain it? She thought her mother saw at least *something* of what went on. Of how unhappy Tori was and how badly Matt treated her. Or could she not see past her rose-tinted glasses where her son was concerned? She wanted to tell her everything - about Matt, Tori *and* Hunter, but her mother was nowhere near the right state of mind.

'I had to do something,' Carmen said quietly.

'Matthew did *everything* for that woman!' Susan snapped.

Carmen shook her head. This wasn't working. 'That's not true, Mum. You're n...'

'Where's Victoria?'

'I can't tell you that,' Carmen said quietly.

Susan sighed. 'You won't, you mean? Why ruin your brother's marriage? Isn't it enough that he's lost his child?' Without warning she burst into tears, the sobs racking her entire body.

Carmen pulled her mother close and gently stroked her wool-like hair. 'Oh Mum...' How would she *ever* tell her she hadn't been a grandmother at all.

'That poor little boy! It's too awful for words...'

'I know Mum, I know.'

'And Matthew... he's in such a state. He won't go to work, won't eat. He won't do *anything*. I've never seen him like this and I don't know what to do. Even though you were the one to squirrel his wife away and cause half of these problems, you have to help. He's your *brother.*'

Carmen frowned. There was no way Matt would be so upset about Tori leaving or the child. It was all for *show*. She knew him too well. A glimmer of unease formed. *Or was his upset down to guilt?*

Her heart sank further. Even though she hated her brother, she didn't want her suspicions over the baby to be correct. She wanted to be wrong about that more than she'd ever wanted anything. Just the thought of him being capable of that made her feel sicker than she thought possible. She had to see him for herself. Had to see his face. If he *did* have something to do with the death of Andrew, then Tori and Hunter deserved to know the truth, but she needed to be sure it *was* the truth before she breathed a word.

'Let me speak to him, Mum,' Carmen said. 'It might help. Tori's lost her child too. Maybe they can make things better?' Tori would never return to Matt, but she'd say what was needed to get in to see her brother.

• • • •

MATT TOOK A SWIG from the whisky bottle he kept in his wardrobe and seethed further. He'd seen with his own eyes his mother getting into his sister's car earlier. Now even *she* was siding with Carmen.

Carmen must have waited until their father had left before taking her chance to call. And what was her plan? To poison their mother's mind with more stuff?

Matt shivered with apprehension. If she'd said anything about him not being the father of the baby, then he'd do Luca's job for him and wring Carmen's bloody neck himself. He didn't want his mother knowing that embarrassing detail. Besides, if she knew, she'd never speak to Tori again and it was imperative things returned to normal as soon as possible. But what happened if Carmen was telling their mother exactly *why* Tori got pregnant in the first place, or why she'd been involved with Hunter?

Matt grasped for his whisky. That couldn't happen either. He needed his mother on side. Carmen may be banished as far as his father was concerned, but clearly not from his mother's perspective. He needed all of this to hurry up and come together.

Reaching across his bedside table, knocking the clock to the floor, he dragged the telephone towards him. Focusing on the numbers in his address book, he punched in Carmen and Luca's home number and after several rings a French voice answered.

'Er, hello,' Matt said. 'Can I speak to Luca?'

'Who is calling?'

'Matt. I'm his brother. No, I mean, brother-in-law,' Matt garbled, thankful that whoever he was speaking to also spoke English.

'I'm sorry, Sir, Mr LeVere is not here.'

'When will he be back?'

There was a pause. 'I do not know, Sir. Mr LeVere did not state where he was going, but did say he may be absent for some time.'

'Thanks,' Matt mumbled, quickly replacing the receiver, a thin smile spreading across his face. That sounded like Luca was on his way. He hoped so. Carmen would dearly pay for what she'd done - as would Hunter, but not until he'd got his delightful sister to work in his favour once more.

With any luck his mother was telling Carmen right this moment how dreadfully upset he was and urging her to talk to him. Matt smiled widely. He hoped so. In fact, he was *counting* on it.

Carmen had to be persuaded that the death of the child made him realise how unfair he'd been. She didn't know he'd worked out he wasn't the father. Oh, no, she'd think him far too stupid for that, but once Tori was back, all he had to do was relax and wait for both Carmen and Hunter to get their comeuppance.

He'd say what had happened had opened his eyes. If he played it well enough, she'd believe him. He just needed a little something extra to make her believe how 'genuinely' contrite he was over his behaviour, but what was that extra something?

There was also another thing he wanted. A bit of an insurance policy, he supposed. He didn't know what his father's issue was regarding Luca, but it was obviously *something*. Not that he liked to admit it, but Matt wasn't sure he entirely trusted his father anymore. If the man could kill a baby to make things easier, then he needed a bit of backup in case his father ever turned on him. Not that he would of course, but having a bargaining chip never hurt. Wasn't that what he'd always been taught?

Opening the drawer of his bedside cabinet, Matt grabbed his notebook and pen and began to write. Quickly scrawling as detailed an account as possible of what his father had earlier admitted, he signed and dated the page. Ripping the note from the pad, he folded it and put it in an envelope. He'd post it in the morning to his solicitor to hold for safekeeping, should he need it in the future.

Feeling a little more in control, Matt leant back against the headboard. Yeah, he'd tell Carmen he wanted to apologise to Tori. He'd promise to be nicer to her from now on and act like a husband should. He'd say anything she wanted to hear so when she saw Tori she'd pass it on and then they could get on with things.

Matt took another swig from his whisky bottle. Even though Tori was now with that moron, when she realised her own husband would treat her better, then she'd see sense. They'd been together a long time and were married, so she wouldn't throw that away.

She'd never be happy with Hunter - he knew her too well. The fact that the thug had killed her father must play on her mind whatever she said. It was obvious she was only with the prick because she was desperate for attention. That loser wouldn't provide for her like he could. She hadn't been brought up to accept the dregs of life and live a hand to mouth existence.

For God's sake, she hadn't even properly seen their new house or what it looked like with all their stuff in it. If Carmen could convince Tori to listen, then he'd talk her round. Maybe they could even try for another baby – properly this time. That would make her happy.

Once she was safely back where she belonged, he'd make her pay for what she'd put him through. This time there would be no one and nowhere to run to. He'd make sure of that.

Hearing a car pull up Matt leapt towards the window, watching as both his mother and Carmen got out. His heart raced. So he was right. Carmen had been guilted into coming to see him. *Bravo, mother!*

His eyes darted around the room. What more could he do to make them believe his life was collapsing around him? Something *really* hardcore and believable.

Matt's eyes lit up. That was it! They'd come up to his room and if they believed he was suicidal then they'd both be on Tori's back. It was simple. *Fantastic!*

Stumbling over to the wardrobe, he rummaged around. He had to be quick, he needed to time this exactly right for when they walked in, otherwise he'd lose his chance.

*Come on, it's in here somewhere*, he thought, frantically and with relief, pulled out a long piece of rope.

After three bad aims, Matt threw the rope over the faux beam spanning the high apex of his ceiling. He'd always hated those stupid false beams that his mother described as 'features', but now he was extremely grateful for them.

Securing the rope tightly, he tugged at it. He had to make sure it looked the part.

Matt realised he didn't have much time when he heard footsteps downstairs and began making a loop with the other end of the rope, forming a noose.

*Shit! Wait! He needed to write a suicide note. Something convincing.*

He glanced up, hearing footsteps on the stairs. *No time to write much.*

Grabbing the notepad, he scrawled a couple of lines and threw it back on the bed before wheeling his desk chair below the rope.

Clambering onto the chair, Matt wobbled as the castors struggled to grip against the polished boards of his bedroom floor. Satisfied he'd steadied himself enough, he quickly poked his fingers in his eyes to make the tears flow on cue.

He looked up at the noose. *Christ, this was high. Would he be able to get his head in this thing? Come on, come on!*

Pushing himself up on tiptoes, Matt finally shoved his head through the noose, uncomfortably aware that his neck was now at a very unnatural angle. He hoped they wouldn't knock and receiving no answer, leave him to it. He didn't want all this palaver to have been for nothing.

That was it – when they knocked, he'd shout, *'Go away'* and sob loudly. That would get them running in for sure. Yes, that's what he'd do.

He couldn't wait to see their faces. They'd be horrified to realise he was so distraught he'd been about to take his own life. After that they'd fall over themselves to make Tori see sense.

Matt almost chuckled to himself over his brilliant idea and shifted his weight to ease the chafing pressure on his neck.

As one of the castors suddenly rolled, Matt could do nothing but yelp as the chair scooted out from under him, leaving him to kick out wildly in panic.

## FIFTY FOUR

RICHARD DIDN'T CARE if Susan didn't like the fact that he'd gone out. He'd had enough and this latest stunt Matthew had pulled was the final straw. However, he'd been pleased at the reaction his presence caused at the Conservative Club. People fell over themselves offering condolences and of course, he worked it well. He'd nodded his thanks for the bountiful sympathy bestowed on him - as well as the drinks.

He glanced around the wood panelled room, ensuring he wore the expected look of silent, but resolute sorrow. He'd only have a couple more drinks - just enough to take the edge off the stress of living in that bloody house of his. After all, he'd got to be careful. He didn't want to risk letting his guard down in public by cracking a smile or looking like he was enjoying himself. He couldn't afford to let his act slip.

He also needed a bit of time to think about what the hell he would do regarding the bombshell Matthew had dropped on him regarding Luca. What was the stupid boy thinking? If he didn't nip this in the bud, then he dreaded to think what could happen.

It stood to reason that understandably, Luca would be back in this country very shortly, if not already, on the search for his errant wife. He gritted his teeth. He could wring Matthew's neck for this, he really could. The boy had no idea what trouble this would cause if it wasn't intercepted.

Richard jutted out his chin. No, as usual *he'd* have to sort it. He wasn't sure how yet, but he'd think of something - he always did. That's why he was so successful. The trouble was, if Luca didn't immediately come looking for Carmen, or worse – for *him*, wanting to know why and how his daughter was allowed to go back on their arrangement, then he hadn't the first clue where to find him.

The only details he knew about Luca's life, apart from the small matter of being involved in a large London gang, were the ones he'd provided himself for this new identity. Richard had, of course, asked for details at the time, but it had been made crystal clear that some things were not up for discussion - that being one of them. The money Richard was handed ensured he'd quickly lost interest in irrelevant details and happily garnered further kudos with the bank for bagging another 'elite' investor. Now he sorely wished he knew *something*.

Still, Richard thought, forcing himself to look on the rather unlikely bright side, it might not have come across as bad as Matthew made out. It shouldn't be too difficult to convince Luca his son was rendered insane with grief and didn't know what he was talking about.

Whatever happened, Richard needed to make sure he was ready for it and whether he wanted to or not, he had to speak to Carmen. He'd let her know what her husband had been told and find out whether any of it was true. *Judging by his daughter's turnaround of late it probably was.*

He scowled with distaste as the unwelcome thought of Carmen parting her legs for a greasy Reaper seeped into his mind.

What was it with the Reapers? First Jack Jacobs, then Tori and now his own bloody daughter! It was like Jacobs had laid a curse, leaving him with a hideous legacy of the Reapers being involved with every single facet of his life as payback.

It was no use, he'd have to see Carmen as soon as possible and find out exactly what the score was. And whatever it was, make sure she was primed to lie to her husband the minute she clapped eyes on him.

At least that was one thing. Carmen now had no choice but to return to Luca. Not unless she wanted the world to know of her infidelity – which of course she wouldn't. What woman would? Not to mention he couldn't risk another one of his offspring being involved with the bloody Reapers.

Richard downed his third whisky, his frayed nerves gradually calming. There was never anything that didn't work itself out. Nothing had ever come of that hoo-haa with Bob Greaves just as he'd expected. He must stop overworrying all of these things.

· · · ·

'HE'S IN THERE, I know he is,' Susan whispered to Carmen as they stood outside Matt's bedroom door, waiting for a response.

Carmen scowled. They'd knocked twice and there was still no reply. Past the point of messing around, she hammered on the door as hard as possible. She didn't need one of his hissy fits. 'Matt! Stop being ridiculous. We need to talk, so let me in! You're upsetting Mum.'

Still receiving no response, Carmen turned to her mother. 'That's it. Let's just go in.'

'We can't do that, dear. It's rude. You don't walk into someone's bedroom - it's private.'

Ignoring her mother, Carmen tried the door, grateful to find it unlocked. Pushing it open, she rushed in. 'Matt, I need to sp...'

Freezing to the spot, she took in the sight of her brother hanging from the ceiling beam, his face bright red, his bulging eyes staring lifelessly from their sockets and his head lolling at a strange angle. 'Oh my God,' Carmen whispered.

'What is it?' Susan followed into the room, letting out an

ear piercing scream as she took in the scene in front of her.

Carmen rushed forward, grabbing Matt's legs to take his weight from the straining rope. She knew it was pointless, but she had to try. She had to do *something*. Sweating with exertion and panic she looked at her mother paralysed with fear in the centre of the room. 'Mum, you need to help me!' she screamed.

Her daughter's desperate voice shook Susan from her trance.

'Take his weight,' Carmen cried, tears rolling her down her face. '*Quickly*! I need to cut the rope.'

Once Carmen was satisfied her mother had successfully taken the strain, she raced to her brother's desk. There had to be something here she could use.

Books and paperwork clattered to the floor as she frantically swiped through Matt's belongings. *There! A Swiss army knife – that would have to do*. Her fingers fumbled as she pulled the blade into place.

'Carmen, I can't hold him much longer… I…'

'You *must*!' Carmen grabbed the chair and pulled it to where her mother crouched pushing against her son's weight. 'I need to cut the rope, I need…' Panting in a combination of panic, fear and adrenalin she clambered on the chair, wobbling as the castors skimmed the floorboards.

Regaining her balance, she avoided looking at Matt's face as she hacked and sawed at the rope. She could however not miss the rope cutting into his neck, the skin around it livid and purple. Involuntarily, her eyes wandered up to his sightless eyes, his tongue protruding from his mouth and nausea flooded her. 'Shit!' she muttered, wobbling again.

Blinking rapidly, Carmen continued hacking at the rope. It was futile – it wouldn't change anything, but she had to get Matt down. She couldn't leave him here, hanging like a piece of meat. He was her brother, her baby brother…

*Come on, come on – nearly there.*

With a final burst of energy, Carmen sawed through the rest of the rope, the one remaining group of threads snapping and

Matt's body fell heavily to the floor on top of Susan.

'Is he alright? Is he alright?' Susan wailed, hope still bright in her eyes.

Carmen jumped from the chair and rolled her brother to one side, hastily checking for a pulse even though she knew there wasn't one. Her eyes slowly met her mother's and she watched the realisation dawn.

'NOOOOO!' Susan shrieked, her hands raising to her mouth.

Carmen placed her arm around her mother's trembling body and gently lifted her to her feet. She led her across to the bed and carefully sat her down. *What should she do*? She'd have to call the ambulance even though Matt was dead. Wasn't that what people did in these circumstances? With shaking fingers, she groped for the phone on the bedside cabinet.

'Carmen?' Susan sobbed, picking up the notepad on the bed. 'Look – he… he left a note…'

Carmen forced herself to look at her brother's writing:

> *'I'm sorry. Tell everyone I'm sorry. I can't live with what I've done.'*

Carmen swallowed, feeling even sicker as her brain processed what was staring at her in black and white. *So few words but they explained everything.*

Blood rushed ferociously in her ears. This was Matt's admission, wasn't it? She'd been right. Matt had killed that baby and his conscience had got the better of him. The note said so, didn't it? Not in as many words, but *she* knew what it meant. *Oh Jesus!*

Susan's sobs grew louder and Carmen felt her heart plummet further. *Her mother would never get over this.*

She placed the notepad back on the bed and took her mother's hand. 'Let's go downstairs,' she said quietly. It wasn't helping anyone remaining here. When they got downstairs she'd call an ambulance and then call her father at the club.

Helping her mother up, Carmen didn't notice the envelope that she'd unknowingly kicked under the bed.

. . . .

'EVENING, RICHARD.'

Richard glanced up as a man sat down in the empty chesterfield armchair next to him, recognising him as one of the many who frequented the Conservative Club on a regular basis. Damned if he could remember his name though, apart from he was one of those people no one took any notice of. One that never had anything interesting to say.

Richard forced a smile. 'Evening, erm…'

'Brian.' The man extended his hand and shook Richard's firmly. 'Just wanted to say how deeply sorry I was to hear… about… well… the dreadful…'

'Yes, yes,' Richard muttered dismissively, quite sick of listening to the same thing. 'Dreadful business.'

'How's your son? And his wife?' Brian continued.

'Oh, you know…' Richard said, beckoning to the bar steward for a refill. He wasn't planning on another one, but what the hell. 'As you would expect under the circumstances.'

He bit back his irritation. The man was now unsure of what to say - the classic awkward silence after condolences. He glanced back towards the bar to see how long it would be before his fresh drink arrived.

'Don't know what the world's coming to. All these terrible things…'

Richard hid the slight roll of his eyes. 'Indeed.'

'And then there was that grisly discovery today. Did you hear about that?' Brian continued.

Richard nodded his thanks to the bar steward as a fresh whisky was deposited on his side table. 'I haven't heard much news lately.'

'No, I don't suppose you have, what with everything you've been dealing with.' Brian smiled kindly. 'I picked up a paper on my way back from work – the late edition of the

Evening News. Dreadful…'

Richard stared at the man, wondering if he would ever get to the point.

'They've found remains - all by accident, I might add. No one would ever have found out about it had the incinerator not broken down. Imagine something like that never being discovered. Awful, just awful…'

A frisson of tension ran up Richard's spine. *Incinerator, did he say?* He sat up stiffly. 'What was that?'

Brian sipped at his brandy. 'Yes, awful business… The hospital incinerator broke down, so they called the engineers…' He paused for effect as if he was telling a group of children a ghost story.

'Yes, and?' Richard snapped, overriding the need to loosen his collar.

'Well, the engineer was trying to find out what had caused the incinerator to stop and found parts… as in *body* parts…' Brian continued, enjoying for once in his life that he'd got a captive audience.

'*Body parts?*' Richard spluttered. *Oh Dear God…* 'Have they… have they…'

Brian raised his eyebrows. 'I mean, what sort of person wou…'

'Who was it? Who did they find?' Richard interrupted. *Jesus Christ. If they'd identified that woman…*

'The paper didn't say. Just body parts. No mention of *whose*. They were only discovered today, so I expect it will take them some time to work it out – that's if they ever do. God, I hope it isn't anyone *we* knew.'

'Why would it be anyone we knew?' Richard barked. This didn't mean anything. They'd never identify someone from a couple of bits. Most of that stupid woman would have already been reduced to ash.

Brian shrugged. 'Well, it *might* be someone we know. Why shouldn't it?'

Richard fidgeted uncomfortably. He wished the man would

shut up. He was hot. *Far* too hot. His neck was burning. He needed to get some fresh air and then get himself home. There was no way he could continue a conversation with this man now – whoever the bloody hell he was.

Why did people always make things worse? He'd only come here to calm himself down and now *this*?

He got to his feet, his legs horribly stiff and like they didn't belong to him. 'I'd best get going. Susan, you know… I should get back.'

Brian nodded. 'Yes of course. Please give my best regards to your wi…'

'Sorry to interrupt, gentlemen.' A bar steward pushing a polished walnut wheeled trolley holding a telephone approached. 'Mr Stevens, Sir. I have a phone call for you.'

Richard swung around. 'For me?'

'It's your daughter, Sir,' the bar steward continued, looking uncomfortable for being the cause of interrupting one the club's most esteemed clients. 'She said it's important.'

Richard's eyes narrowed. *Carmen*? *How did she know he was here?*

His lips pursed together as the reason dawned. The sneaky little bitch. The only person who knew he was coming to the club was Susan, so Carmen must have visited the house the minute he'd left. She knew she was never to step foot in his home again. And as for Susan letting her in? He'd *told* her to have nothing to do with that girl and what had she done the minute his back was turned?

'Sir?' The bar steward handed the receiver to Richard.

Richard snatched the phone from the man's hand, ignoring the quizzical expression on Brian's face. *Nosy bastard.*

He'd speak to Carmen. He needed words with her about this Luca business anyway so it may as well be now. He irritably raised the receiver. 'Yes?'

Brian stared in horror when Richard Steven's face suddenly crumpled and he began howling in anguish.

## FIFTY FIVE

TORI PUT TWO pieces of toast on a plate and scooped the scrambled eggs out of the saucepan. She tried to bypass the thought that in a short space of time she should have been making something like this for her son and walked across to the little kitchen table and placed the plate in front of Hunter.

Everything she did and everything she thought morphed into what she *should* be doing had things been different. But they weren't different and there was nothing she could do about it.

'Are you not having any?' Hunter asked as Tori sat down opposite and picked up her cup of tea.

'No, I'm not hungry.' Tori aimlessly blew on her tea even though it was only lukewarm.

'Tori…'

'Don't worry. I'm not avoiding eating. I'm genuinely not hungry this morning,' Tori said, giving Hunter's hand a little squeeze.

It was true. It seemed unlikely she would ever properly regain her appetite, but at least she'd moved past the phase of not caring whether she starved to death. She was a long way from being ok – that's if she ever would be, but she wasn't in the same place as she'd been two weeks ago. Partly because her focus now, since Carmen had delivered even more unexpected news last week was to keep Hunter on a level pegging.

Tori sipped her tea. Her first reaction to hearing Matt had committed suicide had been relief – much to her own shame. However much she despised the man, she thought she should feel bad that he was dead, but she didn't. Her immediate thought was that she'd driven him to it, but Carmen had made it very clear that it was not anything to do with her and she was right.

Nothing could have prepared Tori for the next bombshell Carmen dropped. She'd also suspected Matt of having something to do with Andrew's death, but worse - the note he'd left gave ultimate proof of his guilt.

*Matt had killed her baby.*

Tori had been angry, devastated, sick. All of those things at the same time. Seething to the point that she'd thought she may even spontaneously combust. Andrew had lost his life because of the mess they'd caused and Matt's need for revenge.

Yes, she'd been inconsolable, but it was because of Hunter that she'd had to put things straight in her head.

Fighting through the desolation, Tori realised there was nothing she could do about what had happened. Nothing at all. Matt was dead and even if he hadn't been, there had been too much pain – too much hurt and she wanted it to stop. *Needed it to stop.*

Her whole life had been forced to revolve around the actions of others' hatred. What had happened to her child was the final straw. Regardless of how desperate she was to go back in time and change things – *so* many things – she couldn't and no amount of reprisals or hatred would alter that.

Out of respect to Andrew, as well as her own sanity, she needed it to end now and stop the cycle, but Hunter wanted revenge. Revenge on Matt's family. Revenge on *everyone.*

He'd been so angry he'd all but thrown Carmen out. *'Why was she protecting that bastard if she suspected him?',* he'd screamed. *'I should have gone straight for Matt when you said about it.'*

Tori's logic broke through like a shining beacon that day. Carmen hadn't wanted to make things worse until she knew for certain whether there was any truth in her suspicions. She understood that. Carmen had done the right thing. There was no doubt Hunter would have killed Matt, but he was too late. Carmen had arrived only a couple of hours after Tori had raised her own suspicions and Matt would have already been dead by the time Hunter got chance to get his hands on him.

And that was the problem now and the cause of her new-found focus – Hunter had been robbed of his revenge. *Again.* And it was not sitting well.

Tori stared at the man she loved, studying the deep creases over his forehead. All of this had aged him about ten years. It probably had done the same to her too, not that she'd bothered looking in the mirror.

Just the thought of what would have happened if he'd caught up with Matt made her feel nauseous and shaky. She'd have lost Hunter too. He'd have been sent to prison for definite and she'd already lost enough. *Far too much.* It would be more than she could bear.

Tori eyed Hunter nervously. 'You meant what you said last night, didn't you?' she asked quietly, almost afraid to hear his answer.

Hunter put his knife and fork down and locked eyes with Tori, but remained silent.

'Please, Hunter, you *promised.* I can't take any more,' Tori said, her voice desperate. 'It won't change anything, you know that. We talked about this…' She grasped his hand, running her fingers across his scarred and calloused knuckles. 'I need the pain and hatred to stop. You said you'd leave it.'

'Yes, I did,' Hunter said slowly. He knew how she felt and what she wanted him to do – or rather what she wanted him *not* to do, but it wouldn't be possible. *Not this time.*

'I've already lost my father and now I've lost my son,' Tori said bitterly. 'I don't want to lose you as well.'

Hunter stiffened and rage crept along his spine like a red line. 'I know.' Yes, he was responsible for killing Tori's father and he'd failed her again by being robbed of taking revenge on the real culprit. Now, yet again, he'd been robbed of what mattered. He'd been robbed of the small consolation – whatever it was worth, of revenging Andrew's death. He'd failed his son too.

'So, you'll leave it? You won't go on some crusade?' Tori pressed. 'There's been enough misery.'

Hunter squeezed Tori's hand as her big blue eyes seared a hole straight into his brain. 'I said so, didn't I?' She was right on that front. There had definitely been enough misery.

He hadn't yet mentioned that he'd seen an article about the gruesome discovery at the hospital. Instinct told him that the body parts belonged to Jeanie. Matt may be dead, but someone was responsible for what had happened to Jeanie. If he couldn't avenge the killing of his child, then he sure as hell could do it something about Jeanie. And he wouldn't be letting that one go.

He'd told Tori a long time ago that he couldn't promise he'd never hurt or kill again if the desperate requirement arose and he'd meant it. But all of this – his child, Jeanie – *everything*, most certainly counted as a desperate requirement.

Hunter smiled at Tori. He'd say whatever she needed to hear if it made her feel better. If it helped her to believe he wouldn't go after anyone, then so be it. He didn't want to make anything worse for her.

Standing up from the table, Hunter walked behind Tori, scooped her hair away and planted a soft kiss on her neck. 'I won't be looking for trouble, ok?'

Tori nodded, but didn't turn around. What he said wasn't the same as saying he *wouldn't* do anything.

• • • •

NOEL FELT LIKE a fish out of water. He wasn't used to this sort of thing. He'd *never* been used to this sort of thing and he didn't particularly want to be either, but Carmen was here. In his place. And whether it had been foisted on him or not, wasn't the point.

Against his will, despite his initial intentions, Carmen had lodged herself in his brain as well as his flat and regardless of whether he was happy about any of it, for once in his life he was unable to do anything.

Noel watched Carmen, her sobs reduced to hiccups as she forced air into her lungs. Wasn't he supposed to do something to make her feel better?

He scowled. How the hell would he know? He'd never felt the urge to be around upset people. The opposite, if anything. In a normal situation, anyone expecting sympathy would be rapidly told to sling their hook, accompanied by a swift slap round the chops, but this was *Carmen*.

Noel ran his hand over his slicked back hair and cleared his throat, sweat forming on his back. Was this what it felt like to have feelings for someone? He wasn't sure. He'd made a promise a long time ago not to allow himself to feel anything, but it seemed he'd failed.

'Have a drink,' he muttered, pushing a bottle of vodka in Carmen's direction. *People died all the time, didn't they? At least in his world they did.*

Without looking up, Carmen shook her head and pushed Noel's hand and the bottle away.

Noel ran his fingers across his stubbly chin. Anyone rebuffing his kindness would earn an ejection by the hair for their ungratefulness, but he wouldn't do that to her. He wanted to make her feel *better*, but didn't know how.

He could hardly pretend to be bothered because that jumped-up prick of a brother of hers had dropped off the twig. It was no secret he didn't like the arrogant shite, so what was he supposed to say? Everything he wanted to utter was laced with sarcasm, so he thought it best to say nothing, but remaining silent was not helping the overall situation.

Noel cleared his throat again, self-consciously reaching for Carmen's hand. 'I know you're upset about your brother,' he mumbled.

'No you don't!' Carmen snapped, then softened sensing Noel biting back his irritation. 'Sorry,' she whispered. She didn't want to take her weird combination of emotions out on him. He was the only thing in her life keeping her sane these past few months. 'I mean, I *am* upset,' she continued. 'But I didn't like him. I'm sad, yet relieved.'

She couldn't believe she'd actually uttered those words out loud. Was she really relieved Matt was dead? Didn't that make her a terrible person?

Noel blinked. 'He was a prick, I'll give you that!'

Carmen tensed. *She* was allowed to say that, but not anyone else. Ripping her hand away from Noel's, she stood up angrily. 'You know nothing about it. You haven't got a clue what's been going on.'

Beginning to lose patience, Noel's eyes narrowed. 'That'll be because you're playing cloak and daggers. Maybe you've got something you want to tell me? I wouldn't hide things if I were you. It's no bones to me whether you're here or not, lady.'

Ok, so he lied. It did bother him, but worse - now he sounded like a jealous dickhead and he didn't appreciate *anyone* having the power to make him act like that.

'And you wonder why no one likes you?' Carmen yelled. If Noel wanted to throw stuff at her, then let him. She wouldn't be jerked around by a man again – the whole lot of them could go to hell.

'People think I'm crazy for being with you and half the time, so do I! You think I haven't heard about your dodgy deals with my brother and running Hunter out of town? Don't you *realise* that no one wants you to be the President? Are you that stupid?'

She'd heard many things and let it all go over her head. It was none of her business, but she might have known Matt would have been involved. Jeremy let slip a while ago about a contract thing they'd all been involved in and it wasn't rocket science to work out that Noel had been at least partly connected with Hunter's disappearance either.

Noel had heard enough. Grabbing the half full bottle of vodka, he launched it against the wall where it splintered into a thousand pieces. 'And what's your interest in Hunter?' he growled. 'How come you seem to know so much about him? Think you're so fucking clever, do you? Calling *me* stupid? You've no idea what he di...'

'He seems decent enough to me,' Carmen shrieked, before belatedly realising she wasn't supposed to mention anything about Hunter to Noel. *Damn.*

Noel's eyes burnt black holes of fury and a vein throbbed relentlessly in his temple. 'You've been meeting with *Hunter*?' he roared. He knew Sarah was lying when he'd collared her about it and Carmen was part of it too?

He lurched towards Carmen, his eyes wild. 'Have you been sleeping with him, is that it?'

Carmen glared at Noel. 'Don't you dare get in my face, Noel. I'm not scared of you.'

Noel stopped in his tracks, his jaw clenching. How did this woman have this effect on him? No woman ever told him what to do before, so why the hell was he allowing this?

'I don't know the ins and outs of what went on between you two and I don't particularly want to,' Carmen spat. 'And no, I'm *not* sleeping with Hunter. I love *you* and I'm just trying to help wi...'

Carmen broke off her ranting in shock. She'd heard what had just come out of her mouth. Had she really just told Noel she loved him? Did she? Feeling shaky, she realised she probably did.

Noel regarded Carmen strangely. She hadn't meant to divulge that information. So, she loved him, did she? If a woman tried that it caused nothing but irritation - merely a way of getting them to do things he wanted, but with Carmen it was... *different.*

'I'm trying to help Tori, Noel. She's lost her baby, remember?' Carmen said, hoping to gloss over her gross mistake.

'I gather that and I'm guessing that's why your Matt topped himself – because of losing the kids?' Noel asked, forcing himself to calm down. 'But what's that got to do with Hunter?'

'Tori left Matt for Hunter,' Carmen said. She knew she shouldn't be saying anything, but it would all be out in the open soon. It had to be now Matt was dead. It would be impossible for her parents to brush this under the carpet any longer.

Noel grinned. 'So, she's shacked up with Hunter, has she? Where the fuck's he hiding?'

'Oh, give it a rest! Whatever your beef is with him, I don't want to know. Just leave them be, for God's sake!'

'What the fuck for? I've got unfinished business with that man! He'll get to me first otherwise. Don't you get it?' Noel roared. 'If you've got so much of a problem with everything, maybe you coming here was a bad idea. You could stay at the White Hart with your *friend*, Sarah!'

'Jeanie's friend is there at the moment, so there's no room.' Carmen snapped.

'Who the hell is Jeanie?' Noel fumed.

Carmen shrugged. 'Something to do with Hunter from when he was a kid from what Sarah said.'

Noel felt a rush of cold flood over him. *He'd heard his mother's best friend was a woman called Jeanie. Could it be?*

'Matt's guilty,' Carmen said suddenly, interrupting Noel from his frantic thoughts.

Noel narrowed his eyes. 'Guilty? Guilty of *what*? Apart from being a complete tosser who topped himself because his wife left him for a biker and his kids went and died on him? I think I'd probably feel the same if he was *my* father!'

Carmen's anger surged. 'You think this is *funny*, do you?'

Noel looked suitably contrite. She was right. He shouldn't have said that. 'I'm sorry… I…'

'Matt killed that child…' Carmen knew she shouldn't say it, but she had to. She had to get it off her chest. She would explode otherwise. It was all too much.

'What?' Noel raised his eyebrows. *Matt had killed a kid? And it was quads, wasn't it? Everyone had seen the paper.* 'Wait, the *child?*'

'There was only one. There had only ever been one. The quads thing was bullshit.' Carmen flapped her hand. 'Don't ask… Long story…'

'But why kill his own kid? That doesn't make sense.'

'Oh yes it does,' Carmen said, her eyes brimming with tears. 'The baby wasn't his. It was *Hunter's…*'

Noel slumped into his chair. It was like someone had smashed an axe over his head and all the resentment for Hunter flowed from him like someone had slashed his throat.

'Noel?' Carmen watched Noel's eyes narrow into slits. She could see that thing again. The thing that lurked there. The thing she couldn't put her finger on.

Noel waved Carmen's concern away and grasped the bottle of vodka. Angrily unscrewing the lid, he raised it to his mouth and gulped down several mouthfuls. Whatever had happened in the past between him and Hunter was now strangely insignificant. This was out of order. Totally out of order. There were some things that were never done and killing a child was one of them. *That wanker, Matt, had killed Hunter's child.*

Noel felt his nerves burning as his rage soared. Hunter wasn't lying when he'd said he'd been trying to find out who really attacked his mother either.

He ran his hand through his hair. He'd got it all wrong, hadn't he? The man had been trying to sort everything out and now his kid had been murdered?

*It was time he put this right.*

# FIFTY SIX

Hunter remained rigid, the only sign that his veins were filled with blood rather than concrete, was the one visibly pulsing in his neck as he clenched his jaw to keep his concentration focused.

He forced his arm to move to place it reassuringly on the small of Tori's back as she trembled beside him.

Tori grasped Hunter's hand, relieved they had been able to give their son a send-off and it was one thing she was thankful for.

After Matt's death, Carmen found little difficulty in arranging the funeral without opposition from Susan or Richard. She hadn't even informed them it was taking place today. Susan was so incoherent over the loss of her son she wouldn't have taken it in anyway.

Despite everything, Tori felt a little bad – after all, Susan had looked after Andrew and cared for him well, but her need to bury her son with dignity with none of that family, apart from Carmen present, overpowered her guilt over Susan not being invited.

As for her own mother being excluded, Tori felt no guilt whatsoever. No, it was just her, Hunter, Carmen, Colin and

Sarah and of course the vicar.

She brushed away her quickly forming tears and glanced back at Hunter, seeing the steely determination in his eyes as he held his emotions in check. She'd watched him carry their son's coffin and thought her heart would shatter. It still might.

Tori tried to concentrate on what the vicar was saying as his voice echoed around the church. She wasn't taking in what he was saying – all she could focus on was the tiny box placed on the trestle to the side of the pulpit. She tried not to picture her baby who, at this very moment, was lying inside, but it was all she could see in her mind whether she wanted to or not.

If she could choose what she wanted, she'd rip the lid of the coffin off and take Andrew out of there.

Tori closed her eyes in desperation. It was a mistake because Andrew wasn't dead. He was alive and smiling. She'd take him home and everything would be alright. It was only one of those awful dreams…

Aware the voice in the background had stopped and Hunter was squeezing her hand, Tori knew she must open her eyes. She didn't want to because the horror that this wasn't a dream at all would smack her in the face and she didn't want to be faced with the reality. *Her* reality – the one where Andrew was safely back in her arms and very much alive, was where she wanted to remain.

Aware that her tears were running from her face and soaking the front of her blouse, Tori opened her eyes and returned to the reality she didn't want to be part of. She found her hand linking with Sarah's as they moved robotically behind Hunter as he stepped forward to pick up the coffin to take it outside for the burial.

Even though she didn't want to move, her legs propelled her forward like an automaton. She didn't want to go outside to the grave. *It was all too final.*

• • • •

Looking even tinier than usual in the overcast light that this most depressing day had to offer, Hunter made sure Tori was alright. This gloomy weather was more acceptable than it being sunny. Somehow it would feel even worse burying a child on a sunny day. Sunny equalled happiness in most people's minds and today was the polar *opposite* of that. It was misery and dark. That's what today was and that was exactly how he felt.

Clenching his jaw as the tiny white coffin was lowered into the earth, Hunter felt Tori sway as if she were about to pass out. He knew how she felt. He'd thought when he'd carried the tiny coffin into the church for the service that his legs may go on him, but they hadn't. He'd steadily walked to the front of the church with the son that he'd never seen contained in the box in his arms.

Hearing the vicar speaking the final words, Hunter focused on what was being said, rather than the thoughts divebombing around his speeding brain. This was worse than hard. It was horrendous. Burying Georgie, with his unborn child had been bad enough... but *this*... this was something else. *Andrew had been murdered.*

Hunter's teeth gnashed, rage spiking along his back, up to his eyeballs. He knew Tori was watching him and that he'd promised he wouldn't go looking for trouble, but trouble found *him*. He didn't want to make this any harder for her than it already was, so he'd let her believe he'd got his feelings under control. *Which he had, just not in the way she wanted...*

But he couldn't let this go. Not in a million years.

When the service finished, the others walked away from the graveside, leaving Tori and Hunter alone for the last few minutes with their son.

'Goodbye, baby,' Tori whispered, her voice barely audible over the rustling of the trees.

Hunter placed his arm tightly around Tori and held her close. His eyes were as cold as ice and after taking a final look into the deep hole in front of him, he gently led her away from the graveside, holding her steady as she sobbed against his side.

As they walked towards the others, Hunter's eyes wandered

through the graves to a clump of trees opposite and came to rest on a figure.

A figure he would recognise anywhere by his silhouette alone. *Noel…*

When Noel stepped forward from the shadows, Hunter translated the expression on his face like words had been shouted from the rooftops.

Tori froze, clutching Hunter's hand. 'W-What's he doing here?' she cried, panic ripping through her. 'He hasn't come to cause trouble, has he? Not today? Oh please, Hunter, tell me Noel won't cause tr…'

'There'll be no trouble,' Hunter muttered, his eyes not breaking with Noel's. 'Go and wait with the others and leave this to me.'

Looking pleadingly first at Hunter and then at Noel, Tori returned her eyes back to Hunter.

'I mean it, Tori. It's fine,' Hunter said, squeezing her hand. 'Go on, let me deal with this.'

He waited whilst Tori walked in the direction of Sarah, Carmen and Colin waiting in the church car park and it was only when she'd successfully reached them, did he move towards Noel.

As Hunter approached, Noel's eyes conveyed everything that could be said. Stepping forward, he put his hand on Hunter's shoulder.

'I heard what happened,' Noel said, his voice thick with emotion. 'Let me help.'

Hunter knew, reading between the lines as they'd learnt to do over the years they'd all been Reapers, that Noel was saying despite what had happened in the past, he'd come to help him serve revenge.

For once in a very long time, Hunter was glad to see the man who had caused so much trouble. Admittedly, it would take a lot more than a few words in a churchyard to put their history right, that's if it ever could be and he wasn't sure if that was something he even wanted, but the desire for revenge overtook thinking about peripheral issues that could wait.

Hunter stared at Noel, gauging whether the man was on the level, or whether he was using this dreadful time as a below the belt opportunity of getting at him. He didn't see any evidence of that. The resentment Noel had always held seemed to have disappeared.

As if sensing the distrust, Noel stepped back. 'I mean it. I'm here and when you're ready, we'll talk. Whatever you want or need, I'm in. Ok?'

Hunter nodded and after watching Noel retreat back up the path towards the trees, he turned and walked over to join the others in the carpark. This was not the time or the place to sort anything out, but the perverse relief it afforded him, knowing his old second-in-command would help him achieve his revenge was strangely soothing.

Hunter smiled. Noel was just who he needed right now to help him get all of this shit equalled out. He'd get revenge for Tori, for his child, for Jeanie and for himself.

And *nothing* would stop him.

# EPILOGUE

**Charles de Gaulle Airport - Paris**

NEIL SPARKS GLANCED in his Louis Vuitton hand luggage. He couldn't be arsed poncing about checking the luggage in. It would only slow him up and after what he'd been told, he wasn't wasting a *moment* longer in getting his hands on his sly, cheating bitch of a wife. Nor would he dally with getting his hands on that twat of a father of hers. And last but not least, his hands on whoever had been sticking their dick in his missus, but he'd be doing things differently this time around.

Ok, so it had taken him a week or so to get everything in place for his arrival, but everything was ready now.

Neil plastered on the smile he was accustomed to using. Oh, he'd got it down to a fine art – he'd had long enough to practice it, but inside he was fuming. Absolutely bloody *livid*.

He plonked his hand luggage on the scanner. It hardly weighed a thing. Almost not worth bringing. He didn't need much. Everything else he required he'd easily pick up the other end when he turned up in his usual haunt.

He wasn't concerned about returning after all this time. Any problems he'd had had died down a long time ago. The men would be glad to see him again after all these years and he was looking forward to seeing what position things were *really* in. He'd kept up to date with everything from over the water via telephone and messages, but nothing *really* compared with seeing how the land lay with his own eyes. And if any of them hadn't been completely kosher with the truth, then God help them.

He didn't think that was the case. His guys were loyal and straight up. Yes, they'd be glad to see him, but there was a hell of a lot of people that wouldn't. And *those* people wouldn't know what had hit them.

Neil glanced at the man behind the security desk. He could see the envy as his eyes scanned the exquisitely-tailored designer suit he wore. Poor sod. He'd have to work another hundred years before he could afford togs like these and that was just the shirt. Still, that was *his* problem. This guy had made his own choices in life, as had pretty much everyone else on the planet, so there was little point in bleating on about it.

Neil's teeth clenched. Only he was aware of the throbbing vein hidden just under his collar which was a giveaway of his anger. Some people's choices had been more than fucking stupid, which they'd discover to their detriment soon enough once he'd got his feet down on terra firma the other side of the channel.

Nodding at the man who had waved him through the body scanner, Neil casually retrieved his holdall and walked towards the gate. He could have chartered the plane himself should he have wished, but didn't want any undue attention. Not yet, at least. On this occasion he was quite happy to slum it for once, even if it was first class.

Reaching the gate, Neil flashed his bright white smile at the woman.

'Boarding pass and passport, please Sir,' the girl said, colouring slightly at the handsome man standing before her.

Neil passed the girl his documents, making sure his fingers lingered just that *little* bit too long before releasing them. *It never hurt to make a woman feel wanted, did it?*

'Thank you, Mr LeVere,' the girl smiled, handing back the paperwork. 'Have a pleasant flight, Sir.'

'Thank you,' Neil smiled. He'd be having a pleasant flight, alright. And once he landed back in London, he'd no longer have to parade around under the guise of Luca LeVere – which was good. He *hated* the name, *hated* the stupid accept he'd adopted and *hated* the fucking French!

His first port of call after seeing the boys would be visiting his wife, wherever her lying arse was resting. He patted the leather-bound address book in his suit jacket's inside pocket. The name and address of a flea pit dive where she drank with her *boyfriend* was in there.

That ponce, Matthew – the jumped up twat that he was, had given him all the info required. Why, Neil wasn't sure, but whatever bone the spoilt tosser had with his slut of a sister was only of benefit to him, so he wasn't complaining.

Carmen would be his first visit, then on to her boyfriend. Who did Matthew say Carmen had been shagging the last few months? That was it – some prick called Ash Hunter. Ash Hunter, who thought himself a bit of a kingpin biker dude. Ash? What sort of a fucking name was that? Still, it might be quite fitting. After all, it would be what the wanker would be reduced to after he was finished.

Neil smiled as he was ushered to his large reclining seat in first class and nodded his thanks, accepting the proffered flute of champagne.

What was even more amusing was this Ash Hunter was something to do with the *Reapers*.

Neil sipped at the ice-cold champagne, a slight tinge of a sneer on his lips. He hadn't thought he'd hear that name again. *The Reapers*. It had been a long time. A *very* long time, but a name he most certainly had never forgotten.

The stunt the Reapers had pulled over that drug deal all that time ago was what had caused him to have to go into bloody exile. Oh, they'd done him up like a kipper. Killed two of his best fucking men as well and they'd had enough on him to be able to put him away for the rest of time, which he couldn't chance.

Now that was over because the Reapers that knew the score or had been involved were long dead, but from *his* side it certainly wasn't over. He'd got a *huge* fucking score to settle with that bunch of wankers and what was even more ironic, yet perfect in a perverse kind of way, was that unknowingly one of the stupid fucks had bedded his wife.

Time was a virtue and he'd waited a *long* time for his revenge on the Reapers, full stop. After he'd dealt with his own slag-faced wife and then the biker boy, he'd be paying that fat old cunt, Richard, a visit too. The old duffer had been stupid. He hadn't kept to his side of the bargain, had he and now he would pay for that.

They were *all* going to pay.

# THANK YOU!

Thank you for reading *The Family Legacy*. I hope you enjoyed reading it as much as I did writing it!

If so, would you please consider leaving a review on Amazon and/or Goodreads.

Reviews from readers are SOOOO helpful and especially important to us authors and without you we would have nobody to write for!

Thank you once again and hope you enjoy the rest of my books.

*Edie xx*

# MORE FROM THIS SERIES

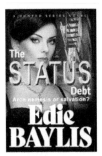

### #1: THE STATUS DEBT

Lillian Morgan would do anything to regain the status she lost by marrying beneath her and to cover the sordid details of her husband's death. This includes blackmail and the hand of marriage of her own daughter.

Tori thought her life couldn't get much worse, but someone is not being honest and secrets have the power to rip everyone to shreds.

Especially when life is built on lies.

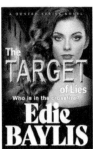

### #3: THE TARGET OF LIES

Neil Sparks has a score to settle. In fact, he has several… His first port of call when returning from France after a five year exile is to catch up with his estranged wife. Secondly, Neil wants to even a score with the people instrumental in his departure and thirdly, he wants an explanation from the man who promised his marriage would be free from hassle. The trouble is, he's not the only one with an agenda…

There are too many people about to become caught in the crossfire and everyone could become a target.

# More From this Author

## RETRIBUTION SERIES:

### #1: AN OLD SCORE

**Three families… One prize…**

Teagan Fraser had no idea what she was getting herself into when she took on an assignment as a live-in carer for Dulcie Adams – a retired dancer from a Soho club. Dulcie has waited forty years for a time that never came and left looking after something important, which Jonah Powell and his firm want back.

A lot can happen in the space of two weeks and Teagan might wish she'd never become involved.

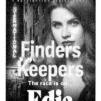

### #2: FINDERS KEEPERS

**The race is on…**

When Saul Powell is released early from prison, it causes mayhem for the family firm. His brother, Jonah, has enough problems trying to keep semblance amidst the chaos, not to mention his fast approaching unwanted marriage.

Teagan Fraser is also facing a dilemma – one which could ruin her life completely. Can anyone come out of this nightmare unscathed?

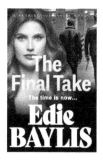

### #3: THE FINAL TAKE

**The time is now…**

Even knowing Ron O'Hara is somewhere in the vicinity, Jonah Powell feels it's time to finally get rid of the diamonds which have haunted his family for decades and caused so much trouble.

However, other problems start to arrive from unexpected and additional sources, some of which Jonah didn't expect.

But what does it all mean? It may be apt to call time on the curse plaguing his family and of those around him, but how can this be achieved while so many other things are at stake?

# MORE FROM THIS AUTHOR

## ALLEGIANCE SERIES:

### #1: TAKEOVER

Samantha Reynold hadn't bargained on unexpectedly needing to step into her father's shoes and take over the family casino business and known nothing about the rules of this glamorous but deadly new world. But she won't let her family down, especially when it looks like they could lose everything to their biggest rivals – the Stoker family.

Eldest son Sebastian hasn't got time to pander to pretty girl Samantha as she plays at being boss. Rumours are swirling around the streets of Birmingham that have the power to rip the Stoker family apart and destroy everything they've built.

### #2: FALLOUT

With the odds stacked against her, Samantha Reynold is determined to prove she's tough enough to be the boss. But when a secret from the past threatens to ruin Sam's reputation, she suddenly feels very alone in this dark new world. There's only one man she can turn to – rival club owner, Sebastian Stoker.

Seb knows first-hand how secrets and lies can tear a family apart. He wants to protect Sam at all costs, but siding with her could threaten his own position as head of the Stoker family and risk accusations of betrayal.
With loyalties divided and two families at war – the fallout could be deadly.

### #3: VENDETTA

Once bitter enemies, Samantha Reynold and Seb Stoker's powerful alliance enables their firms and casinos to go from strength to strength. With the families no longer in opposition, it seems that Sam and Seb are untouchable…

But not everyone is happy with the new power couple of the club world.

Unbeknownst to everyone, someone new wants to see Sam's perfect life ruined. And they will stop at nothing to seek their revenge – even if it means destroying everything - and everyone - in their path.

## DOWNFALL SERIES:

### #1 - UNTIL THE END OF TIME

Dive into Seth and Jane's train wreck of a life, where drugs, alcohol and obsessional love means this downright dangerous pair will do *anything* to ensure nothing gets in their way.

They do bad things. *Very* bad things and their promise to love each until the end of time turns into a war against each other.

A war neither of them can win.

### #2 - ESCAPING THE PAST

Things have changed and Jane has got on with her life.

Well, not *entirely...*

Embroiled in a bitter feud between two rival firms, it is clear that not everyone is who they proclaim to be.

The net is closing in and some things just can't be changed.

### #3 - VENGEFUL PAYBACK

There is something missing. Something *very* important and no one is above suspicion.

Past vendettas are gaining pace and it is vital that whoever is behind this never-ending stream of cleverly engineered payback is discovered before it is too late and everything held dear is ripped apart.

*\*\* This series contains written depictions of graphic violence, sex and strong language. It also contains some themes that may be uncomfortable for certain readers. \*\**

# About The Author

Over the years Edie has worked all over the UK as well as in several other countries and has met a lot of interesting people - several of whom have supplied ideas for some of the characters in her books! She has now settled back in central England with her partner and children, where she is pursuing writing her gritty gangland and urban fiction novels.

Edie is currently signed to Boldwood Books for a 5-book gangland fiction series set in Birmingham. The first three in the *Allegiance* series, *Takeover*, *Fallout* and *Vendetta* have been released and the fourth in the series, *Payback*, is due to be released in January 2023. She is also concurrently writing the *Scarred* series - the first titled, *Mirrors Never Lie*.

Edie's other series are the *Retribution* series, the *Hunted* series and the *Downfall* series - all trilogies.

When she isn't writing, Edie enjoys reading and is a self-confessed book hoarder. She also enjoys crochet and music as well as loving anything quirky or unusual.

Visit www.ediebaylis.co.uk for the latest news, information about new releases, giveaways and to subscribe to her mailing list.

CWA MEMBER

# Connect with Edie

https://fb.me/downfallseries

https://www.goodreads.com/author/show/17153586.Edie_Baylis

https://twitter.com/ediebaylis

https://www.amazon.co.uk/Edie-Baylis/e/B075FQHWCZ/

https://www.bookbub.com/authors/edie-baylis

https://ediebaylis.co.uk/

info@ediebaylis.co.uk

https://www.fantasticfiction.com/b/edie-baylis/

https://www.instagram.com/ediebaylis/

https://www.tiktok.com/@edie747

https://www.pinterest.co.uk/ediebaylis/

# Join Edie's Mailing List

Subscribe to Edie's mailing list for the latest news on her books, special offers, new releases and competitions.

**https://ediebaylis.co.uk/signup.html**

gangland | crime | urban

THRILLER AUTHOR

# ACKNOWLEDGEMENTS

Thanks to the people that kindly read my drafts of *The Family Legacy* – you know who you are and I appreciate your time and feedback.

Printed in Great Britain
by Amazon

27429219R00249

# WITCHBLADE

## REBIRTH
### VOL. 1

*Witchblade* created by:
Marc Silvestri, David Wohl,
Brian Haberlin and Michael Turner

published by
Top Cow Productions, Inc.
Los Angeles

# WITCHBLADE

## REBIRTH VOL. 1

writer: Tim Seeley

penciller: Diego Bernard

inker: Fred Benes with Alisson Rodrigues

colorist: Arif Prianto of IFS

letterer: Troy Peteri

For this edition, cover art by: John Tyler Christopher

Original editions edited by: Filip Sablik

For this edition, book design & layout by: Vincent Kukua

---

**IMAGE COMICS, INC.**

Robert Kirkman - chief operating officer
Erik Larsen - chief financial officer
Todd McFarlane - president
Marc Silvestri - chief executive officer
Jim Valentine - vice-president

Eric Stephenson - publisher
Todd Martinez - sales & licensing coordinator
Jennifer de Guzman - pr & marketing director
Branwyn Bigglestone - accounts manager
Emily Miller - administrative assistant
Jamie Parreno - marketing assistant
Sarah deLaine - events coordinator
Kevin Yuen - digital rights coordinator
Tyler Shainline - production manager
Drew Gill - art director
Jonathan Chan - design director
Monica Garcia - production artist
Vincent Kukua - production artist
Jana Cook - production artist
www.imagecomics.com

To find the comic shop
nearest you, call:
1-888-COMICBOOK

COMIC SHOP LOCATOR SERVICE
888-COMIC-BOOK
888-266-4226

**For Top Cow Productions, Inc.:**

Marc Silvestri - CEO
Matt Hawkins - President & COO
Filip Sablik - Publisher
Bryan Rountree - Editor
Elena Salcedo - Events & Logistics Coordina
Jessi Reid - Social Marketing Coordinator

Want more info? Check out:
**www.topcow.co**
for news & exclusive
Top Cow merchandise!

**Witchblade: Rebirth Volume 1 Trade Paperback.**
May 2012. FIRST PRINTING. ISBN: 978-1-60706-552-6, $9.99 USD.

Published by Image Comics, Inc. Office of Publication: 2134 Allston Way, Second Floor, Berkeley, CA 94704. Originally published in single magazine form as WITCHBLADE 151-155. Witchblade © 2012 Top Cow Productions, Inc. All rights reserved. "Witchblade," the Witchblade logos, and the likenesses of all characters (human or otherwise) featured herein are registered trademarks of Top Cow Productions, Inc. Image Comics and the Image Comics logo are trademarks of Image Comics, Inc. The characters, events, and stories in this publication are entirely fictional. Any resemblance to actual persons (living or dead), events, institutions, locales, without satiric intent, is coincidental. No portion of this publication may be reproduced or transmitted, in any form or by any means, without the express permission of Top Cow Productions, Inc. Printed in U.S.A. For information regarding the CPSIA on this printed material call: 203-595-3636 and provide reference # RICH - 434008.

# Table of Contents

Reborn" ......................... 4

Unbalanced
Pieces" Part 1 ......... 11

Unbalanced
Pieces" Part 2 ......... 33

Unbalanced
Pieces" Part 3 ......... 54

Unbalanced
Pieces" Part 4 ......... 77

Unbalanced
Pieces" Part 5 ......... 98

Cover Gallery ......... 121

Timeline ......... 142

# WITCHBLADE

## REBIRTH

## "Reborn"

"...THAT'S *NOT* THE WORLD. NOT THE WORLD AS IT'S SUPPOSED TO BE.

"THERE ARE THIRTEEN *ARTIFACTS,* THIRTEEN OBJECTS OF SUPERNATURAL POWER, EACH IN THE HANDS OF A BEARER. *I* HAVE ONE OF THEM.

"THERE WAS A MAN WHO *WANTED* TO DESTROY THE WORLD, THE ENTIRE UNIVERSE, SO HE COULD BRING BACK A UNIVERSE HE'D LOST.

"THE *KEY* TO THAT UNIVERSE WAS INSIDE HIM. WE TRIED TO STOP HIM..."

...BUT WE DIDN'T. NOT REALLY.

"THE THIRTEEN ARTIFACTS CONTROL THE FATE OF THE WORLD. IF THEY'RE BROUGHT TOGETHER, THEY CAN *DESTROY* THE WORLD.

"THEY WERE.

"AND THEY DID.

TURNED OUT THAT MY *DAUGHTER,* MY CHILD WITH ONE OF THE OTHER BEARERS... A COP, IF YOU CAN IMAGINE...

"... CONTAINED THE KEY TO *OUR* UNIVERSE."

...I'M THE ONLY ONE WHO KNOWS IT.

YOU BEEN SAMPLING YOUR OWN PRODUCT, ESTACADO? THIS IS *CRAZY TALK.*

WHAT DOES *ANY* OF THIS HAVE TO DO WITH THE TERRITORY BEEF BETWEEN YOUR PEOPLE AND MINE?

WHY ARE YOU EVEN *TELLING* ME THIS?

I HAD TO TELL *SOMEONE...*

...AND YOU WON'T LIVE LONG ENOUGH TO REPEAT ANY OF IT.

# WITCHBLADE

## Rebirth

## "Unbalanced Pieces" Part One

SCREEK

The sounds.

Metal on metal. The rickety friction of the cell door sliding through its track.

CHK

TING TING

The satisfying impact as the door kisses the frame of the cell.

The almost sweet jingle-jangle of the keys on the ring, as the lock is turned.

Together those sounds made the perfect end theme to a job well done.

It was the music that played over the credits when a cop had ended the crook's story.

I heard that tune a lot when I was A cop. But I'm not A cop anymore...

I'm a suspect.

The song has ended. Instead of clapping, there's the sound of footfalls as the officers walk away, leaving me to the sterile silence...

Of course, I'm not just some average perp. I'm Sara Pezzini...

Bearer of the **Witchblade**: sentient Artifact and weapon-- The **balance** between the **Light and** the **Darkness**.

I could blast my way out of here. I could let the Witchblade make its own symphony of fire and metal.

No. I may not be a cop anymore. But I'm not an **outlaw** either.

WELL, LOOKEE HERE. IF IT AIN'T MY FAVORITE SKINNY BITCH.

I BET YOU'RE WISHIN' YOU'D NEVER LEFT NEW YORK CITY.

A million retorts went through my mind in a second, most of them dealing with her big fat ass.

But, I kept it in. Because the fact was, she was right...

OFFICER WOSNICKI.

KINDA SURPRISED TO SEE YA OUT HERE, PEZZINI. "TRIXIES" LIKE YOU DON'T USUALLY COME OUT IN DIS KINDA WEATHER. NOT ENOUGH SKIN ON YER BONES TO KEEP YA WARM.

I'VE GOT THE PROPER PERMITS AND LICENSES SO LET ME SAVE YOU SOME TIME IF YOU'RE LOOKING TO RUN THAT ANGLE AGAIN.

AW, C'MON, NOW. THIS IS JUST A FRIENDLY VISIT FROM YOUR FRIEND, *BIG WOZ,* TO REMIND YOU TO STAY TOASTY.

OH, AND ALSO TO REMIND YOU THAT I'M THE *REAL* COP HERE, SO DON'T GET THE URGE TO DO ANYTHING OTHER THAN "PRIVATELY INVESTIGATE." DON'T WANT YOU AND YOUR LITTLE *HUNCHES* MAKING ME LOOK BAD DOWN AT THE PRECINCT.

LOOK, JANE, I'M NOT TRYING TO STEP ON YOUR FEET. I WAS A COP TOO, BACK IN NEW YORK...

*"WAS",* PEZZINI. NOW YOU'RE JUST ANOTHER *DICK...*

...STICKING YOUR *TITS* IN MY BEAT.

I HAVE TO GET GOING.

WHAT, YOU GOT SOME MORE CHEATERS TO TAKE PICS OF?

NAH.

GOT ANOTHER ONE OF MY HUNCHES.

The first thing I noticed was the temperature. A room formerly warm enough for undies was now colder than the February air outside.

The second thing I noticed was the smell. There should have been the lingering scent of cheeseburger Hot Pocket and sweaty balls. Instead the place smelled like a butcher shop. A charnel house. Acrid and sweet.

And the third thing...well...

The Alderman wouldn't be dry humping his hand, or diddling any secretaries. And he was definitely not going to get re-elected. It looked as if he'd been dead for at least a few days. But I knew he'd been enjoying "Real Housewives" just a few minutes before.

And whoever had done the deed had gotten away fast and clean.

Or, maybe not so clean.

**BREEEP BREEEP**

PEZ INVESTIGATIONS.

MS. PEZZINI. DORIS SPIEGEL.

OH, MRS. SPIEGEL. I'M SORRY---

SORRY? I THINK YOU OWE ME A LITTLE MORE THAN THAT. THE FORENSICS MAN SAID MY HUSBAND WAS DEAD FOR SEVERAL DAYS AT THE LEAST.

AGAIN, MY CONDOLENCES--

MS. PEZZINI, I'VE BEEN PAYING YOU FOR THE LAST WEEK TO SEE IF HE WAS GETTING BUSY WITH THAT MEXICAN TRAMP. YOU KEPT TELLING ME HE WAS WORKING.

RIGHT--

HE WASN'T WORKING. HE WASN'T PORKING HIS SECRETARY. HE WAS DEAD! WHAT KIND OF RACKET ARE YOU RUNNING OVER THERE?!

AH. I SEE WHAT YOU'RE GETTING AT. I'LL...I'LL GET YOU A REFUND.

NEO

EVENTS

OH, YOU BET I WILL. NICE DOING "BUSINESS" WITH YOU, MS. PEZZINI.

Another week without a paycheck. It wasn't a great start to a day that was only going to get *worse.*

But I'd found a clue and a place to start digging for more. A goth club...

I needed something **black.**

I wasn't sure what to expect from a club which I'd discovered from a matchbook belonging to someone who'd **sucked the life** out of a man.

It smelled of Nag Champa incense and spilled beer. The music pounding through the speakers sounded like a box of screws dumped into a blender to me. (I'm more of a Stones or Dylan girl, myself.)

But, at first glance the denizens were typical of these kind of places.

**Weekend wiccans. Hobby Satanists.** People with a mild kink or two. Medieval and military fetishes, depending on the aesthetic. Nice, normal people who liked to occasionally air out their **dark side.**

But the Witchblade told me there were others here to. **Street witches. Urban Shamans. Cyberocculists.** Real arcanists hiding amidst the night-lifers.

I figured it was probably for the best. I wasn't there to fall in love. I was there to search for a killer.

And that's exactly what I was going to do.

As soon as I walked off that bruised ego.

The hardest thing about being an occult investigator with a mystic Artifact attached to your wrist...

Was realizing that despite all the amazing, impossible things you'd seen...

No matter how many demonic creatures you'd stopped from taking over the world.

You couldn't beat time.

NOW, HOW ABOUT YOU AND I HAVE A NICE LITTLE TALK ABOUT THE ALDERMAN, AND MAYBE WE'LL GET AROUND TO EXPLAINING WHY YOU ATTACKED ME--

WEARING WHAT LOOKS LIKE THE MILITARIZED VERSION OF LADY GAGA'S MEAT DRESS.

PUT YOUR HANDS WHERE WE CAN SEE THEM!

NOW, GENTLY PUT GRANDMA DOWN, AND BACK AWAY!

GRANDMA?

*The sounds. The wet squish of snow underneath boots. The click of a holster being unbuttoned. And the trembling whisper of my own voice...*

OH, THIS LOOKS BAD.

From the Journal of Jericho Jorgenson

4-29-1972

Dear future spawn. Sorry. It still feels weird to write these things to someone who doesn't exist...hell, someone who may never exist if I keep at it.

Anyway, today was the first real day of spring. The thermometers crept just above 75 degrees, and the whole city jumped into life, joyously and fearlessly like a little kid into a puddle. Sure, you can get sunshine and warmth every day of the year in San Diego or Los Angeles. But in those places, people take it for granted. Here, a whole metropolis full of people has been cooped up in apartments and houses for the better part of four months. When that first bit of pure sunlight hits their skin, you better believe they appreciate it.

And that's how you get to the best part of the first real day of spring. The girls. The liberation of spring affects the girls the most. Cooped up housewives shed as many layers as they can to push a stroller down the Lakeshore path. The innocent Catholic college girls over at DePaul wear tank tops and short shorts. They walk in small tribes down Fullerton Avenue to the beach to smile at boys, whom their parents would certainly disapprove of.

Like me.

I was leaning against my '65 mustang, the keys still in the ignition, so I could play Pink Floyd on the eight-track player. She walked by, looking over her shoulder, about eleven minutes into "Echoes." Her pale skin was practically translucent, standing out in sharp contrast to her ink black hair. I was a sucker for a dark-haired girl, which I admit might be some left over affection for the movies I watched as a kid like "Bride of Frankenstein." Movies hosted by Maila Nurmi who scared the hell out of me while making my little boy parts tingle as 'Vampira.'

She smiled, and turned back to her friends. The Floyd and the dangerous car had done its job. It was the hook. Now I needed to reel her in; take off my jacket, smoke a cigarette, put in some Sabbath. She wouldn't be able to resist.

Except I was on the job. Grandfather had a line on a vein that some poor stiff had dug into while breaking ground for a gas station near Evanston. The medical report had said he'd had a heart attack, but I knew the truth that he'd choked to death when he'd suddenly sprouted a whole host of new organs that filled his chest when he broke into the vein with his backhoe.

I muttered the short incantation of a marking cantrip that'd allow me to follow up with Catholic College Vampira, and hopped into the 'Stang, hoping the girl saw me leaving and felt a moment of disappointment.

I took neighborhood streets and back roads north instead of the Drive, deciding that if I had to be on Grandfather's time, I'd at least take the opportunity to get an eyeful of ladies laying out in their small yards on rickety lawn chairs.

I made my way through the wooded grove between developed neighborhoods and park land, where the breach had occurred and found the site. It was typical of spots where someone had inadvertently tapped a vein, barricaded off and littered with signs proclaiming it a danger zone. A large white tent covered the spot itself. I stepped under a rope, and was assaulted by the smell, like the dumpster outside a butcher shop on a hot summer day.

I heard a low growl and turned in time to see the thing leap at me. I only had time for the quickest defensive spell I knew, which stopped the thing's heart a moment before its distorted jaws dug into me. It fell to the ground, still spasming; it's extra heart pumping tainted blood into its own stomach. A squirrel or, a former squirrel anyway. I could tell already this vein was too corrupted for Grandfather's use, but he'd never accept my assessment without a sample.

Just then I heard voices. I crouched behind a fallen tree, and watched as several figures exited the white tent. They wore grey body suits, and World War 2 era gas masks, giving them the alien appearance I'd seen before. One of the men poured salt on the ground, as another lifted his arm, and drew back his sleeve to cut a short line across his wrist. Yellow smoke poured from the salt. His appearance was so fast it seemed to occur between the blinks of my eyes. I ducked down the moment I recognized him, short of breath, and more afraid than I'd usually like to admit.

Esquivel. He was MAL Analytics' elite agent, a former bullfighter, who'd taken a horn to the heart, and awoke from a coma with one leg in the Afterworld. He'd sense me in a second, and I'd die with his hairy knuckled hands around my throat. I'd be buried in the hole left when MAL excavated the vein, never to feel the first day of spring sun on my face again.

I snuck back across the grove to my car. I leaned back, and listened for the quiet notes of my cantrip. The girl was still at the beach. I popped Black Sabbath, by Black Sabbath into the eight-track player, and I took the Drive back downtown. If I'm going to have to keep writing these, maybe I should get to work on that spawning thing. Or, at least, get in some practice.

Transcribed by Tim Seeley, 12-13-2011

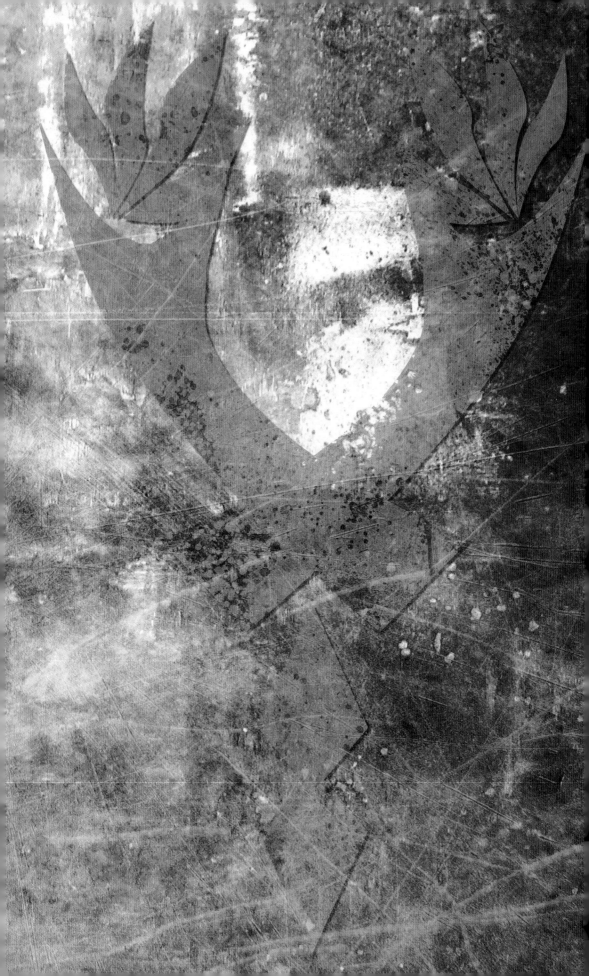

# WITCHBLADE

## REBIRTH

"UNBALANCED
PIECES"
PART TWO

THAT GIRL, *MIRANDA SMALLS*, THE ONE WHO ATTACKED YOU. SHE CAME TO A FEW OF MY SHOWS. I KNEW SHE WAS INTO SOMETHING WEIRD. JUST DIDN'T KNOW SHE ACTUALLY QUALIFIED FOR *AARP* DISCOUNTS.

YEAH, I PLAN ON DROPPING IN ON GRANDMA TOMORROW FOR TEA AND EXPLANATIONS.

YOU DON'T SEEM ALL THAT FREAKED OUT FOR A GIRL THAT JUST GOT HASSLED BY A WOMAN WHO WENT FROM G-STRINGS TO ADULT DIAPERS IN SECONDS.

I WORKED A FEW *"SPECIAL CASES"* WHEN I WAS ON THE NYPD. I KNOW SOME STUFF GETS LEFT OUT OF POLICE REPORTS BECAUSE IT'S A LITTLE TOO GRIMM'S FAIRYTALES.

ANYWAY, I'M PRETTY SURE I CAN HANDLE WHATEVER *"THE SECOND CITY"* CAN THROW AT ME.

CAREFUL. CHICAGO *ISN'T* NEW YORK. NEW YORK HAS LONG *SHADOWS*, BUT CHICAGO'S ARE *DARKER.*

HERE, CORRUPTION DOESN'T JUST *GREASE THE WHEELS...*

IT KEEPS THE LIGHTS ON.

SO I GUESS YOU'RE NOT JUST A CLUB HOPPING SMOOTH TALKER, CAIN JORGENSON.

WHAT IS IT YOU DO, EXACTLY, BESIDES PAYING THE BAILS OF GIRLS YOU JUST MET?

NO...

NO. STOP.

WHU--?

I HAVE TO GO.

WAIT. CAN'T I GIVE YOU A RIDE?

I'LL GET A CAB.

AT LEAST TAKE THE JACKET. IT'S FREEZING FOR CHRIST'S SAKE!

I DON'T NEED IT--

MY 'PERSONAL MAGIC' WILL KEEP ME WARM.

LAKE VIEW THEATER

TAXI

Crap. So distracted I went **'home.'** Should have just gone in to the office.

Well, as long as I'm up and caffeinated, I can so something I should have done weeks ago.

All this stuff, thrown into boxes and dragged half way across the country.

The sight of each item jogs a few memories, swishing them off the bottom of my mind like a shaken snow globe.

It feels like all the right pieces.

But something about the way it all **comes together** feels awkward.

Someone beat me to a visitation.

And whomever it was can take a 30-foot fall as well as Smalls can in her *bacon armor*.

I try not to smile too much...

But the truth is I'm one happy little P.I.

I love it when I have no choice but to use the Witchblade to solve a problem...

And the Witchblade loves it, too.

12-9-1958

I first became curious about these diaries when I was only David's assistant, still flushing when I'd catch him looking at me out of the corner of his eye. I thought them fiction; manuscripts scrawled by some devious writer to be sent in to a pulp magazine for the entertainment of men with unrefined tastes in literature. After David's injury, I came to know them well, each by weight, and feel, and where each fit into the strange chronology of the Jorgenson family line, as I retrieved them for David's trembling hand. And now, as his injuries make even holding the journals difficult, I know them for their invaluable advice in surviving encounters with the Cataract. Yes, I am quite familiar with these diaries. I know what they are for. I know they're for the future of the Jorgenson line, and really this is written to the child of my child's child. They are for you, whomever you might be, some relative of mine; a grandchild, a great grandchild, perhaps you are even my own son. These are intended to act as field notes, observations, and advice.

But, well, frankly, I find it difficult to approach these reports in a such a clinical manner this day, when I know my son Jericho will one day be putting his life in danger. Perhaps the imagery on the front pages of the newspapers these past weeks, the Our Lady of Angels fire is still fresh in my mind. Perhaps the loss of so many children has put me in mind to wonder how I would survive were I to lose my own son. David has done much to train Jericho for his future job, driven by his own passion to ensure none suffer the injuries he had in pursuit of the bizarre treasure that is the lot of the Jorgenson line. But the images haunt me. The heavy black smoke. Melted desks. The firefighter carrying the limp body. The grieving parents standing in the snowy street, their faces contorted by a grief I hope I never know. I will do my best to put all this aside, and report the event for posterity's sake. In the midst of the flurry of headlines associated with Our Lady, one article went largely unnoticed. It described a break-in at a small scrap yard on the west side of the city, by unknown assailants and the death of the dog, which had been tasked with guarding it. Of no great concern to a city which had so recently lost 92 of its children, but David thought it curious since we had found several veins in that neighborhood.

I put Jericho to sleep, and set David up at the window with the field radio. We no longer owned a car, and could ill afford one that could transport David in his condition, so I took the bus east. I noted the strange looks by the other passengers when I got off at my stop. Likely an unpopular place for white women in their mid-forties.

The street was empty of passers-by, allowing me to make my way to the chain link gate without incident. I have no skill with magic, but David has enchanted a few items for me. I found my slippers, invested with a limited form of levitation, to have enough lift to clear the fence. The police had been through the day before, and the remains of their hasty investigation were still evident.

I set my bait, a ball of suet, cooked in excretions made by the bizarre mushrooms we'd encountered near other veins in the area. I crouched behind a rusty barrel, and waited, hoping I wouldn't be waiting long in the cold December air. As I waited, I swore I was able to still smell the smoke from Our Lady only a few blocks away. The longer I waited there, the more my mind wandered to dark place flashes of terrible images. I was glad to be brought back to reality by the appearance of something that could only have been described as "unreal." Crawling towards the suet was what appeared to be an old radio, wires from its interior acting as spider-like legs. It was an unsteady contraption, barely able to pull its weight. After the shock of its appearance wore off, I determined what I was looking at. It was one of the shadow-children, as David called them, likely expelled from tainted soil nearby. The things didn't survive long by themselves, vulnerable to light as they were, and usually bonded themselves to some other small living creature a rat or a cockroach to form a parasitic relationship. This one, perhaps sensing some spark in the remains of the radio had chosen poorly, and was now dying under the strain of trying to animate structures never intended for the purpose it had chosen.

It's compatriots, likely the perpetrators for the break-in, and murder of the dog, were long gone now, leaving this one to fend for itself.

I determined the thing would provide little sustenance, certainly not enough to warrant the difficulty of transporting in home. I walked up to it, bringing along a metal post that had been laying nearby. I thrust the post through the brittle plastic shell of the old radio. The thing struggled, but the soldered connection of its wires could never replicate the effect of nerves, and it clearly felt no pain. I waited for the bus, content that the sun coming up in a few hours would eradicate the shadow creature haunting the wires and leave behind an ordinary broken radio.

I received even stranger looks on my return trip, but was pleased that the night's activities were of little danger save for the cold, and the biting stares of strangers on a late night bus ride.

I woke up Jericho for school, and cooked him a breakfast of eggs and ham. I watched him walk down the sidewalk on his way to school, as I took down the notes in the journal, I knew he would someday read. I hoped he would see through the advice, and the observations. Through the bizarre details of walking appliances. I hoped he would think of his mother, watching him sleep, her eyes brimming with tears.

(As written by his wife, Estelle Jorgenson)
Transcribed by Tim Seeley, 12-13-2011

# WITCHBLADE

## Rebirth

"Unbalanced
Pieces"
Part Three

**KRAK**

HUK!

SHRRAAAK

The conduits throb, echoing the heaving of lungs. Sometimes I feel short bursts of...emotion isn't the right word, coming from the Witchblade.

Familiarity enough that the 'blade knows what to do.

Right away the Witchblade goes to work absorbing whatever's pumping out of the end of her wand.

AGH!

SHO

I can feel the thin, metal veins activating to disperse the excess energy like a city storm sewer.

As it disperses the spellfire, there's a sense of confusion, and surprise, followed by a light inkling of familiarity.

WHOA!

FRRRROOOOMM

I will the Witchblade to take out her tires, but it resists, still collecting itself. I figure it deserves a rest...besides, I'm not here for the easy rider. I'm here for--

YOU AGAIN...

SHOULD NEVER A' LET SPIEGEL HAVE THAT LAST CIGARETTE. YOU'VE BEEN STUCK TO MY ASS SINCE YOU FOUND MY MATCHBOOK.

YOUR ARMOR. WHAT'S THIS ALL ABOUT?

HEY! WHAT THE HELL IS GOING ON HERE?!

WHAT ARE YOU DOIN'?!

I NEED SOME INFORMATION....

AND I DON'T NEED AN AUDIENCE.

THE HELL?

I'VE SEEN THIS ON TV. IT'S ONE OF THEM HIGH TECH EMERGENCY COCOONS.

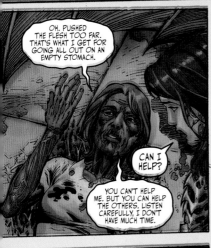

OH. PUSHED THE FLESH TOO FAR. THAT'S WHAT I GET FOR GOING ALL OUT ON AN EMPTY STOMACH.

CAN I HELP?

YOU CAN'T HELP ME. BUT YOU CAN HELP THE OTHERS. LISTEN CAREFULLY, I DON'T HAVE MUCH TIME.

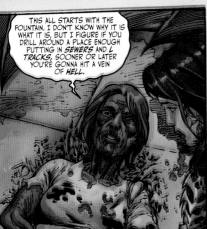

THIS ALL STARTS WITH THE FOUNTAIN. I DON'T KNOW WHY IT IS WHAT IT IS, BUT I FIGURE IF YOU DRILL AROUND A PLACE ENOUGH PUTTING IN *SEWERS* AND *L TRACKS*, SOONER OR LATER YOU'RE GONNA HIT A VEIN OF *HELL.*

THIS OLD FELLA, *LEON GOLD* FOUND IT FIRST. DISCOVERED THAT WHEN HE DRANK HE COULD BECOME YOUNG AGAIN. SO HE LET SOME HIS NEIGHBORS IN ON IT. ALL OLD FOLKS LIKE MYSELF.

MORE YOU DRANK, THE YOUNGER YOU GOT. CALLED THE EFFECT THAT CAME WITH IT...THE 'ARMOR', *THE FLESH.* KINDA TOOK IT AS A NAME FOR OUR CREW TOO. MOST OF US WENT BACK TO OUR TWENTIES. LEON, HE FIGURED HIS BEST DAYS WERE AS A BOY.

"THING IS, NOTHING'S FREE, AND PRETTY SOON WE FOUND THERE WAS A PRICE FOR YOUTH. TO STAY YOUNG, WE HAD TO SUCK THE LIFE FROM OTHERS.

"NOW, WE WERE ALL GOOD CITIZENS, MIND YOU, SO WE PICKED THE WORST PEOPLE AROUND TO EAT UP THEY WEREN'T USING THEIR LIVES TOO WELL ANYWAY, WE FIGURED. HAD THE NEIGHBORHOOD GANG PROBLEM LICKED IN A COUPLE A' MONTHS.

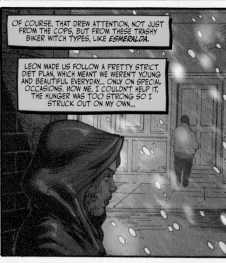

OF COURSE, THAT DREW ATTENTION, NOT JUST FROM THE COPS, BUT FROM THESE TRASHY BIKER WITCH TYPES, LIKE *ESMERALDA*.

LEON MADE US FOLLOW A PRETTY STRICT DIET PLAN, WHICH MEANT WE WEREN'T YOUNG AND BEAUTIFUL EVERYDAY... ONLY ON SPECIAL OCCASIONS. NOW ME, I COULDN'T HELP IT, THE HUNGER WAS TOO STRONG SO I STRUCK OUT ON MY OWN...

IN OTHER WORDS, I GOT GREEDY AND DUMB, WHICH JUST GOES TO SHOW YOU THAT YOU CAN WATCH OPRAH FOR 20 DAMN YEARS AND STILL NOT GET THE MESSAGE.

I NEVER MARRIED. NEVER HAD KIDS. WAS USUALLY TOO AFRAID TO TRY MUCH OF ANYTHING NEW.

GUESS I LOOKED AT THE LIFE I LIVED AND DECIDED I HADN'T LIVED ENOUGH. WOULDA DONE ANYTHING TO KEEP TRYIN'.

YOU'RE STILL YOUNG. DON'T YOU GO DOING WHAT I DID...HAVE LOTS OF FRIENDS, DRINKIN' BUDDIES. HAVE SOME GREAT LOVES AND ALL THE GOOD STUFF THAT COMES WITH IT, IF YA KNOW WHAT I MEAN.

AND HAVE A BIG OL' FAMILY, EVEN IF THEY DRIVE YOU NUTS ONCE IN A WHILE.

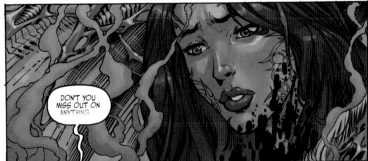

DON'T YOU MISS OUT ON ANYTHING.

HURRY UP! WE GOTTA CUT THOSE WOMEN OUT OF THERE--

WHAT THE HELL?

So, Cain was right. **Corruption** does run deep in Chicago. And sometimes it comes bubbling back up out of the ground.

I'm thinking about that, and what Smalls said about not missing out on life as she aged into dust right in front of my eyes...

And I guess I'm pretty much on auto-pilot because I end up right in front of Cain's theatre.

LAKE VIEW THEA

Maybe I don't have much of a life. No family. But maybe it wouldn't hurt to have a friend. A drinking buddy...

And even if I don't have a "great love" anymore, it doesn't mean I can't maybe have a bit of "the great stuff that comes with it..."

"... if ya know what I mean."

The second I get up the steps, I notice something is wrong. The door to his apartment has been forced open.

Instantly, I'm in detective mode.

Basic deadbolt. The door and lock broken by extreme heat.

Footprints in the snow. two to three hours old. Combat boots. Women's size 8. Also, women's size 6.

Two distinct tire tracks in alley. Motorcycles.

Biker witches.

CAIN!

YOU CAN ALWAYS TAKE IT UP WITH THE CPM. COPS DON'T EVEN MANAGE THE FINES IN THIS TOWN. MAYOR SOLD PARKING TO A PRIVATE COMPANY.

HECK, THEY MIGHT FIND IN YOUR FAVOR. OF COURSE, IT MIGHT TAKE A COUPLE WEEKS TO GET THE BOOT OFF IN DA MEANTIME.

*Sure, I may do my best to never become an "outlaw..."*

GOSH, I BET IT'LL BE PRETTY HARD TO DO YOUR P.I. WORK WITHOUT A CAR, EH, PEZ?

CLMP

*...but that doesn't mean I can't **play dirty** every once in awhile.*

HUH. GUESS YOU NEED MORE PRACTICE ON ATTACHING THOSE.

WHAT THE--?

ANYWAY, LIKE I SAID, I'M IN A HURRY. DO LET ME KNOW ABOUT THOSE PARKING TICKETS, JANE.

*I think I'm starting to get this city.*

HEY THERE, BOSS. LONG TIME NO SEE. WHAT, THEY GOT NO SHADOWS AT ALL OVER THERE?

I WAS ON A VACATION WITH MY FAMILY.

I CAN SMELL THAT SUNSHINE ON YA. NASTY STUFF. OR MAYBE THAT'S THE SMELL OF YOUR WIFE'S--

MY GUY, JERRY, SAYS SHE'S BEEN KEEPING LATE HOURS. SPENDS A LOT OF TIME AT WORK, NOT A LOT AT HOME. LIKE YOU USED TO BEFORE YOU GOT WHIPPED.

SARA. I WANT MY REPORT.

DID HE SAY HOW...HOW SHE LOOKED?

HOW SHE LOOKED? YEAH. SAID SHE'S GOT AN ASS LIKE A 12-YEAR-OLD BOY AND A RACK HE WANTS TO MOTORBOAT. OR IS THAT NOT WHAT YOU MEAN, BOSS?

YOU STILL A LITTLE SWEET ON THE BITCHBLADE, BOSS?

THAT'S ENOUGH. HAVE JERRY MAINTAIN HIS SURVEILLANCE FOR A FEW MORE DAYS.

YEAH? YOU WANT ME TO TELL HIM TO EVALUATE HER MENTAL STATE FOR YA?

I SAID...

THAT'S ENOUGH.

FRIGGIN' SMUG SIZE 2, CHICKEN LEGGED...

KRRSH HEY, WOZ, YA WANNA MEET US FOR LUNCH?

NAH, NOT TODAY.

WHAT? BIG WOZ TURNIN' DOWN LUNCH? YOU HEARING THIS, TONY? WHAT, YOU ON A DIET?

REAL FUNNY. NAH, I'M RUNNING SOME ERRANDS.

ON THE SOUTHSIDE.

WHY WERE YOU IN SUCH A BIG HURRY TO DRIVE ALL THE WAY TO THE SOUTHSIDE, PEZ?

YOU AIN'T THE ONLY ONE WHO GETS HUNCHES. I DIDN'T THINK HOODS LIKE THIS WERE YOUR KINDA THING. MUST BE SOMETHING HERE THAT TICKLES YOUR TAINT.

THIS WHERE YOUR DEALER HANGS OUT? OR MAYBE YOU'RE INTO THOSE SWINGER PARTIES, WHERE A BUNCH A' GOOD LOOKING PEOPLE MEET UP FOR ANONYMOUS PORKIN.' WHATEVER IT IS, I'M BETTING IT'S SOME WEIRD...

SHMMMPH!

From the Journal of
Dr. Timothy Jorgenson
8-13-1917

## OBSERVATIONS MADE OF VEIN-GENERATED DEVIATIONS no.33: OFFAL MEN

(Note to future sons of the Jorgensen bloodline: Observations in this field book pertain simply to those phenomena observed without speculation into biological significance. For more in-depth hypotheses, see Index: OFFAL MEN; BIOLOGICAL INFERENCES AND IMPLICATIONS.)

6:30 pm - While in my office at the University of Chicago, I received a visit from Detective O'Shaughnessy. He informed me of a body discovered at the Union Stockyard in that morning. Body belonged to adult male, early 20s. Cause of death unknown. The Detective suggested that the body may have been brought to the Yard with the intent of disposal. State of body reminiscent of a case I had worked with the Detective earlier in the year (ref: See VAMPIRE HARLOT MURDERS) The Detective informed me that his department had ruled the death to be of natural causes. The officer had doubts though, after our encounter with Ms. Waters, and asked me to follow up on his concerns. He noted that the press had not been yet notified of the death. Since the man was a recent immigrant, it was unlikely it would be noted, allowing for significant time should the perpetrator decide to return to scene.

9:30 pm - Exited railcar in New City and promptly purchased box of ammunition and black cape. Previous encounters with Offal

Men demanded discretion and proper armament. Also purchased three (3) mason jars, medium.

OBSERVATION: At this time of year, smell of Yards perceptible at two miles away.

10:30 pm - Waited outside American Pork Products site of body, until night shift changeover. Entered. OBSERVATION: Majority of Yard workers are Irish or Polish immigrants. Many are missing fingers, leading me to question the content of American Pork Products' Thuringer.

2:30 am - Observed interaction between two yard workers. Red headed man (40s) and Black haired man (20s).

Conversation hushed, but assumed discourse implied one man telling new employee of secret nightly meeting concerning formation of a Union. Meeting location very near to location of body.

3:15 am – Meeting occurs.

OBSERVATION: Rendering Machine nearby is extremely loud. Poor choice for a meeting. Black Haired Man (hereafter referred to as BHM) looks alone and concerned. Attack occurs. I have listed the methodology of the Offal Man for future reference:
- Offal Man, clothed in "Offal Man Armor" descends from perch on ceiling. Agility and strength clearly heightened to levels beyond peak human.
- Offal Man utilizes prehensile armor appendages to pin BHM. Secondary appendages cover BHM's mouth.
- Offal Man kisses BHM. After several seconds of profane embrace, BHM begins to noticeably change. BHM's hair displays effects of advanced age. Skin dries and tears. Body bloats as if in state of advanced decay. Smell is strong. Smell of Yards on summer day seems pleasant by comparison.

3:24 am – Observe Offal Man retract appendages. As expected, Red Haired Man (hereafter referred to as RHM) is revealed as the perpetrator. Observe RHM drag body to rendering tank, where this morning's body was discovered. Rendering Machine even louder as it processes BHM. RHM looks strong, healthy and vital.

3:28 am – Unload four slugs into back of RHM's head while he rests. Observe generation of "Offal Man Armor" upon impact of shell into brain pan. Rendering Machine covers sound of gunfire.

OBSERVATION: Though it would likely have been easier and more expedient to use a spell, there is a certain satisfaction knowing that I dispatched of one of the creatures with a modern and practical means.

3:30 am – Sever RHM's carotid artery and collect blood in Mason Jars for consumption by Grandfather. Blood is thick, and purplish. It smells of strangely pleasant. Similar to the indescribable scent of newness attributed to babies.

6:30 am – Exit Rail Car at Police Department. Report to Detective O'Shaughnessy that I observed nothing, save the normal nightly workings of a Stockyard meat-processing plant. Describe my own disappointment in detail to defer any suspicions. The Detective accepts my report, but it is clear to me, that he is a man of above average intelligence, and were he not quite certain I had dealt with his problem, he would press me further.

OBSERVATION: Difficult to focus on conversation at hand after I notice blood stain on cuff of right sleeve.

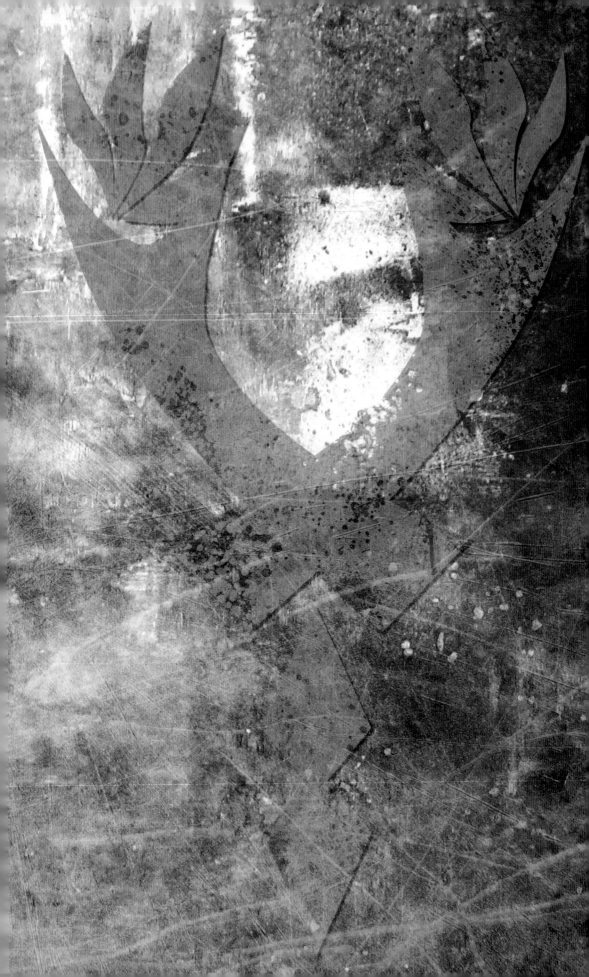

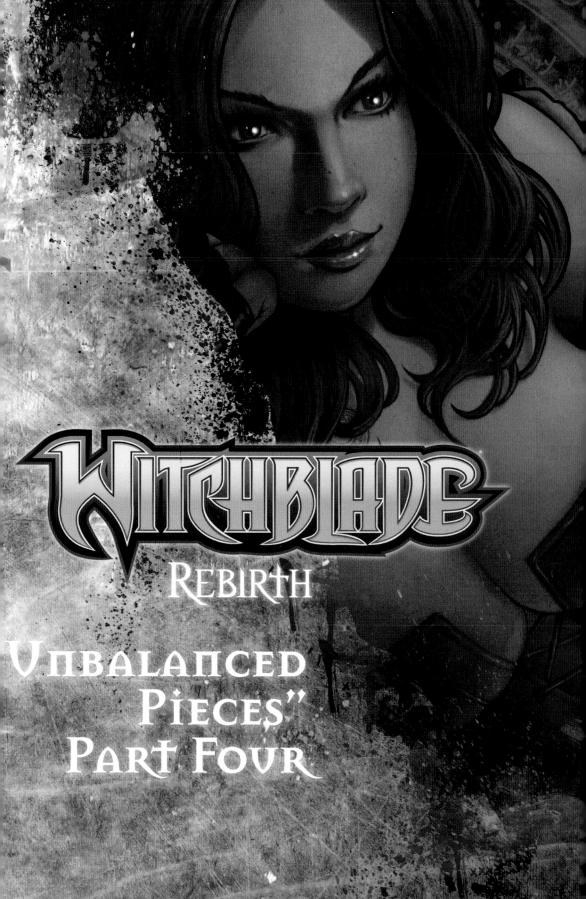

# WITCHBLADE

## Rebirth

# Unbalanced Pieces"
# Part Four

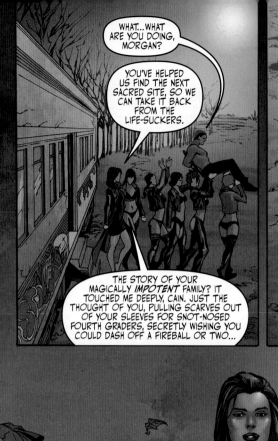

WHUH...DID... DID I JUST GET PUNCHED OUT BY A KID?

WHAT. THE. EFF?

I GOTTA... GOTTA SIT DOWN.

SPLT

SKLUT

DID YOU GET A LEAD ON YOUR MAGICIAN?

NO.

GOOD, THEN HOW ABOUT WE HEAD BACK UP NORTH? MAYBE YOU'LL HAVE ANOTHER ONE OF YOUR HUNCHES AND YOU CAN RUIN SOMEONE ELSE'S DAY INSTEAD OF MINE?

SORRY, JANE.

WHAT'S THIS?

MISSING PERSONS. THESE PEOPLE HERE SHOULD BE CONSIDERED SUSPECTS IN THEIR MURDERS. BRING 'EM DOWNTOWN.

JEEZ

CHARLES

HOLANDA PETERSON

BARRO EMMET

LEE JACKSON

JORGE RUIZ

BRENT FOWLER

WELL... GO ON. I CAN'T DO IT.

I DON'T HAVE A WARRANT.

THEY TRIED TO SUCK YOUR BLOOD.

TOUCHÉ.

ALL RIGHT PEOPLE. LISTEN UP! YOU'RE UNDER ARREST FOR THE MURDER OF JORGE RUIZ, HOLLAND PETERSON, LEE JACKSON, BRENT FOWLER...

MS. PEZZINI...I THOUGHT WE HAD AN UNDERSTANDING?

CHARLES "CHUCKY" LAWSON, CLAY EMMET,...JEEZ THERE'S A LOT OF THESE.

From the Journal of Howard Stearnes
10-11-1893

It was a most lovely day. Leaves swirled about in multi-colored eddies. The dwindling sunlight, though not so warm as it had been only a month before, still dazzled upon the cheeks of happy children, running amongst the crowd, wands of candy floss gripped in their sticky hands. All manner of people were in attendance today, and it was clear simply by the diversity that the Columbian Exposition had truly made Chicago a "City of the World".

It was the first day I'd had to myself in several weeks. With so many people swarming into the City over the past several months, my duties as coroner had been much in demand. After all, such an influx of life inevitably meant an increase in death. And Eidolon's need to feed, though lessened over the years, still provided me with a mission that consumed most of my non-working hours.

I had seen and done much already: witnessed moving pictures on Muybridge's zoopraxiscope, blushed at the sight of a beautiful snake charmer's dance, listened to minstrels and orchestras, and toured ships from around the world. I'd still intended to see Hickock's Wild West Show, and end my excursion with a ride upon the Ferris Wheel so I could see the entire White City in all it's glory. But my attention was pulled away from the sights, smells and sound of the Exposition by a strange buzz, faint at first, then growing in intensity, soon shifting from an auditory sensation to one that encompassed my sight and sense of smell as well.

I had experienced this beforeÖit was one of Eidolon's gifts, a kind of sixth sense that alerted me to the presence of the Vein, or something corrupted by it.

I stumbled through the crowds, no doubt looking like a drunk, driven by the sense. I stopped, and leaned against a tree, darting my eyes about to locate the cause of my otherworldly anxiety. That is when I saw him. He was of medium height, and quite unexceptional in appearance, with a long mustache, heavily lidded eyes, and a dusty suit and cap which had likely not seen the domestic touch of a woman in quite some time.

He was talking to a young man, his wife and their child. They were foreigners... Nordic by the looks of them, carrying bundles and likely in need of shelter for the night. I did not know who this mustached man was, or why his appearance had elicited such a reaction in me. But I knew it was my duty to observe, as whatever he had said to the young couple had convinced them to follow him.

I kept a distance behind the group; my attention focused raptly upon the mustached man to quiet the powerful buzzing, and followed them out of the Exposition. Maintaining my cover was easy at first amongst the crowd, but as we moved into the surrounding blocks of the Englewood neighborhood, the crowds thinned, and I was forced to maintain a safe distance. After a walk of several miles, we arrived at the man's intended destination just as the sun dipped below the horizon.

It was a three-story building, encompassing a city block. The bottom floors contained a variety of small businesses, servicing the local community, while a canvas sign hung across the upper floors advertised the "World's Fair Hotel." Twenty-five years as a coroner had given me a kind of familiarity with death, an almost preternatural sense of its presence. This combined with Eidolon's gifts made the deluge of images invading my mind at the sight of this "castle" nearly unbearable. Terrible, unspeakable things had happened here. I knew Eidolon would want me to leave. If there were an accessible vein here, it would be best to regroup, concoct a plan and return. But there was the family. And the young child.

I entered the "hotel" just as the mustached man was using a gun to force the young family into one of his dungeon-like rooms. The smell of old death and fresh lye assaulted my nostrils as I attacked this slayer of innocents. I used what cantrips and spells Eidolon had taught me, but I had never excelled in the use of the combative arts. Some dark force protected this murderer, and I was quickly subdued, placed in shackles, and imprisoned along with the family.

Now, my powers are diminished, weakened by contact with this mustached man and his dark influences. But I can summon my remaining mana, and cast one last teleportation spell, to transport the child, Timothy, away from here to Eidolon. Eidolon will teach him his ways. Without me, all three would have died, but instead I trade my life for the child's.

As I finish this entry, and prepare for the spell to free the child, and this journal with him; I hope that future servants to the Eidolon will remember that though we are first in service to him, we must never forget that we are, also in service to all of mankind. We trade servitude for power, but we must never forget our other master: Chicago, City of the World. I write this now, with no regrets. Though my interference has cost me my life, I know now it was the correct decision. For as I wait with the Jorgenson family, in a room lined with dessicated bodies and bare skeletons, I am filled with peace at the knowledge that one life will continue on, even as three are extinguished.

It was a lovely day.

Transcribed by Tim Seeley
2-11-12

# WITCHBLADE

## REBIRTH
## "UNBALANCED PIECES"
## PART FIVE

The sounds. The dull friction as the sharp metal traces a line down the jaw of **Officer Jane "Big Woz" Wosnicki,** an enemy turned ally.

I DON'T CARE WHAT YOU SAY PEZZINI, YOUR BOYFRIEND IS GONNA BE AN ASS-PET TO SOME VERY BIG INMATES FOR THIS!

The fast, ragged breathing of **Cain Jorgenson,** an ally turned enemy, possessed by the black magic of the Brunhilda biker witch gang.

And the cacophony of an **arcane gang war** going on all around me. Screams. The hisses of an impossible creature, and the intensifying growl of motorcycle engines, circling closer and closer like a flock of carrion birds.

ut for the moment I ave to put all of that ut of my head; push ut all the distraction, nd figure out how to ave Woz's life. And Cain's soul.

CAIN. I LOOKED THROUGH YOUR NOTES. ALL THAT RESEARCH, TRYING TO FIND THE SITES OF "THE CORRUPTION CATARACT." PLAYING RANDI AND ESMERALDA. YOU WANT POWER.

JANE! NNF! GET THE HELL OUT OF HERE, NOW! CALL FOR BACKUP! THIS IS GOING TO GET MESSY!

WHAT WAS YOUR FIRST CLUE? THAT SOMEONE LET LOOSE A FUCKING LION?

FRRGHH!

YOUR BOYTOY IS GOING DOWNTOWN!

I SAVED YOUR ASS. LET'S CALL IT EVEN, AND TRUST ME THAT WHAT CAIN NEEDS RIGHT NOW IS NOT TO BE ARRESTED.

NOW GO! THERE ARE BACK DOORS THAT WAY!

FINE. MY DAMN SHIFT IS OVER ANYWAY.

FSSH HSSS!

I GOT IT!

LEON!

MRROWWWR~

WHUHF!

MEW.

THERE'S MY LITTLE POOPS. DID THOSE MEAT-MONKEYS TRY AND HURT YOU?

**AIEEEAGGH!**

*I'm in the middle of another war.*

Wars are always the same. Someone wants something someone else has. Land. Oil. Power. Immortality.

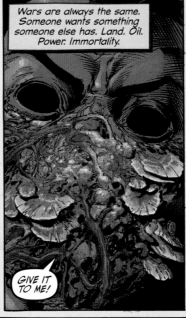

**GIVE IT TO ME!**

Cain is infected; his body slowly being warped by some alien being's approximation of The Darkness.

The Witchblade is the Balance between **The Darkness** and the Artifact of the Light, **The Angelus.** Its job is to keep the opposing forces from destroying each other, and by proxy, everything else.

The Witchblade was designed to right wrongs perpetrated by both sides and to punish them if need be. It knows both forces intimately, the way a hunter knows its prey.

There are times I ask myself why I keep the Witchblade. It got me fired. It uprooted my life. It's not like there aren't a whole lot of people who'd gratefully step up and take it.

I always come back to the same answer. I keep the Witchblade, because I don't trust anyone else with it.

MEW?

VRRROOOOOMMM

HRRRRRKKKK!

SPPLTCH

KA-ROOOM

As soon as I entered the room with the creature, I could feel it excitedly probing my mind.

SHLK

I could feel its disdain, for beings it thought of as nothing more than tools. It had learned in its time here, that humans were easy to bend to its will.

It wasn't like anything I'd ever felt before. Something so alien and foreign, that I didn't even have a concept for it.

Immersed in the water, immersed in the creature, I can see the past.

I see the bearers, three people who hate each other bearing three Artifacts that hate other even more.

Together, their strength is greater. They create an impossible force. One capable of sealing a tear in space.

One capable of setting the world on fire.

But I was away from any other Artifact bearers. I was away from the New York Police, from Gleason. I was in my own little universe.

SHREEeeEE!

But I wasn't truly alone. I have the Witchblade. Two Artifacts in one. Together, our strength is enough.

I reject the creature's gift.

FRACHOOM

Later.

SO, I'M RUNNING A FEW ERRANDS RIGHT? I PICK UP AN ITALIAN BEEF, AN' ALL A' SUDDEN, I FEEL LIKE THERE'S SOMETHING UP.

SO, I DRIVE HERE, AND I SEE THIS PLACE GO UP IN FLAMES, JUST AS SOME CHICKS ON BIKES TAKE OFF.

YOU'RE A REGULAR BLOODHOUND, WOZ.

NAH. I JUST GET THESE "HUNCHES..."

I'M SORRY, LEON...I DON'T THINK ANY OF YOUR FRIENDS CAME OUT...

*I'm not sure **anyone** got out besides us.*

THE GODDESS DELIVERED US FROM DEATH, NOW WE WILL OFFER HER REVENGE.

I'M NOT GOING TO CRY FOR THEM. NOT GOING TO CRY FOR MYSELF EITHER.

LAKEVIEW THEATRE

GRANDFATHER?

CAAAAIIN. WHY DO YOU DISTURB ME?

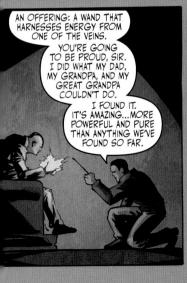

AN OFFERING: A WAND THAT HARNESSES ENERGY FROM ONE OF THE VEINS.

YOU'RE GOING TO BE PROUD, SIR. I DID WHAT MY DAD, MY GRANDPA, AND MY GREAT GRANDPA COULDN'T DO.

I FOUND IT. IT'S AMAZING...MORE POWERFUL AND PURE THAN ANYTHING WE'VE FOUND SO FAR.

IT'S CALLED "THE WITCHBLADE."

I'm sitting in the small study at the front of my cramped apartment, smelling of soot, and smoke. My lungs ache, and with each new cough, I produce a thicker and blacker mucus that I fear will remain with me to the end of my days. My hand is cramped and blistered from the writing of hundreds of coroner's reports and death certificates. But I must record the events of this day, and were my hands burned off in the conflagration, my impetus would still be so strong that I would scrawl this missive with a pen clamped between my teeth.

The fire had begun only two days previous (writing that now, the notion that a scant forty-eight hours was enough to turn my city into a black scar seems impossible. But, believing in the impossible has become a new profession for me these past few days). Fire was nothing new in Chicago, but as it moved beyond the farms and immigrant ghettos, it became evident this fire was not common. A dry fall, high winds, and a beleaguered fire department, already exhausted from a fire fought the day before created a lethal combination of factors. From my small balcony, I first watched the smoke rising from the south of the city with wonder. Concern followed as I begin to smell the blaze, and when tiny, bright embers began to float upon autumn breezes past my nose, I began to feel a deep and certain dread.

I began on the Northside, following firefighting crews like a buzzard after a pride of lions, circling behind the carnage. By the early morning of the 10th, I had determined (with relative ease) the death of over 50 people, their corpses blackened and curled into nearly unrecognizable forms. My quest south brought me past scorched tenements, bars, factories and mansions.

No caste had been spared, and my aching hand noted the death of paupers, immigrants, aldermen, policemen, priests, and whores.

I arrived at the O'Leary farm on DeKoven Street early this morning. The October sun had not yet fully risen above the soldering ruin of a once thriving city. Little remained of the O'Leary barn, and the surrounding buildings, save black wooden skeletons. Rumors had already begun circling that this small, unassuming Irish immigrant owned barn was the epicenter of the holocaust. The Chicago Republican had already run stories blaming a cow, which had kicked over a lantern, but the paper's sensationalist tendencies instantly made me suspicious of bovine indiscretion.

I stopped, exhausted, having been awake for the better part of two days, at the edge of a small stream at the edge of the field, which had likely produced corn or wheat. The stream, now running black, trickled out of a mound of earth. Only a few days before, the scene was likely quite beautiful, colored leaves falling from trees and gently landing atop the running water, carried on towards the Chicago Rivers, bound for the Mississippi.

Though I dared not drink from the stream, the spot seemed almost a tropical island respite compared to the

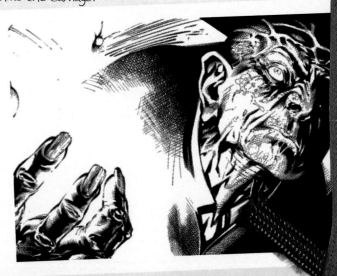

...ng line of shriveled bodies I would likely ...counter at the edge of the farm where ...ighbors were placing their former friends.

Looking upon it now, it seems almost a ...eam, and perhaps, in my exhaustion-addled ...ind, I imagined the whole thing. As I sat, ...rched at the edge of the small onyx river, ...y attention was drawn to the mound from ...hence the trickle originated. It was moving... ...ulsing, as if being pushed from the inside. ...s I stared in disbelief, the mound erupted in ...spray of sediment. And, from the remaining ...rater, did walk three of the most unusual ...ople my eyes have ever laid eyes upon. First ...me a well-dressed man in his early 20s, the ...rious, grim expression in his face belying his ...ars. Next came a girl with jet-black hair, ...lling over her slight shoulders. She was ...essed in some kind of ornate habit, bearing ...spear that shown brightly in the early light, ...spite being covered in some kind of dried ...ood. And, last emerged a stern Negro woman, ...ho pulled herself from the ground unaided by ...e man. So confident and graceful was she, ...took me a few seconds to register that the ...oman was a cripple, missing her right hand.

The three bickered amongst each other, ...blivious to my presence, until the stern man ...w my dumbstruck form. As the two women ...alked away, the man flashed a smile I can ...ly call "disturbing" and then raised a finger to ...s lips to indicate I make no sound. He then ...rned and followed after the women, a motley ...ew to be sure.

I am unsure how long I remained in my ...tunned silence, but when I regained my ...enses, I made my way to the farm. As I ...uspected, my duties lie in front of me like a ...im parade. I spent the next 14 hours, doing ...y best to identify distinguishing features ...pon the victims to aid in their identification, ...d determining their causes of death. As night ...scended I came to the last body. Eyes blurry, ...y mind was still clumsily trying to understand ...e three strange people who had emerged from ...eneath the earth like visitors from Hades.

The body was that of an elderly man, likely an ...ish farmer who had left his mother country ...hopes of a better life. The heat had withered ...s wrinkled skin, pulling his lips over his teeth, ...d contorting his already bent body. He was ...e least burned of the corpses I had seen ...at day, and it seemed likely he had died of the ...moke filling his already weak lungs. I began to ...ll out my ledger, sympathy for the poor man ...elling up in my heart...

When he spoke.

The voice did not seem to come from the grimace that was his mouth, but rather from within, pulled from some deep inner chamber of the twisted corpse. I could not determine exactly what he had said, just that he had addressed me... KNEW me as some old acquaintance. I looked around, squinting in the diminishing light to see if any of the others had heard it. The voice came again, illustrating a desire to leave this place of the dead, insisting that a great reward awaited me for taking him him out of this hell. I rubbed my eyes, shook my head... the three strange visitors, a talking corpse... was exhaustion overtaking me? Was the sight of so much suffering and death finally dragging me into insanity? I felt panic and fear overtaking me, pushing upon my chest, disassociating me from the acrid smelling reality around me...

The next real memory I have is placing the blanket wrapped body of the old man upon my duvet. Apparently I had readily followed his requests, and though I knew not how, I had carried him across the razed city to my home. I felt no ache in my arms, while in contact with him. As I backed away from what had once been a human body, but was surely now something else, quiet, confident words echoed from his cracked lips.

"You serve me now."

As I backed away from the room, retreating to my study, the ache in my arms returned. My lungs ached. My eyes stung. My hands cramped. I knew I should have collapsed in exhaustion, hoping to awaken the next day to find I had simply imagined all of it, caught in a bizarre hallucination that would be cured by a deep sleep.

Instead, I flexed my hand. I reached for my journal. I reached for a pen.

Transcribed by Tim Seeley
2-11-12

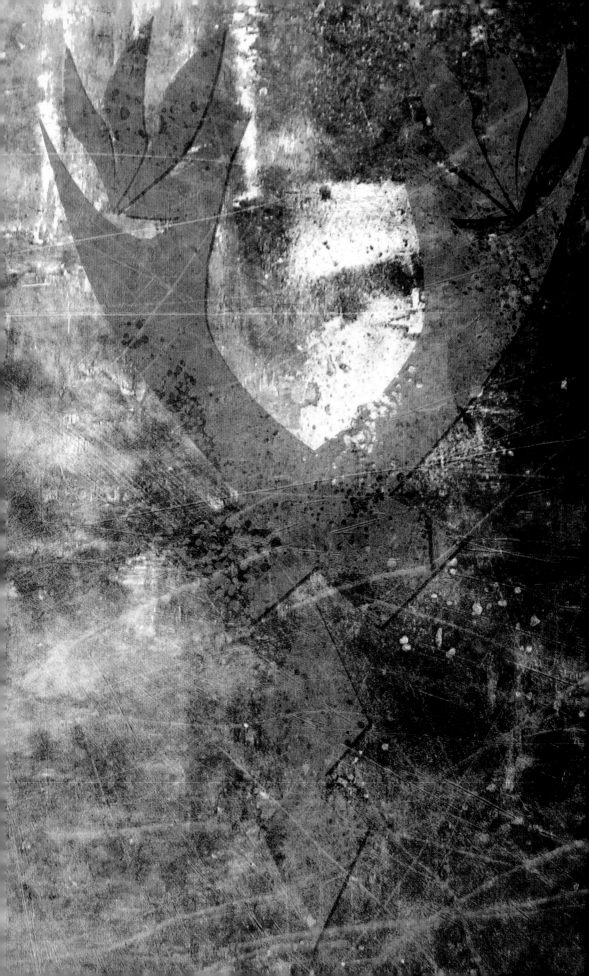

# WITCHBLADE

## Cover Gallery

Witchblade issue #151 Cover A & D, art by: *John Tyler Christopher*

Witchblade issue #151 Cover B, art by: *John Tyler Christopher*

Witchblade issue #151 Cover C, art by: *J. Scott Campbell*

Witchblade issue #151 Cover E, art by: *Diego Bernard, Fred Benes, & Arif Prianto of IFS*

Witchblade issue #152 Cover A, art by: *John Tyler Christopher*

Witchblade issue #152 Cover B, art by: *Diego Bernard, Fred Benes, & Arif Prianto of IFS*

Witchblade issue #152 Cover C, art by: *Dennis Calero*

Witchblade issue #153 Cover A, art by: *John Tyler Christopher*

Inset: Witchblade issue #153 Cover B, art by:*Diego Bernard, Fred Benes,*
*& Arif Prianto of IFS*

Witchblade issue #154 Cover A, art by: *John Tyler Christopher*

Witchblade issue #154 Cover B, art by: *Diego Bernard, Fred Benes,*
*& Arif Prianto of IFS*

Witchblade issue #155 Cover A, art by: *John Tyler Christopher*

Witchblade issue #155 Cover B, art by: *Diego Bernard, Fred Benes, & Arif Prianto of IFS*

# WITCHBLADE

## Timeline

**Witchblade Origins Vol. 1**
*collects Witchblade #1 - #8*

**Witchblade Origins Vol. 2**
*collects Witchblade #9 - #17*

**Witchblade Origins Vol. 3**
*collects Witchblade #18 - #25 + "Family Ties"*

**Witchblade Compendium Vol. 1**
*collects Witchblade #1 - #50*

**Witchblade Compendium Vol. 2**
*collects Witchblade #51 - #100*

First appearance of Witchblade in Shi/Cyblade #1

**#1** – Sara Pezzini acquires Witchblade /
Death of partner Michael Yee

**#10** – First encounter with Jackie Estacado,
bearer of the Darkness

**#19** – Loses the Witchblade to Ian Nottingham

**#25** – Reacquires the Witchblade

**#39** – Sara begins to understand
and control the Witchblade

**#42** – Introduction of the Pez Killer

**#51** – Ian Nottingham revealed to have killed
Sara's father

**#53** – Ian Nottingham confesses his love to Sara

**#62** – First encounter with The Magdalena

**#75** – Death of Kenneth Irons/
Sara's sister, Julie Pezzini arrested

**Witchblade Vols. 1-8**
*collects Ron Marz' run of Witchblade #80 - #130*

**First Born Arc**

**Broken Trinity Arc**

**Artifacts Arc**

**#76** – Sara encounters Celestine, future Angelus bearer, for the first time

**#80** – Detective Patrick Gleason assigned to Sara

**#82** – Sara introduced to The Curator

**#87** – Sara transferred to Special Cases Division

**#92** – The Witchblade's origins are revealed to Sara

**#98** – Sara arrests Ian Nottingham

**#100** – Death of Detective Jake McCarthy/ Sara discovers she's pregnant

**#102** – Sara relinquishes the Witchblade to Dani Baptiste

**#1** – Jackie Estacado revealed to be the father of Sara's child

**#3** – Birth of Hope Pezzini; Witchblade becomes divided between Sara and Dani

**#119** – Sara's first confrontation with Aphrodite IV and Lt. Phipps of Internal Affairs

**#3** – Death of the Angelus host, Celestine

**#125** – War of the Witchblades begins

**#128** – Julie Pezzini released from prison

**#130** – Sara reclaims the whole of the Witchblade; Dani becomes the Angelus

Angelus Arc **#1** – Dani moves to New Orleans

**#1** – Death of Julie Pezzini; Hope abducted by Aphrodite IV

**#144** – Lt. Phipps begins his investigation of Sara Pezzini and the Witchblade

**#150** – Sara leaves the NYPD

**Witchblade: Redemption Vols. 1-3**
*collects Witchblade #131 - #145*

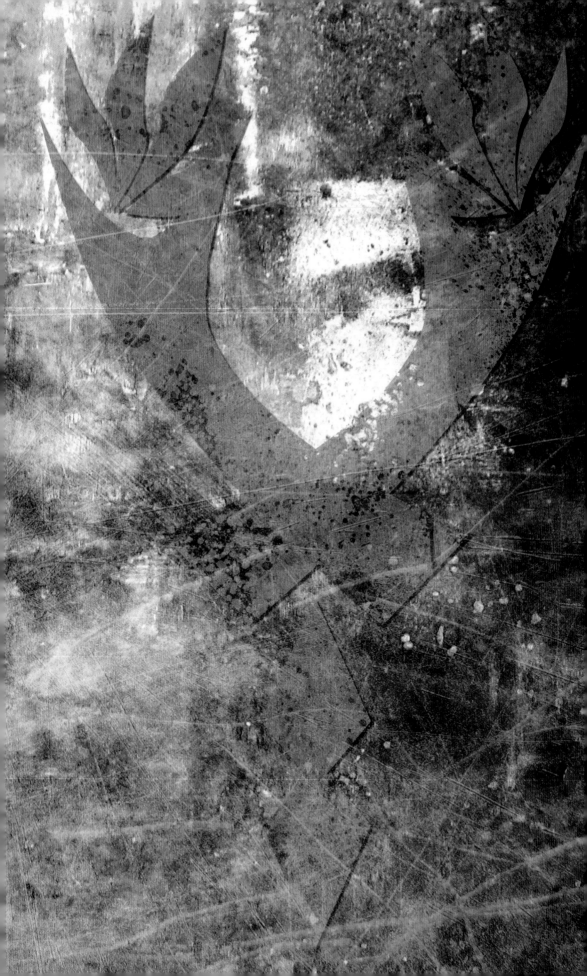